The Darkness Within

The Darkness Within

Graeme Hampton

hera

First published in the United Kingdom in 2021 by Hera Books

This edition published in the United Kingdom in 2022 by

Hera Books
Unit 9 (Canelo), 5th Floor
Cargo Works, 1–2 Hatfields
London, SE1 9PG
United Kingdom

A CIP catalogue record for this book is available from the British Library.

Print ISBN 978 1 80032 854 9
Ebook ISBN 978 1 912973 53 8

Look for more great books at www.herabooks.com

Printed and bound in Great Britain by Clays Ltd, Elcograf S.p.A.

1

For Tracey

Prologue

I'm not sure if it's him at first. He looks older. His hair is greyer and his skin is looser.

But when I get close enough I know it's him.

And then it kicks in.

The hatred. Even after all this time, it hurts to look at him. Seeing the man who destroyed my life walking down a suburban street without a care as though what happened to me never mattered.

My heart races. I should let it go, but I can't. Something inside me stirs. I can feel the hatred clawing at my chest and burning my stomach, and I clench my fist in my jacket pocket.

He heads down a side street. I cross the road and follow him, keeping my distance; not wanting him to see me, but curious too as to what would happen if he did.

Then I hurry my step and quickly make a plan in my head. I'll walk past him, perhaps accidentally barge into him and mutter an apology as I pass. I'm not ready for a full-on confrontation, not yet.

But he turns round unexpectedly. For a brief second, our eyes meet. Is there a flicker of recognition there? If so, what does he feel? Guilt? Regret? Fear?

He opens his mouth to speak.

Then the red mist descends and everything goes blank.

Chapter One

It was the smell that hit him first. The stale, rancid stench of something sour yet sickly sweet greeted him before he'd even walked through the front door of the dingy flat.

The flat was on the second floor of a grim concrete block in the middle of Hackney's notorious Bedgebrook Estate. Over the years, the estate had earned itself a reputation for drugs and violence, most of which was gang-related and near impossible to police. Uniformed officers used to patrol its maze-like streets in pairs. Then the cuts began to bite and they stopped patrolling them altogether. There had been plans to regenerate the estate after the 2012 Olympics, but either the money or the enthusiasm had run out long before the work had ever started.

He was standing in the pokey living room at the back of the flat. It overlooked an abandoned playpark complete with broken swings and broken glass. Beyond the playpark, the London Overground stretched between Dalston and Stratford in a near-straight line.

The room stank of despair as well as rotting flesh. The only furniture was an old brown sofa, a second-hand sideboard, and a table in the corner with a bulky television on top. And a battered leather armchair beside the window, in which was slumped the body of an elderly man, an ugly gash running across his throat like a serrated smile.

Detective Inspector Matt Denning had seen his share of murder victims over the years, but each one still hit him like a smack in the face. It was the pointlessness of it that bothered him: the futile waste of a life for reasons that were usually fairly prosaic.

The room was busy with white-suited Scene of Crime Officers, but no one had looked up when Denning entered. He was on the point of announcing his presence when he spotted DS Deepak Neeraj standing in a corner speaking to one of the SOCOs. Neeraj was in his mid-thirties, the same age as Denning, and dressed in his trademark leather jacket, his jet-black hair gelled into a trendy style. He jerked his chin at Denning by way of a greeting.

'Morning, boss. Pretty grim, huh?'

Denning nodded his acknowledgement and walked over to get a closer look at the body. He'd already put on a pair of paper booties, and had slipped on some slim-fitting blue Nitrile gloves. He hated wearing the gloves as they always made his hands feel clammy.

The victim was in his late seventies and painfully thin, almost emaciated. Matted strands of grey hair were smeared across his scalp, almost as though his hair had been painted on as an afterthought. His left arm dangled in mid-air, the skin loose on the hand like a glove that was about to suddenly slew off. The deep gash across his throat was flecked with speckles of dried blood. More blood had stained the front of his grubby shirt, turning it crimson, and had formed a congealed puddle at his feet. A short strip of what looked like masking tape had been placed over his mouth.

Dozens of angry flies buzzed around the body, or bashed against the window in a fruitless attempt to escape.

'Do we have a name?' Denning asked, trying to ignore the incessant buzzing in his ear.

'Not yet,' Neeraj replied. 'We're trying to find ID, but if this is a robbery, then chances are his wallet and phone will have gone walkabout.'

Robbery was certainly a possible motive, but Denning never liked to make assumptions until he was in possession of all the facts, and they were a long way off that point right now. 'What about time of death?'

'Going by the state of rigor and the loss of blood, I'd say this wasn't recent.' The question was answered by the Crime Scene Manager, Sheila Gorton. Gorton was Canadian and in her fifties. She was courteous and professional, just the kind of person Denning liked working with. She lowered her mask as she approached. 'Good morning, Inspector Denning,' she said with a wry smile. 'One day I hope we'll meet in slightly more inviting surroundings.'

Denning wasn't sure if Gorton was flirting with him whenever their paths crossed, or if this was simply her attempt at humour.

'The smell alone says he's been dead for a while,' Neeraj added. 'Not to mention those bloody flies.'

Gorton made a tutting noise, then said: 'I would estimate he's been dead for anything up to a fortnight, and certainly more than forty-eight hours. Cause of death is a cut to the throat, severing the carotid artery. He would have bled out in seconds. Of course, this is all strictly off the record. The pathologist is on his way – stuck in traffic, or something – so until he gets here and offers up his official verdict, look upon me as the warm-up act and not the main event.' She threw Denning another smile. 'We're also still waiting for a Scene of Crime photographer, so I

4

would appreciate it if you didn't disturb the body any more than is necessary.'

Denning promised they'd be as careful as possible. He sympathised with Gorton. Recent cuts to the service had made her already difficult job even harder. And giving an exact time of death was always tricky, even for an experienced pathologist.

He studied the body closely. According to Dr Arpad Vass, a dead body passed through four distinct stages of decomposition: livor mortis, bloating, putrefaction, and finally skeletonization. This much Denning knew. The first stage of decomposition saw enzymes eat their way through the body's cells from the inside out. During the second stage, bacteria caused gases to become trapped in the lower intestines, giving the body a bloated look. He guessed they were clearly into the third stage with this body, where the skin began to slip, allowing the trapped gases to escape. This was the reason for the putrid smell. Denning had done a short course in forensic pathology shortly after joining the Met. The course had covered the basics, but it had given him a useful insight into the crude mechanics of a post-mortem. He remembered one pathologist describing the smell of death as like a bucket of fish having been left out in the sun.

'One of the neighbours complained about the smell,' Gorton continued. 'It took a couple of days for the council to find a spare set of keys. Got quite a shock when they unlocked the door and saw our man sitting there.'

'The door was locked from the inside?' Denning asked.

'It's a simple Yale lock, so the door would have locked when our killer closed it behind him.'

'No obvious sign of a struggle,' Denning noted.

'Perhaps he was pissed.' It was Neeraj. He looked pointedly at an empty bottle of whisky lying on the floor beside the armchair, splattered with the victim's blood. 'Maybe he was already out for the count, and whoever did it managed to take him by surprise.'

'Why tape his mouth shut?'

Neeraj pulled a face. 'Maybe they tortured him first?'

'Any chance we could open a window?' Denning asked. The combination of the smell of the corpse, the noise of the flies and the general feeling of claustrophobia was making his head throb.

Gorton nodded. She turned to speak to one of her colleagues, while Denning tried to push open a window that had been crusted shut with years of paint. After a moment, he gave up and inwardly cursed.

He returned his attention to the victim. The blood-stained shirt was frayed and a couple of buttons were missing. His eyes were shut, as though he was asleep. If it wasn't for the slashed throat and the tape across his mouth, he would have looked peaceful. Apart from the knife wound, there didn't appear to be any further injuries, but he would wait for the post-mortem to confirm this. There was no sign of the knife, suggesting whoever did it had taken the knife with them.

'Did the council give us a name?'

'Yes, boss,' Neeraj said. 'That was a bit of a story. According to their records, the flat was leased to a bloke called Joseph Jupp, but they reckon this Jupp geezer was sub-letting to our man there. Apparently Joseph Jupp is in his early thirties. Seems Jupp paid his rent every month and never said jack shit to no one.' He jerked his head towards the body sitting on the chair. 'Probably after taking a few quid off that poor sod and making himself a bit on the side.'

Denning nodded at Neeraj. They'd been working together for the best part of a year now and he was used to his colleague's bluntness. Neeraj didn't mean it, or so Denning had managed to convince himself, it was just his way. Occasionally Neeraj would overstep the mark and he would be forced to say something, only for Neeraj to offer up an indifferent shrug and pull a blank face. Sometimes it was easier just to let it pass. 'We'll need to speak to this Jupp character,' Denning said. 'It's possible he may know our victim.'

'He could have done it himself for all we know,' Neeraj offered. 'I mean, think about it: if he's illegally sub-letting this dump, maybe our man found out he's been ripping him off, there's a bit of argy-bargy and it turns nasty.'

'Then why tape his mouth shut?'

Neeraj shrugged. 'To stop him from screaming when he rips his throat open?'

'Well, I don't suppose we'll know until we speak to him,' Denning said.

'On the other hand, this does smell like a robbery, boss,' Neeraj continued. 'Why else would someone want to top a harmless old bloke?'

Denning glanced around the shabby room. There was no sign of the place having been ransacked. Apart from the wallet and the phone, it was unlikely there would have been much worth taking in the first place; even the telly looked old enough to be have been a Logie Baird prototype. But people had been murdered for less.

Sheila Gorton approached them. 'Sorry to interrupt your mothers' meeting, gents, but we've found the victim's wallet. It was in a tin in a kitchen cupboard, of all places.' There was a worried look on her face, which unsettled Denning.

'We found this in it.' Gorton handed Denning a slightly faded bus pass. He checked the photo: it looked like a younger, healthier image of their victim. The name on the pass was Frank Buckfield.

'Frank Buckfield,' Gorton said aloud, just in case Denning couldn't read the name. She pursed her lips and looked from one detective to the other, clearly expecting a reaction. When none came, she said: 'I should have recognised him, though it's been more than twenty years since I last worked with him, and then I was just a junior SOCO so we barely exchanged two words.' She glanced over at the elderly man sitting dead in his armchair, and Denning hoped she was about to come to the point.

'Frank Buckfield,' she repeated, shaking her head at their evident ignorance. 'I knew him as DCI Buckfield.' She stood with her hands on her hips, like a DC Comics superhero. 'He's one of yours, gents. He's an ex-copper.'

Chapter Two

'I think your hormone levels may be slightly out of balance. Stress, perhaps.' Dr Klaus checked the notes on her computer screen. 'I see you have a stressful job. Sometimes that can affect how our body behaves in certain situations.'

Detective Sergeant Molly Fisher smiled at her GP and agreed that her job was, indeed, stressful. However, she was unlikely to be changing career anytime soon.

'Fair point.' Dr Klaus recommended a combination of yoga and vitamin supplements. 'If you still feel out of sorts after a week,' she added, 'you should make another appointment.'

Molly thanked her GP and agreed that she would see how she felt in a week's time.

She left the health centre and headed for the bus stop on nearby Hornsey Rise.

As she swiped her phone off silent mode, she noticed there was another text message. She slipped the phone into her jacket pocket without reading the text. She knew who it was from without even looking at the screen.

The first message had arrived yesterday evening just after dinner. As soon as she'd clocked the sender's name she'd deleted the text unread. And now another one had arrived today. She hoped the sender would take the hint and give up. But she doubted it.

Molly turned into busy Hornsey Rise and checked her watch. Depending on how quickly the bus arrived, she could be sitting behind her desk within the hour – an hour and a half at most.

She'd told work she was going to the dentist rather than the doctor that morning. A trip to the dentist would elicit fewer questions from colleagues than a GP's appointment, and she could do without well-intentioned concern right now.

She arrived at the bus stop. According to the display board, there would be a number ninety-one along in five minutes. She sat on the cold, hard bench and waited.

"Out of sorts". That was one way of putting it.

Molly had done two tests: both negative. But her period was late, and she was never late. She had to make sure.

She'd breathed a silent sigh of relief upon having it confirmed. And yet, deep down, she couldn't help feeling slightly deflated. It was like the time she wasn't picked to play the recorder at a school concert when she was ten years old. The thought of having to do it had made her sick to the stomach for weeks, and her relief when the music teacher opted for slim and pretty Jennifer Moulsen had been palpable. But then, so had the disappointment at not being picked.

But a baby…

It would have been wrong on so many levels.

For a start, there was her job. She'd only recently been promoted from regular CID and offered a place with the Major Investigation Team. MIT – *the Murder Squad*, the cream of Met policing, or so she'd thought when she'd first joined. She was still trying to prove herself within the team, and taking time off to have a baby wasn't likely to do her career prospects any favours in the long term. No matter how forward-looking the Met liked to think it was, it had yet to provide its officers with crèche facilities. And the idea of carrying junior about in a papoose whilst she poked around a murder scene was just not practical.

Then there was Jon, her partner. The prospect of introducing a child into their complicated relationship would be like prising open a very sticky can of worms.

It would either bring them closer together. Or pull them apart.

Either way, she wasn't willing to take the risk.

The phone bleeped again. Another text. Sighing, she took it out of her pocket and looked at the screen, already knowing who it would be from.

Mags.

She slid the phone back into her pocket.

Their paths had first crossed nine months earlier, during a blisteringly hot summer when a maniac was murdering women on the streets of London. Magda Kilbride was a freelance journalist who had offered to help Molly with her investigation. But it had turned out that Mags – as she liked to be called – had another agenda. Actually, she'd had several, not least of which was trying to split up Molly and Jon. She hadn't succeeded, and Molly had left Mags in no doubt as to what she thought of her.

They'd had no contact until now, and Molly was happy to keep it that way. But what could be so imperative that she felt the need to get in touch after all this time?

Molly pushed back the worm of curiosity that wriggled in her brain. Mags meant trouble and that was something she could do without.

A trilling sound from her pocket indicated her phone was active again; this time it was a call rather than a text.

Thinking it might be work checking up on her ETA, she took out the phone and looked at the name. Another sigh. Perhaps there was only one way to end this.

Swiping the phone to answer, she put it to her ear.

'What do you want, Mags?'

There was no preamble, or felicitous greeting, just: 'I need to talk to you. It's important.'

Molly glanced up at the display board: her bus was only a minute away.

'Mags, I haven't got time for your nonsense. If you don't stop hassling me, I'll—'

'I've got information about a murder. And it's big. Meet me after work at—'

But Molly had already ended the call. She didn't have the headspace for Magda Kilbride. Not today. Not ever.

Chapter Three

The killing of a cop, even an ex-cop, sets all number of alarm bells ringing.

Within ten minutes of Denning phoning it in, DCI Liz McKenna was scraping the tyres of her Renault Megane against the kerb outside the flat.

Denning watched as she climbed out of the driver's seat and locked the car behind her. She flashed her ID at a young PC, who lifted the police tape and let her through.

McKenna was in her mid-fifties, so not long until she could collect her gold watch, if retiring police officers still received gold watches. Not that McKenna had plans to retire any time soon; at some point the Met Police had stopped being just a job for her and had become a way of life.

She threw a nod of acknowledgement at Denning when she spotted him standing by the communal entrance, and marched up the short path to greet him.

'Buckfield,' McKenna said as soon as she was within earshot. 'The new Detective Chief Super is taking an interest, so no fuck-ups. What do we know?'

'Not much. The pathologist is on his way: should be here any moment. Neeraj is leading door-to-door enquiries, and the SOCOs are finishing up inside. No sign of the murder weapon. Possible robbery. We've found his wallet, but there's no sign of his phone, or the murder weapon.'

They headed into the building, Denning leading the way, filling her in on what they'd discovered so far.

He'd just finished when they reached the door to Buckfield's flat. 'Buckfield,' McKenna repeated, very slightly out of breath. 'I recognise the name, though I'm pretty sure our paths never crossed. I know of his reputation though. He was SIO on a number of high-profile cases. A couple of them even made the headlines. I'm pretty sure he was given some kind of commendation for catching a serial killer.' She let the significance of her words hang in the ether, then turned to Denning. 'An ex-copper, Matt. We have to find the bastard who did this.'

McKenna stood at the doorway to the living room and took in the depressing scene, probably thinking the same as Denning: how did a once-successful copper end his days in a grotty flat with nothing but his memories and a bottle of Famous Grouse for company? Was this what the future held for them?

She nodded a greeting at Sheila Gorton, and headed over to take a closer look at the body. Denning watched her from the doorway as she and Gorton chatted.

McKenna gave little away. Despite having worked with her for some time now, even having shared the odd post-work drink on rare occasions, most of what he knew about his DCI came from rumour and gossip. She hailed from Motherwell just outside Glasgow, and at some point in her career had earned the nickname Betty Taggart; a sobriquet only ever uttered out of earshot. Beyond that, she kept her personal life to herself.

'Get your report to me ASAP,' she told Gorton. 'And chase up the pathologist. I need both cause of death and, more importantly, time of death confirmed sooner rather than later. Until we know when the poor fucker was killed, we're pissing with the light off.'

Gorton nodded her agreement. McKenna turned back to address Denning.

'Have you spoken to the other residents?'

'Only three of the flats in this block are occupied. The usual "wall of silence" stuff so far,' Denning said. 'Seems Buckfield kept himself to himself and could be a bit of a rude beggar when the mood took. And a boozer too, by all accounts.' Denning jabbed a thumb at the empty whisky bottle lying on the blood-soaked carpet. 'According to the young couple downstairs, he flooded the bathroom on more than one occasion. If they complained, he just gave them a mouthful of abuse.'

'Speak to them again, Matt. I want official statements from everyone in this building. We need a detailed insight into Buckfield's movements: where he went, who he met. Did anyone come to visit him here, and if so, were there any arguments or threats? Maybe get onto Control, see if uniform were ever called out to deal with Buckfield or any of the neighbours. Could be he pissed off the wrong person and they decided they'd had enough.' She stood in the centre of the sparse living room and rubbed a hand through her hair. 'Do you buy the robbery motive?'

He shrugged. 'It's possible. Someone broke in, couldn't find anything worth taking, then ended up killing him out of frustration.'

'He would have had a decent pension, maybe even a bit of money in the bank.' She glanced around the dreary room. 'Then again...'

McKenna had clearly seen enough. She turned on her heel, left the flat and clattered down the concrete stairs. Denning followed, offering Gorton a farewell wave of the hand.

Once they were outside, McKenna said: 'Tell Neeraj to question everyone in this block, and speak to the immediate neighbours.' She looked around the soulless estate. Eyes peeped out from behind several windows; a group of children on bikes were watching them from across the street, one or two of them edging closer to McKenna's car. 'But let's not go overboard on general door-to-door enquiries. Round here it's a case of "see no evil, hear no evil, speak no evil". There's an unwritten code.'

'Maybe if we tell them he's an ex-policeman? Let them know we're taking this seriously.'

She shot Denning a withering look. 'Get hold of his next of kin, Matt. At the very least we'll have to find someone to officially identify the body.'

Denning nodded and dug his phone out of his pocket. He would contact Neeraj, ask him to scale back the house-to-house and return to the station for a briefing. McKenna got back into her car and started the engine before driving off at speed, causing the kids on bikes to scatter.

Denning looked around the drab estate, scarred by neglect and awash with litter and graffiti. This was the other side of Hackney. The side that was hidden from the inhabitants of the gentrified squares and overpriced apartment blocks that had redefined the borough from urban decay to fashionable enclave. London was a city in constant social flux, where wealth and poverty sat cheek by jowl; one largely oblivious to the existence of the other.

Bedgebrook only saw the poverty. A place where life expectancy was low and crime was high. He could sense a sea of unsmiling faces watching him. McKenna was right: this estate was home to the Three Wise Monkeys.

Chapter Four

'OK guys, when you're ready.' Denning cleared his throat and waited for the room to quieten down before he began the briefing.

'Francis George Buckfield.' He nodded at the photos of Buckfield that had been pinned to the whiteboard: an official 'portrait' shot of him taken a few months before his retirement contrasting sharply with the post-mortem photo of him with his throat slit. They looked like two different men. 'Formerly Detective Chief Inspector Buckfield,' he continued, 'found murdered in his flat on the Bedgebrook Estate.'

A low murmur spread round the room at the mention of Bedgebrook.

Denning ignored it and continued, filling the team in on what they'd discovered so far; highlighting relevant points on the whiteboard. 'Probable weapon was some kind of knife, which we still need to find. Probable motive is something we need to establish, though at this stage, we can't rule out robbery. His wallet was found, but his mobile phone is missing. We need to find his phone. At the moment, we don't have a lot to work with: if robbery was the motive, why the need to kill him? The time of death has yet to be confirmed, but we're looking at a likely window of between forty-eight hours and two weeks. Once we know when Frank Buckfield was killed, we can start looking over any CCTV in the area. In the meantime, we need to get as clear a picture as we can of Buckfield's life and his movements. Deep, did house-to-house throw up anything useful?'

Neeraj glanced over his notes and looked around the room. 'About as useful as I expected it to be, which is not very. Apparently Buckfield had lived there for a couple of years, but mostly kept himself to himself. Some bloke did say he used to chat to Buckfield down the local boozer, but he never mentioned anything about having been a copper. This bloke said he would never have spoken to Buckfield if he'd known he was an ex-cop.'

'If he was living on the Bedgebrook, then he'd have kept his head down. Anyone in that cesspit had found out he used to be one of us, they'd have kicked his head in.' DS Dave Kinsella, a sweaty bear of a man in his late forties, offered up his opinion.

'Someone did worse than that, Dave,' quipped DC Trudi Bell. 'They cut his throat.' She threw Kinsella a cheeky smile, which he countered with a flick of his middle finger.

'Emphasising my point,' Kinsella retorted.

Denning smiled while the team laughed. It was good to encourage banter among the group: it helped to develop a strong team dynamic, or so he'd read somewhere. 'OK, guys,' he said as soon as the laughter subsided. 'Anything else, Deep?'

'He confirmed that Buckfield liked the booze. In fact, this bloke reckoned he was a bit of an alkie. There was never any trouble, though. Buckfield would get a bit shouty sometimes, but he'd calm down if the landlord told him to button it. None of the neighbours had much to do with him, apart from the odd bout of aggro with the couple downstairs, However, it seems uniform were never called out, so it's likely it never went beyond a bit of verbal.'

'It might be worth paying a visit to the landlord at Buckfield's local and find out if he had any friends, besides the occasional drinking buddy.'

Buckfield belonged to the generation where drinking was such an ingrained part of police culture it was almost not worth commenting on. But that didn't necessarily turn police officers into alcoholics. However, it did help to explain the empty whisky bottle lying next to Buckfield's chair at the flat. 'What about this Joseph Jupp character?'

'Spoke to him a few minutes ago,' Neeraj said. 'He was a bit cagey at first until I told him this was a murder inquiry and we could bring him in if we wanted to. He admitted he's been illegally sub-letting that dump to Buckfield for the past couple of years. Says he was doing Buckfield a favour as he had nowhere else to go. He used to drink in the same pub as Buckfield and took pity on him after he was evicted from his last place. The rent was paid by housing benefit directly into Jupp's bank account every four weeks.'

'Wouldn't the council have checked that the flat wasn't being illegally sublet?' Trudi asked.

'You'd like to think so,' Kinsella said, 'but I expect they have neither the resources nor the inclination to double check how they spend tax-payers' money.'

'It's likely Jupp has done this sort of thing before,' Molly said. 'I imagine he'd probably prepared a fake lease, or even said he was a lodger. I worked on a couple of housing benefit fraud cases a few years ago: these guys are good at covering their backsides.'

'So it looks like Mr Jupp's only crime is property fraud,' Denning said. 'We'll pass the details onto the appropriate agencies and let them chase this up. But as soon as we have time of death established, we'll need an alibi from Jupp, just to make sure he's not hiding something from us.'

'Housing benefit?' Trudi said. 'Wouldn't a retired DCI have a decent pension?'

It was a good point, and something that had occurred to Denning while they were in Buckfield's grotty flat. 'Dave, get onto HR and see if they still have anything on file. I know it's been a few years since he worked for the Met, but hopefully they'll have some contact details for him. And whilst you're speaking to them, ask about a next of kin. I know he lived alone, but that's not to say he didn't have family out there somewhere.'

Kinsella nodded. 'I'll get on to them.'

Denning looked around his team. They were a disparate bunch, but they worked well together, despite their differences. He liked to push them, encourage them to lead on an investigation rather than rely on him to provide all the answers. 'Anyone got any thoughts they'd like to share?'

'No sign of forced entry. That suggests he could have known his attacker and let them in.' It was the turn of DC Ryan Cormack. Cormack was the youngest in the group, and – like Denning – a fast-tracked graduate. He tended only to speak when he had something useful to say, a trait Denning appreciated.

'Then again,' Neeraj noted, 'security at that dump wasn't exactly tight. Anyone could have just walked in off the street.'

'I'm assuming Buckfield kept the door to the flat locked,' Denning said. 'And there was no sign of damage to the door. However, even if Buckfield did let his attacker in, that doesn't necessarily mean he knew them.'

Denning was about to continue when he spotted DS Fisher waving a Biro in his direction. 'Molly?'

'Do we think it could have been premeditated?' she asked. 'Cutting someone's throat. And then that whole thing with the tape over the mouth. It feels very...' She searched for the word. '...deliberate.' She was looking at the photos on the whiteboard, tilting her head slightly to one side to study them more closely. 'I might be talking out my backside, but I don't think this was a random murder.'

All eyes in the room were now fixed on the whiteboard. There were photos of the depressing flat as well as the body. The sadness of Buckfield's empty life was plain for all of them to see, but the flat hadn't been disturbed: nothing was out of place, nothing broken. If this had been a straightforward burglary, Denning would have expected the flat to have been ransacked. The only thing missing was Buckfield's mobile phone, but that didn't prove anything.

The photos of the body had been taken from different angles. Buckfield's pale, thin face looked like a death mask; only the flecks of dried blood added a token splash of colour. Molly Fisher was right: someone had entered that flat with the sole intention of killing Buckfield. But why?

'A revenge killing?' Trudi suggested.

'In which case, it could be anyone.' Kinsella sat back on his chair; thick arms folded across his barrel of a chest. 'Buckfield was a copper for over thirty years. It'll take months to go through every case he's ever worked on.'

'What do we already know about Buckfield?' Cormack asked. 'I mean, was he ever involved in any high-profile cases, for instance?'

'We need to look into everything,' Denning said. 'And not just the high-profile cases. If this is about revenge, it could be for something seemingly trivial. We need as detailed a picture of Buckfield's life and career as we can get.'

'A mate of mine in Hendon worked under him back in the late nineties,' Kinsella said. 'He was your typical DCI by all accounts.' He flicked a glance in the direction of McKenna's office door at the far end of the room, and lowered his voice. 'He'd break your bollocks if you stepped out of line, but he'd cover your arse when you needed it. He was a good copper. I expect he put away some big-time villains back in his day, but that's part of the job. We know it and they know it. I can't believe someone would go after him now. He was an old man, for Christ's sake.'

'Actually, Dave, now you mention it, wasn't there a story about him being involved in some kind of scandal?' Trudi said. 'I'm sure I remember my dad talking about it some years back.' Denning knew that Trudi's father had been a uniformed sergeant for many years, probably around the same time Buckfield was a detective.

'That was all a load of crap,' Kinsella shot back.

Denning threw him a look. 'Care to elaborate anyway, Dave?'

Kinsella looked shifty. He unfolded his thick arms and scratched an itch behind his left ear. 'There was a rumour he had a run-in with Professional Standards.' He pulled a face. 'But that means nothing.'

'Any idea what it was about?' Denning asked. He had a feeling he was going to have to tease this out of him bit by bit.

Kinsella folded his arms across his chest again and leaned back in his chair. 'Look, we all know it doesn't take much to get those muppets sniffing round us. Some scumbag claims we didn't treat them with enough respect, or we forgot to say "please" and "thank you" when we nicked them, and they put in an official complaint. Standards are duty-bound to investigate it, even if it clearly is a load of old tosh.'

He waited for Kinsella to give details. When he didn't, Denning said: 'So we don't know what it was about?'

'Look, I never knew the guy personally, and unlike some round here, I don't go in for gossip.' Kinsella sat there with his arms folded, making it clear he wasn't prepared to discuss the matter further.

'Trudi?'

She just shrugged.

Denning looked at Kinsella. Either he didn't know what the run-in with the Directorate of Professional Standards was about, or he was refusing to say to protect the reputation of a now-dead officer. But Denning would find out. It would just take longer to do it via the official channels.

He was drawing the briefing to a close, allocating jobs for his team, when he spotted McKenna coming out of her office. She stood at the front of the room, tapped her watch and nodded at Denning. 'I don't want to interrupt, everyone. Just a gentle reminder the new Chief Super wants to speak to us all straight after lunch.'

There was an audible groan from the room. They had just got a major murder investigation off the ground, with days – possibly weeks – of slog ahead of them. The last thing they needed was the unwelcome distraction of a meet and greet with the new Detective Chief Superintendent.

Denning was on the point of saying they were too busy and could she make apologies on their behalf, but McKenna had already disappeared back into her office, the door clicking shut behind her.

Chapter Five

Molly grabbed a seat at the back of the room, furthest from the small stage that had been hastily cobbled together from a couple of bits of rostra. She hoped no one would sit next to her. She wasn't in the mood for small talk right now. If she was honest, she'd rather not be there at all.

As soon as she'd walked into the office that morning, she had seen that the incident room had been jumping like a flea on a hotplate.

'A murder,' Trudi had said before Molly had even sat down at her desk. 'Serious, by all accounts. A former cop.' Trudi had then mimed lighting a cigarette, forgetting Molly had given up some months back. Molly declined the offer to join her, though part of her was tempted. Despite her will power, the cravings had never gone away, not entirely; they still lingered like hunger pangs, or struck unexpectedly, like the urge to go to the loo at inconvenient times.

She'd told Trudi she'd catch her later – perhaps go for a drink one evening, assuming this murder investigation didn't destroy their social lives for the foreseeable. She'd headed to her desk, woken her computer from sleep mode, and checked her emails.

But she'd struggled to focus. Trudi's words had mirrored those of Mags:

'*I've got information about a murder. And it's big.*'

Molly had spent the duration of the bus ride back from the doctor's trying her best to blot out Mags and her phone call, yet the worm of curiosity had wriggled round her brain and refused to go away.

Meet me after work…

She knew Mags, so she knew it would be some kind of fantasy – an embellished half-truth that she would run by Molly, gauging her reaction to see if there was the makings of a story. Molly was determined not to play her games.

And now this…

A meet and greet with the new Detective Chief Superintendent. He wanted to introduce himself personally to all eighteen MITs and familiarise himself with their workloads. It was good management practice, apparently, and the Met was all about good management these days.

They were in what was jokingly called the conference room, located on the ground floor. It had originally been the cafeteria when the building had served as a working police station, before the most recent round of cuts had forced its closure and conversion into office space for the East London MITs. Her own team had been camped out at Stoke Newington Police Station for the past year and a half until the refurbishment of their new home in Barkingside had been completed. The place had been given a cursory lick of paint, and a thin beige carpet now covered the floor. But it was all slightly soulless, and there was a slightly sour smell that had somehow ingrained itself into the fabric of the building and refused to let go.

A couple of dozen chairs had been arranged in a horseshoe facing the impromptu stage. She watched as the room began to fill up.

Denning was sitting at the front chatting to Betty Taggart, their heads locked together in serious conversation.

The new DCS was called Ian Harrison. Molly knew very little about him, except that he'd survived the culling of senior management that had resulted from the Met's latest reorganisation, and was rumoured to have a reputation for not suffering fools gladly.

She glanced at her watch. They were already running late.

Trudi slipped in the door behind her, quickly dropping a packet of B&H into the top pocket of her blouse. She looked around the room, spotted Molly and sat down next to her.

'Alright, Moll. This is a right load of old piss, ain't it?' She tipped her head towards the small stage. 'It's a bit like meeting a new headmaster. And I never liked mine much.'

Molly smiled her agreement just as Harrison entered the room. He strutted towards the stage with a confident swagger that let everyone know he was the new man in charge. Harrison was tall and broadly built, with a weathered face that hinted at someone who liked to spend a lot of time outdoors. He had a severe salt-and-pepper haircut that did little to temper his craggy features.

There was another, younger man with him. He was of a similar height to Harrison, though slimmer, and exuded the same air of self-confidence as the strutting DCS.

Both men walked onto the small stage and the room fell silent.

Harrison's voice was clipped and authoritative, with a strong trace of a South London accent.

'Good afternoon everyone, and thank you for coming along today. I realise you're all busy people and your time

28

is precious, so I'll keep things brief.' He turned to the younger man. 'Firstly, let me introduce Justin Morrow, London Assembly member and Deputy Chairman of the Police and Crime Committee.' Morrow was in his mid-forties and immaculately groomed. He was dressed in a smart Armani suit and pale blue checked shirt, his thick blond hair cut in a trendy style. Molly could almost smell the Tom Ford aftershave wafting off him. He reminded her of a slightly older, slightly more polished version of Denning.

Morrow spoke with the slickness of a professional politician. Unlike Harrison, his eloquent tone suggested he was the product of a private education. He told them that he considered himself to be a friend of the police, and wanted them to know he was on their side. There were a few nods and grunts from the audience, but otherwise most people looked like they'd heard it all before.

When Morrow finished speaking, he handed the baton over to Harrison.

Harrison was fiery and bombastic. He spoke for several minutes outlining the direction he wanted to take the MITs in, referencing his background and experience as a serving police officer. He'd clearly perfected the art of management speak, and spouted it like a practised performer.

Molly let the endless stream of professional bullshit wash over her as her mind returned to Mags. The woman was a seasoned liar: it was what she did for a living. There was no reason for Molly to believe a word she said. So why couldn't she escape the feeling that she shouldn't have been so quick to dismiss her?

She glanced back at the two men on the stage.

Harrison was still talking, while Morrow smiled his support. By now, most of the room had their arms folded, or were fidgeting in their seats. She spotted Betty Taggart sneaking a sly peek at her watch, while Trudi stifled a yawn.

Harrison finally ended his speech to a ripple of limp applause, and asked if there were any questions. But before there was a chance for any hands to rise, a mobile phone tinkled into life. For a second, Molly thought it was hers – another call from Mags – until she remembered her phone was still in her jacket pocket on the back of her chair in the office. All eyes were focussed at the front of the room as Denning removed his phone from his pocket and chatted to someone. A spluttering of conversation rippled through the room and Harrison shot Denning a filthy look. Molly glanced at Trudi, and they both tried not to laugh. Denning finished the call and muttered something to Betty Taggart, who mouthed an apology at Harrison. When he'd finished whispering in her ear, Denning got to his feet.

'Apologies everyone, but we've just been informed by the local CID that there's been a serious assault in Islington. They think it might be an attempted murder.'

Chapter Six

Technically, it was Highbury rather than Islington. Quieter and leafier than its trendier neighbour, Highbury seemed mainly to consist of large residential properties and green open spaces.

The street they wanted was located off Highbury Hill, not too far from the Emirates Stadium. Arundel Road was typical of the area: bay-windowed terraced houses looking onto tidy gardens. The strobing blue lights from a couple of parked squad cars guided them like a beacon to the right address.

A cordon had been set up in front of number twenty-four; police tape stretched between a lamppost and a tree, while uniformed officers ushered members of the public away from the scene.

Denning and Neeraj showed their ID to one of the officers, then ducked under the cordon. They were on the point of asking who was in charge when an efficient-looking woman in a smart grey suit strode over to meet them. Denning guessed she was the CID officer who'd called it in.

'Victim's name's David Cairns,' she said as soon as she was within earshot. 'Lives at number twenty-four.' The CID detective introduced herself as DS Anna Klein. She was in her late twenties, with a cheery face, framed by a pair of metal glasses, which made her look a bit like a librarian. 'He's been the victim of a nasty assault occasioning actual bodily harm,' she added. 'He's in a pretty bad way.'

'Where is he now?' Denning asked.

'He was taken away in an ambulance about ten minutes ago. The paramedics reckon he's got concussion and internal bleeding, not to mention a few broken bones for good measure. They said that if they hadn't got here when they did, we would likely be looking at a fatality.' She let the significance of her words hang in the air. 'One of the neighbours reported it. Heard a noise in the street and glanced out of her front window to see a man running away.' She pointed to a bay-windowed house across the street. 'A Mrs Joyce Lindsey. Uniform have spoken to her but she was unable to give much of a description.'

'I'll have a word with her,' Denning said, 'see if there's anything else she can add. A bit of background on the victim might be useful if nothing else.'

There was a fresh crimson puddle drying on the pavement, a vivid reminder of the violence that had just taken place in broad daylight in a quiet residential street. Denning looked up and down the road; this looked like the land of twitching curtains. Somebody must have seen something.

'Any other witnesses?'

'Uniform have tried speaking to the immediate neighbours, but everyone seems to be out at the moment – at work, presumably. Of those who are in, no one seems to have seen or heard anything until we arrived on the scene. We haven't initiated wider house-to-house yet – we thought it best to wait until you got here. Let the big boys make that call.'

'What about CCTV?' Denning asked.

'Not much round here,' Klein informed him. 'There's little need. Apart from the odd burglary and the occasional spot of car crime, it's a pretty safe area. Popular with families and young professionals.'

'It's pretty posh round here,' Neeraj said, looking at the twin rows of well-kept houses that lined the street. 'Could this have been a mugging? Bloke's almost home – takes out his door keys and his eye's off the ball. Would only take a few seconds for someone to jump him.'

Klein shook her head. 'The level of violence suggests otherwise. Plus he still had his wallet and his watch on him. And his door keys, for that matter.' She threw them a wry smile. 'I'd say this has all the hallmarks of an attempted murder. That's why we called you boys in.'

MIT's remit was strict: murder and serious crime. The high volume, day-to-day stuff was left to CID. There was the inevitable overlap of course, and this looked like it might fall into something of a grey area. If the victim died of his injuries, then they would certainly be looking at a murder inquiry – and it would be their call. But if this was simply a common assault that had got out of hand, then they'd be batting it back into CID's camp quick enough. At this stage, it was too early to tell which way it might fall, so Denning was prepared to keep an open mind.

'Which hospital did they take him to?' Denning asked.

'Whittington is the nearest. Though it'll be some time before he can talk to you.' She arched an eyebrow. 'That's assuming he recovers.'

Denning took her card, telling her they'd take charge for now and get in touch if anything changed. But with the murder of a former cop hanging over their heads, this was one unwelcome distraction they didn't need. And yet, as he watched Klein heading back to her car, something inside his gut told him there was more to this than first impressions suggested.

–

Joyce Lindsey showed Denning and Neeraj into the comfortable sitting room of her terraced home, the wide bay window of which overlooked the scene of the attack.

Joyce, as she insisted they call her, was a well-preserved sixty-something, dressed in a pair of beige slacks and an expensive-looking cashmere pullover. She had a pair of fluffy mules on her feet that looked like they were worn for comfort rather than fashion.

'We've lived here for over ten years,' she said, 'and I've probably exchanged about half a dozen words with him in all that time.' She sat opposite them on a green velvet armchair, while they occupied a matching sofa that faced a faux-marble fireplace, upon which were arranged several porcelain figurines. The living room smelt of lavender Febreze. 'He was always polite,' she continued, 'but never what you would call friendly. He keeps himself to himself, and I've never seen anyone going into his house.' She blushed slightly. 'I don't want you to think I'm nosy, but it's a very friendly street here, or at least it used to be. All the neighbours will tell you the same thing: he's something of a recluse.'

'Do you know how long Mr Cairns has lived round here?' Denning asked.

'Oh, it's *Doctor* Cairns,' she said with a little smile. 'And I only know that because I took in a package for him once.'

'He's a doctor?' Denning asked.

'Not a medical one, I don't think. More a teacher.' She shook her head. 'Not a school teacher. A university one. You know what I mean…'

'An academic?' Denning suggested. His parents were academics: lecturers at Keele University in Staffordshire. While his mother only used her title professionally, his father introduced himself to everyone he met as 'Dr Denning'.

'Yes,' she nodded. 'One of those kind of doctors.' She gave another little smile. 'Though I guess he's retired now.'

'So you have spoken to him?' Neeraj asked.

She looked at him for a moment before she answered. 'I've never had what you'd call a proper conversation with him. I mean, we'd say hello if I passed him in the street, and naturally he thanked me when I took that package in for him.'

'Can you take us through what you saw today?' Denning asked. 'Take your time.'

She toyed with a loose piece of thread on the armchair. 'Well, I've already told the uniformed policeman everything I saw.'

Denning offered her a reassuring smile. 'Would you mind going over it again, for us? It would be very helpful.'

She sat back in the chair, took a deep breath, then noisily exhaled. 'I'd just made myself a coffee and was sitting down to watch the end of *This Morning*, when I heard shouting coming from outside. I thought it was kids messing around at first. But it didn't sound like kids. They should have been at school anyway – it's not the Easter holidays yet, is it?' She looked blankly at the two men, then carried on. 'I got up to see what the commotion was.' She gave a little shudder. 'Dr Cairns was lying on the ground and another man was kicking him, quite viciously. It was horrid. He must have been doing it for a good few seconds before he stopped. Then he just stood there, looking down at Dr Cairns and then he turned and ran off. I dialled 999 straight away. I thought about going out to see if Dr Cairns was OK, but I was frightened that man might come back.'

'Which direction did he run?' Denning asked.

She had to think for a second. 'Towards Highbury Hill.'

'So, south,' Denning said, thinking aloud.

'To the Tube station?' Neeraj suggested.

'Maybe…' Denning looked at Joyce again. 'Are you sure it was just the one man? There was no one else?'

'Oh yes. There was only one.'

'Can you describe him?'

She shook her head again. 'No. I didn't really get a good look at his face. Besides, he was wearing a jacket with the hood up.'

'Please try,' Denning prompted gently. 'Anything you can remember would be helpful.'

She placed a finger against her mouth. 'He wasn't very tall. I think he was young. Well, he wasn't old. I mean he ran quite fast, so he couldn't have been old, could he?'

Denning looked at Neeraj who just shrugged. She wasn't giving them much to work with. He suspected she was already trying to blot the memory from her mind.

'Did he say anything?' Denning asked. 'The man who attacked Dr Cairns – did he speak to him during the attack? Or afterwards?'

'No. Well…' She pressed her finger firmly against her lips. 'He didn't speak, exactly…'

'Go on,' Denning prompted. 'Anything you can remember will help us catch this man.'

She looked over at Denning. 'He was crying.'

'Crying?' Neeraj looked like he thought he'd misheard her.

'Yes,' she said. 'After he'd stopped kicking Dr Cairns, when he was standing there, he turned his head for a fraction of a second, and I thought he looked like he was crying.'

'So you did get a look at his face?' Neeraj said.

Her brow wrinkled. 'Pardon? Oh yes, well. Just for a second. I mean I don't know if I'd recognise him again.'

Denning digested this information. It didn't make a lot of sense, but then so much of what they dealt with didn't make sense, at least not to a rational mind.

'OK, thanks, Joyce. That was very helpful. Maybe you could tell us a bit more about Dr Cairns. For example – is he married? Does he have any family?'

'Not as far as I know. I mean, I've never seen him with anyone, and as far as I'm aware, no one else lives there. Though it is a big house for one person.' She blushed suddenly. 'I don't want to give you the impression that I spend my days spying on my neighbours, but ever since I had to leave work because of my arthritis, I've spent a lot of time at home. And like I said, this is a friendly street.'

Denning gave her another reassuring smile. 'It's fine, Joyce. We need to build up as clear a picture of Dr Cairns as we can. Is there anything else you can tell us about him?'

'Sorry, Inspector. I've told you all I know.' She rubbed a hand over her face. 'It's terrible what happened to him. I mean, attacked on your own doorstep. This area used to be ever so safe when we first moved here. Now you've got people being mugged in broad daylight.' She stared into space for a moment, then sniffed. 'But I'm sure I don't have to tell you all about how bad crime is in London these days, do I?'

Denning nodded. 'Thank you, Joyce. You've been very helpful. We may need to speak to you again if there are any developments.' By that, he meant if this turned into a murder inquiry.

She smiled her appreciation, no doubt happy to have done her civic duty and been able to assist the police. She showed them out.

Once they were outside, Neeraj said, 'What do you think, boss?'

Denning was looking down the street towards Highbury Hill, the direction the attacker had run. Had he known the area, or had chance brought him to this particular street? SOCOs were already poring over the scene, while a couple of uniformed officers remained by the cordon. 'There's no point doing further house-to-house – it's unlikely to yield anything useful at this stage. We'll check CCTV at Highbury and Islington station for a man in a hooded jacket, possibly running. If we can get any decent pictures, we'll ask Mrs Lindsey to have a look, see if anything jogs her memory.'

But Neeraj wasn't convinced. 'I still think this is an attempted mugging. The victim refuses to hand over his wallet, so the guy gives him a good pasting to teach him a lesson.'

'She said he was crying.'

Neeraj was already heading back towards the car. 'I don't think she knows what she saw. More likely he was laughing, not crying.' He'd reached the car, spreading his arms on the roof, waiting for Denning to unlock it. 'This is street crime, boss. Not our bag. CID just wants to get it off their books and pass it over to some other mugs.' He jabbed his thumb at his chest. 'Us.' He gave a cheeky grin. 'And I can't say I blame that DS. Let's be honest, boss, we'd probably do the same in her boots if we thought we'd get away with it.'

'He left the victim's phone and wallet, Deep. He could easily have taken them if he wanted to.' Denning unlocked the car and Neeraj opened the passenger door.

'So, he's a crap mugger. Or maybe he clocked Old Mother Hubbard there and panicked.'

They got in the car and Denning started the engine.

A mugging? Perhaps…

Muggers did strike in broad daylight and quiet streets like this were the perfect spot for an opportunist thief to find a suitable target.

But something didn't fit. A seemingly random assault that didn't feel entirely random.

He thought about Buckfield. Two people attacked, one killed, the other seriously injured: robbery the most obvious motive in both cases, yet nothing was taken.

Was he putting two and two together and coming up with five…?

Either Neeraj was right and this was the work of the world's worst mugger, or it was down to something else. Something personal in both cases.

Chapter Seven

'Let's focus on priorities here, Matt. We have a dead ex-cop chilling in the mortuary, and still no clue as to which bastard put him there. It's only a matter of time before the top brass start kicking backsides. Mine *and* yours.' McKenna wasn't in the mood for taking prisoners. She sat behind her desk with a face like a gathering storm. 'I don't need this right now, and nor do you.'

'We can't simply ignore the attack on Cairns. If we rule out robbery, then we're looking at a deliberate attack. Whoever did it is dangerous and there's a chance they could attack again. We would very likely be looking at a fatality next time.'

McKenna sighed and shook her head. 'Have you spoken to the hospital?'

'He still hasn't regained consciousness, but he is stable. They'll know within the next twenty-four to forty-eight hours if he's going to pull through or not.'

McKenna looked at Denning from across her desk, fixing him with her gimlet stare. She gave another sigh and sat back in her chair. 'As soon as you're able to speak to him, find out what happened. If it's nothing more than an attempted robbery that got out of hand, then we drop it like a hot turd, and it becomes the local CID's problem. Got that?'

He nodded. 'And if it's something else?'

She continued looking at him, like a panther eyeing a gazelle. 'If you're thinking there's some connection here with Buckfield, forget it. The attacks don't even smell similar.'

'I'm not saying there is a connection. But in both cases the most obvious motive was robbery, though neither man was robbed. If we're suggesting they were both attacked for some other reason, then we have to find out what that reason was.'

McKenna was silent for a moment. Denning could sense she was chewing the options over in her head; trying to find the route of least resistance.

'What do we know about Cairns?' she asked.

'Not a great deal at the moment. He seems to be something of a recluse. We know he worked in academia at some point, but we don't as yet know where.' He'd asked Neeraj to do some background checking on Dr Cairns, but he hadn't been able to come up with anything in time for Denning to take it to McKenna. He'd also instructed the local uniforms to resume house-to-house enquiries that evening, once people had returned from work. He wanted to build up as detailed a picture of Cairns and his life as they could get, but he wasn't convinced they were going to find anything useful. He had a feeling Cairns was someone who lived off the radar.

'OK,' McKenna said. 'Keep Cairns on the back burner for now. What about the Buckfield investigation? Please tell me there's been some progress there?'

'We're still trying to track down next of kin. There's an ex-wife around somewhere, though possibly no longer going by the name Buckfield. He hasn't lived at the address HR gave us for some time. We've even spoken to the current DCI at the last station he worked at, but we're going back over twenty years, and memories aren't great. But Buckfield was around for a long time. He worked dozens of cases – some of them high-profile and some not.'

'So, what are we doing?'

'We're looking at anyone who was released within the last few years who might have a credible motive. However, it's going to take time. Even then, we could be totally off-piste. This could have nothing to do with his job.' He pulled a face. 'We don't even know for certain that Buckfield was specifically targeted. This could yet turn out to be a random attack. Like Cairns.'

McKenna ignored the comment. 'Do we have any specifics about the cases he worked on?'

'He led his fair share of murder investigations over the years – this was before the formation of the Major Investigation Teams in 2000 – as well as fraud, armed robbery, all the usual stuff. He was even part of the team who investigated the Security Direct warehouse robbery back in '96, shortly before he retired.'

He noticed McKenna's eyes light up at the mention of Security Direct. She leaned forward on her desk and started twiddling with a Parker pen, a sign she was churning something over in her brain. 'Interesting,' she said after a moment.

'Interesting? How?'

She continued twiddling the pen, seemingly lost in thought, then said, 'Nothing. I just didn't realise he was part of that team.'

'It was a major investigation. From what I understand, it involved several teams from across London, as well as Kent and Surrey. Buckfield was based in West London at the time. As a senior detective, it makes sense he would have helped with the investigation.'

McKenna didn't say anything, and Denning wondered what she was thinking. In the end he decided it would be quicker just to ask. 'Do you think Security Direct is somehow relevant? It's certainly possible his death could have something to do with that. Some of the big players who went down for it would have been due for release around now, assuming they served their full sentences.'

More pen twiddling, then she threw the pen on the desk and sat back in her chair again. 'OK, look into it, but I think it's probably a bit of a long shot. If someone is targeting all the cops involved in that investigation, it's going to be one bloody long list.'

'There is one other thing.' He shuffled awkwardly in his seat. 'It seems Buckfield was investigated by the Directorate of Professional Standards… well, Complaints Investigation Bureau as it then was, shortly before he retired.'

'Go on.'

'Depending on how serious the complaint was, he could have been forced to retire, with the consequences for his pension. It would explain why a retired DCI was living in near penury.'

'It's possible,' McKenna said. 'Though it only tends to be in extreme cases that an officer has their pension forfeited, even then it's usually only if there's a court case involved. What does it say on file?'

'That's the weird thing. The file is marked as restricted. I haven't been able to access it.'

McKenna's eyebrows gave a brief twitch. 'Probably nothing. But I can look into it if you think it might be relevant. I may need to get authority from someone above my pay grade, but if our new DCS means what he says about "streamlining systems" and "increasing efficiency", then let's see him put his money where his mouth is and get some strings pulled.'

Denning nodded. 'Incidentally – and off the record – what did you think of him? Harrison?'

She gave a dry chuckle. 'I've been in this game a long time, Matt. I've seen them come and I've seen them go. Granted, Harrison makes a lot more noise than most, but we'll see how long he lasts.'

'What about the suit who was with him?'

'Morrow?' She pursed her lips. 'Don't know. He's with the Police and Crime Committee, and they're essentially toothless – just there to keep an eye on the Mayor's Office for Policing, at least that's their official role. Though they're not entirely without influence. But I reckon he's just another politician out to make a name for himself. Get the police on-side and it'll look good on his CV. Why?'

He wasn't sure, there was just something niggling him. 'Harrison wasn't the first choice for DCS, was he? There were a couple of other names that dropped out of the running at the last minute, weren't there?'

McKenna gave another throaty chuckle. 'You're not suggesting Harrison nobbled the competition? He wanted the job, and he's certainly qualified – he has a solid background in both MIT and CID, both at senior levels. The Met's no different to any other large organisation – the higher up you go, the more the job's about politics rather than donkey work. That's why I've always been happy to stay a DCI.' She waved her hand at him. 'Relax, Matt. A new broom will always try to mark their territory when they first take over. He'll soon settle down and let us get on with what we're paid to do. Which is to investigate murders, in case you'd forgotten.' She threw him a wintry smile. 'Take my advice, Matt — stick to solid policing and let our elders and betters worry about playing politics. And keep your head under the parapet — it's the easiest way to dodge any flying shrapnel. I'm speaking from experience.'

Denning returned to the main office. He had just sat down at his desk when Neeraj came over.

'I did a PNC check on Cairns.'

'Don't tell me he's got a criminal record?'

Neeraj shook his head. 'That was my first thought. Turns out it's something else entirely.' He waited until he had Denning's full attention. Denning half expected him to mime a drum roll.

'Go on.'

'About twenty years ago,' Neeraj continued. 'Cairns was reported missing. And this is the really interesting bit: according to the report on the PNC, the file was never closed. Cairns is still officially listed as a missing person.'

'Who reported him missing?'

'His sister.' Neeraj looked at the piece of paper he was holding, no doubt trying to decipher his awful handwriting. 'A Mrs Frances Hynd.'

'Then I think we need to speak to Mrs Hynd and inform her that her missing brother has now been found.'

'On the other hand,' Neeraj said, with a sardonic grin, 'perhaps there's a good reason why Dr Cairns didn't want to be found.'

Chapter Eight

The pub was a five-minute walk from St Paul's Cathedral, down a side street that led towards the river. It was already busy with after-work drinkers. They either milled around the bar, getting in everybody's way, or congregated in clumps near the door, talking loudly about work and money. Molly found a table in a corner with a view of the pub's entrance. She sat down and waited. She could see a couple of smokers out on the pavement, puffing away, oblivious to the early-evening chill. For a brief second, she envied them. Right now, more than ever, a nicotine kick would have been very welcome.

Trudi had suggested going for a drink after work. She and her partner, Charys, were going through a rough patch, and Trudi said she needed a sympathetic ear to chew over a couple of pints. Molly had been very tempted.

Instead, she had made an excuse, saying she'd arranged to meet her brother after work, but reassured Trudi they would have their girly chinwag another night.

She felt guilty. Her friendship with Trudi predated her arrival at MIT, and Trudi had been there for Molly when she'd needed a friend not so long ago.

Now she was sitting in a noisy pub staring at a pint of Kronenbourg wishing she'd taken Trudi up on her offer. She'd sent Jon a text to tell him she'd be back late and was on the point of taking her phone out of her jacket pocket to send another one when she was suddenly aware of someone near her table.

'Sorry I'm late.'

Startled, she looked up to see Mags standing there. Her mind must have been elsewhere as she hadn't noticed her come in.

'Hi. That's alright. I've only just got here myself.'

Mags dumped an oversized handbag on the table and rummaged around inside it, eventually pulling out a tiny tartan purse.

'Do you want anything from the bar? Nuts, or crisps?'

Molly shook her head. 'I'm fine with this, thanks.' She looked at her pint glass, from which she'd already taken several sips.

Without another word, Mags headed over to the bar, pushing through the crowd of office workers that blocked her way. She returned a couple of minutes later with a glass of what looked like sparkling water but could have been a vodka and lemonade.

Molly couldn't remember if Mags was a drinker, but part of her wished she'd chosen something non-alcoholic herself as it was always wise to keep a clear head when dealing with a journalist – especially one as slippery as Magda Kilbride.

She looked at Mags. The hair was a slightly sharper shade of red than the last time they'd met, but nothing else had changed. She was still dressed head-to-toe in black: slim-fitting chinos and a tailored shirt, topped off with a dark grey blazer. Her lips were a slash of magenta, which stood out against her pale face. She wore a silver cross around her neck, which Molly thought was ironic, considering Mags always reminded her of a vampire.

'Thanks for agreeing to meet,' she said, sitting on the chair opposite Molly. She dropped the tiny tartan purse back into the capacious bag then placed the bag on the floor. 'I knew you'd come. Curiosity get the better of you?'

'What's this about, Mags?'

Mags sipped her drink, then circled the rim of her glass with a scarlet talon.

'A friend of mine has gone missing, and I'm worried about him.'

'Then you should dial 101 and ask to file a Missing Person's report. You don't need me for that.' Molly drank some of her pint, already sensing this was going to be a wasted evening.

'It's not just that he's missing,' Mags continued. She was still circling the rim of her glass, staring hard at the tabletop. 'He's vulnerable, and I think something might have happened to him. I don't want to make this official and you seemed the obvious choice. What with us being friends.'

Molly wasn't sure if Mags was taking the piss or if in some deluded way she actually thought that what existed between them somehow passed for friendship.

'Mags, this really isn't my area. I'm not CID anymore. And even if I were…'

'If it wasn't for me, you wouldn't even be in MIT. You owe me.'

'I don't owe you shit, Mags.' It was true Mags had been useful once before. Less than a year ago, Molly had been investigating a series of brutal murders without any tangible lead. It had been a clue from Mags that had led them to the culprit, albeit indirectly. But it was a major leap to suggest that Molly 'owed' her. 'Don't push your luck. We'd have caught that bloke with or without your so-called help.'

'Maybe, but it would have taken you longer to get there. And you did all right out of it. You'd still be spending your days directing traffic – or whatever the fuck it is CID do – if I hadn't pointed your investigation in the right direction. Like I said, you *owe* me.' She looked Molly in the eye, making sure she held her gaze. 'And this *is* about a murder, so it is your area, unless MIT's remit has suddenly changed.'

Molly knew Mags well enough to know she was capable of lying, or at least manipulating the truth for her own ends. She had no reason to believe a word that came out of the woman's mouth. Common sense told her to finish her pint and walk away. But something made her think again. If there was even the faintest chance Mags knew something about a possible murder, then Molly felt obliged to hear her out.

'OK,' she sighed. 'Tell me about this alleged murder.'

Mags started circling the rim of her glass again. 'It happened a few years ago. My friend… somebody killed this kid he used to hang around with. He wouldn't tell me his name, or what they did to him. But he says the men who did it said they'd kill him if he ever told anyone.'

'When you say "a few years ago" – how long ago are we talking?'

'About thirty years.'

'Thirty years! That's a cold case, Mags. The chances of us finding someone after all this time is slim, to say the least. Especially if we don't have a name.'

'I've told you all I know.'

Molly wasn't sure. 'If this all happened thirty years ago, why has your friend gone missing now?'

But Mags just shrugged. 'I don't know. Maybe something's happened to scare him.' She looked imploringly at Molly. 'But I really do believe he might be in trouble.'

This sounded more and more fanciful by the second. Molly wondered if Mags was making it up as she went along just to get her attention. Or did she genuinely believe what she was saying? There were times she wished she had Denning's ability to read people.

'How long have you known this friend?' she asked.

'A while.' She paused. 'I went to school with his sister.'

'And he's only just mentioned this murder from thirty years ago?' Molly struggled to keep the scepticism from her voice.

'Look, I know how this sounds. But we kind of lost touch. He's been away...' She took a moment to find the right words. 'I hadn't seen him for some time, then he got back in touch with me a few weeks ago. He was very agitated; claimed he'd had time to think about things, and he wanted to sort his life out. But before he could move on, he had to deal with all the crap that had gone down in his life, including this. He's been living with it for years – frightened to tell anyone, scared of what would happen if he went public with it. I wanted to help him, but I didn't know how. I'm a journalist, not a counsellor – I'm not trained for this kind of thing.'

'So why didn't you and your friend come to us and make this official? You know it's a crime to withhold information from the police.'

'I told you – they threatened him, which is why you need to find him. He could be in trouble.'

Molly took another sip of Kronenbourg, trying to make sense of what she was being told. 'Why should I believe you, Mags? What makes you think this friend's disappearance is something sinister? He could just have gone away for a while.'

'Like I said – I think he's scared.'

'And you've tried contacting him?'

'Well, of course I have. He's not answering his phone, or replying to my voicemail messages.'

'What about social media?'

'He isn't on social media.'

'Have you been round to his address?'

A pause. 'I don't know where he lives.' Her finger stopped mid-circle, and her eyes met Molly's again, staying there for a moment, before falling back to the tabletop. 'He only recently moved to London. I think he's sofa-surfing, or dossing down with mates. He might even be sleeping rough.'

'How long has he been missing for?'

'Just over a week.'

Molly wondered just how well Mags really knew this 'friend', and what it was she wasn't telling her. Her gut instinct was to approach the situation with caution. 'Then my advice is to wait until he gets in touch again. If you haven't heard from him by the end of next week, contact your local police station and report him as a missing person. And I'm sorry, but unless you can give me some hard facts about this supposed murder, I can't take it any further.'

Mags leaned in closer. Molly could smell her perfume: Christian Dior's '*Poison*' – appropriate. 'You don't get it, do you? There's a real possibility something bad could have happened to him. That's why I got in touch with you.'

Another sigh from Molly. Whatever was going on here, the bottom line was that a possibly vulnerable man had gone missing. A man who may potentially have information about a serious crime. It was all very tenuous, but if Mags was telling the truth, as far as she knew it, Molly had a moral obligation as a police officer to take her seriously. Besides, she had a feeling Mags wasn't going to let the matter drop easily.

'Alright. I'll have a look on the system and see what I can find out. But I can't guarantee anything, at least not until I have more information.' She took a pen and pad from her jacket pocket. 'Give me his details.'

'His name's Colin Meek. He's in his late forties. He originally hails from Barnsley, but he no longer has any connections there. I've got his mobile number, and I can email you a photo, if that helps.' She reached over the table and grabbed Molly's hand. Molly wasn't sure if it was a gesture of appreciation or a threat. 'Promise me you'll try and find him.'

Molly pulled her hand away. She put the pen and pad back in her pocket and glanced at her watch. There should be a bus in five minutes, meaning she could be home in half an hour.

She downed the rest of her pint, then grabbed her bag from the back of the chair and slung it over her shoulder.

Getting to her feet, she said, 'OK, Mags. I've said I'll look into it. That's all I can do for now.' Molly told Mags she'd be in touch. She left the pub and headed to the bus stop on Queen Victoria Street. But as soon as she was on the bus heading back to Crouch End, she regretted having said anything at all. Agreeing to do a favour for Magda Kilbride felt a bit like offering your soul to the devil: once you'd signed it away, there really was no hope of turning back.

She had a horrible feeling this was all going to come back and bite her on the arse.

Chapter Nine

The aromatic tang of something exotic greeted Denning as soon as he entered the flat. Sarah was in the kitchen preparing dinner.

He and Sarah had an informal arrangement where each made dinner on alternate evenings, assuming they weren't dining out. They both had demanding jobs and often worked long hours, so they'd agreed early on in their marriage that it was only reasonable they should divvy up the domestic chores as evenly as possible. In reality, it was usually the case that whichever one was home from work first ended up cooking, and more often than not that was Sarah. Not for the first time, Denning wondered what life would be like if he had a more conventional job.

'Busy day?' she asked. She was chopping some vegetables ready to add to the cubes of pork sizzling in a fruity sauce in the Le Creuset casserole dish on the hob.

'So-so,' he replied. Any interest she took in his job was motivated by politeness rather than actual curiosity, and that worked both ways. His wife had no wish to become acquainted with the gorier intricacies of a murder investigation any more than he had an urge to query the tax implications of the investment portfolios she managed on behalf of wealthy clients. Work was rarely discussed beyond the usual cursory enquiries. 'How about you?' he asked.

'Same,' she replied. 'So-so.'

He headed upstairs to the shower room off the main bedroom on the mezzanine level, which overlooked the vast open living space that took up most of the flat.

As he changed out of his work suit and turned on the shower, he thought about Buckfield's spartan flat. The contrast in their living arrangements couldn't have been greater. The lofty Shoreditch apartment he called home was mainly paid for courtesy of Sarah's salary rather than his, but even so they could still have afforded to live somewhere nice on what he earned.

Buckfield should have retired with a good pension, easily enough to have funded a comfortable home to see out his remaining years. So why had he ended up living in that dump?

Before they'd all left for the day, Dave Kinsella told them he'd found contact details for Buckfield's ex-wife. Denning would speak to her tomorrow. Perhaps she could throw some light on her ex-husband's domestic situation, though Denning wasn't holding out much hope.

He stood under the shower, letting the needles of water ease away the day's tension. Ex-wives... that was something he and Buckfield did have in common.

Claire hadn't been in touch for a while. She was planning to take their son Jake down to her mother's in Devon for the Easter holidays. Not that long ago she'd been talking about moving there. That idea seemed to have been knocked on the head recently, but there was always a chance Claire would move away from London, taking Jake with her. He'd wanted to spend a bit of quality father-and-son time together over Easter. Jake's ADHD meant he found it difficult to make friends, and often felt isolated. Denning wanted to prove to Jake that his son could depend on him if he needed to.

He turned off the shower, dried himself, then slipped on a pair of jeans and a woollen pullover, and headed back downstairs.

Sarah was still in the kitchen, adding some chopped tomatoes to the casserole. 'It'll be another twenty minutes,' she said. 'You might as well chill for a bit.' That was code to get out of the kitchen whilst she was cooking, so he took a bottle of beer from the fridge, went into the living room and made himself comfortable on one of the linen sofas.

His thoughts turned to the meeting that morning with the new Detective Chief Super. He still wasn't sure about Harrison; there was something about the man he just didn't like. Maybe it was his condescending manner, or the way he talked about change and efficiency. The Met had undergone a decade of cuts and savings, none of which had helped make the service any more efficient, no matter what the politicians claimed. Crime hadn't dropped, but the workload of the average copper had significantly increased. Harrison had said little – if anything – to address this.

Denning sipped the beer and took out his phone. Curiosity had got the better of him. He logged on remotely to the Met's intranet and looked up Harrison's profile. Most of what he read he already knew: Harrison had joined the Met straight from school as a PC, moving over to CID in his late twenties and steadily progressing through the ranks until becoming a DCI in his mid-forties. His later promotions had come about after a period of restructuring had created gaps in senior management that had been slow to fill. The implication was that

Harrison's success had been down to good timing rather than talent, but perhaps that was unfair.

The picture on Harrison's profile page was at least ten years old. The man who had addressed them today was greyer and more grizzled, his skin more pockmarked than the 'official' picture suggested.

Denning did a further search but could find no information about the other contenders for the DCS post or their reasons for dropping out. Had Harrison received political backing? Detective Chief Superintendents were internal appointments, decided by the Met rather than arranged by the Mayor's Office for Policing, but having an Assembly member on his side probably wouldn't have harmed Harrison's chances.

Still curious, he then googled Justin Morrow. Morrow's page on The London Assembly website gave little away. According to his biography, he'd come from a financial services background, but had always been interested in politics from an early age.

Apart from the Police and Crime Committee, Morrow was a member of two other committees and some kind of special advisory body on crisis planning that reported directly to the Mayor's office. However, there was nothing to link him with Harrison, and no suggestion that the two had known each other prior to Harrison's recent appointment. Perhaps Denning was looking for things that weren't there.

He logged off and placed the phone on the coffee table. Morrow had been smooth. Smooth and confident was how Denning recalled his performance that morning: a well-rehearsed speech that Morrow could probably deliver off pat by now. But what was his interest in the Met Police, and in MIT in particular? The Mayor's Office had recently come up with several community-based initiatives to try and reduce knife crime and gang-related violence in the capital, but that was outside of MIT's remit. True, they had to deal with the aftermath of such crimes, and it would certainly be in their interests to see it drastically reduced, but these initiatives were generally better directed at rank and file policing, rather than overworked detectives.

But if Harrison was planning radical changes to MIT, then having political support behind him would provide some much-needed clout if it came to a fight.

Denning couldn't help worrying that there may be stormy times ahead.

Chapter Ten

Jon was pottering in his 'man shed' when Molly got back to the North London home they shared. She could hear Motorhead's *Iron Fist* oozing across the scrub of overgrown lawn that separated the shed from the house.

The shed had recently been converted from general garden usage into a 'space' for Jon to write and think, though he mostly used it to listen to music and smoke dope. He'd moved an old sofa bed from one of the spare rooms into the shed, along with a desk he'd found in a junk shop, and an old gas heater donated by an elderly neighbour. He'd made the place cosy and homely, to the point where, if he were to add a kettle and a toilet, Molly suspected he'd be quite happy to live in it permanently. She rarely crossed its threshold.

She briefly thought about knocking on the shed door to let him know she was home, but decided against it. Instead, she went into the cluttered kitchen, walked over to the sink and poured herself a glass of water.

Things had been going well between them lately. Jon had spent the best part of a year almost paralysed with depression. It had put a strain on their relationship, no matter how sympathetic she'd tried to be. The situation had been exacerbated by him losing his job as the political editor of a tabloid newspaper, *The London Echo*, along with the ensuing loss of self-worth that went with unemployment. Fortunately, he'd recently turned a corner thanks to medication and regular sessions with a therapist. Plus he was now teaching journalism at a local FE college two days a week and firing off the odd article for the few publications that still accepted freelance submissions. But the risk of a relapse was never far away. There were days when Molly felt like she was treading on eggshells such was her concern that something she said or did could trigger another bout of melancholy. Other times she felt guilty that she wasn't being more supportive. It was a delicate balance.

Then there was her trip to the doctor's that morning. They'd never discussed having children. Molly had tacitly assumed that kids were off the agenda. She had been so focussed on her career since they'd got together, and Jon had never struck her as the paternal type. She knew he had a daughter out there somewhere, although he had lost touch with her and she was rarely mentioned. The prospect of another child might make him run for the hills. Or give him a reason to get up in the morning. Either way, now was probably not the time to try and find out.

She sat at the kitchen table and sipped the water. Drinking a pint of Kronenbourg quickly on an empty stomach had been a mistake. Meeting Mags had probably been a mistake too, but there wasn't much she could do about that now.

Jon suddenly appeared at the back door, his face breaking into a smile when he saw her. 'Heya, when did you get back?' He kissed her on the cheek.

'A few minutes ago,' she replied. 'I didn't want to disturb you.'

He gave a slightly forced laugh. 'It's all right. I was only chilling. Nothing to disturb.' Sometimes Molly felt he was trying too hard to convince her everything was OK. Or perhaps he was trying to convince himself; it was hard to tell.

–

Neither of them fancied cooking, so dinner was a takeaway pizza in front of the telly. Molly sat in the comfy armchair that she'd recently bought from Ikea, while Jon was on the rickety chaise longue that was partly supported by two and half bricks. *Channel 4 News* was doing a piece about the melting polar ice caps, and she could see Jon's eyes focus more on the pizza than the telly. This felt like a convenient moment to share what was on her mind.

'I saw Mags today.' She ate a mouthful of ham and pineapple and waited for his response. Jon and Mags had worked together at the *Echo* several years ago, long before he and Molly met. At some point they'd had a relationship – a full-on affair, according to Mags; a brief and forgettable fling according to Jon. Molly had never been sure which one to believe, and suspected the truth lay somewhere in the middle.

'Mags?' he said, looking up from his pizza to stare at the telly, suddenly interested in melting ice caps. 'What did she want?'

She filled him in on what Mags had told her about the missing 'friend' and the alleged murder, the details of which were too sketchy to make any real sense. She omitted to mention her somewhat impetuous promise to look into it; a promise she was already regretting.

When she'd finished, he was still gazing at the telly, chewing on a slice of pizza. 'Do you believe her?' he asked.

'About the missing friend? Probably, though I would question her use of the word "friend". I'm not sure Mags does friends.' He didn't react to her comment, so she continued. 'About the alleged murder?' She paused. 'I don't know. I suspect the murder story was simply the bait to lure me in.'

'I take it she wants you to find this friend?'

She nodded. 'But I'm not sure I can justify wasting time on what could turn out to be a wild goose chase.'

'But...?'

She nibbled some of the pizza crust. Jon was right; there was a 'but'. 'It was when she said he was vulnerable. I can't help thinking it's possible something *could* have happened to him. And if it has, I'd never be able to live with myself knowing I hadn't taken this seriously.'

Jon sighed. 'Look, if he's a friend of Mags's he probably just wants a break from her. Mags can be a bit full-on sometimes. Maybe she hinted that she was looking for more than friendship and he ran a mile.'

Molly laughed and threw a cushion in his direction. It hit him on the shoulder, then landed beside him on the chaise longue. 'That's such a male response!'

'That doesn't mean it's not true, though,' he said.

She ate the last slice of pizza. 'I think there's more to it than that.' She looked over at Jon, but he was still staring at the TV screen. 'I actually think Mags is genuinely worried about this guy.'

Without taking his eyes off the screen, he said: 'Does that sound like Mags to you?'

'That's what I mean. If she's worried then there must be something wrong.'

He picked up the remote, switched off the TV, and turned to face her. 'Well, it looks like you've got two options. One: you assume this is Mags chasing some story and she wants you to play along. Or two: she's telling the truth – it has been known – and this guy is in some kind of trouble. In which case, you probably need to find him, for his sake as much as for hers.'

She stared at the empty pizza box lying on the floor. She knew Jon spoke sense. Her head said one thing but her gut said another. They had just kicked off a murder inquiry – two murder inquiries if David Cairns didn't survive the night. The last thing she should be doing was running round after a journalist whose credentials were questionable to say the least. But on the other hand, she had given Mags her word…

'Maybe I should toss a coin?' she joked. But in her head, she had already decided what she was going to do.

Chapter Eleven

Denning was the first one in the office next morning. As soon as he was at his desk, he phoned the hospital for an update on Cairns's condition. Still unconscious but stable, he was told. They would let him know as soon as Cairns regained consciousness, or if his condition deteriorated.

Then he logged on to the Police National Computer and checked the Missing Person's report that had been filed for Cairns. According to the report on the PNC, Frances Hynd had reported her brother missing twenty years ago, after failing to contact him for several weeks. Just as Neeraj had said, the case had never been closed, so, technically, Cairns was still officially listed as a missing person. For whatever reason, he had clearly decided not to get back in touch with his sister after all these years. Denning made a note of her contact details and decided to give her a call later that morning. He was just about to close the file, when something caught his eye. Cairns's age was given as sixty-one at the time he was reported missing, meaning he would be over eighty now. Denning had assumed from the way Joyce Lindsey had spoken about him that he was a much younger man.

Next, he checked his emails to see if there was anything from the Directorate of Professional Standards regarding the investigation into Buckfield's alleged misconduct. McKenna had put the request in via Harrison, so Denning should have been granted access by now, but there was still nothing coming up on the system. Maybe McKenna needed to give Harrison another prod.

He glanced up from his keyboard to see Molly Fisher pushing open the glass door to the office. She had her earbuds in, and was carrying a coffee from the McDonald's across the road. She seemed surprised to see him. 'Another early bird,' he said, throwing her a smile.

She removed her earbuds and returned the smile. 'I wanted to crack on with looking over Buckfield's case histories,' she said. She placed her bag on her desk and draped her jacket over the back of her chair. 'I thought it best to do that when the office was quiet.'

'Good thinking.' He returned to his emails. Scanning the most recent messages, he found one from the pathologist confirming the post-mortem had been booked for later that morning, and another from Kinsella sent the previous evening with the contact details for Buckfield's ex-widow. Denning made a note of her address.

He looked over at Molly's desk. She was sipping her coffee. He suddenly wished he'd bought one before coming into work that morning. There was a machine on the ground floor near the entrance that purported to offer tea and coffee as well as cold drinks, but the one time he'd used it the coffee had looked and tasted like something he'd put in his car engine. He briefly thought about popping over and chatting to her. Molly had joined MIT shortly after he'd arrived, and in a way they were both like the new kids on the block. He thought about popping over to speak to her, but she seemed too focussed on what she was doing...

A quick look at the time on the bottom corner of the computer screen told him it wouldn't be long until the rest of the team would start arriving. Ryan Cormack was usually one of the first, and McKenna the last. Perk of being a DCI, he supposed. McKenna wasn't a morning person, and would usually pitch up once everyone else was sitting at their desks. Even then it generally took the rest of the morning and several coffees before she was at her best.

Today, however, was the exception. The clock on the screen said 8:06 when McKenna arrived, dressed in dark glasses and a raincoat, as though she was recovering from a heavy night. She took off her sunglasses as soon as she was through the door, and asked to see Denning in her office.

'I spoke to Harrison,' she said, before her backside had even made contact with her chair. 'Yesterday, just as I was about to leave the office. He likes working late by the look of things. Anyway, he wasn't shy in letting me know his thoughts for the day.' She made sure she had Denning's full attention. 'He wants us to treat Buckfield's murder as our sole priority. Anything else comes in, we punt it over to one of the other teams. From now on, we're responsible for catching Buckfield's killer and nothing else.'

'What about Cairns?' Denning asked.

'Have you spoken to the hospital this morning?'

'First thing.'

'And…?'

Denning knew where this was heading, but he wasn't prepared to walk away without a fight. 'He's still unconscious. They'll get back to me once that changes.'

'So he's still alive,' she said. 'Unlike Buckfield.' She folded her arms and perched on the desk, no doubt warming up to the gimlet stare. 'You see my problem, Matt? We just don't have the resources to prioritise both cases. And Harrison has made himself clear, so unless you can find something to connect the attack on Cairns with Buckfield's murder, which isn't very likely, we're handing this over.'

Denning knew he was being outmanoeuvred and outgunned. This wasn't just Betty Taggart he was locking horns with – this was the new DCS. He was really going to have to stand his ground. He mentioned the Missing Person's report, and how it was still active, but McKenna shook her head.

'What does that tell us? Someone didn't make the effort to follow things up? Or Cairns doesn't want his sister to know he's still alive? If so, that's not our problem. Either way, we know he's not missing any longer.'

He sighed, meeting her gaze and holding it, refusing to back down just yet. 'At least let me speak to Cairns when he regains consciousness. If only to reassure myself that this really was just another attempted mugging. Then I'll happily pass it on to either Islington CID, or another MIT.'

She eyed him for a couple of seconds; the gimlet stare just a heartbeat away. 'All right,' she said eventually. 'You can formally question him, then you make it clear we're handing this over to someone else to follow up. Agreed?'

Denning agreed.

'And we shift our focus onto Buckfield. Harrison is keen to see some progress. The media are already asking questions.'

'On the subject of Buckfield, there's still nothing from the DPS regarding the alleged misconduct investigation. You said you would ask Harrison if he would authorise the request.'

'Oh, yes – that.' She sat back in her chair and steepled her fingers, tapping them against her chin. 'We discussed this in some depth last night. It turns out Harrison is aware of the allegations against Buckfield. He was keen to remind me that nothing was ever substantiated and the investigation into Buckfield was quickly dropped. I'd be surprised if there was anything left on record, at least in any detailed form.'

'So Harrison knows what those allegations were?'

McKenna fidgeted some more. 'He knows what the allegations alleged.'

Denning tried to suppress a smile. 'That's a bit of a tautology.'

But the dark look on McKenna's face suggested she didn't appreciate the humour. 'Matt, you know how damaging false allegations about a serving officer can be. Even when they're cleared, the rumours still linger. It can damage their reputation and destroy careers.'

'But did Harrison actually tell you what the allegations against Buckfield were?'

McKenna clenched and unclenched her right hand, as though squeezing an invisible stress ball. 'This goes no further.' She relaxed her hand and placed it on the desk. 'There were suggestions that Buckfield had been receiving backhanders from someone in exchange for turning a blind eye whenever something went down. Any arrests made would be conveniently dropped. This was all unsubstantiated and naturally the allegations were reported anonymously, but the CIB – as it then was – was duty-bound to investigate them.'

'Yes, I know how it works. A formal investigation is no more proof of guilt than a lack of evidence is proof of innocence.'

'The allegations related to a specific case,' McKenna continued. 'And to a specific individual believed to have been involved in that case.'

Denning decided to grasp the nettle. 'Look, Liz, we could sit here playing hunt the thimble all morning, but as you've already pointed out, we have an ongoing murder investigation hanging over us. Why don't you just tell me what these allegations were?'

She sighed. 'They were made in connection with the investigation into the Security Direct robbery.' She shifted her gaze from Denning to the desktop, a sure sign she felt uncharacteristically uncomfortable. 'They relate specifically to Alfie Kane.'

'Kane!' Denning tried not to fall off his chair. 'That's pretty serious. No wonder Harrison wants it hushed up.'

The gimlet stare returned. 'You just said it yourself, Matt. An official investigation doesn't automatically suggest there's any truth in the claim. And for the record, Detective Chief Superintendent Harrison doesn't want the matter "hushed up", as you put it. He just doesn't feel it's relevant to this investigation.'

Alfie Kane: not quite a Mr Big, but someone whose name had been associated with organised crime over the past three decades, perhaps more if they were to include youthful misdemeanours. He was claiming to be a legitimate businessman these days, but if a leopard didn't change its spots, then neither did a villain.

'What do you believe?'

'I prefer to keep an open mind. But I don't think this is an avenue we should necessarily feel we need to explore. The most likely motive behind Buckfield's killing lies with some slimy scrote he put away. I want us to continue looking into past cases, and especially the big ones. The answer to this lies there.'

Denning smiled and agreed with her. But he wasn't so sure. He had a feeling there was something more than he was being told. Buckfield and Alfie Kane. It was entirely possible there was something there worth looking into, despite what McKenna was telling him. But if he were to go down that particular route, he was going to have to tread very carefully.

Chapter Twelve

Molly had planned to get into work early that morning, hoping the office would be deserted and she could work undisturbed. She hadn't banked on Denning being in at sparrow's fart too. She'd fobbed him off with a story about wanting to sift through Buckfield's old cases, even though she'd spent most of the previous afternoon doing just that, and had failed to come up with anything that could credibly be considered as a motive for killing him.

In reality, she had logged on to the PNC and entered the name 'Colin Meek'. She hadn't been sure what to expect, but had been surprised and slightly shocked at the information that had flashed up on the screen.

Meek had been in and out of trouble more or less from the moment he'd exited the womb. After the death of his mother from a heroin overdose when he was six, he'd spent most of his childhood being bounced between foster homes and residential care. Each time the fostering had come to an end, it was because Meek had either stolen something, hit someone, or made false claims about one of his foster parents. By the time he was fourteen, he had been arrested for shoplifting and assault. By the time he was thirty, he'd served sentences of between two and six years for ABH, fraud and theft.

At first glance, it looked like Meek was a recidivist who had become so entrapped in the system that he was beyond help. But she'd been a cop for long enough to know the facts rarely told the whole story. If anything, the information on her screen showed that Meek was a victim of the system, and had probably been allowed to fall through the net on more than one occasion. His adult life had been set on a course that had pretty much been predetermined by his damaged childhood. He'd become entrapped in a deviant cycle of crime and its consequences.

However, it was the final entry on the page that rang the biggest alarm bell.

Thirty years ago, aged nineteen, Meek had claimed he'd been sexually assaulted by a number of men when he was in his mid-teens at various locations around London. He stated that there had been other boys too, but he didn't know their names. There was no mention of a murder though, and Molly was now convinced that Mags had lied about this to get her attention. If Molly had known the truth, she would have told Mags to go and fuck herself. Rather than being a victim, Colin Meek seemed to be a serial offender.

Meek's claims had been thoroughly investigated at the time and found to be false. There was no evidence to suggest any abuse had ever taken place. Meek was cautioned for wasting police time. According to the information on her computer screen, he had recently been released from prison after serving another five years for GBH. While in prison, he had made a false claim of assault against one of the prison officers, resulting in him having an extra six months added to his sentence. It seemed that not only was Meek a recidivist, he was a compulsive liar too.

The report made for depressing reading.

There was nothing to suggest he'd come into contact with the police since his release from prison four months ago, so it was just possible he was trying to keep his nose clean.

She looked on the MisPer database, but there was no mention of Meek. If there was anyone else in his life besides Mags, they hadn't reported him missing. She noted the name of his probation officer: Marcia Wilson. She phoned and left a message for Ms Wilson to call her back.

As soon as she'd put the phone down, Molly spotted Betty Taggart arriving, looking like she'd had a heavy night. She then disappeared into her office with Denning.

Molly decided to wait until she'd spoken to Marcia Wilson before officially registering Meek as a missing person. Not that they'd be able to do much beyond circulating his details and waiting to see if anything popped up on the system. She couldn't ignore the possibility that Jon was right, and Meek simply wanted to avoid Mags.

The rest of the team was starting to arrive now – computers were being woken from sleep mode, and the room began to fill with the buzz of early morning chatter. She glanced over at Betty Taggart's door. In a moment Denning would emerge and the day would officially begin, the focus of their attention for today and for the foreseeable future being the investigation into Buckfield's murder. The whereabouts of Colin Meek and the reason for his disappearance would have to wait.

But intrigue still nibbled at her. How well did Mags really know Meek? And was her interest in him born out of the scent of a story or genuine concern for his wellbeing? As much as she wanted to forget about Mags and Colin Meek, Molly had a feeling she was about to get sucked into the whole sorry mess. And despite her better judgement, something told her there was a strong chance Colin Meek could be in trouble.

Chapter Thirteen

Denning found the house easily enough. A 1930s semi in suburban Ruislip with a neat lawn and a tidy gravelled path that led to a freshly painted front door. The door was answered by a slender man in his late forties, who greeted Denning with a cautious look. He had a slightly receding hairline and wore a pair of round, black-framed glasses, through which he peered at Denning's ID. Denning told him why he was there.

'I'm Gavin Buckfield,' the man said. 'Frank was my dad. I came round as soon as Mum phoned this morning.' He opened the door further to let Denning in.

His mother was sitting on an armchair in the living room. She was a well-groomed woman in her mid-seventies, and was introduced to Denning as Sally Batcheller, Buckfield's ex-wife. 'Gavin's been looking after me,' she said, after the introductions had been made. 'He's kindly agreed to identify Frank's body. I just couldn't face it. Besides, it's been so long since I last saw Frank, I'm not sure I'd be able to recognise him after all this time.' She immediately put her hand to her mouth. 'God, isn't that an awful thing to say. Not being able to recognise someone I was married to for the best part of twenty-five years.'

Denning sat on the sofa and nodded sympathetically. A uniformed officer had called round earlier to inform

Sally Batcheller of her late ex-husband's death, although technically she was no longer the next of kin. Denning looked over at Gavin Buckfield, who sat on a dining chair, unsmiling. 'It will just be a formality,' Denning said. 'I appreciate these things are never pleasant.'

Gavin Buckfield offered a quick nod of the head. 'The least I can do.'

The house was homely and warm, the antithesis of Buckfield's depressing flat.

'Frank and I divorced over twenty years ago,' Sally Batcheller explained. 'I remarried twelve years ago, and we bought this place. It was a fresh start. Sadly, I lost my husband last year.' There were silver-framed photos on a table of Sally and a grey-haired man smiling lovingly at each other, and another couple of photos on top of a glass-fronted cabinet, featuring Sally and what Denning assumed to be her grandchildren. There were no photos of Frank Buckfield, which was perhaps understandable if he hadn't been a part of her life for such a long time.

'I'm very sorry about what happened,' Denning offered. 'We're doing all we can to find Frank's killer. However, at the moment, we don't have a motive for his murder. Anything you can tell me about him would be helpful.'

She offered a thin smile. 'Frank was a good policeman. A good husband too. But the work always came first with him.' There was a faraway look in her eyes as she spoke. Gavin Buckfield remained impassive. 'I suppose you'll know all about that,' she added, looking over at Denning, 'being with the police yourself.'

He thought about how the job had got in the way of his first marriage. Claire had expected him home at a sensible time, and assumed he could turn the job on and off like a tap whenever it suited. Luckily it was less of an issue with Sarah, who seemed to accept that work took priority over home life if you were to get anywhere in this world. But there were times even she found his job overbearing, though she'd never admit it.

'Being a detective isn't like a normal nine-to-five job,' he agreed. 'And it's often our partners who bear the brunt of that.'

'Do you think my dad's murder had something to do with his job?' Gavin asked. Denning detected an edginess about Gavin Buckfield. Not exactly hostility, more a kind of resentment that he was having to go through this. 'He hadn't been in the police for over twenty years,' he added. 'Why would someone go after him now?'

That was a good question, and one to which they were still struggling to find an answer. 'At this stage, we can't confirm if that's definitely the case, but neither can we discount it as a possibility.' Denning turned his attention to Sally. 'I'm guessing Frank didn't remarry after you divorced?'

She shook her head. 'No. He took the divorce quite badly, to be honest with you. But by then it was impossible for us to carry on. After he retired and the children had left home, we just spent the whole time arguing. About trivial things mostly, but it starts to grind you down when it's happening all the time.'

'Don't worry,' Denning said, 'I understand.' He directed his next question at Gavin. 'When did you last see your father?'

Gavin puffed out his cheeks, then blew the air through his mouth. 'Not for a few years. We kept in touch a bit after he and Mum split up, but I'd moved to Manchester by then, so I wasn't around much. By the time I moved back to London, Mum had remarried and Dad was pretty much off the scene.'

'What about your other children, Mrs Batcheller? Would they have been in touch with Frank?'

He addressed the question to Sally, but it was Gavin who answered. 'There's only my sister, and she lives in France. They exchanged the odd Christmas card, but that was it.' He glanced over at his mother, but wouldn't make eye contact. 'We were never very close to our dad. Not even when we were kids.'

'Frank was always hands-off with the children when they were growing up,' Sally explained. 'He left all that to me. But he was a good husband,' she repeated, as though reciting a mantra she'd learned at an early age. 'And he was a good provider.' She looked over at her son. 'Neither you nor your sister ever went without.'

An awkward silence fell over the room like a pall.

'The last time we spoke was about four years ago,' Gavin said, once the silence was in danger of taking root. 'He asked if he could borrow some money. A hundred quid.' He glanced again at his mum, but she was looking at the floor, refusing to return his gaze. 'I told him to sod off, or words to that effect. Whatever money we have I need for my own kids. He didn't speak to me after that. Told me I was a selfish little prick.' He was still looking at his mother, possibly hoping for a response, but her focus remained fixed on the floor.

'Did he tell you what he wanted the money for?' Denning asked.

'He said he was behind with his rent. I expect he really wanted to piss it up the wall.'

Sally finally looked up at her son. 'You never said anything.'

He ignored her and continued talking to Denning. 'My dad was a piss-head. That's the main reason I didn't want to have much to do with him.'

'That's not true,' Sally argued, but Denning could tell from the look on her face that she knew her son wasn't lying. 'Maybe he did like a drink now and again,' she said. 'Who doesn't? It was a way of switching off from the job. A way of coping.' She searched Denning's face for a reaction, possibly hoping he would offer a nod or a smile that would support her claim. Denning just looked back at her, refusing to confirm what she wanted to hear. Yes, the job was stressful, like so many others. But not all police officers coped with it by drowning themselves and their careers in drink, contrary to many a popular cultural misconception.

'It was more than that, Mum,' Gavin insisted. 'Dad always had a problem with the booze. He was pissed more often than he was sober when we was kids.'

Sally made a shushing motion with her hands.

'Mrs Batcheller,' Denning said calmly, 'it's important I get a clear picture of Frank's life. Especially recently. It's entirely possible his murder could have something to do with his private life. Maybe someone he owed money to, or had fallen out with. The more facts we have about him, the easier it will be to look in the right places to find our answers.'

'He was a bully,' Gavin said suddenly. He looked over at his mum. Sally was shaking her head, visibly denying what her son was saying. 'Oh, come on, Mum. Be honest. He's been out of your life for the past twenty years. You don't have to defend him anymore. Dad was a bully and a cheat. There's no point pretending otherwise.'

'Be quiet, Gavin. You don't know what you're talking about. You were too young to understand.' She looked at Denning. 'He sees everything in black and white. Things are never that simple. Yes, we had our problems, but doesn't everyone? He was a good husband,' she repeated, but with less conviction than before. 'He always tried his best to be a good husband and a good father. But the job…' She shook her head again. 'There were things he wouldn't talk about. Things he wanted to keep from his wife and kids, and what's wrong with that?'

Denning was beginning to see a different picture emerging of Buckfield, one that contradicted their initial understanding of the man: the distinguished and respected police officer seemed to have another side to his character. Taking what his ex-wife and son were saying, along with the corruption allegations, Buckfield was clearly a man whose private face was at odds with his public one.

'There were plenty of things he wanted to keep from us, and it wasn't just the booze,' Gavin said. He looked at his mum who returned his gaze and gave another shake of her head, only more slowly this time, as though she was trying to make a point.

'In what way?' Denning asked. He was addressing Sally Batcheller, but the question was aimed at her son.

'Let's just say, he was a difficult man to live with,' Gavin added. 'And if you want to know the truth, he's been out of our lives for so long now, we're neither of us sad he's dead.'

The silence returned, filling the room with its awkward bulk. Somewhere in the street outside, Denning could hear a dog barking.

He wasn't going to get anything else for now, at least not while Sally was present. There was clearly only so much dirty laundry she was willing to wash in public. Whatever had really gone on in her first marriage, she wasn't prepared to share it with a stranger.

'I really am very sorry to have brought all this up again,' Denning said. 'We only want to find the person who killed Frank. Thanks for agreeing to do the formal identification; I know these things are never pleasant. Please get in touch if there's anything else you can think of.' He handed Gavin his card. 'I'll let you know as soon as his body can be released for the funeral.'

Gavin saw him out. Once they were in the hallway, he closed the living room door. 'I shouldn't have said all that in there, not in front of Mum. It's just…' He shook his head. 'I hope you find my dad's killer, I really do, but don't expect either me or my mum to be at his funeral.'

As Denning headed back to his car, he reflected on Gavin Buckfield's comments about his father. He wondered what his own legacy would be. He thought about a grown-up Jake spilling his bile about him years from now: a good detective, he might say, but a useless husband and father too perhaps.

He opened the car door and shuddered. That certainly wouldn't be a generous assessment of him, but would it be an accurate one?

Chapter Fourteen

Later that morning, Denning pushed open the heavy glass door that led to the mortuary suite. He'd already been buzzed into the main building after giving his name to the voice on the other end of the intercom at the staff entrance. He walked along a whitewashed corridor until he reached the room he wanted.

Dr Baker was just finishing off the post-mortem. One of the mortuary assistants was helping him out of his gown. Denning tapped on the glass wall of the examination room and raised his hand to let Baker know he was there. Baker acknowledged Denning with a brief tip of his chin.

He looked to see if Sheila Gorton was there. It was usual for a member of the SOCO team to attend the post-mortem, but these days Gorton seemed happier delegating that particular pleasure to a junior officer. There were a couple of men standing near the door to the examination room, neither of whom Denning recognised, so it could have been one of them. They would prepare their own report, which would be sent on to Denning later that day.

Denning waited for Baker in his office at the end of another whitewashed corridor. The building was in the basement of a teaching hospital in West London, and little in the way of natural light managed to filter its way to the lower levels. He always wondered how the staff were able to work in these conditions. There must be times when they felt totally cut off from the outside world.

Baker's office was small and furnished with a desk, a couple of filing cabinets, a couple of chairs and a book-case. There was a small fridge in one corner with an old battered kettle on top along with a couple of chipped mugs, which probably wasn't very hygienic for such a sterile environment. On the wall above the desk there was a calendar featuring pictures of different lighthouses around the UK. Denning wondered if Baker had a thing for lighthouses, or if the calendar had simply been a random gift from someone he knew.

'DI Denning,' Baker said, pushing open the office door with his foot. 'Apologies for keeping you waiting. There was something I had to double check.' He headed over to the fridge and removed a bottle of sparkling mineral water, unscrewed the top and took a lengthy swig. When he finished, he offered the bottle to Denning.

Denning shook his head. 'Many thanks again for doing this as a priority. We really do need to pull all the stops out on this one. I'm sure you can appreciate the pressure we're under.'

Baker guffawed and sat down at his desk. He was a heavy-set man in his early sixties, with a neat grey beard and an unruly head of hair.

'Obviously you'll have everything in the report as soon as I've had a chance to type it up.' He gestured at a small Dictaphone that he'd just placed on his desk. 'I'll aim to have it completed this afternoon, but that depends on whether or not I'm sent another body to cut open.' He gave another guffaw, and gently stroked his beard.

'In the meantime,' Denning said, 'I'd appreciate the basic gist of what you found, just so we have some idea of what we're dealing with.'

Baker nodded and continued stroking his beard. 'Death was caused by sustained blood loss resulting from the severing of the carotid arteries, as you already know. I would say it was very precise, almost neat. This would suggest someone who was calm and collected when they committed the murder, rather than someone who was panicking. Time of death is something I'm always unwilling to be drawn on – pinpointing it to an exact second as you lot always want is beyond the skills of a mere quack like myself – but judging by the state of decomposition and rigor, I'd say he's been dead for ten days. I'm afraid I can't be any more precise than that.'

'OK, that's a help. At least we have a date to work backwards from.'

'I can also confirm that the weapon of choice was a knife: serrated, and very sharp. Unfortunately the only DNA on the body was the victim's.'

'What about the tape over his mouth?'

'Standard packing tape available from any stationer's shop or DIY store. Again, no DNA traces on it, except for the victim's.' Baker stopped stroking his beard and scratched his ear. 'The other thing to note is the high level of alcohol in his bloodstream.'

'We know Buckfield was an alcoholic,' Denning said.

'It's worse than that. His liver was damaged beyond repair. He would have needed a transplant sooner or later, and my money's on sooner.'

'You're saying Buckfield was seriously ill?'

'No. I'm saying he was dying.'

'Dying?'

Baker stroked his beard again. 'He had advanced and chronic cirrhosis. I've never seen scarring like it on a liver, at least not for a long time. I'd say he had six months. Maybe a year if he was lucky.'

Denning considered this. 'Do you think he knew?'

Another guffaw. 'Inspector Denning, I'm a pathologist, not a psychic. You could speak to his GP, or ask to see his medical records. But if I were to hazard a professional guess, then I would say it was very likely he knew something wasn't right. His stomach was swollen, he would have been vomiting blood. Then there are symptoms like fatigue, loss of appetite. He would have been seriously ill, and getting worse.'

'So what you're saying is, if Buckfield hadn't received a liver transplant, he would have died, and probably fairly soon?'

Baker nodded. 'His chances of qualifying for a liver transplant would have been pretty slim too. According to official guidelines, anyone should be eligible for a transplant. But in reality, the younger and healthier you are, the more likely you are to get on the waiting list. His age, taken together with his general poor health and alcohol dependency, would have put him at the bottom of a very long queue.' He nodded again. 'I know, it's unfair, but you have to appreciate the shortage of available donors out there, and how surgeons are forced to prioritise and make difficult choices. To put it bluntly, Buckfield wouldn't have had a hope in hell.'

Denning thought about the significance of what Baker had just told him. Why kill a man who was already dying? Obviously the killer didn't know. But did Buckfield? And was it in some way relevant to their investigation?

He thanked Baker and headed for the exit. He was almost back at his car when his phone rang: it was the hospital – David Cairns had regained consciousness.

Chapter Fifteen

'DS Fisher?'

'Speaking.'

'This is Marcia Wilson. You left a message to phone you about Colin Meek.'

The phone call had caught her slightly unawares. Molly had been completely absorbed in something Denning had asked her to do, and had almost forgotten about her phone call to Meek's probation officer earlier that morning.

'I'm not sure what this is in connection with,' Marcia continued, 'and I don't want to get him into any trouble.' She paused, waiting for Molly to fill the space.

'It's nothing serious, Ms Wilson. I just need to speak to him about a minor matter. He isn't in any trouble.'

Marcia Wilson sounded harassed, like this was one of many phone calls she would be making that day. The probation service had recently undergone privatisation and had seen a lot of staff leave their jobs, never to be replaced. Like the Met, there were fewer people doing more work.

'I haven't seen Colin for over a week,' Marcia said. 'We were supposed to have had a supervision meeting yesterday, but he failed to turn up for it, and hasn't been answering his phone. I have left several messages asking him to call me back, but he hasn't so far.'

'Could something have happened to him?' Molly asked.

'It's possible he simply forgot about the meeting yesterday,' Marcia reassured her. 'It does happen, especially when someone has just been released from prison – all that freedom and lack of routine takes a bit of getting used to.'

'Do you have an address for him?'

'Yes, but I don't want him to think that I've reported him for failing to attend yesterday's meeting.'

Molly reiterated that he wasn't in any trouble. After some more prevarication and a token acknowledgement of client confidentiality, she gave Molly his address. Molly made a note of it. She would call round this evening after work, speak to him, then tell Mags that everything was OK. Then she could get on with the job she was paid to do.

'Fancy a natter?'

Molly looked up to see Trudi standing by her desk. She flicked a glance at her watch. A coffee break would go down a treat right now. 'You've twisted my arm.'

Although Molly had given up smoking, Trudi still claimed it was one of the few pleasures she had left in life, and often reminded Molly that they all had to die of *something*. Molly joined Trudi in the car park at the rear of the building, having first purchased something coffee-like from the machine near the entrance. She sipped the acrid liquid while Trudi puffed on a B&H.

'You still up for a bevvy one night?'

'Definitely.' She waited while Trudi took another puff. 'Sorry about last night. I just couldn't get out of it.'

She hated lying to Trudi, but she didn't have the energy to go into the whole tortuous story of Mags and her wild claims right now.

Trudi blew out some smoke. 'I think me and Charys might be splitting up.' She pulled a face. 'I think she's seeing someone else. She hasn't said anything, but she's been behaving kinda weird lately – agreeing with everything I say, not being bothered about anything when I ask her something. Looking at her phone all the time.' She took another drag on her ciggie. 'You know, the little things that tell you something's not right.'

Molly made a sympathetic noise. Trudi and Charys had been a couple for as long as she could remember. She couldn't imagine them not being together. Some people just belonged in a relationship.

'I'm sorry to hear that,' she said. 'You know you can always chat if you want to get anything off your chest.' Someone else's problems were a welcome distraction from her own, and she knew Trudi would do the same for her. 'It could be you're seeing things that aren't there. I can't say I know Charys all that well, but she's never struck me as the sort to be unfaithful.'

Trudi shrugged. 'Maybe. Then again, you just get a feeling, don't you, when something isn't working?'

Molly wasn't sure what to say. She could never claim to be an expert on relationships. Before Jon, most of the men she'd dated had been self-obsessed and immature. Even Jon had his moments, but at least he was older. His age alone gave him an air of maturity, even if his behaviour sometimes didn't. But she'd always known when a relationship was coming to an end. Trudi had a point about the signs being there, if you chose to look for them.

'I saw this documentary on Channel 5 once,' Trudi said. 'There was this woman who'd been married to the same man for over forty years. Swore blind she knew him – knew everything about him. Then when he died, she discovered he had this whole other life. Another woman, kids. Another house. She'd been married for all that time and never had a clue. I mean, you'd have to be blind, wouldn't you? Or very stupid.'

'It's not always that simple,' Molly argued. 'People can deliberately blind themselves to something if they don't want to see it.'

'But married all that time. She only found out the truth after he died.' Trudi finished her cigarette then ground the butt under her heel. 'Speaking of which, I see Denning's gone off to speak to Buckfield's ex-wife.' She kicked the cigarette butt in the direction of a drain. 'What's your take on the whole Buckfield story? I still reckon it was some junkie, broke in, killed him for the hell of it.'

It was Molly's turn to shrug. 'It's possible.' She finished the remainder of the so-called coffee and scrunched the plastic cup in her hand. She'd drop it into a bin once they were back inside. 'Denning seems to think it's got something to do with Alfie Kane.'

'Kane?' Trudi's voice rose half an octave.

Molly regretted saying anything as soon as the words were out of her mouth. Denning had specifically asked her to keep it to herself for now. 'Look, forget I said anything. It's just that he's got me looking into the Security Direct warehouse robbery. He seems to think there's a connection between that, Kane and Buckfield.'

Trudi opened her mouth to speak, then closed it and shook her head. 'He's not serious, is he? That was decades ago. How is that relevant to Buckfield?'

'He worked the case.'

'Half the flaming coppers in London worked that case. Even my dad was part of the team for a while.'

'Six men went down for the robbery,' Molly added, showing she'd done her homework. She'd been living in Sydney at the time, so it was all news to her. It may have made the papers in Australia; she really couldn't remember. She'd had other things on her mind in 1996, like her parents splitting up. 'Most of the gang were already known to the police,' she continued. 'But there's no mention of Kane.'

'Kane's slippery, like an eel. There were always whispers he had a bent copper in the Met passing him info.' Trudi looked at Molly, mouth falling open slightly. 'That's it, isn't it? The allegations about Buckfield – the ones Dave was being so cagey about? They're to do with Alfie Kane?'

But Molly just shook her head. 'I don't know. Denning didn't go into detail. He just said to look into Security Direct and see what I can find. I've looked, and so far I've found jack shit.'

'They only recovered about a third of the stolen loot, so there's a few million quid's worth of gold bullion stashed out there somewhere.'

She threw Trudi a wry smile. 'If you're suggesting Buckfield had some of it hidden under his mattress, then I think you might be barking up the wrong lamppost.'

Trudi laughed. 'Not Buckfield, maybe, but Kane.' She lowered her voice a fraction. 'You know he's gone legit now. I mean no one really buys it, but he's a proper respectable businessman these days. Does a lot for charity – hangs out with minor celebs and sports people. Shit no longer sticks to Alfie Kane.'

Molly knew of Alfie Kane by reputation. His youngest son, Gregor, had been arrested for drug dealing less than a year ago, and she'd been part of the CID team that helped put him away.

'That's assuming Kane was ever involved,' Molly said. 'He's either very clever, or very lucky. Either way, the chances of finding anything to link him to Buckfield's murder are somewhere between slim and anorexic.' She shrugged and glanced at her watch. 'I can't help thinking Denning's backing a loser with this one.'

Trudi punched the entry code into the panel beside the heavy steel door, and they headed back inside.

'Do you want to tell him, or shall I?'

Molly pulled a face as the door shut behind them. 'I might just let that one go. If it does all turn out to be a massive waste of time, it's on his head, not mine.'

Chapter Sixteen

It was just after lunch when Denning arrived at the hospital. He purchased a cheese and tomato bagel from the Costa just off the hospital's reception area and stuffed it into his jacket pocket to eat later. The grumbling in his stomach told him he wouldn't manage to keep hunger at bay for too much longer, but lunch was probably going to have to be eaten on the hoof today.

Cairns had been moved out of intensive care and into a private room at the end of a corridor on the third floor.

'He's awake,' one of the nurses told Denning. 'We've given him strong painkillers, so he might be a bit woozy, but the doctor's been round and says he's otherwise OK.' She fixed him with a stern look. 'You can speak to him but not for too long.'

He gave a light tap on the door, and pushed it open.

Cairns was sitting up in bed. A fresh dressing had been applied to one side of his face. The remainder of his face was purple with bruises; his top lip was swollen and his left eye half closed. And these were just the injuries Denning could see. There were internal ones too, apparently – including broken ribs and damage to his liver. He'd taken quite a beating. And all for what? Hopefully Denning was about to find out.

Cairns glanced over at him, but didn't acknowledge his presence for several seconds. 'Dr Cairns,' Denning said softly, 'I'm Detective Inspector Denning. I'm with the Met's Major Investigation Team. Would you be up for answering some questions about the assault you suffered yesterday?'

A faint groan came from the direction of Cairns's bed. 'Who called you in? I didn't ask for you.' His voice was croaky, as though it hurt to speak.

There was a plastic jug of water on the table beside the bed, along with two glasses. Denning poured some water into one of the glasses and pressed it into Cairns's right hand. He took a couple of sips then placed the glass back on the table.

'Thanks.' He looked at Denning for a moment, then slid his eyes away. 'I asked why you're here?'

'We were called to the scene yesterday, Dr Cairns.' There were a couple of hard plastic chairs in the corner by the window, but Denning preferred to stand. 'You were attacked outside your house. Do you feel up to talking me through what happened?'

'I can't remember.'

'Perhaps you could try,' Denning coaxed. The prospect of going back to McKenna empty-handed wasn't something that appealed to him. Even if he could just conclusively draw a line under this, that would at least be something.

Cairns sighed and shook his head. 'I'd just popped out to post a letter. I was about to go back into the house, when some bloke jumped me. After that, it's all a blank.'

'It was definitely a man?'

'I imagine it was. I don't reckon a bit of skirt did this, do you?'

'Did you get a look at him?'

94

Another shake of the head. 'No, I didn't see anyone. It all happened very quickly.'

'Did he say anything, either before or during the assault?'

'Like I told you – I don't remember.'

Denning looked at Cairns. His hair was greying, mostly around the temples, and was thinning on top, but there were flecks of dark brown still clearly visible. And although it was hard to see beyond the bruising and the gauze bandage dressing that covered so much of his face, David Cairns didn't look like a man in his eighties. Denning would have put his age at around mid-sixties; late sixties at most. As he'd suspected, there was a notice-able discrepancy between the age listed on the Missing Person's report and the age of the man currently lying in the hospital bed in front of him. There could be a perfectly innocent reason for this, so why did he feel it was somehow significant?

'Can you think of anyone who would want to harm you?' he asked.

'Of course not.' Cairns's brow wrinkled in concern. 'You're not suggesting this was deliberate, are you? It was a mugging, wasn't it? Why would somebody...' His gaze flitted to the door, then settled on Denning. 'Why are you here if this was just a mugging? You said you were "Major Investigations".' He flicked another glance at the door. 'What's this all about?'

'The assault on you was particularly violent, Dr Cairns. If you hadn't survived, we'd now be investigating a murder.'

His words made Cairns wince. His battered face seemed to twist like a corkscrew. 'Murder? Are you saying someone tried to kill me?'

'It's a possibility.' He gave it a moment before he continued, trying to gauge Cairns's reaction. 'Has anyone threatened you recently? Or have you been aware of anyone watching you, or hanging round outside your house?'

'No. No, nothing like that.' He composed himself. 'Look, I'm sure you've got this wrong. It was a mugging. Simple as that.'

'Except you still had your phone and wallet when the local police found you.'

Cairns looked shocked. 'Well, maybe someone scared them off.'

'But not before they had a chance to give you a good going-over.'

Denning studied him. There was something in his face, and not just the bruising: confusion? Fear? It was hard to say for certain, but he had a feeling Cairns knew more about the attack than he was letting on. If he didn't know who was responsible, Denning suspected he had an inkling as to why he had been attacked.

'I don't understand...' Cairns was looking worried, but then quickly composed himself. 'Look, whatever it was, I'm alright now. A few bruises and I'm a bit sore, but I'll live. I'm sure you've got more important things on your plate than an attempted mugging.'

'You had concussion, Dr Cairns. And internal bleeding. According to the paramedics who treated you, you're lucky to be alive.'

'I don't care.' He looked at Denning, his one good eye staring up at him from the bed. 'I want you to drop this. I'm the victim here, and I'm asking you not to take this any further.'

'You've been the victim of a serious assault. Surely you want us to catch the person responsible?'

Cairns turned his bruised and battered face away from Denning. There was a small speck of blood on the pillow, a little smudge of red set against the starched white material like an ugly blemish. 'I've told you,' Cairns said, 'I'm fine now. I just want to forget about it.' He was becoming agitated, raising his voice and rubbing his hand over his face. 'I want you to go now. I don't have to speak to you if I don't want to. You said it yourself – I'm the victim here, not a suspect. You can't speak to me if I don't want you to.'

Denning had a feeling Cairns was about to press the buzzer by the bed to summon a nurse. It was unlikely he was going to make much progress with Cairns, so it was probably better to leave.

'OK, Dr Cairns. If you don't want to take things any further, that's your decision. I can't force you.' He paused and waited until Cairns turned his head back to face him. 'I just have a couple more questions before I go. Did you ever know a man called Frank Buckfield?'

For a moment, there was just the briefest flicker of something; not recognition perhaps, but something that suggested he'd heard the name before. Then he shook his head. 'Who? No, I've never heard of him. Why?'

'No reason. Just curious.' He smiled at Cairns. 'Finally, were you aware that you're still officially listed as a missing person?' If Denning was hoping his words would elicit some kind of reaction, he was disappointed.

'Well, I'm obviously not missing any more,' Cairns said. 'Am I?'

And Denning couldn't argue with that.

As Denning left the hospital, he suddenly remembered the cheese and tomato bagel in his jacket pocket. He reached into the pocket and touched it at the same time as his stomach gave another grumble.

There was a small seating area that bordered a neat gravelled garden not far from the hospital entrance. It was a mild spring day, with a nod of sun poking through the sporadic cloud cover, so he decided it might be nice to have his lunch outside.

He sat on a wooden bench and unwrapped the bagel.

Something wasn't quite right about Cairns. It wasn't that Denning was a snob, but Cairns hadn't come across as he had expected a retired academic would. Educated, and articulate… Cairns hadn't struck him as being either.

'*A bit of skirt…*'

Perhaps he was being a snob. According to his parents, some of their colleagues could be surprisingly uncouth when the mood struck. Then there were the celebrity academics that fronted so many pseudo-intellectual programmes on TV these days: laddish, boorish and playing up for the cameras. Academics were probably no different to detectives: a disparate bunch whose personalities couldn't be easily pigeonholed.

But there was something else that still bothered him.

The age discrepancy.

That could be easily explained: an overworked member of the Met's support team hitting the wrong key when inputting the original data, for instance; an error sadly not as uncommon as it should be. He once knew of a suspect who'd escaped a murder conviction because an 'o' had been mistyped as a zero on an evidence sheet.

Police support staff were as human as anyone when it came to making mistakes.

The bagel tasted bland: the bread was too chewy and the cheese had a decidedly plastic quality about it. Or perhaps he wasn't as hungry as he'd thought. He forced himself to finish eating it though – anything to keep his stomach quiet – then tossed the cellophane wrapper in a bin beside the bench.

Something just didn't feel right here. He had left a message with Cairns's sister, but until she returned his call and cleared up the confusion surrounding the Missing Person's report, his hands were tied.

He'd promised McKenna he'd walk away from this case if it turned out to be nothing more serious than an attempted mugging, and according to Cairns, that's exactly what it was.

So why didn't he believe him?

He took his phone from his pocket and called Molly. There was something he needed her to do.

Chapter Seventeen

Molly was shown into a cluttered office at the end of a long corridor. The plate on the door said Dr Helen Noonan: Senior Lecturer – School of History.

Dr Noonan was finishing a phone call when Molly entered. She smiled warmly and indicated for Molly to take a seat on one of the two chairs that sat at right angles to her desk. Helen Noonan was in her early sixties: charcoal grey hair swept back off her face, a fussy, flowery blouse, and piercing blue eyes that looked like they never missed a trick.

Denning had called asking her for a favour. There was something about David Cairns that didn't add up: could she get a bit of background on him and try and fill in the blanks? He also asked that she keep it from Betty Taggart for the time being.

Intrigued, she'd headed over to Queen Mary University on Mile End Road. A quick google of the name 'Dr David Cairns' had led her to the university's School of History, where he was listed as having once been on the teaching staff. She'd contacted the faculty administration office, and been put through to Dr Noonan. Noonan was a former colleague of Cairns and had agreed to spare her five minutes between tutorials.

The walls of the small office were lined with shelves, all of which overflowed with books: some looked new, while others looked like historical artefacts themselves. Molly had never seen the appeal of university herself: neither of her parents had been academically inclined, and she had always thought that three years of partying just to emerge with a load of debt and a piece of paper was probably not a productive use of her time.

'I remember Dr Cairns well,' Helen Noonan said before she'd even replaced the phone's receiver. 'It was over twenty years ago, and I hadn't been here very long. He was a nice man who took the time to introduce me to the department and the disparate personalities who taught here at the time – a lot of whom had been here since the university was first established as the London Hospital Medical College in 1785. Or so it seemed at times.' She gave a light, tinkly laugh. 'My apologies – I shouldn't be flippant. Being a history lecturer can feel like a way of life sometimes.'

'What was Dr Cairns like?' Molly asked. She noticed a pile of marking stacked on the doctor's desk, while the screensaver on her computer depicted Bodiam Castle. Molly remembered visiting Bodiam with Jon two years ago. They'd had a picnic lunch overlooking the moat, until a sudden heavy shower had forced them to take shelter under a nearby oak tree.

'A very quiet man,' Dr Noonan said. 'I'd almost say shy. He could have been – some might even say *should* have been – Head of Department, but I don't think the idea appealed to him.' Her sharp blue eyes seemed to dance as her memories were reignited. 'His main area of research was the late Victorian and Edwardian era, so we had a lot in common. I specialise in early twentieth-century history,' she explained, gesturing towards some hardback books that sat on a table near her desk. The breeze block of a book on top of the pile was titled: *Europe Before the Great War: 1899-1914*. It didn't look like light reading. 'We did once discuss the possibility of working on a paper together on the great social reforms of the Asquith government,' she continued. 'But it wasn't to be.'

'What happened?' Molly asked.

'To the paper or to David?' The blue eyes twinkled at Molly. 'Nobody really knows. That's the real mystery.' She looked at Molly, her face adopting a serious expression. 'Sorry, I don't mean to sound so dramatic. It's not often I receive a visit from a detective, so forgive me for playing up ever so slightly.' She sighed. 'We had all returned from the summer break and were preparing for the autumn term, but there was no sign of David. Then somebody said he'd decided to take early retirement. However, it was very out-of-the-blue. He hadn't mentioned anything to me about retiring, and I did think he might have at least mentioned it in passing before the summer break, particularly as he'd already been allocated his teaching quota for the autumn term. There was a rumour he'd left due to ill health, but I couldn't say if there was any truth in the rumour. One of the admin staff organised a card and some flowers which were sent on to his home. I did think he might have come back and said goodbye to everyone. He didn't even empty his office before he left. And then we had to find someone to cover his teaching at short notice.'

'When you say "ill",' Molly asked, 'do you know what might have been wrong with him?'

'I don't know exactly. David did suffer from depression, but to my knowledge he was coping with it. But then, depression can be a debilitating illness – very often people who suffer from it become experts at hiding it.'

Molly nodded, silently agreeing with her. She wanted to say that she was all too familiar with the coping strategies used by people with depression, and the levels to which they would try to conceal their true feelings. She'd experienced it so many times with Jon.

'So nobody actually saw him, or spoke to him prior to his departure?'

'Universities were different places twenty years ago. We didn't have summer schools then, or students returning to do resits. The whole campus more or less shut down over the summer months. Just a skeleton admin staff and the occasional academic popping in to use the library. Apparently his partner contacted HR and informed them that David had decided not to return to work. I imagine HR handled all the requisite paperwork at their end. I'm afraid I wasn't privy to such information so I can't confirm the details,' Dr Noonan continued. 'He was in his early sixties, so he was only a few years off retirement anyway. I imagine he thought "why not go early?".'

'He had a partner? You wouldn't happen to know their name?'

She shook her head. 'I was surprised to hear he had a partner, to be honest with you. I mean I often suspected David was gay – he never said anything, but you know within five minutes of meeting a man that if they're not trying to mentally unbutton your blouse they're more than likely playing for the other side, or whatever the expression is. But David never discussed his private life with me and I never asked him about it. I had no reason to assume he didn't have a partner, it just felt strange to hear that he did.'

Molly digested this information. The more they discovered about David Cairns, the more layers of his life they seemed to peel away. But that so often applied to the victims of crime: secrets were quickly exposed as the most private aspects of a person's life were pored over in forensic detail. 'This may seem like a strange question, Dr Noonan, but can you think of anyone who had a grudge against Dr Cairns? Perhaps a former student who resented him for some reason? Or another academic he had fallen out with?'

She gave another tinkling little laugh. 'David wasn't the type of person who attracted grudges. He would have gone out of his way to avoid an argument.' She smiled at Molly. 'I think the favoured expression is "wouldn't say boo to a goose".'

Molly smiled. 'Did you try to get in touch with Dr Cairns after he left?'

Dr Noonan splayed her hands in front of her. 'If I remember rightly, I did phone and leave a couple of messages on his answerphone. Partly to see if he was still interested in working on a paper with me, but also to see how he was.' She looked like she was trying hard to rekindle an old memory. 'Thinking back, I was slightly concerned when he left so suddenly. I had thought we were... well, perhaps not exactly friends – David was too private to let anyone from work get that close to him – but I would certainly have said we got on well together, and I would have liked to have kept in touch.'

'Did you follow it up?'

'Sometimes I wish I had. Unfortunately this all happened at the worst possible time for me – I had been planning to go off on sabbatical the following year and there had been some glitch with the paperwork, which meant it hadn't been signed off in time. I was so focussed on trying to get that sorted, plus I had an impending deadline for a book I'd agreed to contribute to, so unfortunately David slipped from my mind.' She offered Molly a sympathetic look. 'I'm sorry to hear about what happened to him. A friend of my mother's was mugged a few months ago. It really does knock your confidence when you're elderly.'

Molly agreed that it did, but reassured her Dr Cairns had now regained consciousness and seemed to be on the road to recovery, at least according to Denning. 'Is there anyone else at the university who might have known Dr Cairns when he worked here?' she asked.

Dr Noonan shook her head. 'I wouldn't have thought so. Certainly as far as this department is concerned, I'm the only member of staff who was here at the same time as David. I don't think he had much to do with anyone from other departments.'

Molly wasn't sure if any of this would answer Denning's niggling questions about David Cairns. As she thanked Dr Noonan and then tried to find her way back to the main entrance, she was suddenly aware that as well as trying to discover who attacked Dr David Cairns and why, they now had the added mystery of why he had left his job so suddenly.

Chapter Eighteen

McKenna was behind her desk. There was a copy of the post-mortem report on the desk, half poking out of its manila folder, McKenna's name in bold capitals on the cover. Baker must have typed it up and had it biked over first thing that afternoon. They were certainly pulling out all the stops with this one.

Denning had wanted a quick chat with Molly Fisher before he went in to see McKenna, but she still wasn't back from Queen Mary University, so he'd have to wait to get the lowdown on Cairns. He was still determined to fight his corner with McKenna, though admittedly with slightly less ammunition in his arsenal than he would have liked.

'Now we have a date – if not a time – for Buckfield's death,' McKenna said, pointing at the manila folder. 'We can start going over whatever CCTV is working on that estate. Anyone going into, coming out of, or hanging round Buckfield's flat, we need to trace them and eliminate them.'

'We're still no closer to finding a motive,' Denning offered.

McKenna rubbed a hand through her raven hair. 'Then keep digging. It's there somewhere.'

'I think Kane is worth looking into,' Denning said. 'The PM report as good as says this was something akin to a professional killing. That's very much his territory.'

She gave a throaty laugh. 'Mr Kane is – as both he and his lawyer are keen to remind everyone within earshot – a respectable businessman these days. Anyway, what would the motive be?'

'The Security Direct robbery? It links the two men.'

There was a sharp shaking of the head from McKenna. 'Forget it, Matt. Any link is tenuous at best. Kane was rumoured – but never proved – to have been involved, and Buckfield was one of literally dozens of officers who worked the case. And besides, I don't see how the Security Direct robbery could be considered a credible motive, even if we could prove Kane was involved, which even the investigation team at the time were unable to do. And then why now? It doesn't make sense. We need to look for something more concrete.' She sat back in her chair and steepled her fingers, bashing them against her chin. 'Besides, the post-mortem didn't exactly say it was a "professional killing". It just says that it was neat. We want to be careful we don't read too much into this.' She offered him a thin smile. 'I suggest you look elsewhere for your motive. What about the family? Did your visit throw up anything interesting?'

'Both claim they hadn't had any contact with him for some time. His widow has clearly moved on with her life, but there's no love lost between Buckfield's son and his late father.'

'Can we rule either of them out at this stage?'

He shrugged. 'I think we can safely assume Buckfield's widow had nothing to do with it. As for his son…' He gave another shrug. 'Unlikely, but I couldn't honestly say for sure.'

'OK. Find out where he was the day Buckfield was murdered. If he has a credible alibi, then we can leave him alone. Otherwise, he goes on the board as a person of interest.' She rested her hands back on the desk. 'Is there anything else?'

Denning decided to grasp the nettle. 'I've spoken to David Cairns.'

She stared at him for a second; her eyes meeting his without flinching. 'What did he have to say?'

He gave her an edited recount of his hospital visit. 'He told me he doesn't want to take things any further,' Denning concluded, already second-guessing McKenna's response.

'Right, then we drop it.' She fixed him with the gimlet stare. 'That's what we agreed, Matt.'

'I'm not sure it's that straightforward. For a start, Cairns was so doped up on painkillers I don't think he knew what he was saying. Secondly, he's lying – I don't know what about, but he's definitely holding something back. There's the Missing Person's report, which highlights an inconsistency in his age.' He scratched at an itch on the back of his neck. She would try her best to shout him down over this, but he would lob his biggest grenade at McKenna and hope the explosion would have the desired effect. 'And then there's the fact he recognised Buckfield's name when I mentioned it.'

McKenna didn't miss a beat. 'Hardly surprising. His murder's been all over the local news. Half of London will have heard the name "Buckfield" by now.'

'Yes, but Cairns has been unconscious since yesterday afternoon. He wouldn't have seen or heard the news.'

'Maybe he overheard some of the nurses talking about it this morning?'

'Perhaps…' He could still feel the itch on the back of his neck. 'I still think there's more to this than Cairns is letting on.'

She fixed him with another gimlet stare. 'You have to let this drop now, Matt. OK, maybe there are discrepancies with his story, and maybe he does know who attacked him and why, but if he wants the investigation dropped, then we have no choice but to go along with his wishes.'

'We can't let this whole thing drop. Cairns was attacked and left for dead on his own doorstep. There's a dangerous individual out there who needs to be caught.'

She shook her head, more slowly this time as if to emphasise her point. 'Even if we were to get someone for this, the CPS will be reluctant to proceed if the victim's unwilling to press charges. You know how it works.' McKenna leant forward and drummed her fingers on the desk. 'I don't want to get shitty about this, Matt, but I will if I have to. Forget about Cairns. He was the victim of an attempted mugging. And even if he wasn't, he's asked you to drop this, and now I'm telling you to drop it.' The gimlet stare was burrowing into him like a dentist's drill. 'I take it you haven't seen this?'

There was a copy of that day's *London Echo* under the folder on her desk. She slid it out from underneath the PM report and pushed it across the desk at him.

Killer Targets Ex-Cops? the headline blared, next to a grainy picture of Buckfield taken some time ago. The story, from the few sentences he managed to read, hinted that whoever had killed Buckfield had a grievance against former police officers and may be about to go after others. It was very carefully worded to suggest this was simply a theory and not one that was backed up by the police. But it would have served its purpose: generate fear and sell papers.

'It sends out a worrying message, implying it's open season on police officers, retired or otherwise. Besides,' she sat back in her chair again and sighed. 'Harrison's been doing his nut. He's threatening to take personal charge if we – if *I* – don't get a quick result.'

Denning could feel his eyebrows pointing towards the ceiling. 'He's not serious?'

'Deadly. He claims that now the press is running with these kinds of batshit crazy stories, then it's only a matter of time before this whole thing explodes in our faces.' She reached out and grabbed the newspaper, pulling it back to her side of the desk. 'But, between you, me and the goalpost, I reckon it's got more to do with him wanting to make a name for himself.' She lowered her voice, even though no one else could hear them. 'I was chatting to a mate over at Scotland Yard last night. It seems Harrison was considered a rank outsider for the DCS's job until Morrow put a good word in for him. It would appear that Justin Morrow is not a man without influence.'

'What's it got to do with Morrow?' Denning asked, barely managing to conceal his surprise. 'Are they friends? In any case, he shouldn't have that kind of influence. The Mayor's office only has any say over senior appointments: Commissioner, Deputy Commissioner. A DCS appointment is usually an internal decision. And Morrow isn't even part of the Mayor's office, he's only on the committee that oversees it.'

It was McKenna's turn to shrug. 'Who knows how their minds work? The Met is certainly a lot more political these days than it ever used to be. But ours is not to reason why, et cetera.' She shot him a serious look. 'I mean it, Matt – I've got Harrison kicking my backside over this, so I'm kicking yours. I want all efforts focussed on finding Buckfield's killer. We need to be seen to be doing fucking *something*.' She leant on her desk again and offered him another thin-lipped smile. 'Forget Cairns. If either of us wants to keep our jobs, then Buckfield takes priority.'

–

When Denning returned to the main office, Molly Fisher was just sitting down at her desk. He was on the point of heading over to speak to her when Neeraj waved at him.

'I've heard back from Islington nick,' Neeraj said. 'Uniform have finished doing the door-to-door around Cairns's place. Nothing much to report. Most neighbours confirm that he was a recluse who never spoke to anyone. Someone said he was an unfriendly bugger who wouldn't give you the time of day; someone else said he was rude to her once when she asked if he wanted to join the neighbourhood watch.' Most of this Denning already knew, or wasn't surprised to hear. And now that McKenna had put the kybosh on any further investigation, the whole exercise was academic, no pun intended. 'One old geezer in the next street said he and Cairns used to play bridge sometimes,' Neeraj continued. 'This was years ago apparently, then Cairns suddenly cut off all ties: didn't answer the phone, was never in whenever he called round. He hadn't seen him for ages and was surprised to hear he was still alive.' Denning nodded, waiting for him to finish before telling him to hand the whole thing back to Islington CID, when Neeraj glanced down at his notes and said, 'But this is the interesting bit. Seems this old geezer says he thought Cairns had had a lodger living with him at one time. Didn't know any more details. Says he never met this lodger and couldn't tell us anything about him.'

'Him? So the lodger was male?' Denning was turning this over in his head when Molly Fisher suddenly piped up.

'Sorry, boss, I couldn't help overhearing that last bit. I've just got back from the uni where Cairns used to work. Not much that was useful, but I think I can clarify the lodger situation. It seems that Cairns had a partner. Kept himself to himself at work as much as he did with his neighbours. Nobody at the uni knew about his private life, but a colleague definitely remembers mention of a partner around the time Cairns retired.' She briefly looked at Neeraj before returning her gaze to Denning. 'Could be worth trying to trace this lover/lodger and hearing what he has to say about the assault on Cairns? Maybe there was some unfinished business there.'

Denning wanted to agree, but McKenna had spoken: this was no longer their concern. However, if Fisher's lovers' tiff theory had any meat on it, then it was more likely they were looking at a possible attempted murder rather than a random mugging. It might also go part of the way towards explaining why Cairns was so keen to drop the investigation. And there was another searing question that needed to be answered.

'Did this colleague say how old Cairns was when he retired?'

'Early sixties. Why?'

That tallied with the age on the Missing Person's report, which clearly hadn't been an admin error after all. 'When was this?'

'About twenty years ago.'

'So around the same time he was reported missing by his sister?' Denning was thinking aloud, attempting to join together lots of dots. 'Meaning Dr David Cairns would be in his early eighties now.'

'I guess so.'

He could see Fisher and Neeraj exchange quizzical looks, trying to figure out where he was going with this. He glanced over at McKenna's office. She'd been adamant that Cairns was now off the agenda as far as they were concerned, but he was now almost certain that they were looking at something more sinister than an attempted mugging. If McKenna wouldn't OK it, then he would have to speak to Harrison directly, and either ask for them to work on this in tandem with the Buckfield investigation, or at least get another MIT involved.

'Deep, speak to DS Klein at Islington CID and get an address for this old bloke who knew Cairns from their bridge days. We need the name of the man who lived with him at the time the Missing Person's report was filed.'

'OK, boss, but even with a name, there's no guarantee we'll be able to trace him.'

'Just do it anyway,' Denning barked. 'We need to find this man.'

But Denning was certain the man they were looking for was the same man who had been attacked in the street the other day and was pretending to be David Cairns.

He just had to work out why.

Chapter Nineteen

Harrison was currently occupying an office at the rear of the building, which had previously been inhabited by the borough commander. He was spending a week with each area MIT to observe them in operation and try and identify any areas of improvement, and to familiarise himself with the detectives on each team. This week it was the turn of the East London MIT. So far as Denning could gather, it seemed Harrison had only managed to familiarise himself with DCI McKenna, but perhaps it was a top-down process.

Denning had initially thought about phoning Harrison, but decided a face-to-face meet might be more direct. Plus it would give him the chance to state his case persuasively. Now he was heading to Harrison's office, however, serious doubts began to gnaw at him.

Going over the head of his DCI wouldn't do his long-term career prospects any favours. He'd quickly earn a reputation as someone who couldn't be trusted, even a potential trouble-maker. And it wouldn't be fair on McKenna. Despite her flaws, she was a good DCI, who always put her team's interests first, and would fight their corner with all the ferocity of a lioness defending her cubs if it came down to it. She had been placed in a difficult position, and by the very man Denning was about to speak to.

But he couldn't let this pass. The situation with David Cairns had changed. It now looked likely that something had happened to Cairns, and the man currently lying in a hospital bed was very probably responsible.

Except getting proof would be near impossible. They struggled to find the resources to investigate current murders, and trying to justify launching an investigation into a possible murder from twenty years ago would be a hard sell.

He was in the corridor outside Harrison's office. He had to make a quick decision. McKenna would want confirmation that he'd handed the Cairns case over to local CID. He could walk away from it here and now, or go behind her back to Harrison and formally request that he be allowed to continue with the investigation, inviting the wrath of a furious DCI in the process…

Before he had a chance to reach a decision, however, the door to Harrison's office opened. Denning was surprised when Justin Morrow came out.

Morrow spotted Denning and raised a hand in acknowledgement.

'It's Matt, isn't it?' He was smiling warmly at Denning. Not the professional smile he'd been wearing the previous day when he'd appeared in his capacity as Harrison's support act, but a genuine smile, as though he meant it. He offered his hand for Denning to shake.

'I spotted you yesterday, but didn't have a chance to talk to you,' he said. 'It's good to see you again. How's it going?'

Denning twitched his mouth into a smile and returned the handshake, trying like fury to work out why the hell Morrow was greeting him like they were old friends.

'Good,' he said quickly. 'Busy.'

'Great. And how's Sarah?'

It took Denning a moment to pick himself up from the floor and acknowledge the fact that Morrow knew his wife's name. 'She's good too, thanks.' Denning was trying to keep his voice level. Had Morrow been checking up on him? Leafing through his personal file for whatever purpose? Was he even allowed to do that?

He glanced towards Harrison's office, remembering his reason for being in the corridor in the first place. Morrow was still talking at him.

'Listen, I can't chat now, I've got a meeting over at County Hall, which I'm already running late for.' He pressed the button for the lift and the doors immediately opened for him. 'But we must catch up sometime.' Morrow headed into the lift and pressed the button for the ground floor.

Denning watched as the lift doors slid shut, still not entirely sure what had just happened.

–

When he returned to his desk, his first thought was to phone Sarah and ask if she knew Morrow.

He'd been replaying the conversation with Morrow over and over in his head as if it were on a loop. Morrow had clearly implied that he knew Sarah, and Denning, too. He'd racked his brains, but he couldn't remember having ever met Morrow previously. It was possible he could have arrested him at some point, or spoken to him in connection with an investigation, but surely he would have remembered.

And what was Morrow doing in Harrison's office? He was pretty sure the remit of the GLA's Police and Crime

Committee didn't allow for visits to Met departmental offices, especially ones where Major Investigation Teams were based.

He was tempted to look up Morrow's page on the London Assembly website again, but he had other matters to focus on right now.

In the end, he'd decided not to approach Harrison, at least not quite yet. If they could make some kind of breakthrough on the Buckfield case, maybe then he could justify asking to look into Cairns. Or if he could find some evidence to prove that Cairns had come to harm, he might be able to persuade Harrison and McKenna to launch an investigation.

In the meantime, he'd do what he'd promised McKenna, and concentrate on finding Frank Buckfield's killer. And there seemed an obvious place to start.

Molly Fisher had left a folder on his desk. He opened the folder and leafed through her notes. On the first page it said: Security Direct.

Denning was already familiar with the general background to the robbery. He wanted to know the details.

And the details were pretty stark.

In the early hours of Saturday twenty-third of June 1996, eight armed men had broken into a warehouse near Heathrow Airport and left two hours later with over thirty million pounds in gold bullion – worth around fifty-six million pounds in today's money. Four security guards had been tied up and threatened with petrol and a lighter; enough to guarantee their cooperation. The men had all worn balaclavas, and the CCTV sprayed with black paint.

There were the inevitable comparisons with Brink's-Mat, and it was rumoured some of the same characters had been involved in both robberies.

After a year-long investigation, six men had been arrested and charged, either with being part of the armed gang, or having handled the stolen bullion. Just under ten million pounds of bullion had been recovered; the investigating officers surmised that the remainder had been melted down, smuggled out of the country, or hidden. It was believed there had been over a dozen people involved in the robbery in total; from planning it, to helping dispose of the bullion. Most of those involved had evaded justice, including – so it was rumoured – Alfie Kane.

Kane had taken great care over the years to distance himself from those rumours. In 2001, he had successfully sued a newspaper that had implied he'd been part of the gang, and in 2009 he had managed to block a Channel 4 documentary about the robbery, in which it had been implicitly suggested he was one of the men behind it and had been in receipt of some of the bullion.

Denning read on.

One of the arrested men had initially pointed the finger at Kane as part of a plea bargain, but had subsequently changed his story, rather suddenly and without explanation. A year later, acting on an anonymous tip-off, police searched Kane's house but nothing was found that could link him to Security Direct. Kane had threatened to sue the police, and news of the raid had been kept out of the press under threat from Kane's solicitors.

There were photos in the file too: grainy pictures from the warehouse's CCTV, including an image of one of the robbers spraying black paint over the lens, and other pictures showing the two vans that had been used in the raid parked outside the entrance to the warehouse. The vans had later been found burnt out and abandoned in a field in Kent. There were several photos of the warehouse itself, both its interior and exterior, as well as some of the men arrested. All the photos had either been downloaded from the internet, or uncovered from the data on the police computer.

Denning closed the folder. Molly had done a thorough job, but there was one area where the information was still sketchy. The bones were there, he just needed to put some flesh on them.

He googled the name Alfie Kane.

The most recent articles focussed on Kane and the new charity he was launching, all carefully avoiding any reference to his questionable past. He clicked on some of the images: Kane on a yacht: a tanned, toned man in his mid-sixties, exuding confidence; Kane's luxury mansion near Epping Forest. There was a photo of his wife, clearly younger than Kane: blonde and tanned and wearing a designer suit. The article stated that she was Kane's second wife. There was no mention of his first.

There was a brief story from the previous year about the arrest of Kane's youngest son, and another short piece covering the subsequent court case. Denning remembered Kane's son, Gregor: His ex-girlfriend had been murdered and Gregor Kane had briefly been considered a suspect, until a solid alibi had put him in the clear. Gregor had been cocky and sure of himself. A chip off the old block? Or had he been rebelling against his father's reformed character act?

Anything that came up about Alfie Kane now would show the successful businessman: the new image he had carefully cultivated. He would need to go back further to uncover anything interesting. Back nearly thirty years, to the days before Kane ran a haulage firm based in

Dagenham. The days when his various business interests consisted of less legitimate enterprises.

He scrolled down the page.

There was an obscure website called *Great British Crimes – The Truth*, in which Kane's name appeared.

He clicked on the section about Security Direct. Skimming over the content, most of which was hearsay and speculation, he checked out the photos at the bottom of the page.

There was a picture of a younger-looking Alfie Kane taken from a distance. He was leaving his house; not the impressive mansion he lived in now, but a smaller semi-detached property, though still substantial. He was walking to his car, scowling at the camera with a posse of solid-looking men beside him. Denning stared at the photo. One of the men, walking immediately behind Kane's right shoulder, looked familiar. It was probably taken in wintertime as the men were all wearing thick coats. He tried to enlarge the photo, but couldn't.

He stared at the photo, not quite believing what he was seeing.

The image wasn't clear, but he peered hard and was sure he recognised the figure.

According to the names listed under the photo, the man in question was called Gordon Lomax and he was described as being an 'associate' of Alfie Kane.

But the more Denning stared at the photo, the more he was sure he was looking at a younger and less bloodied image of the man currently lying in a hospital bed and calling himself David Cairns.

Chapter Twenty

The address Marcia Wilson gave for Colin Meek turned out to be a bedsit on traffic-heavy Tulse Hill. Molly rang the bell beside the peeling front door of the three-storey terraced house, and waited for an answer. From somewhere behind the front door, she could hear the steady thump of a garage beat.

A man in his early twenties with greasy hair tied back in a ponytail and a face covered in tattoos opened the door on the third ring.

'What do you want?' He had several piercings about his nose and ears, and looked like he had just woken up. If he had been asleep, she wondered how he'd managed to sleep through the deafening din. The garage beat was louder now, threatening to drown out any conversation. It was matched by the powerful stench of some pretty strong skunk that emanated from inside the dingy building.

'I'm looking for a man called Colin Meek,' she said, not quite shouting, but talking louder than felt comfortable. 'I was told he lives here.'

He gave her a quizzical look. 'Who wants him?'

She could have told him the truth but she imagined as soon as she said she was police, he would tell her to fuck off. 'I'm a friend of a friend,' she ended up saying. It was close enough to the truth to sound convincing.

The man stared at her for a few seconds, sizing her up, wondering if he should take a punt and believe her. 'He's not here,' he said eventually.

'Do you know when he'll be back?'

The man shrugged. 'I dunno, luv. I'm not his secretary.'

'Thanks. Thanks for your help.' Molly turned to go.

Then, almost as though his conscience had suddenly kicked in, he said: 'There's a park, about five minutes from here. He sometimes likes to hang out there.' He told her how to get there and she headed off, following his directions.

It took her closer to ten minutes than five to find the park. The roads around South London were noisy with rush hour traffic and heavy with exhaust fumes, but the park was a haven of quiet. The trees and shrubs that bordered it managed to insulate the mellow space from the urban clatter that surrounded it.

It was still light, but the park was almost empty, apart from a couple of dog walkers and a lone male jogger. There was no sign of Colin, and as all she had to go on was a vague description and an out-of-date photo Mags had emailed her, she wasn't even sure she'd recognise him.

Molly wandered round the park for a few minutes, appreciating the eerie calmness and the twittering of birdsong that preceded dusk. The sound of nearby traffic filtered through the greyness. It was spring and the park was just coming back to life; trees were prickling with the green shoots of new growth, and bright yellow daffs bowed their heads in neatly-tended borders. She remembered that the clocks went forward that weekend, bringing a welcome hour of extra daylight to help lift the gloom of winter.

The further into the park she went, the quieter it got. Soon the sound of city life was just a distant thrum. There was no one else around now, except for the jogger, who was circling a small lake some way ahead of her. She was on the point of giving up, when she found herself beside a low metal fence that bordered a children's playpark. She spotted a middle-aged man sitting alone on one of the swings. He briefly looked up from the ground when Molly approached, then immediately dropped his eyes back to the thin grainy sand under the swing. He was wearing a black beanie hat and a faded grey hoodie. There was an elaborate tattoo of a spider's web on his neck and a scar on his face running from his temple to just above his left ear. His muddy trainers scratched at the sand beneath the swing.

She sat on the swing next to him and said hello. He looked up at her, slightly curious. She wasn't entirely sure how she was going to play this.

'Colin?' She smiled at him. Even though she knew he was in his late forties, there was something childlike about him. 'I'm Molly,' she said. 'I'm a friend of Mags.'

'Mags?' He looked at her. He was unshaven; not quite a full-on beard, but getting there. His breath was sickly sweet.

'She said you were a friend of hers. She's concerned about you.'

He didn't speak for a while. 'Mags,' he said eventually. 'You mean the woman from the newspaper?'

'Yes. She was worried something might have happened to you.'

He stared into space for a minute, then shook his head. 'Are you a cop?' he asked.

She nodded. 'I'm a detective with the Met's Major Investigation Team, but that's not why I'm here.' She wanted to reach over and touch him reassuringly, but thought he might misconstrue her action. Her hands remained by her side. 'I'm here because Mags hasn't seen you for a while and asked me to help find you. Your probation officer is also concerned that you missed an appointment. Don't worry, you're not in any trouble, at least not yet. But you will need to get in touch with her.'

'Did she send you?'

'Miss Wilson?'

'The woman from the newspaper. Mags?'

Why did he refer to her as 'the woman from the newspaper'? Wasn't she meant to be his friend? Molly was beginning to suspect Mags had given her half a tale. Possibly not even that much.

'Look, why don't we go for a walk?' she suggested. 'I've never been here before. It's a nice park.' She couldn't help feeling sorry for him. He seemed alone and lost, and a part of her could relate to that.

'It'll be dark soon.'

'Not for ages yet.' She got off the swing. 'We can head back towards the street if you'd feel more comfortable.'

He thought about it for a moment. 'OK.' He got off the swing and they headed towards the main path. 'I come here most days. It's peaceful and it gives me time to think.'

They wandered through the park, heading in the vague direction of the gate where Molly had entered. The jogger had disappeared. There were just the two of them in the park now as far as she could see. She reminded herself he'd been in prison; done time for GBH, God knows what else. But she had been a police officer long enough to know better than to make hasty judgements about people that could easily turn out to be false.

She told him a bit about herself, underplaying her job as a police officer in case it spooked him.

'How long have you been Filth?' he asked when she'd finished talking.

She tried not to smile. She hadn't been called that for a while. When she'd first joined the police, her brother had jokingly referred to her as 'the Filth' for a time. The joke had quickly worn thin.

'About twelve years,' she said.

'Do you enjoy it?'

'The job? Yes, I suppose I do. Most of the time. I like helping people.'

He seemed keen to talk. But then, living in a lonely bedsit, he would likely be glad of the chance of some company.

'And you think that's what you do?' he asked suddenly. 'Help people? You don't think you make things worse for them?'

It was a strange question. 'I hope not,' she said. 'Maybe we don't always get things right, but I honestly believe we do the best we can. Why?'

He walked ahead for a while. 'You lie, when it suits you. You're supposed to be on the side of the good guys, but that's not always true, is it?'

She was having to hurry to keep up with him. He walked quickly, with his head down, as though frightened the ground was suddenly going to swallow him up. 'What do you mean?'

He stopped and turned to face her, looking her in the eye. 'I came to you lot for help once and instead, you destroyed my life.'

They were standing next to a duck pond now. She guided them towards a bench where they both sat.

'Talk to me, Colin. Tell me what happened?'

He stared into space for a moment, then shivered very slightly. It was cooling into a chilly evening, and his thin hoodie wouldn't be enough to keep out the cold. The birdlife had quietened down now; a growing silence filled the air as dusk began to fall.

'I told the police, but they didn't believe me.' He scuffed the ground with his trainers. 'I was only fifteen when it started.'

'Do you want to tell me about it?'

He looked at his feet as he spoke. 'We used to hang around an arcade near Piccadilly Circus. Other boys, same age as me mostly. A man would come there. He would offer us money if we'd meet up with men he knew. Older men.'

'What can you remember about this man?'

'He looked ordinary. Nothing special. He was quite posh. I think he was friends with the man who ran the arcade. He would chat to us. He would ask us where we lived and if our parents knew where we were. Then he would ask if we wanted to earn a bit of easy cash. That's what he would call it: "easy cash".'

'Where did you meet these men?'

'In houses, or flats. Sometimes hotels.'

'Can you remember anything about them? Anything that stood out, or might give some clue as to their location?'

He shook his head. 'No. We would get picked up in a car and driven to wherever we were meeting them. Sometimes there would be other boys there too. I think some of them might have come from care homes, or borstals. I don't know. We were never allowed to talk to the other boys. Then the car would drop us back at the arcade afterwards.' He thought for a moment. 'I remember there was a nice flat by the river. We went there a few times. It wasn't far from the Houses of Parliament. Then there was a big house in the countryside, with crests on the gates, but I don't know where it was. There was another one near London Zoo that was full of antiques. It used to smell funny: a bit musty.' He shook his head again. 'I can't remember much else.'

It was all so hazy. He was providing little in the way of hard evidence, and nothing that could be put before a jury. But if there was even the faint possibility he was telling the truth, then he deserved justice. The very least she could do was listen to his side of the story. 'Tell me about the men.'

'They were very nice to us at first. They'd chat to us, and they were friendly. And there was always drink. Drugs too, if you wanted them. But things would get out of hand sometimes. There were a couple of men in particular... I think one of them was one of your lot. Quite high up too. And there was the judge. We nicknamed him Judge Dredd – you know, like in the comic.'

Molly was familiar with the film of the same name, and was vaguely aware it was based on a comic from the 1970s.

'Some of the boys called him that because they used to dread it whenever he was there. He would take the boys into a room one at a time. He never picked me because I was too old. I was nearly eighteen by the time he came on the scene. He liked them a bit younger.'

Molly wanted to keep him talking. 'Go on. Tell me everything you can remember.'

'One of the boys – I only knew him as Tommy – was a particular favourite. Anyway, one day he wasn't there anymore. Someone said he'd been killed. They said Judge Dredd and one of the others had killed him because he threatened to tell on them if they didn't give him more money. I never saw Tommy again after that.'

'Are you sure this boy was killed?' she asked quietly.

Colin was still staring at the ground, shuffling his feet. 'I don't know. One of the other boys said they told him, and that they would do the same thing to anyone else if we threatened to tell.'

She wasn't sure how much to believe. Even if he was telling her the truth, trying to prove the abuse had taken place would be hard enough. But trying to prove a teenage boy had been murdered when there was a total lack of any evidence would be almost impossible. 'When was this, Colin? Can you remember exactly?'

He shook his head again. 'I don't know. I was eighteen by then, so I was already considered to be too old for most of the men.' He looked up at her, eyes burning. He was still shaking. 'The late-eighties. I can't remember exact dates.' Another shake of the head. 'I've spent so long trying to forget it.'

Molly was churning it over in her head, trying to make sense of it all. 'What about this judge? Did you ever hear anyone call him by his real name?'

'We all had to call them "Sir". Sometimes the older ones liked to be called "Uncle", or "Daddy" if they were really pervy. We never knew anyone's names.'

'How old were these men?'

'I don't know. Fifties. Sixties. Maybe older.'

'Did you recognise any of them? Had any of them been in the papers, or on the telly?'

He looked at his feet. 'No. Well, except for the MP. The one who was involved in that scandal with a rent boy. I can't remember his name, but I'd seen him there sometimes. He wasn't one of the regulars, but he would come along for their parties.'

Molly would check this out. It wouldn't be too difficult to discover the name of the MP in question, especially if he had been involved in a public scandal. Even then, though, it still wouldn't give them much to work with.

'How did you get out?' she asked.

'I moved away from London. I lived in Brighton for a while. A few years later, a friend persuaded me to go to the police. I was back in London by then. It was when that MP was in the papers. I spoke to a couple of policemen. I told them everything I knew, including about Tommy. They said they'd investigate it. They came back to me a few months later and said there was no evidence to back up what I'd told them. The following month I was arrested for assault. I already had a conviction for GBH. I'd stabbed a man in Brighton after he'd tried to attack me. The police used this against me. They told lies about me in court. I was sent down for two years.'

Molly was trying to take this all in. There was so much here that didn't make sense. 'But the police did investigate what you've just told me? The abuse, and the disappearance of this boy Tommy?'

He shrugged. 'They said they did. They said another witness had come forward. Then suddenly they told me they were dropping the case because of the lack of evidence. They even accused me of making the whole thing up.'

'Did they tell you the name of this witness?'

'No. I don't know who he was.'

She could find out though. His details would be on file. But why would they drop the case if there were two separate witnesses? It was clear that if Colin didn't know the identity of this other witness, then there was no possibility of collusion. 'Who did you speak to, when you went to the police?'

'I don't remember. I spoke to different people at different times.'

She was shocked. The Met had specialist teams trained to deal with child abuse these days. But it would have been a different story thirty years ago, when hardened cops like Dave Kinsella would have been asked to listen to details that would have made them feel uncomfortable. And if the men they were being asked to investigate were anonymous, it would have been almost impossible to build a convincing case.

'And Mags. How does she fit into this?'

Another shrug. 'She approached me when I was last inside. She told me she'd heard about the story and did I want her to look into it for me? She said she'd help me bring the men who abused me to justice. I wasn't sure at first, but she persuaded me. She wanted me to go public with it. I wanted to believe her, but I wasn't sure I could trust her. But she kept pushing me and pushing me. I just needed some space to get my head sorted before I spoke to her again.'

Molly could imagine what Mags would have been like. Hunting the scent of a story; not letting something like vulnerable emotions get in the way. 'Don't let Mags bully you. If you don't want to talk to her, there's no way she can force you to.'

He looked like he was going to cry. 'I want to trust her, but it's difficult. It's difficult knowing who to trust.'

He looked at Molly; a look that said he was unsure if he could trust her either.

'Colin, I promise you I'll look into what you've told me, but I have to be honest: as it was such a long time ago, and has already been officially investigated by the police, I can't promise we'll be able to find these men now.'

It was a lot to ask, after all this time. If the men responsible were in their fifties and sixties thirty years ago, most of them could be dead now.

It was starting to get dark. The park felt strangely empty as the fading light began to dim.

She walked him back to the bedsit on Tulse Hill, and gave him her card. She already had his mobile number, courtesy of Mags. She promised him she would get in touch the moment she'd found anything out. But she wasn't optimistic. If she was honest, she wasn't even certain she believed his story.

Chapter Twenty-One

The nurse recognised Denning from his earlier visit. She was just about to come off shift, but confirmed there had been no change in the patient's condition. The doctor had said it would be another few days before he could be discharged. 'You can speak to Dr Cairns,' she said, 'but don't upset him.'

Cairns was sitting up in bed, half reading a motoring magazine when Denning entered. He glanced over at Denning and sighed.

'Not you again. I told you last time – I don't want to press charges.'

Denning stood by the bed, looking down at him. 'Not that simple, Dr Cairns. I think it would be in both our interests for you to start being honest with me.'

'What are you talking about?' He threw the magazine on the bed. 'Look, just get lost. I still can't remember what happened, and I've got nothing else to say to you, so you might as well piss off.' He picked up the magazine and began flicking through it, trying to find the page he was reading before Denning pitched up.

Denning leaned over and grabbed the magazine out of his hand and tossed it onto one of the chairs in the corner.

'Your old colleague Dr Noonan was asking after you.'

'Was he really?'

'She.'

Cairns didn't answer.

Denning perched on the edge of the bed. 'You specialised in late nineteenth and early twentieth-century history, didn't you?'

'Amongst other things.'

'What's your take on the early female suffrage movement? Why was Asquith so reluctant to support it? Or the Great War? Was it an inevitable consequence of unfettered colonialism?'

Cairns looked blank.

One of Denning's parents' colleagues taught history at Keele. Denning remembered him talking about a book he was writing on the early 1900s. He'd had forgotten most of what the professor had told him, but it was obvious he knew more about the subject than the man lying in the bed.

'OK, how about an easier question: do you recognise the name Gordon Lomax?'

He didn't flinch. If Denning's words had had any effect, then he didn't let it show. 'Never heard of him. Now give me back my fucking magazine.'

'Gordon Neil Lomax,' Denning continued. 'A former associate of Alfie Kane. I presume you've heard of Alfie Kane.' He smiled at Lomax, who scowled at Denning in return. 'I've done a bit of digging, and it's thrown up some fascinating information. But do you know the most interesting fact? Gordon Lomax disappeared around the same time David Cairns was reported missing by his sister.' He gave the man in the bed another smile. 'It was assumed he was dead. However, you're not dead, are you? But David Cairns is still officially missing. Care to explain that one?'

'You're talking shite. Now get lost before I call for a nurse.'

'I need to know two things before I leave you alone with your thoughts.' He waited until he had the man's full attention. 'What happened to David Cairns, and was Alfie Kane responsible for putting you in here? Because we both know, Mr Lomax, that was no mugging. Someone wanted to kill you, and I suspect Kane would have a very good motive.'

'I've never heard of Alfie Kane. Or Gordon Lomax, for that matter.' He gave a dry laugh. 'I have to admire your imagination, but I'm afraid you've made a mistake. My name is David Cairns, and unless you can prove otherwise I'm going to have to insist you leave me alone.'

Denning waited until Lomax had finished and then threw him another smile. 'OK. If that's how you want to play it. I will find out the truth, so there's no hurry.'

He knew they were both playing a game of bluff. Unless he could prove Lomax wasn't David Cairns, and come up with some solid evidence to show that Cairns had come to harm and Lomax was somehow responsible, Lomax would get away with this charade, and the truth would never be uncovered.

'This isn't over, Mr Lomax.'

He was interrupted by the arrival of a nurse; not the same one he'd spoken to when he'd arrived, but an older one with a stern look about her. 'Is everything alright?' she asked.

'No.' Lomax was looking agitated now, rubbing a hand over the side of his face in an exaggerated manner. 'I'd like this man to go.'

The nurse turned to Denning. 'I'm sorry, sir, but I'm going to have to ask you to leave.'

Denning looked from one to the other. He could make it official, insist he had to question her patient in connection with a crime. But what would that crime be? Impersonating a possibly-dead academic? That was the best he had to go with at the moment.

'OK,' he said. 'I can come back another time. I've got some further questions for Mr Lomax.'

He barely registered the look of confusion on the nurse's face when he left the room.

Chapter Twenty-Two

'Do you believe him?' Jon asked.

They were sitting in the living room, eating Spaghetti Bolognese off trays in front of the telly. Jon had cooked, or at least he'd opened the jar and added it to the mince in the saucepan.

Molly twirled the spaghetti on her fork, trying to muster up the enthusiasm to eat it. It wasn't that there was anything wrong with the food; she just didn't seem to have any appetite.

After her chat with Colin, she'd gone for a coffee to clear her head and think over what he'd told her, and the potential consequences. It was late by the time she'd got back. Her head was still a muddle.

So she'd told Jon. She had to unburden herself to someone, and if she were to tell anyone at work, there was always the risk it would be made official, and she wasn't ready to do that just yet.

'I don't know,' she said. 'It's an extraordinary story.' She ate a forkful of spaghetti, chewing it while she thought. 'That doesn't mean it's not true, though.'

Jon was staring at the telly. *Channel 4 News* had finished. They were watching a documentary on Sky about Watergate and the fall of Nixon. Fortunately, Jon had muted it.

'It does prove one thing.' He switched his gaze from the silent telly to her. 'Mags was telling the truth.'

Mags. She realised she hadn't phoned her to let her know Colin was OK. She wasn't even sure that was the right thing to do. Colin hadn't seemed keen to talk to Mags, and the idea that they were friends, as Mags had claimed, was clearly a fallacy.

'The jury's still out on Mags. Whatever else he is, Colin Meek is a damaged individual. I think Mags is in this for herself.'

'It sounds like you do believe him,' Jon said.

She didn't know the answer to that. She'd been pondering it on the way home. Colin had seemed credible. When he was talking to her in the park, the raw emotion with which he spoke felt real, as though it was being spewed straight from the gut rather than whittled from a distorted memory. But now she'd had time to digest it, she wasn't so sure.

'It's possible Mags has offered him some kind of financial incentive to ensure he provides her with the juiciest version of what happened. And now he is having second thoughts, which is why he is avoiding her?' She toyed with some more spaghetti. 'That's assuming it happened in the first place.'

Jon was staring at the oversized TV screen again. There was a picture of Richard Nixon mouthing something at the camera, looking forlorn, guilt stamped on his face like a boot print. If there was any truth in what Colin had told her, were the men responsible for abusing him feeling guilty for robbing him and others of the final bit of their childhood?

Then she remembered. 'He mentioned an MP who resigned around that time after he was caught up in some scandal involving a rent boy.'

'Could be talking about Robin Sims,' Jon said. 'That *was* a scandal.'

She didn't recognise the name. It was likely she'd been living in Sydney at the time, or perhaps she'd just been too young to take any interest. 'Care to share the details?'

He turned his attention from the documentary and looked at Molly. 'Robin Sims. MP for Haversham East. We'd all heard the rumours for years, but no one was ever brave enough to put anything into print. When the story did finally appear, sadly it wasn't us that broke it. *News of the Screws* got in there first, I think. Or *The Star*, I can't remember now. We did do a follow-up, but the story was going stale by then.'

She put her plate on the coffee table, leaving the rest of the spag bol uneaten. 'Any chance you could elaborate?'

He folded his arms across his chest. 'It was the dying days of the Thatcher government. Sims was a junior minister at the Department of Trade and Industry. Not a big player, but he was making a name for himself. There were even whispers he might make leader one day. Like I said, there had been rumours about Sims for years. Him and young lads; rent boys mostly, but other stories too. Nothing that had a hope in hell of fighting its way through a libel court though, so everyone preferred to tread carefully. Then one day a boy came forward and claimed he'd been having a sexual relationship with Sims off and on for over a year.'

'Boy? How old are we talking?'

He shrugged. 'Seventeen, eighteen?'

'Not exactly a boy.'

'Maybe not, but still below the legal age of consent for gay men at the time. Anyway, this boy – young man – had proof: photos of the two of them together, or so he claimed. Apparently there was even a video he'd got a friend to take of him and Sims in bed. I can leave the details to your imagination. The paper ran the story – including a full interview with the boy, grainy pics of him and Sims on holiday somewhere hot, even quotes from one of Sims's neighbours saying how he'd seen boys going in and out of Sims's London flat at all hours. Sims denied everything, of course. Insisted both the photos and the video were fake; the neighbours were lying, and he was the victim of a tabloid set-up. He threatened to sue, as they always do when they've been caught with their pants down. But he never did in the end. His career was finished, though. He resigned from the government straight away, then stepped down as an MP at the next general election.'

'What about the photos and the video? Assuming they were genuine.'

'I imagine Sims paid handsomely for their return. I expect the whole thing was nothing more than an attempted blackmail that got out of hand.'

'Blackmail?'

'Pay up, or I take this to the press, that kind of thing. Sims stood his ground, so the boy carried out his threat. Sims likely thought he was bluffing at first. Or maybe he thought he could threaten the boy into keeping quiet, who knows? Either way, it spelt the end of Sims's career in politics.'

'Why didn't he go to the police, if he was being black-mailed?'

'I'm afraid that's one question you'll have to direct at Sims, Detective. Though I imagine there are days when he probably wishes he had.'

Molly was thinking this over, trying to tie it with what Colin had told her.

'What were the other rumours?'

'Rumours?'

'About Sims?'

He yawned and scratched his bald dome of a head. 'There was some story about him being cautioned by your lot after he was caught hanging round Hampstead Heath in the wee small hours. It was kept out of the press at the time, though we all knew about it. There were other stories about him and the son of a constituent who helped out at the local party office. Until the rent boy scandal, there was never anything concrete, and to be honest, this wasn't really my area. I mean, there was obviously a political angle while he was an MP and then a government minister, but once Sims had resigned, it ceased to be about politics and became more about sensational gossip. It's possible Mags would know. That was more her kind of bag. Like I said, we did cover the story once it was out there, though not in any great detail. Partially because it quickly became old news, but mostly because there was a real chance Sims was going to sue. We didn't want to get dragged into what could have been a costly libel case.'

'So these rumours had nothing to do with Sims being part of a paedophile gang?'

He laughed again. 'All I know is that he liked boys. If you're asking if he could have been one of the men Colin Meek was talking about, then I don't know.'

'What about this young man who claimed he'd been involved with Sims? Can you remember his name?'

'Christ, Molly – it was thirty years ago. Why don't you ask me what I had for breakfast the morning the story broke?'

He'd been seventeen, eighteen… The age Colin would have been thirty years ago. 'So Sims used rent boys?' she asked. 'Regularly?'

'Apparently. But there's a world of difference between paying for sex and abusing vulnerable teenagers.'

Molly wasn't so sure. She thought a very thin line separated the two, but now wasn't the time for that discussion.

'Will you speak to Mags?' he asked. 'Tell her about Colin?'

She thought about this. 'I'm not sure what to say to her. OK. Maybe she didn't lie. But at the same time, she didn't exactly put me in the full picture.'

He gave another indifferent shrug. 'It's your call. At least it would get her off your back.'

Molly nodded. But if she was honest, she wasn't in any hurry to face Mags again. An encounter with her always felt like a battle, and Molly always seemed to come off worst.

Chapter Twenty-Three

Sarah was listening to Classic FM when Denning arrived home. A Mozart piano concerto, though he wasn't sure which one. No doubt if he were to ask Sarah, she'd be able to tell him.

She was sitting on one of the sofas, tapping at her laptop. 'How's your murder investigation going? There was something about it on the news earlier.'

'Oh yes, what?'

She was still focussed on her laptop, typing an email that looked more like a short novel. 'Rumours that someone might be targeting ex-police officers.' She looked up at him and smiled. 'As long as they don't start going after serving officers.'

He perched on the arm of the sofa she was sitting on. 'You should never believe everything you hear,' he said. He glanced at the kitchen. 'I'll get changed and start on dinner in a minute. What are you in the mood for?'

She'd finished writing the email and was now reading over it. 'Surprise me.'

He yawned, stretching his back and easing out the stresses of the day. He stood, then sat down again.

'Do you know a man called Justin Morrow?' he asked.

She clicked *send* and the email disappeared from the screen, probably landing in an inbox on a computer somewhere in New York. 'Justin?' She closed the laptop. 'That's going back a bit.'

'So you know him?'

'He used to be my boss when I first started at Bishop & Willett. In fact, Justin interviewed me for the job. Why?'

He told her about his meeting with her former boss and his new position with the GLA, and how he'd been slightly poleaxed when Morrow asked after her.

'You met him once,' she said. 'Do you remember?'

He shook his head. 'I've never seen him before yesterday.'

'Christmas drinks party at the Dorchester. About five years ago.'

Denning had a vague recollection of a Christmas party some years back. A posh room full of sharp suits talking about school fees and second homes. He had never warmed to Sarah's work colleagues. Their take on life seemed so at odds with his own. He dealt with the unvarnished truth of the real world, something their wealth and privilege insulated them from for the most part.

But he didn't remember Morrow. If they'd met, Morrow had failed to make any kind of impression. Though it was possible the memory had been dulled by alcohol consumption. If he was thinking about the right night, he seemed to recall there being a free bar: attentive waiters topping up his wine glass with the sleight of hand of the average magician. Though clearly Morrow had remembered him. Had he said something he shouldn't have? Behaved inappropriately? It was unlikely.

If Morrow had been Sarah's boss at the time, there was bound to have been some kind of formal introduction, about which Denning had no memory.

'I haven't heard anything about him in years,' Sarah said. 'He was a good boss – encouraged promotion and always believed in gender parity, which was pretty unusual in those days, especially for a man.' She rubbed a finger along the lid of her laptop. 'Funny though, he never struck me as being very political. I never even knew he was a GLA councillor.'

'I think they call themselves "Assembly members",' Denning corrected her, 'but I don't know if it's politics that motivates him, or if he just sees it as a stepping stone to bigger and better things.'

'That's a bit cynical.'

He gave another yawn, realising he was tired and he hadn't eaten. Neither of them would be eating if he didn't get his backside into the kitchen sharpish. 'Where do you think his interest in politics comes from? I mean, what would motivate him to give up the high-flying world of corporate finance to become a lowly member of the London Assembly?'

Sarah had opened the lid on her laptop, checking to see if there had been a reply to the email she'd just sent. 'I think he left to set up his own investment company. Maybe he sees politics as a way of making useful contacts. But good luck to him. Politics isn't for the faint-hearted, is it?'

But Denning didn't know, or care. He'd met too many Justin Morrows: ambitious, motivated by self-interest and full of empty promises. And this one didn't seem any different.

Sarah closed the laptop again. 'He was a good boss,' she added. But Denning had stopped listening. He headed into the kitchen to make a start on dinner.

After dinner he Skyped Jake.

His son was initially reluctant to chat; arguing that he wanted to watch something on the telly, but after a bit of prompting from Claire, he started chatting away, telling Denning all about his day at school and his plans for the Easter holidays. He was looking forward to seeing Granny in Devon and building sandcastles on the beach. There was no mention of spending time with his daddy, and Denning tried not to take it personally. Jake tended to focus on what was happening in his own little world, rather than having any concept of the bigger picture. In fairness to Claire, she regularly reminded Jake that he had a daddy who loved him and was a part of his life. But Jake liked to compartmentalise his life. Unless you were part of his immediate environment, he tended to sideline you, and fit you in only whenever he felt comfortable. Or whenever he was prompted to.

'Give my love to Granny,' Denning said. He said goodbye to Jake then chatted to Claire about her plans for Easter, explaining that his involvement in a major case at work might impact on the time he would have with Jake. Despite this, he would make an effort to see him whenever he could, and would endeavour to make up for any missed time as soon as the case was over. Claire nodded, briefly closing her eyes: a look that showed she was not surprised at this familiar situation. He no longer felt obliged to apologise for his job. Claire knew the score, and there was no point in wasting energy reheating the same old arguments over and over again.

He finished Skyping, and was about to close his laptop when the niggling voice in his brain reminded him of something. He googled Gordon Lomax. There were predictably few photos of Lomax, and very little in writing about him. He had worked hard at keeping his head below the parapet. What photographs Denning could find were at least twenty years out of date, but behind the bruises and the bandage, he was sure the face he could glimpse matched that of the man who had been pretending to be Cairns.

He looked up Alfie Kane again. There was a piece on the BBC News website about the arrest of Kane's son Gregor the previous year, and a reference to Alfie Kane's new charity, which he was about to launch amid much fanfare…

And then there was Frank Buckfield. Somehow they were all linked: a murder and a possible attempted murder. The connection with Security Direct. At the heart of it all was Alfie Kane, sitting like a spider in his impressive Essex mansion. He didn't know much about Kane, but he knew he was clever. Clever enough to make sure anything that did link him to those two crimes would be effectively buried.

Chapter Twenty-Four

The following morning, Denning pulled up in front of a pair of ornate metal gates, through which he could see an imposing brick mansion. The house was surrounded by an eight-foot-high wall that gave the impression of a fortress. At the far end of the road he could glimpse the greenery of Epping Forest. Living out here, London must have felt like it was a world away.

He pressed the button on an intercom that had been built into a brick pillar beside the gates, and announced who he was. A moment later, the heavy gates swung inwards and he drove up a short mono-block driveway with a wide expanse of lawn on either side.

The house had been built from reclaimed bricks and designed to resemble a Georgian mansion. Two double-storey rows of sash windows sat either side of a stucco-pillared front door. The pictures on the internet hadn't done it justice. It had only been completed a few months ago, built on the site of an old country hotel that had mysteriously burned down a couple of years back.

Off to the left of the house there was a three-car garage, in front of which was parked a Mercedes S-class saloon, a Land Rover Discovery and a stylish E-class cabriolet.

He parked his own humbler Ford Focus on the driveway, got out and rang the doorbell. He was aware of the unblinking eye of a camera lens gazing back at him.

McKenna had warned him off chasing up the attack on Cairns, and with only a tenuous connection to link him with Buckfield, Denning knew he was taking a risk talking to Kane. But he couldn't ignore the feeling Kane had something to do with this whole thing. His name kept cropping up, and that couldn't just be a coincidence.

Eventually, the heavy front door was opened by a thick-set man in a designer suit. Too young to be Kane, he was most likely some kind of security-guard-come-butler.

The man led Denning through a double-height, marble-floored hallway and into a large mock-Victorian conservatory at the rear of the house.

Kane was sitting at a glass-topped table finishing a breakfast of croissants and fruit juice.

He looked up as soon as Kane's henchman announced Denning's presence in a broad estuary accent.

'Inspector Denning, good morning.' Kane gestured to one of the sturdy wicker chairs that sat around the glass-topped breakfast table. 'Coffee?' Before Denning had a chance to say anything, Kane had poured out a cup of coffee from a cafetiere and pushed the cup towards Denning. 'How do you take it? Better still, help yourself.' He indicated a white ceramic milk jug and matching sugar bowl. Denning, who took his coffee black and unsweetened, declined the offer of milk and sugar.

'How can I help you, Inspector? I don't believe we've met.' He extended his hand towards Denning. Denning returned the handshake, noting Kane's firm grip. According to the news stories he'd read, Kane was sixty-four, but regular gym visits and a healthy tan trimmed a good decade from his age. His accent was cultured, as though the rougher edges had been chiselled away. He remembered how Gregor Kane's polished accent had taken him by surprise. It seemed as though the family was keen to erase any reference to their working-class roots.

'Just a few questions about a former associate of yours. A Gordon Lomax. Do you have any contact with him?'

He laughed. 'Gordon! Christ, I thought he was dead.' He looked at Denning, the laugh ending and a serious look appearing on his face. 'Are you saying he isn't?'

'Mr Lomax was recently the victim of a serious assault. He's currently in hospital.'

Kane's face contorted into a moue of sympathy. 'Well, I'm very sorry to hear that, naturally I am. However, I haven't seen Gordon for the best part of twenty years. Not that I believe you're suggesting I had anything to do with what happened to Gordon. I mean, why would you think that?' He looked Denning squarely in the eye. Not quite McKenna's gimlet stare, but not far off it.

'I'm not suggesting anything at this stage, Mr Kane. Just trying to establish a few facts. Did you know Mr Lomax has been living under a different name for the past twenty years?'

Kane didn't look especially interested. 'No. Why would I know that? As I told you, I hadn't seen Gordon for a long time. I have no idea what he's been up to, and to be frank with you, Mr Denning, I don't want to. Gordon Lomax was an employee of mine, a long time ago. And not a very reliable one either. I've moved on in my life and I imagine he has too.'

'When was the last time you saw Mr Lomax?'

'Like I said, it must be over twenty years ago.'

'So around the time of the Security Direct robbery?'

If Denning's comment hit a raw nerve, Kane didn't let it show. There wasn't even a flicker. 'So you've been doing your homework. I'm impressed. But if you were being thorough – and you strike me as the kind of man who is always very thorough, Mr Denning – you'd know I had nothing to do with that particular endeavour. I can't, of course, speak for Gordon Lomax.'

Kane was one cool customer, Denning had to give him that. 'So your last contact with Mr Lomax was around twenty years ago, and you haven't seen him since?'

'I think we've confirmed that now.'

'Lomax would be how old now? Fifties? Early sixties?'

Kane looked puzzled for a moment and a little wary, possibly wondering if Denning was trying to catch him out somehow. But again he gave little away. 'He's about the same age as me,' Kane said. 'Why is that relevant?'

'It's not relevant at all. I just wanted to confirm something.'

'In that case, is that everything? I'm a busy man, and I'm sure you are too.'

'Just one last question, Mr Kane: what was the exact nature of your relationship with Frank Buckfield?'

Again, no reaction from Kane, not even a flicker of emotion. 'You'll have to remind me, Mr Denning – who is Frank Buckfield?'

Denning found it hard to believe Kane didn't know the name. If nothing else, it had been all over the news for the past two days. 'I expect you would have known him as DCI Buckfield. He was found murdered two days ago. I understand you and he knew one another. Your name certainly came up when we looked into his background.'

Kane pulled a face, very slightly exaggerated as though unsure if Denning was being serious. 'You have me at a disadvantage here, I'm afraid. To my knowledge, I've never met a DCI Buckfield, so again, sorry, but I can't help you.'

Denning nodded. He knew when he was being outmanoeuvred, and he suspected Kane was a past master at it. 'OK, thank you for your time, Mr Kane. You've been very helpful.'

As though summoned by magic, the same security guard that had shown him in appeared and showed him out again, the front door closing with a firm click behind him.

He got back into the Focus and drove towards the electric gates. There was a minute before they swung open to let him out: more brinksmanship from Kane – keeping him waiting before allowing him to leave the property was another reminder of who was calling the shots here.

He glanced in the rear-view mirror as he turned off the driveway and onto the street: the visual display of opulence, the suave, self-assured arrogance of the Alfie Kanes of the world made him sick. Even if he worked beyond his retirement, claimed all the overtime going and factored in Sarah's inflated salary, there was no way he could ever afford to live somewhere like Kane's ostentatious monument to vanity. He was sure if they investigated Kane's finances thoroughly enough, they could find enough gaps and questions to go after him for something. Al Capone had been brought down by the taxman. But Kane was clever. He'd used his brains to keep one step ahead of the police all his adult life. It was very likely he'd made sure there was no shit that could potentially stick to him. Had he been working hand in glove with Buckfield? Possibly. But in the end it hadn't done Buckfield any favours, dying as he had in a sorry flat on a grotty estate while Kane lived it up in his opulent mansion. Not for the first time, Denning mused on the unfairness of life.

Chapter Twenty-Five

Molly was first in again. She was pleased to see she had the place to herself this time. Denning was either elsewhere or running late. She didn't care, as long as she could work in peace.

She joggled the mouse and woke her computer from sleep mode, then tapped in her ID and password and logged onto the PNC.

Despite doing a detailed search, she could find no reference to a murdered child corresponding with the time that Colin claimed Tommy had been killed. Taking a bit of a punt, she searched for the name 'Tommy' on the Missing Persons site, but again, nothing came up. It didn't help that Tommy was unlikely to be his real name, and without a surname to go on, there was little chance she would be able to take it any further for now. She fired off an email to a colleague at the National Crime Agency, asking if there were any unsolved Missing Persons cases on file that might match Tommy. The NCA had now been given overall responsibility for all Missing Person's reports, even historical ones. She also requested information regarding any unidentified bodies that may have turned up fitting the vague description she had of Tommy. She didn't hold out much hope. This would be like looking for the proverbial needle in a haystack.

She then checked the report on the investigation into Colin Meek's claims of sexual abuse.

Colin had approached the police in January 1990, some two and a half months after the Sims story had broken, and the investigation had been handled by Hammersmith CID. The case had been dealt with by a DS Coughlin and a DC Flynn. Neither name rang a bell with Molly. The entry on the PNC was short and to the point. Colin's claims had been thoroughly looked into as part of a six-month investigation, but there was no evidence to support any of his accusations. A witness, named Jason Wainwright, had come forward quite early on and backed up Colin's claims, stating that he had been one of the boys abused by the gang, and had offered some pretty explicit details. Then, without warning, Wainwright had subsequently retracted his statement after he confessed to having lied about the whole thing. This had resulted in serious doubt being cast on Colin's claims, which, taken along with the lack of evidence, had resulted in the case being dropped in the summer of 1990. The official conclusion had been that Meek had made the story up in an attempt to cash in on the Sims scandal. Reference had been made to Meek's criminal record and how he "wouldn't make a reliable witness should the case ever get as far as a courtroom". Molly grimaced at the wording: Colin's criminal record should never have been an influencing factor when making this kind of decision; the case should have been judged solely on the evidence available. However, she had to accept that the case seemed weak at best and the noticeable lack of evidence, combined with Colin's flawed character, would have resulted in some unconscious bias on the part of the investigating team.

She didn't know what to make of it. Certainly there was nothing there that would convince CAIT – the Met's Child Abuse Investigation Team – to look into it again in any official capacity. After a series of high-profile cases being dropped in recent years – along with several thousand being paid out in compensation for wrongful arrest – they'd learned to subject all claims of historical sex crimes to rigorous scrutiny before committing to an investigation. She could contact someone from CAIT and ask for their advice, but that was dangerously close to making the whole thing official.

Maybe she could run it by Denning or McKenna and gauge their response, to test the water. But that would mean admitting she'd been looking into this at least partly in police time – something that was hard to justify at the best of times, and almost impossible during an ongoing high-profile murder inquiry.

Perhaps if she could get hold of this Jason Wainwright, she could ask why he'd confessed to lying. Had someone put pressure on him? Or had he only ever been motivated by the prospect of money, thinking there might have been some kind of pay-off at the end of it?

Then there was the whole question of how Mags had come to hear of the case. She may have covered the original story, depending on how much had been revealed to the press at the time, though Molly suspected that whatever information was leaked at the time would have been very light on detail. Had Mags been researching the case out of curiosity, or had someone tipped her off? If the latter, then who – and more importantly, why? What was to be gained by reopening allegations of sexual abuse dating back more than three decades? Was this someone with an agenda? Or was it about revenge – exposing the men responsible and going after them?

The more she thought about it, the more she thought Mags had some serious explaining to do.

She looked up to see Denning standing over her. Her initial thought was that he'd clocked what she was doing and was going to ask what the hell she thought she was playing at using the PNC for personal use. Instead, he surprised her by asking if she wanted to go for a coffee.

She glanced at her watch. 'Yes, why not?'

They went to the McDonalds across the road. Denning ordered an Americano, and a caramel latte for Molly.

The restaurant area was quiet, with most people coming in for takeaways before starting work. They sat at a table near the window. Denning stared at his drink. 'We haven't really had a chance to chat lately,' he said. 'I just wondered how you were getting on.'

Molly wondered if this was some kind of unofficial appraisal. She hadn't yet been with MIT for a full year, and technically Denning was her line manager. But if that was the case, why would he have suggested McDonald's?

She sipped her latte and smiled. 'Yes, fine, thanks.'

'Good. We've neither of us been here for very long. I suppose, in a way, we're both still seen as outsiders by the rest of the team.'

Denning had joined the team a few months before she had, but she knew it took time to become fully accepted by a team of detectives. It had been the same story when she'd been in CID. 'They're a good team,' she said. 'I think we're both respected.' In fact, she was never very sure if Betty Taggart fully respected her being part of MIT, but then McKenna played her cards so close to her chest that no one really knew what she thought of the detectives under her command. Molly often found it difficult to second-guess Denning too, but at least he seemed more human. She just couldn't quite figure out what made him tick. There was a steely confidence about him that belied his quiet calm. In all the time they'd worked together, she'd only ever heard him raise his voice on a couple of occasions.

'What's your take on Harrison?' he asked.

She was slightly wrong-footed by the question, and wondered if he was trying to catch her out. 'It's too early to form an opinion,' she said. 'He's new and he's obviously keen. Why do you ask?'

Denning stared at his coffee for a moment, then took a sip and grimaced very slightly. 'I don't know. There's just something about him.'

Molly wasn't sure if she was being tested in some way. Detective Chief Superintendents came and went. Some made their presence felt and others had little impact on the day-to-day running of the Met. Harrison clearly wanted to be seen as falling into the former category, but that wouldn't impact on them. 'He talks the talk, but we'll see if he manages to walk the walk.' She didn't know what he expected her to say.

'Look, forget it,' he said. 'I just get a bit jittery whenever we have a new boss. The job is demanding enough without having to negotiate awkward personalities.' He sipped some more of his coffee, before pushing it to one side. 'And I forgot to say, thanks for speaking to David Cairns's colleague. However, I'm pretty sure David Cairns is not who he claims to be.'

'Seriously! What's the story there?'

'It's too early to say for sure, but I believe his name's Gordon Lomax, and he's an associate of Alfie Kane's.'

'Kane? You think this could be linked to Buckfield somehow?' she asked.

He shrugged. 'At this stage, I'm not sure. But McKenna wants us to pass it over. She says it's not our bag, and I'd rather keep that between us for now. At least until I can find some way of proving it.'

Molly agreed she'd keep it to herself. But if Denning was right, and Alfie Kane was somehow involved, then they were in for a bumpy ride. 'I'm not sure I see Kane as a link to Buckfield. I mean any possible connection between them was years ago. Then again, Alfie Kane strikes me as someone who doesn't like loose ends. It's just possible he saw Buckfield as one.'

Denning nodded quietly, but didn't say anything.

She finished her latte and wondered if she should offer to buy them both another couple of drinks. She wanted to talk to him about Colin Meek. She would have liked to have sounded him out and get his opinion on whether she was on to something, or whether he thought she was chasing shadows. She was about to tentatively broach the subject when Denning suddenly stood up and announced it was time to return to the office.

–

Denning decided to call another briefing. Progress was slow – too slow. And Harrison had made it clear he wanted results.

The team was getting twitchy too. The first forty-eight hours of a murder inquiry were the most crucial. They would soon be passing that mark.

'We now have the date of death confirmed as March sixteenth. It was a Saturday, so there must have been people around. Unfortunately, we can't get an exact time of death due to the decomposed state of the body, but it does give us a good timeframe to work around.'

'OK. Deep, has the CCTV at the Bedgebrook Estate come up with anything?'

Neeraj scanned his notes. 'Nada, boss. We're still looking, but half of it's not working, and what is working isn't of the best quality.'

'Keep looking.'

'Will do, boss.'

Denning turned to the whiteboard. 'We also need to keep looking into Buckfield's background. I still think this is personal, and not necessarily connected to any cases he's worked.'

'Did Gavin Buckfield's alibi check out?' he asked Trudi.

'Yup. He was where he said he was. CCTV can confirm it.'

'So we can rule him out?' Neeraj asked.

'We can rule him out,' Denning said. He had never believed Gavin Buckfield had murdered his father. In some ways, he wished he had: it would have tied things up quickly. But the truth was about what was right rather than what was convenient. They were going to have to look elsewhere for their murderer.

'What about Joseph Jupp?'

'Again his alibi checks out, boss,' Trudi said. 'He was in Bristol ten days ago attending a stag do. We've got CCTV of him at Temple Meads station. And witnesses who can confirm he was with them that weekend.'

'Let's widen the field. Dave, you were going to speak to some of Buckfield's former colleagues. What did they have to say?'

'Pretty much backed up what I already said: a decent copper. He was respected by those under him, and got on with the job. Most agreed the DPS investigation was a load of bollocks and Buckfield was the victim of "Met politics" as one retired DI put it.' Denning knew the Met Police was like any organisation: rife with petty jealousies and office politics. Yet there was something about Buckfield's departure that didn't feel right. He wasn't ready to dismiss the possible link to Kane just yet. Not until he knew for certain there was no truth in the corruption allegations.

He noticed Trudi Bell had her hand in the air. 'Yes, Trudi?'

'What about the attack on David Cairns? Are we still looking into that, or are we focussing solely on Buckfield now?'

On a separate whiteboard, he'd written the name David Cairns, next to which was a old photo of Cairns that had been provided by the university. He looked unremarkable: slightly serious, with greying hair and a wrinkled frown. If Lomax had been Cairns's lodger all those years ago, it would explain how they knew one another. But Denning still felt there was more to it than that.

He asked Molly to share what she'd found out from Cairns's colleague at Queen Mary, adding the points to the whiteboard. 'Have we managed to interview the bridge-playing neighbour yet?' he asked.

'I'm liaising with Islington CID on that,' Neeraj said. 'They spoke to him this morning, but he can't remember much about this lodger. Said he never actually met the bloke, he just remembers Cairns saying he'd moved in. He did say he thought it strange as Cairns hardly ever let anyone through his front door. Said he was a very private man.'

'We're certainly getting that impression,' Denning said. He wanted to share his thoughts with the team: tell them that David Cairns and the man who had been attacked the other day were two different people, but without proof, and as long as McKenna was snapping at his heels to pass the Cairns case onto CID, the whole thing would have to go on the back burner for now.

'Good,' he said. 'Well done everyone. For the time being, we concentrate on Buckfield. But if anything comes up, we'll keep going with the investigation into the attack on Cairns.'

He looked again at the names on the two separate whiteboards: Buckfield and Cairns. He was convinced there was *something* that connected them, but whatever it was, it still wasn't jumping out at him.

Despite McKenna's reservations, there was one obvious place to look. And that was exactly what Denning planned to do.

Chapter Twenty-Six

The nurse stationed outside Lomax's room greeted Denning with a wary smile, but agreed he could speak to David Cairns as long as he wasn't in there for too long.

Denning was amused by the fact that people still assumed the man lying in the bed in the private room was called David Cairns. There was now no doubt in Denning's mind that he was Gordon Lomax.

Lomax was sitting up in bed reading a copy of *The London Echo* when Denning entered the room. He rolled his eyes as soon as he saw Denning and groaned. 'What do you want now? I thought I'd seen the back of you yesterday.'

'That's not very polite, Mr Lomax. I've made a special effort to come and see you this morning, because I've got plenty I'd like to talk to you about. Starting with my recent conversation with Islington CID. They've spoken to a former friend of Dr Cairns, who informs us that Dr Cairns had a lodger around the time he disappeared. I'm willing to bet that lodger was you.' Denning stood at the top of the bed looking down at Lomax, reading his face and gauging his reaction. 'It's certainly not going to be difficult to prove, so I wouldn't bother continuing to deny it if I were you. What I really want to know is why you felt you had to disappear so abruptly in the first place, and then let the world think you were dead.' He put his hands in his pockets. 'And more importantly, what happened to the real Dr Cairns?'

It was a few minutes before Lomax spoke. He'd tossed the paper on the bed and was lying back on the pillow with his eyes shut. Either he was pretending to be asleep, or he'd just hoped that if he kept his eyes shut for long enough, Denning would have got bored and pissed off. But that wasn't going to happen.

'He topped himself,' Lomax said, suddenly opening his eyes and looking up at Denning. 'David Cairns is dead. He died twenty years ago this September.'

'OK,' Denning said, finally feeling they were getting somewhere. Perhaps he had managed to convince Lomax there was nowhere left to hide. 'Why don't you tell me about it?' he asked. He grabbed a chair from the stack in the corner by a small handbasin, and placed it beside the cabinet next to Lomax's bed. If this was going to be a long story, he might as well make himself comfortable.

Lomax rubbed a hand over the part of his face that wasn't bandaged, and breathed out through his nose. 'I knew David from way back. I helped him out with some research for a book he was planning to write. He let me stay with him when I was down on my luck. My marriage had ended, my missus chucked me out and I had nowhere to go.' He closed his eyes again as he remembered the events. 'David was a nice man. Not the kind of person I was used to associating with. He was cultured. He knew about wine and books and art and stuff. He used to try and teach me about that sort of thing. Before I lived with David, I'd never even read a book.' He opened his eyes and gave a hollow laugh. 'But David had another side to him too, especially when he'd been drinking. He wasn't just a connoisseur of wine, he used it to blank out his dark thoughts. And those thoughts visited him often. In the end it was obvious he was struggling to cope with life. I came back from the pub one evening and there was a note on the kitchen table saying he couldn't go on any more and I wasn't to feel sorry for him. And that was that. I never saw him again.'

'What happened?'

'I don't know.' He looked across at Denning. 'That's the honest truth. Whatever he did, wherever he did it, his body never pitched up.' He touched his face again and winced slightly. 'I reckon he ran into the sea and then disappeared, like that bloke back in the seventies.'

'John Stonehouse?' Denning offered, referring to the British politician who, in 1974, had famously faked his own death by drowning.

'Reggie Perrin,' Lomax said. 'I always thought he'd done a Reggie Perrin.'

It was Denning's turn to roll his eyes. 'Why didn't you contact the police? If you suspected he'd come to harm, you had a duty to let someone know. His family, for instance, were concerned about him.'

'He only had a sister, and he hated her. This seemed like the obvious answer. He was talking about leaving his job, so that was boxed off. I used to run errands for him, so I knew the PINs for his bank cards. He'd paid off the mortgage on that house. He hardly had any friends to speak of and he never spoke to any of the neighbours. I'd totally fucked my life up. I was up to my arse in debt, my ex-wife was after me for more money. And there were some people I was keen to avoid – let's call them former associates. For the first time in my life something good had come my way. I wasn't going to let it pass.'

'Except you lied. You pretended to be someone else. You fraudulently claimed his pension. You're squatting in a house that isn't yours. Not to mention the small matter of failing to report a suspected fatality.'

Lomax stared at the ceiling. After a moment, he closed his eyes again. 'So what are you going to do? Arrest me for impersonating a dead man? I'll deny it. I'll say Cairns said he'd leave everything to me in his will. And let's face it, you can't prove he's dead. Not unless you plan to dredge the English Channel.'

Denning waited a couple of seconds before asking his next question. 'On the subject of former associates you were keen to avoid, how does Alfie Kane fit into all this?'

Another laugh. Slightly more forced than last time. 'He's got nothing to do with anything. I hadn't worked for Alfie for years by the time all this happened.'

But Denning didn't believe him. 'David Cairns disappeared in the late nineties, just a few years after the Security Direct robbery. Is that a coincidence?'

'You're not suggesting Cairns had anything to do with that?'

'Not Cairns, Mr Lomax, you. Or more to the point, Alfie Kane had something to do with it. And I think that's the real reason behind your vanishing act. Did you know too much? Did Kane want you silenced? If Kane discovered you were still alive, he could have been responsible for the assault on you the other day. Paid someone to give you a good going-over to teach you a lesson for running out on him?'

He shook his head. 'That's not Kane's style. He'd have confronted me himself: face to face, man to man. Alfie's never been afraid of confrontation. Besides, I think you're overstating my importance in Alfie Kane's life. I worked for the bloke for a while. One of many employees over the years. One of many, and equally forgettable.'

'Well, there's got to be something more to this than you're admitting to,' Denning said. 'By the sounds of it, it's unlikely Dr Cairns had many enemies, so even if someone had assumed you were him, I can't see them having a good reason to assault you. Whereas Kane...' Denning sat back on the chair, hearing it creak under his weight. 'Why don't you tell me about the Security Direct robbery? We know Kane was involved, and I suspect you could probably name names if pushed. It might count in your favour if you find yourself in need of police protection.'

Lomax was staring at the ceiling again. His eyes were still open, but focussed solely on a dark spot to the right of one of the light fittings. 'You're talking crap. Either arrest me for pretending to be David Cairns, or just leave me alone. I'm not going to tell you anything about Alfie Kane that isn't already common knowledge. If you want to use someone to get to Alfie, then find some other muppet, because I'm just not interested.'

Denning stood up, placing a hand on the back of the chair. 'What are you so frightened of? If it's Kane, we can give you protection. If it's something else, then you need to tell me. Because this isn't finished. Not by a long chalk.'

Lomax turned his gaze from the spot on the ceiling to look at Denning. 'Except it *is* finished, at least as far as I'm concerned.' He was still looking Denning squarely in the eye. 'I have nothing more to say.' With that he picked up the copy of *The London Echo* that was lying on the bedclothes and began reading it again.

Denning noticed the headline on the front page: *Police Still No Closer to Finding Cop Killer.* There was the same out-of-date picture of Buckfield in his full police regalia that had appeared in the press releases. But underneath there was another picture. One of Denning leaving the mortuary the previous day. It had clearly been taken from a distance and from an unflattering angle. At first glance, Denning looked considerably older than his thirty-four years.

Despite Lomax's admission, they were still no further forward in finding Buckfield's killer. And he was still convinced Lomax hadn't given him the full story. But with McKenna on his back, there was little chance of him being allowed to follow this up for now. He thought about passing it over to Anna Klein, but what did he actually have? Suspicions that Lomax had lied about what had happened to Cairns? Without any proof, there was no way of telling what had really happened to Cairns, and all they had at the moment was whatever Lomax chose to tell them.

Chapter Twenty-Seven

Denning headed back to his car. As he pulled out of the hospital car park and turned onto the main road, he glanced in his rear-view mirror. A grey Toyota Corolla had pulled out of a parking space at the same time and was now following him down the road. There were two men sitting in the front, neither of whom he could see clearly: the driver was wearing a pair of shades, while the passenger had a baseball cap pulled down over his face. The sun reflected off the car's windscreen, making it even harder to get a clear view of their features.

He reached a set of traffic lights and the car pulled up behind him. The man in the passenger seat was speaking on a mobile phone, but looking straight ahead at Denning.

The lights changed and he moved off.

As he pulled away, the car followed him. The number plate was partially obscured by mud, and he could just about make out the first three letters, but the numbers were unreadable.

The car followed him down Holloway Road. It stayed close all the way into Highbury. He was tempted to phone the local plod and get someone to pull the car over, but that really would be giving in to paranoia. This could be nothing more sinister than someone innocently leaving the hospital car park at the same time as him and heading into central London. But there was something about the whole thing that made him feel uneasy.

He slowed as he approached the next set of traffic lights at Highbury Corner. The lights changed as he was almost upon them and he briefly accelerated, turning left onto St Paul's Road at the last second without indicating.

He checked the rear-view mirror again and saw that he'd managed to lose the car.

Denning knew it could be his paranoia getting the better of him. But he couldn't ignore the fact that this had happened so soon after he'd spoken to Kane. Was it a warning? *We can follow you and find out where you live?*

He turned into a side street just before Balls Pond Road to make sure the car was no longer following him.

His hands were trembling on the steering wheel. If Kane was threatening him then it made him all the more determined to bring him to book.

Chapter Twenty-Eight

Dave Kinsella was in the middle of making a phone call when Denning arrived back at the office, slightly shaken. He sat at his desk thinking over what had just happened, and was determined to dismiss it as nothing more than rampant paranoia. He could take it further, and confront Kane. But without any proof, he was unlikely to get very far.

Once Kinsella had ended the call, Denning headed over to his desk. There was an old saying that said if you wanted to know about something, ask someone who was there, and Kinsella had been around for donkey's years. He may not know where the bodies were buried, but he would have a good idea where to start digging.

'Dave, do you fancy a coffee?'

Kinsella looked momentarily taken aback, probably thinking it was a trick question. Then his face broadened into a smile. 'OK, boss. I wouldn't mind a break from this.'

They headed to the coffee machine on the ground floor. Denning selected a latte with two sugars for Kinsella and an Americano for himself.

They sat in the empty conference room.

'How's it going?' he asked Kinsella. 'Uncovered anything interesting in Buckfield's past?'

Kinsella sipped his latte and pulled a face. 'Just what you would expect. Nothing's rung any alarm bells so far.

And CCTV from that rat's nest of an estate is worse than useless.'

Denning waited for a moment. 'What about Alfie Kane? Has his name come up yet?'

'Kane?' Kinsella narrowed his eyes. 'Not in relation to anything specific. Why?'

Denning told Kinsella about his meeting with the reformed gangster that morning. He didn't mention being followed from the hospital, focussing instead on the rumours linking Buckfield to Kane. He wasn't sure how much Kinsella knew about the DPS allegations, and whether Kane had ever been mentioned by name, or how much was just hearsay. But Kinsella was around at the time and was familiar with the state of play back then. 'There's not much on the PNC. I know you're familiar with Kane's activities from way back, before he officially turned his back on the dark side. I thought, maybe, you could give me a bit of an insight into Kane?' He took a sip of his coffee and tried to ignore the acrid taste. 'I'd really like to know the stuff that isn't flagged up on any police system. For a start, where did he get his money from?'

Kinsella pulled another face. 'His main business is the haulage firm. But he's had a finger in a lot of very different pies over the years.'

'Any of these pies likely to attract interest from us?'

He shrugged. 'Revenue and Customs, maybe, but I reckon his business dealings are mostly – if not entirely – legit these days.'

Denning had looked Kane up on the Companies House website. The haulage firm was certainly profit-able, judging by the previous year's annual returns, but profitable enough to pay for the swanky mock-Georgian mansion with the view of Epping Forest? He was sure there had to be something they were missing.

'Going back further. The not so legitimate aspects of his business empire, where did they come from?'

'Apparently he was just your average tearaway in his youth. Then he got ambitious: nicking cars for bank jobs, hiding stolen goods, that kind of thing. He started hanging out with some of the big boys, doing odd jobs for them, running errands. After a few years, he wound up working for Bernie Michaelson. I suppose that gave him his first taste of the gangster lifestyle.'

'Bernie Michaelson?'

Kinsella chuckled. 'Before your time, boss. Michaelson was an old-school villain who made his name in the sixties and seventies. A known associate of the Krays when they still called the shots, as well as other lesser-known players. Unlike them, Michaelson preferred to keep his name and face out of the limelight. By the mid-seventies, he had an empire that covered Soho and West London, a lot of it inherited from the twins after they went inside. Casinos, knocking shops, strip joints. Even owned a couple of bars and a nightclub – *Smokey Joes* on Wardour Street. Someone put a bullet in his brain in the early eighties. We never got anyone for it. Then again, maybe we weren't looking too hard.'

'And Kane worked for this Michaelson character?'

'For a while. Hatchet man, gofer, that kind of thing. I think he ran one of Michaelson's casinos back in the late seventies. Kane was still in his twenties at the time; a right cocky little so-and-so by all accounts. He bought up a lot of Michaelson's properties after his death, then sold them off a few years back for a tidy profit.'

But there was something Denning had to know. Something that had been bothering him ever since the name Alfie Kane was flagged up on his radar. 'How come we never got Kane for his part in the Security Direct robbery?'

Another chuckle. 'He's too clever. You can guarantee his paw prints would have been kept well off that. He helped plan it, maybe – and I'd bet my pension some of that bullion found its way into his possession – but he'd make damn sure there was nothing that led back to him.'

'But you're certain he was involved?'

'Word at the time was that Kane was certainly part of the food chain. But then so were half the faces in London, if you were to believe all the whispers.'

Denning nodded and sipped his coffee. 'Does the name Gordon Lomax mean anything?'

'Lomax?' Kinsella's mouth twitched to form an upsidedown 'u'. 'Can't say I recognise the name. Was he linked to Security Direct?'

'Possibly. He's certainly connected to Kane. Or at least he was.'

Kinsella drank the rest of the rancid coffee. 'You still think there's a connection between Buckfield and Kane? You think that was what all that crap with the DPS was about: Buckfield was taking backhanders from Kane?'

'Do you? It's likely Kane knew someone in the police. It can't be a coincidence that he got away with so much as often as he did. I'm not saying it *was* Buckfield, but we can't overlook the possibility he was somehow involved. Or at the very least, he knew about it and deliberately turned a blind eye.'

'Think about it, boss: if Buckfield was on the take, what happened to all the money? You saw that flat. He wasn't living the life of Rockefeller, was he?'

Denning finished his coffee and threw the plastic cup into a bin by the door. 'Then we keep looking, Dave. We find something that connects the two men, even indirectly. And start with Gordon Lomax. I reckon he's the weak link here.'

'Whatever you say, boss.'

Kinsella didn't sound convinced, but Denning knew he'd do it anyway. Kinsella may not have been the sharpest of detectives when it came to following a hunch, but he was the sort who would gnaw away at something until he found what they were looking for.

Denning couldn't help feeling this whole thing had Kane's fingerprints all over it. It couldn't be a coincidence that two people closely associated with Kane had been attacked: one murdered and the other in hospital. It was like he was trying to silence anyone who could directly connect him to his dodgy past now that he was trying to persuade the world he was a reformed character. At the moment, he had nothing more than a hunch to work on. Finding the evidence to nail Kane wasn't going to be easy.

He was about to head back to his desk, when he noticed a text from McKenna:

> Wherever you are, get your arse back here pronto! Harrison wants to see you in his office – and he's one unhappy bunny.

–

Harrison was behind his desk, a look of thunder spread across his face like a nappy rash. They were in the office Harrison had commandeered at the rear of the building, with the view of the car park.

'How's the investigation going into Buckfield's murder? Found his killer yet?'

Direct and to the point. His face remained unsmiling. Denning knew a bollocking when he was on the receiving end of one. He just wasn't sure why he was being treated to it and not McKenna.

'We're making solid progress, sir,' he said. 'We're exploring a number of possible avenues, and I'm confident of a breakthrough soon.'

'Close to making an arrest?' Harrison's voice rose very slightly at the end of the sentence.

'Not as yet, sir. Like I said, we're—'

'"Exploring a number of possible avenues". Yes, I heard you. Only I've heard that kind of twaddle before. It usually means an investigation is stalling. Is that the case here, DI Denning? Are things stalling?'

Denning sensed he was being backed into a corner. Harrison would keep pushing until Denning told him what he wanted to hear.

'Well, to be honest, sir, we're not making the kind of progress I'd like. We now know when he was killed, so we're going over CCTV from the day in question, but that all takes time. Plus we've still to establish a clear motive for DCI Buckfield's murder.'

Harrison pressed his hands against the arms of his chair. 'Just a suggestion, but perhaps if you spent more time looking into likely motives and less time harassing people who have no connection with this case, you might find progress was a bit sharper.'

Denning had a pretty shrewd idea where this was heading, but opted to play along.

'Sorry, sir, I'm not with you?'

'Alfie Kane, Denning. I believe you spoke to him this morning.'

'It's true I interviewed Mr Kane in connection with the inquiry.'

'Why? Is he a suspect?'

Denning struggled to keep his voice calm. 'He has a connection to DCI Buckfield, and I wanted to know the nature of that connection.'

'And you think this "connection" is enough of a motive to murder him? Because I can't see it myself.'

'Until I spoke to Mr Kane this morning, I had no way of knowing whether or not there could have been a motive.'

'And your conclusion? Did you uncover the nature of this alleged "connection"?'

Denning made a conscious effort to let his shoulders relax before answering. 'Kane told me he had never met DCI Buckfield.'

Harrison splayed his hands on his desk. 'You're a good officer, DI Denning. I note that since you've been here you've impressed DCI McKenna with your dedication and your leadership qualities. There are, however, some issues regarding your team spirit. I'm sure you realise policing at this level is all about teamwork. A team is only as strong as its weakest member.' He paused, giving his words a moment to fully hit their target. 'You've also still got a lot to learn about on-the-ground policing, which is often the way with graduate recruits to the service. There's a lot to be said for learning the job from the beat up. Characters like Alfie Kane need careful handling.

We don't go charging in there like a bull in a china shop throwing around unsubstantiated accusations.'

'With the greatest respect, sir, I had good grounds for speaking to Kane this morning. His name came up as part of an ongoing murder inquiry; specifically his links to allegations made about Buckfield in light of the Security Direct robbery in 1996. I wouldn't be doing my job properly if I didn't follow up on all our leads.'

Harrison sighed and rubbed a hand over his eyes. 'All I'm saying is, tread carefully, that's all. If you do feel the need to speak to Kane again, and I don't see any reason for you to do so, then run it by me first. It might be better if either me or DCI McKenna talk to him. He might respond less aggressively if approached by a senior officer.'

Denning couldn't quite believe what he was hearing. 'Sorry, sir, but I would have thought a detective inspector is senior enough. And I'm sure you wouldn't want me to run my list of suspects before you?'

The thunderous look had returned to Harrison's face. 'I'm not saying that, and I'm not sure I appreciate your attitude here, DI Denning.'

Denning knew he ought to be treading carefully around Harrison, but there was something about the man that pressed all the wrong buttons with him. Moreover, he wondered why Kane had felt the need to contact his superior in the first place after what had been nothing more than a routine inquiry.

'If that's everything, sir, I'll head back to my desk?'

Harrison looked at Denning. He folded his arms across his chest, as if he was trying to make himself look bigger. 'That's all for now. But remember what I said. It takes a wise man to know his limitations.'

As Denning closed the office door behind him, he only just managed to stop himself from telling Harrison that it was very good of him to admit it.

—

Back in the main MIT suite, he spotted McKenna standing by the door to her office. She called him over.

'What did he say?' she asked as soon as they were safely seated in her office.

'DCS Harrison? Oh, nothing much.' He gave her an abridged account of his bruising encounter with Harrison. 'I'm just wondering why Kane went running to the DCS. It's almost as though he's got something to hide.'

She sat back on her chair. 'We *know* he's got something to hide. But I'm inclined to agree with Harrison on this score: I don't think he's hiding any involvement with Buckfield's murder.'

'Then why put in an official complaint to Harrison?'

The gimlet stare was back. 'Be careful, Matt. Harrison may look like he's all bluff and bloater, but he bites too. A bit of respect wouldn't go amiss, even if you don't mean it.'

'I called him "sir". What else does he want?'

Her chilly reaction signalled her lack of appreciation for his humour. 'I'm just saying don't piss him off if you can help it. I've already had one run-in with him, but I haven't got long till I'm out of here. You've got your career ahead of you. Don't screw it up. It's a lonely old world out there for an ex-cop without a pension.'

'Thanks for your concern, which is duly noted. Can I get back on with my job now, while I still have one?'

She didn't bother to respond, but he could sense her reproachful look all the way back to his desk.

As soon as he sat down, he felt guilty. McKenna was simply looking out for him; even if she went about things with all the subtlety of a sledgehammer, she clearly had his best interests at heart. He owed her an apology, but it could wait. It wouldn't do any harm to let her think he was pissed off with her.

Chapter Twenty-Nine

Molly didn't have long to wait until Mags appeared. They'd arranged to meet that evening in the same pub as last time. There was a group of people bustling around the immediate vicinity of the bar, and Molly had to wait a few minutes before being served.

She found a table near the back of the pub and sat down with her pint.

Mags was carrying her usual oversized bag and started to speak before she'd even sat down. 'You found him! That's brilliant. How is he?' There was no offer of a drink this time.

'I've spoken to him,' Molly said coldly. 'And what I found was a damaged and vulnerable man.'

'How did you find him?' she asked, dismissing Molly's concerns with a wave of her hand.

'I contacted his probation officer. He wasn't too hard to trace.'

'So why won't he return my calls?'

Molly sighed and sipped her pint. Mags's lack of self-awareness astonished her sometimes. 'Maybe he doesn't want to speak to you, Mags. Maybe he's fed up being used.'

'What? What are you talking about?' She finally sat down, taking stuff out of her capacious bag like she was about to have a picnic.

'He needs help, Mags. If even a fraction of what he says is true then he needs counselling and support, not harassment.'

'Oh, it's true alright. And I'm not harassing him. I'm trying to help him.' She placed her tiny tartan purse on the tabletop, but showed no signs of heading towards the bar. 'He went to your lot years ago and you chewed him up and shat him out.' She said the words 'your lot' like the police were some kind of dangerous cult.

'I accept there may have been failings during the original investigation,' Molly said calmly, 'but if I can persuade Colin to talk to us officially, I can guarantee he will be listened to this time. If there's any evidence to back up his claims, they will be thoroughly investigated.'

Mags made a cackling noise. 'Yeah, I can just see him doing that. Especially after the kid-gloves treatment your lot gave him last time.'

'That was thirty years ago, Mags. A lot has changed since then. The Met now has a specialist team that was set up specifically to look into historical sexual abuse claims.'

Mags looked at Molly, her face contorting into a mask of derision. 'Yeah, and a right dog's breakfast they've made of it.' She placed her bag on the floor. The tartan purse still sat on the table unopened. 'Look, it's not me you need to convince, love. It's Colin. How is he, by the way? Is he up for speaking to me again?'

'I told you: I think he should speak to a counsellor. Some of the things he was saying were… well, I'm not sure how much of it was real and how much could be affected by some kind of false memory syndrome, but he needs to talk to someone to try and come to terms with whatever's going on inside his head.'

Mags was unimpressed. 'He needs to talk to *me*. The best thing for Colin is for what happened to him and those other poor sods to be made public. Expose the dirty bastards responsible and then it's up to your lot whether or not things get taken any further.' She reached out for the purse, shot a glance at the crowd standing by the bar, and decided to leave it where it was. 'If Colin goes back to the police, what's to say the matter won't be swept under the carpet after a few mealy-mouthed promises to "look into things again"? Or worse, he finds himself being accused of all sorts of things he didn't do? He has no reason to trust you.'

'He has no reason to trust you either, Mags. What's the real motive behind your interest in him? He's clearly not a friend as you claimed, and I can't imagine you breaking sweat for a stranger unless there was a decent pay-off at the end of it. So what's in this for you?'

Mags toyed with a beer mat, twisting it round and round like a card trick. 'His story needs to be told. The nationals won't touch this – they were warned off last time, or were just too weak to run with it. It needs someone with enough guts to put it out there.'

'And that person is you?'

'Why not? Whatever you might think of me, I'm a damned good journalist. Colin Meek was a victim of the system. That, and some powerful men. Men who've gone unpunished for too long.'

It sounded like a well-rehearsed speech that she'd used as a personal justification for chasing the story in the first place. Molly leant on the table so her face was only a few inches from Mags. 'Then take what you know to the police. Make it official.'

She shook her head. 'That's not how I work. For a start, I don't trust you lot. You'll bury this like you did last time, especially as there are clearly some big names involved; possibly even some people close to home.'

'You trusted me enough to find Colin for you.'

She laughed again. 'And now that you've found him, I'm very grateful. You can go away knowing you've done your bit to help get justice for Colin.'

Molly could feel the heat rising in her cheeks. But she knew Mags would take any public display of anger as a personal victory. She took a deep breath. 'So what now?'

'Now I speak to him again. I persuade him to share his story and we expose these bastards for what they are.'

It sounded good, almost convincing. There was still one question that needed answering though. 'How did you find out about all this? The story's decades old. Did Colin come to you, or did you go after him?'

'That's not important.'

'But you'll tell me anyway.'

There was a lengthy silence. Mags eventually realised the only way to end it was to tell Molly what she wanted to know. 'It was easier if I said he was a friend.' She was still playing with the beer mat. 'I tracked him down. He was in prison, so he wasn't difficult to find. I wrote to him, met with him inside a couple of times. Then when he got out, I made him an official approach. He begged me not to bring you lot in. He said he'd had enough grief from you last time. He was terrified he was going to end up back inside on some trumped-up charge. It wouldn't have been the first time.' Her eyes flashed at Molly. 'It took me a long time to gain his trust and confidence.'

'So you could use him. Get your story, then ditch him once he'd served his purpose?'

'You have a very cynical view of me, Molly. Comes of being a police officer, I expect. Your job breeds mistrust in people.'

Molly was determined she wasn't going to rise to the bait. 'This is nothing to do with me and what I do, Mags. This is about you and a vulnerable man.' She lowered her voice, suddenly aware that the people at the next table were looking over at them. 'You still haven't told me who tipped you off about all this in the first place?'

But she just looked over at Molly, her lips tightening into a narrow line of vermillion. 'That doesn't concern you. All you need to know is that Colin is the victim here, and he's not the only one. There are very likely other people out there who didn't have the courage to speak out for fear of receiving the same treatment he did.'

That reminded Molly. 'What about this other witness: Jason Wainwright? The one who later admitted he'd made the whole thing up?'

A shrug of her slender shoulders. 'Who knows? He either had some kind of agenda, or he was frightened into withdrawing his statement.'

'Have you spoken to him?'

'I've tried to contact him, but without any luck. Besides, whatever the case, it doesn't detract from what Colin told me. I believe him, even if you would appear to have your doubts.'

'I deal in evidence, Mags. Hard evidence, not supposition and hearsay. And so far I don't see a lot of evidence. I'm not saying Colin's lying, I just think we need to be very careful we don't set in motion something that could potentially do a lot of damage to a lot of innocent people. And when I say "we" I mean you.'

Mags was gazing at a poster on the wall advertising an upcoming jazz band. 'There you go again, pissing all over this because it's easier to do nothing than risk stirring up a hornets' nest. And you wonder why people don't trust the police.' She shifted her gaze from the poster and on to Molly. 'Your little Miss Goody Two-Shoes act might fool Jon, but it's never fooled me. You'd be happy enough to use someone if you thought it would benefit your stupid career. You only tracked Colin down because you thought you could take a juicy murder to your bosses and show them how clever you are.' She started playing with the beer mat again; spinning it round over and over, making Molly want to grab it out of her hand and chuck it on the floor. 'It's taken me months to get to this stage with Colin. Persuading him to trust me. Convincing him it's in his best interests to let me run with this story. Then you go thudding in with your great big copper's boots and likely scared him off. He'll probably never speak to me again.' She gave a slightly too theatrical sigh. 'All this because of what happened to Rebecca Owen. You failed to save her, so everything you've done since has been about trying to redress that. But you can never change what happened. Get over it. She's dead. Move on.'

Molly knocked back the rest of her pint. She was struggling to keep a lid on her temper. She could feel the heat prickling her face again, as anger threatened to rise inside her like a red-hot tidal wave. 'You're a hard-faced bitch, Mags. I knew it was a mistake to get involved with you again. You're like a poison. You seep into people's lives and infect them. And then get a sick pleasure out of sitting back and watching them suffer.'

She was aware she'd got to her feet and was shouting but she didn't care. She was fed up with being a reluctant participant in Mags's game-playing. The group at the next table had stopped talking and were staring at them. Even the crowd at the bar were glancing over in their direction.

Mags sat there looking ice-cool. 'You might want to keep your voice down, love. You're making a twat of yourself.'

But Molly had had enough.

'Go to hell, Mags. And don't contact me again. Ever.'

Chapter Thirty

Denning and Sarah had arranged to go to the theatre that evening. There was a Pinter revival on at the National: *The Homecoming* was playing in rep along with *The Birthday Party*. Sarah had bought the tickets, and Denning couldn't remember which one they were seeing.

He was waiting for her in the main café bar on Level 3. They'd agreed to have something to eat before the show, but Sarah had already texted to say she was running late.

So he'd ordered a bottle of Italian beer and a mushroom and walnut quiche with a mound of salad that was partly falling off the plate. Sarah could grab something quickly when she got there. His stomach had already decided it could no longer wait for sustenance.

The café bar overlooked the river, with Waterloo Bridge off to the left. The late evening rush hour traffic was grinding its way inexorably across the bridge, while a couple of pleasure boats gently glided along the Thames, their illuminated decks bustling with tourists.

There were days when he wished he wasn't a copper. Today was one of them.

It wasn't so much the job as the inevitable politics that went with it. Harrison's attitude had riled him; the resentment he had felt towards Denning, simply because he represented a new breed of Met detective: degree-educated and fast-tracked. It wasn't something he'd ever felt the need to apologise for, nor attempt to justify, even if some people in the force resented what they wrongly saw as a short-cut to a senior position. It was the direction of travel for the Met Police these days, and people like Harrison were just going to have to accept it.

He wondered about McKenna's own run-in with Harrison. McKenna was a tough cookie, but she chose which fights to pick. An approach he should consider adopting if he wanted to survive in the Met.

'God, what a day.' Sarah threw her briefcase down on the empty chair next to Denning and kissed him on the cheek. 'I thought that meeting would never end.' She nodded at Denning's food. 'I see you've already ordered.'

'Sorry, I couldn't wait. And I wasn't sure what time you'd get here.'

She quickly looked over the menu and ordered her food at the bar, returning a few moments later and slipping into the seat opposite Denning. She took her phone from her jacket pocket, placed it on the table, then took a small glass bottle of scent out of her handbag, removed the top and liberally sprayed her neck and wrists. Denning caught a whiff of Tom Ford's '*Black Orchid*'.

'That's better.' She replaced the top and slipped the bottle back into her bag. 'How was your day?'

He tried not to think any more about Harrison. 'Well, let's just say I survived it, and leave it at that.'

Sarah gave a half smile and checked her phone for messages. 'I won't even tell you about mine. Except to say that I had a phone call from Justin Morrow this afternoon.'

'What did he want?'

'Just to confirm dinner.'

'Confirm…?'

She fiddled with her phone, then placed it back on the table. 'I emailed him last night after you mentioned his name. I was curious about him. I told you he'd set up his own investment company? Turns out he's doing rather well for himself. He might be able to put some useful contacts my way. Anyway, I suggested dinner and he called today to say he and Emma would love to meet.' Her phone bleeped. She picked it up and hurriedly read a text message before pulling a face and dropping the phone back on the table. 'Emma's his wife. I think she's some kind of lawyer, if I remember rightly. Anyway, he suggested tomorrow evening.' She looked at Denning for confirmation. 'There's a Thai place he and Emma like. It's not far from here actually. I think we've been there once. Or maybe I went with a client.'

'Thai?'

'You like Thai, don't you?'

It wasn't the choice of restaurant that bothered him, it was the company. An evening with Morrow and his wife; everyone talking investment portfolios. It was the last thing he needed to finish off a stressful week. On the other hand, if things were to get tricky with Harrison, it wouldn't hurt to have a member of the Assembly's Police and Crime Committee onside. Perhaps when it came to Met politics it was better to play the big boys at their own game. 'Yes, OK,' he said. 'Let's do that. We'll both try and finish work early.'

She nodded, checking an email on her phone. 'That sounds like a plan.' She finished reading the email and slipped the phone back into her pocket. 'Have you spoken to Claire about Jake's plans for the holidays? I could have a word, if that's easier.'

After some initial animosity, Sarah and Claire now got on well together, and Sarah was genuinely fond of Jake. But he didn't like people organising his life for him. Jake was his son, and therefore his responsibility.

'Thanks,' he said. 'But there's no need. I'll give her a call tomorrow.'

Sarah smiled and patted his elbow. Then a waiter arrived with her food, just as a voice announced that Act One of *The Birthday Party* would be starting in five minutes.

Chapter Thirty-One

It had rained heavily the night before, bringing a splash of freshness to the morning air. It was still drizzly when daylight broke, and some early commuters could be seen scurrying along pavements beneath umbrellas, or wearing anoraks with the hoods up.

Denning was standing in a car park behind a sports centre in Bethnal Green, dressed in protective overalls and booties. Deep puddles had formed on the tarmacked surface. One was the size of a small pond, and Denning suspected there was a blocked drain somewhere. Another significant spell of rain, and the whole car park would be partly submerged.

'A dog walker found the body this morning,' Gorton said, her mask tucked under her chin. 'Apparently she uses this as a short cut to get to a nearby park. Well, to be more accurate, the dog found it. The walker merely established it was a body and phoned 999.' Denning was never sure how to take Gorton's sense of humour. On the one hand it always seemed inappropriate, but on the other hand, if it helped her cope with the demands of the job, who was he to grumble.

'Don't suppose you'd care to have a guess at an approximate time of death?'

'Probably at around the same time she was murdered.' A wry smile played on her lips. 'Sorry. I'm not a morning person, as you've doubtless already twigged.' She clutched at her mask, unhooking it from behind her left ear. 'The body's still relatively fresh. There's no sign of any insect activity and I'd say it's still in a state of autolysis, so a good estimate would be less than twelve hours ago. Once she's on the slab they'll be able to give you a more accurate assessment, but she hasn't been dead long.'

'And killed here?' Denning asked, looking at the body.

The victim was lying on her side, blood pooling around her head. The lower half of her left arm was lying in a puddle, and the sleeve of her jacket was soaked with bloodied water. She was a fairly young woman, probably late thirties, maybe slightly older. Her hair and face were wet with rain; glassy eyes staring at her wet sleeve.

'Carotid arteries have been severed.' Gorton pointed at a gaping raw gash that ran along the victim's throat. There was a soggy piece of brown masking tape hanging half across her mouth. Just like Buckfield. 'The rain will have inevitably washed away a lot of evidence, which always makes our job harder.' Gorton was kneeling now. She gently turned the victim's head with a gloved hand. 'Judging by the amount of blood still present around the body, and allowing for the level of rainfall we had last night, I'd say she was very probably killed right here.'

Denning glanced over at the SOCOs in their rain-spattered suits. One of them was carefully videoing the crime scene, just in case any further evidence was lost.

'Where's the dog walker now?' he asked.

Gorton got back to her feet and pointed to a woman in her fifties sitting on a bench under a canopy by the entrance to the sports centre. She was being comforted by a female police officer. A black Labrador lay silent at her feet. 'She's very shaken, but she's up for giving a statement.'

He would speak to her as soon as he'd finished with Gorton, but it was unlikely she could tell them anything they couldn't already see for themselves. 'What time does the sports centre open?'

'Eight thirty according to the notice on the door. Why? Are you in the mood for a game of footie?'

Denning just caught the twinkle in her eye as he glanced at his watch: almost another hour until the place opened.

'There's CCTV,' he said, jerking his head towards a couple of cameras mounted on a pole attached to the side of the building. 'We'll need to examine it.'

Gorton looked over at the cameras. 'Unless the range is particularly good, I doubt they'd cover this part of the car park. But you might be lucky.'

They were in a far corner of the car park, furthest from the entrance. The area was bordered by dense shrubbery, beyond which the sound of trundling tube trains could be heard.

'To get here both victim and killer would have had to pass the cameras. There's no other way to get to this part of the car park. Plus we'll need to know when the place closed last night and what time the staff left. It's possible somebody could have seen something, depending on the time of the attack.' He looked around the car park. What was their victim doing here? Perhaps she'd been coming out of the sports centre and was walking to her car when her killer struck. But apart from the various police and SOCO-related vehicles, the car park was empty. It was possible the attacker had taken her keys and stolen her car, but until he could see over the CCTV footage and interview the members of staff who were on duty last night, this was all just speculation.

'She could have been killed while the centre was still open,' Denning said. 'But equally, it could have happened after it closed. You said the time of death was anything up to twelve hours. I'm assuming it could easily have been less.'

Gorton nodded. 'I agree that a narrower timeframe would help, but you know it's not up to me to do the pathologist's job for them. I can offer you an approximate window based on the evidence available, that's all.'

Denning was all too aware that there was a fine balance between pushing the CSM for quick answers and letting them do their job at their own pace. He would have to wait until the post-mortem before he'd get a more accurate time of death and even then it was never exact, it just gave them a shorter window to work with.

'Do we know the victim's name?'

'Well, that is one consolation,' Gorton said. 'We found the victim's bag beside her. According to her NUJ card, her name was Magda Kilbride.'

Chapter Thirty-Two

Molly had barely been in the office for ten minutes when she spotted a stony-faced Denning arrive. She had planned to come in early again that morning, but she'd forgotten to set the alarm the night before and had had to rely on Jon to wake her, by which time it was nearly eight thirty. Already running late, she had managed to spill a glass of orange juice over her skirt during breakfast and then dropped her phone in a puddle on the way to the bus stop. She'd had better starts to her working day.

With only the briefest glimmer of eye contact, Denning asked if he could have a word with her in McKenna's office. She'd dutifully followed him in, trying to guess what it could be about.

Betty Taggart was sitting behind her desk looking even more stony-faced than Denning. Denning stood against the wall, still trying his best to avoid looking her in the eye. She sat on the hard chair opposite Betty Taggart, whose sharp black eyes – unlike Denning's – seemed to bore into hers like a dentist's drill.

There was a noticeable chill in the office, and it wasn't down to a lack of heating.

'How well do you know Magda Kilbride?' Betty Taggart asked.

Molly felt her heart thudding in her chest. Had Mags made an official complaint about her? It wouldn't have been the first time she'd gone running to Denning telling tales. At least last time, Denning had had the good sense to know he was being played. Judging by the look on his face, this time he seemed to be taking matters more seriously.

'She's a journalist,' Molly heard herself saying; her voice sounding slightly cracklier than usual. 'She's a known trouble-maker, and I wouldn't take anything she says seriously.'

'So you wouldn't describe her as a friend?' Betty Taggart asked.

'No. She's certainly not that.' She clocked Denning and McKenna exchanging glances. 'Why? What's she said now?'

'She hasn't said anything.' McKenna replied coldly. 'She's been murdered.'

'Murdered?' Molly was aware her voice had suddenly risen an octave. 'When?'

'Her body was found earlier this morning,' Denning said. 'In a car park next to a sports centre in Bethnal Green.'

'How? I mean, what was she doing there?'

'That's a very good question. I can see why you wanted to be a detective.' McKenna's face was a mask of granite.

'Sorry?'

'At this stage it looks like she was attacked sometime after she left Jericho's Bar yesterday evening,' Denning said.

'That would be some time after she met *you* at Jericho's Bar yesterday evening, DS Fisher.' Betty Taggart was still staring at her, as though trying to burn a laser beam into her soul. 'Perhaps you could join up some of the dots for us?'

Molly looked at McKenna and then Denning. She wanted to open her mouth and say something but her throat felt like the Sahara.

'It seems that Miss Kilbride used an old-fashioned Filofax-type diary,' Denning said, filling the silence. 'SOCO found it in her bag. The entry for yesterday evening states that she had arranged to meet you in the Jericho Bar off The Strand.'

Molly had to focus. She knew if she started talking without giving some serious thought to her words, there was a danger she would start gabbling and sound like an idiot. Or worse, sound like somebody with a motive for murdering Mags. She was still trying to get her head round the fact that Mags was dead. Another silence seemed to be growing out of nowhere and slowly filling the room with its empty fug. Her brain was ticking faster than a metronome on acid. Was she being accused of something here? Was she being accused of murdering Mags? Did they know about Mags and Jon, and thought somehow that gave her a motive?

'I met her last night,' she found herself saying. 'At the Jericho, after I'd finished work.' She wanted to ask for a glass of water, instead she whipped her tongue round the inside of her mouth and continued. 'It was in connection with a story she's working on. She wanted to run it by me first. Get my opinion.'

Another look danced between Denning and McKenna. 'Your opinion?' McKenna asked dryly. 'You're sure that's all she wanted? Not information?'

'No. Look, she wanted me to find someone for her. A man she was working with in connection with this story. I said I'd help find him. She thought something might have happened to him. I met her last night to tell her that I'd met him and he was OK, and that was it. I wasn't going to help her any further.'

'You looked for this man in your own time? Or in our time?' Denning asked. He was giving her eye contact now, but his face still resembled a bottom that had just been spanked.

'In my own time,' she emphasised. 'I didn't have too much difficulty finding him. I spoke to him, and passed the details onto Mags... Magda.'

'What was this story she was working on?' Denning asked.

'I'm not sure it's relevant to anything.'

'The woman's been murdered, DS Fisher. I would say everything is relevant at this stage.' McKenna's voice was still icily calm, but Molly knew it wouldn't take much for her to explode without warning. She was in danger of pushing her luck and pushing herself out the door if she wasn't careful. Perhaps, under the circumstances, the best way out of this mess was to spill her guts about why she'd really met with Mags in the first place. No matter how bad the truth might sound, it was probably preferable to whatever her two senior colleagues were thinking.

So she told them about Colin; his wild allegations and his involvement with Mags. When she finished, another silence filled the room. From outside the double-glazed window she could hear a car alarm wailing, the sound slowly burrowing into her skull.

'I'm slightly stunned, DS Fisher,' McKenna said eventually. 'You do realise you had no right to contact this man Meek. You should have reported your suspicions to a senior officer – either DI Denning, or myself, or passed it over to the Child Abuse Investigation Team. You know the rules, and you know why CAIT exists.'

'I understand. But when she mentioned a murder, even a historical one, I couldn't just let it pass.'

'Except we have an ongoing murder investigation that needs our attention at the moment,' McKenna said. 'And as of this morning, we now have another one that may or may not be connected with it.'

'Did you find anything to support Colin Meek's story about this boy's alleged murder?' Denning was calmer than McKenna, but there was a look of disappointment on his face. She found herself cursing Mags: even in death the woman was causing her grief. Then she felt guilty, thinking of Mags lying alone and dead in some car park. Even she hadn't deserved that.

'I can't find anything on the system,' she said. 'But there could be lots of reasons for that.'

'One of them being that Colin Meek is a known recidivist and a liar,' McKenna said coldly. 'While I can see this wouldn't necessarily be an issue for a journalist, it is a matter of concern for a serving police officer. I only hope for your sake that if Magda Kilbride had run this story, she'd have kept your name out of it.'

Molly felt she was being unfairly treated. She had tried to do the right thing here, even if she had bent some of the rules in the process. She would have expected Denning and McKenna to have at least understood that her motives had been sincere. 'If there was any truth in what Colin Meek said, then I had to take his claims seriously.'

But McKenna's face suggested this wasn't an opinion she shared. 'Unfortunately, unlike what's left of the UK press, we can't operate on rumours. Colin Meek's claims were, to my knowledge, fully investigated at the time. There was no evidence found to support his allegations. The matter was closed.'

'It's just possible Mags has found some new evidence. She wouldn't have gone after this story if she didn't think there was some truth in it.' She looked at McKenna, and then Denning. 'Are you saying there could be a connection between her murder and Buckfield's?'

'We don't know that at this stage,' Denning replied. 'But it can't be ruled out.'

'Did you discuss Buckfield's murder with Ms Kilbride?' McKenna asked.

'No, of course not.'

'And you admit your relationship with Ms Kilbride could be difficult at times?' Denning asked.

'I didn't have a *relationship* with her. I met with her a couple of times to talk about Colin Meek. That's all.'

'But you as good as admitted you didn't like the woman,' McKenna said.

She looked at them. 'I admit, we didn't always get on. And, yes, I disliked her. But you can't seriously think I killed her?'

It was Denning who spoke. 'Of course we don't think that.'

She noticed there was no similar offer of reassurance from Betty Taggart.

'But you did have an association with her. You're certainly one of the last people to see her alive. And it could even be argued that you had a grudge against the woman. You see the difficult position this places us in?'

She opened her mouth to speak, but didn't trust the words that might come out. She inwardly counted to ten before she answered. 'If there is a connection between Mags's and Buckfield's murders, then we should be exploring any possible links between them. Colin Meek *could* be a link.'

'We'll be looking at every aspect of Magda Kilbride's life,' Denning said. 'Including any stories she was working on.'

'However, unfortunately, you won't be part of that team, DS Fisher.' It was McKenna this time, her fingers steepled under her chin, like a cartoon baddie. 'I have no option but to suspend you on full pay until the investigation into Magda Kilbride's murder has been concluded. I suggest you contact your federation rep if you wish to discuss the matter further.' She offered a thin smile in Molly's direction. 'In the meantime, please clear your desk and leave the building. We'll be in touch as soon as your suspension has been lifted.'

Molly returned to her desk in a heavy mood. She could see Trudi mouthing something to her, but the words never reached her ears. She smiled at Trudi and said she'd catch her later. She collected the few personal belongings she had on her desk, took her bag and jacket from the back of the chair, and left the building. As she walked to the bus stop, she suddenly realised she was shaking. An elderly couple walking past stopped and looked at her. She thought she heard one of them ask if she was alright, but she carried on walking. By the time she reached the bus stop, she was struggling to keep the tears from rolling down her cheeks.

Chapter Thirty-Three

By the time Denning returned to the main office, Molly had already left the building.

After their meeting, McKenna had wanted to discuss the Magda Kilbride situation with him, even though he'd made it clear he was still waiting for more information to come through. He'd promised to keep her informed of any progress.

And then there was Gordon Lomax and Alfie Kane. Denning wasn't ready to let them off the hook just yet...

He'd hoped to speak to Molly before she left. He wanted to explain that her suspension wasn't anything personal, and McKenna was simply following procedure. Despite this, he felt McKenna had been overly harsh with Molly. He accepted Molly was a bit of a maverick, and McKenna clearly liked things played by the book. He did too, if he was honest, but every now and again it paid to go out on a limb and listen to your gut. Unfortunately, Molly Fisher liked to make a habit out of it. But she was a good officer, and now the team was one member down, and at the worst possible time.

Perhaps he'd phone her later. Or perhaps it was better to leave it for a while and let the water cool before he waded in with any offers of sympathy.

By early afternoon, enough information had begun to trickle in to convince Denning it was time to call his team together for a briefing.

He began by explaining that Molly was on temporary suspension due to her connection with the victim, but didn't provide further details. He didn't need to; the rumour mill was already filling in any blanks.

'Magda Jane Kilbride, thirty-nine, a freelance journalist,' he said. 'She was discovered earlier this morning with her throat cut.' Magda Kilbride's photo had been pinned to the whiteboard. They'd found a few pictures of her on her website. She was even smiling in one of them. There were photos of the rain-soaked crime scene too. 'She left the Jericho Bar around seven thirty yesterday evening,' Denning continued. 'CCTV has her heading in the direction of Temple tube station. We can confirm that she returned to her flat in Vauxhall shortly after eight o'clock. At some point later that evening – and we still have to establish exactly when – she ended up in a car park in Bethnal Green, where she presumably met her killer.' They still hadn't received the CCTV footage from the sports centre. Denning had stressed the urgency of the situation, but the manager had seemed more concerned about reopening the centre car park for his customers rather than helping the police find who was responsible for killing someone on his premises. After some firm persuasion, he'd promised to email it over that afternoon.

'Are we assuming she'd arranged to meet her killer there, rather than this being a random attack?' Trudi asked.

'Even if she had arranged to meet someone there, it doesn't automatically follow that that person was her killer?' Neeraj said. 'It's possible they didn't turn up, or she was killed after she'd met with this person.'

'So we need to find out who it was she'd planned to meet, and why,' Trudi said. 'To eliminate them from the investigation, if nothing else.'

'My money's on a lover,' Kinsella said, ignoring the audible groan from Trudi. 'Well, it's an obvious place to meet someone discreetly: quiet, out of the way. Supposing the bloke she was meeting was married? They'd want to go somewhere low key.'

'You're making a bit of a broad assumption there, Dave,' Trudi said.

'That she was meeting a lover?'

'That her lover's a bloke,' Trudi replied caustically, casually winking at Denning.

There was a general murmur of laughter from the team.

'OK, everyone,' Denning said once the laughter had subsided. 'Once we get the CCTV from the sports centre and the results of the post-mortem, we'll hopefully get a better idea of who she was meeting, and what time. There's very little CCTV in the streets surrounding the sports centre, but we'll look over what there is. In the meantime, we can't rule out Dave's theory, however wild it might seem. It's likely she arranged to meet someone she knew, but we shouldn't assume that person killed her. As yet, we know very little about Magda Kilbride's private life, and not a great deal about her professional life either, for that matter.'

'I looked her up on the internet,' Ryan Cormack said. 'Seems she's ruffled a few feathers over the years. Even way back when she worked for *The London Echo*. She's no big fan of us either. She's done a couple of stories about alleged police corruption. She even contributed to a book about police brutality and racism.'

'One of those sorts,' Kinsella muttered, partially under his breath, but loud enough to ensure everyone heard.

'We know she was working on a story at the time of her death,' Trudi said. 'That could be relevant.'

Denning nodded. He told them about Colin Meek. He mentioned the historical sex abuse allegations, but kept the finer details sketchy and airbrushed out any mention of Molly. 'We'll obviously need to speak to this Colin Meek character, though I don't think we should necessarily regard him as a suspect at this stage.'

'Even though he's got a criminal record longer than Penny Lancaster's legs,' Kinsella said, sitting back in his chair with his arms folded across his barrel of a chest.

'We should keep an open mind when we do speak to him,' Denning said. 'By all accounts he's a vulnerable adult and may need handling with care.'

Kinsella pointed his eyes at the ceiling. 'And what exactly is this woman's connection with Molly?' he asked.

'The boss has explained that, Dave,' Trudi countered. 'She knew the victim. Nobody's suggesting there's anything more sinister. And I'm sure she'd like to know she has the support of her colleagues.' She looked at Denning, who nodded again.

'Our victim had met Molly in a bar earlier that evening. According to witnesses, Molly was seen and heard arguing with this Magda Kilbride.' Kinsella looked around the room, but everyone was either staring at the floor, or had their eyes facing front towards Denning. 'How do we know it wasn't Molly she'd arranged to meet at the sports centre later that evening?'

'We can rule DS Fisher out of this, Dave,' Denning said, hoping his tone of voice would be enough to draw a line under the matter. 'She has an alibi and no motive.' He wasn't willing to admit he hadn't checked whether Molly actually had an alibi, but he wasn't going to share this with the team. He trusted his detectives, and he didn't expect to have his judgement questioned.

'Look, I'm not saying she did it,' Kinsella argued, refusing to take the hint. 'All I'm saying is we know she had a connection with the victim. If it was anyone else, we'd be dragging her in for a formal interview. Especially as she was one of the last people to see the victim alive. And she clearly had some beef with this Magda Kilbride. Like it or not, that gives her a motive.'

'Let it drop, Dave,' Trudi said, staring him down. 'Molly didn't kill her. End of. It's going to be tough enough trying to find this bastard without us suspecting each other of being murderers.'

Kinsella opened his mouth to say something, but cast a look round the room and decided against it.

'Right. Well said, Trudi. If you're happy now, Dave, perhaps we can move on and concentrate on finding her killer.' Denning nodded to Neeraj who had his hand raised.

'Anything from her mobile phone?' Neeraj asked.

'It wasn't found with her belongings,' Denning replied. 'So we're assuming her killer took it. Her purse was still in her bag, so it was unlikely that robbery was the motive.'

'So if we're discounting robbery as a motive, what we're saying is that Magda Kilbride was deliberately targeted.' It was Ryan Cormack, highlighting the obvious elephant in the room. 'A murder where the obvious motive looks like robbery gone wrong, but there's no evidence of a robbery.'

'And then there's that weird thing with the tape over the mouth,' Neeraj said, staring at the photos on the whiteboard. 'Same as Buckfield.'

Denning nodded slowly. 'This is something we can't ignore.' He looked at his team. He had their full attention. 'This means that it's more than likely they were killed by the same person.'

'In which case we have to explore the possibility we have a serial killer out there,' Kinsella said.

'Maybe.' Denning wasn't sure. 'The masking tape feels...' He searched for the word. '... additional, somehow, as though whoever did it *wants* us to think this is the work of a serial killer targeting people at random. I have a feeling whoever is doing it is trying to throw us off the scent.'

'Do we know of any connection between Buckfield and Magda Kilbride?' Trudi asked. 'It's possible they were targeted specifically.'

'There's no obvious link between them, and I'm taking it as read that Magda Kilbride's name hasn't come up in connection with our inquiries into Buckfield's case histories?' There was a general shaking of heads. 'It's possible she could have spoken to him regarding an article she's written. However, Trudi's made a good point. It is possible there's something that directly connects the two of them. Something that isn't immediately obvious. If there is, we need to find it.'

There was something else. Something he wasn't yet willing to share with his team. Initial inquiries had told them that Magda Kilbride lived alone and had few friends. She was a loner. Like Buckfield.

He gave them a moment to digest what he'd said. It was Dave Kinsella who was the first of the team to speak. 'So what now, boss?'

'Now we look at every police-related story she ever covered, and any cases Buckfield investigated that may have crossed over with one of her stories. We see if anything matches. And that's going to take time.'

'There is another possibility.' Kinsella waited until all eyes were on him. 'That your gut feeling is wrong, boss. This is just a coincidence and there's no connection between them. In which case we've got a maniac out there killing people at random and taping their mouths shut just for the hell of it.'

It was unlikely Kinsella even heard the mass groaning from the rest of the team.

—

It was later in the afternoon when they finally got a break-through. Denning checked the time on the bottom of his computer screen: it was almost five thirty. He stretched the tension from his shoulders and remembered his dinner date with Morrow that evening. He would give it another ten minutes and then call it a day.

The sports centre had finally forwarded on the CCTV, but Gorton had been right, the range hadn't covered the murder scene, just its periphery. He would get his team to examine it in detail over the weekend, but a cursory glance hadn't shown up anything of interest. There was no sign of Magda Kilbride entering the car park, let alone any footage of her talking to anyone. They'd check any CCTV on the roads that approached the sports centre, but there was no guarantee it would throw up anything useful.

Kinsella and Neeraj had been dispatched to interview the sports centre staff and track down any customers who might have been in the vicinity of the car park yesterday evening, but so far it seemed none of the staff had seen anything suspicious. The centre had mostly been occupied by a couple of five-a-side football teams, who had packed up and vacated the premises by nine thirty. The staff had locked up and left shortly afterwards. The assistant manager had been the last to leave, and the car park was deserted when he'd pulled out of it at around ten p.m.. Security lights covered the area around the entrance, and were movement sensitive, but the lighting in the car park itself was on a timer and went off at ten thirty, perhaps slightly before.

Denning was flicking through the CCTV, fast-forwarding from the moment the assistant manager's Toyota Yaris pulled out of the car park, when Trudi came over to his desk. 'I've been looking through Buckfield's cases again and there's definitely nothing that connects him to Magda Kilbride. It doesn't look as though their paths ever crossed.'

'OK. Well, thanks anyway, Trudi. It was always going to be a bit of a longshot.' He was hoping she might have had something more constructive to offer, as he was unwilling to countenance Dave Kinsella's theory about a maniac attacking strangers.

'But I thought I'd take a bit of a gamble on a hunch,' Trudi continued. 'I was curious about Colin Meek. I vaguely remember the case. I was based at Hammersmith for a while, and was pally with one of the DSs who was around at the time. She seemed to think something wasn't right about the original investigation. Nothing definite, just a feeling she'd had. Anyway, I looked into it. Meek's claims were investigated by a DS Coughlin and a DC Flynn.' Denning nodded. 'Flynn left the force ten years ago, but Coughlin is now a DI in Barnes. I gave him a call. He remembers the case. He was a bit reluctant to talk about it at first, perhaps understandably under the circumstances, but after a bit of prodding he told me the senior investigating officer at the nick in question was DI Buckfield.'

Suddenly Denning no longer felt tired. 'You're sure, Trudi?'

'Positive. In fact, according to the report, the case was dropped on Buckfield's say-so.'

Chapter Thirty-Four

The restaurant was next to Borough Market, not far from London Bridge. Every few minutes trains rumbled overhead. The taxi dropped Denning and Sarah off a few minutes early.

The restaurant was slick and classy, with a slate-tiled floor and whitewashed walls. Subtle music played in the background. Denning would have described it as pretentious, but it had a friendly charm that shaved the edge off its flashiness.

Morrow had booked the table. The maître d greeted them with an ebullient smile when Denning mentioned their name. He remembered Sarah saying the Morrows were regulars at the restaurant, and he suspected they were generous tippers.

Sarah was wearing an impressive Dior dress, with a simple gold necklace he'd bought her for her birthday last year. Denning had opted for smart casual: a beige linen jacket and tailored navy shirt. He didn't want to feel overdressed.

A waiter showed them to their table and took a drinks order from them.

'This is nice,' Sarah said. He wasn't sure if she was referring to the restaurant or the fact they were dining out.

He was trying not to think about work. Sometimes it was good to switch off and remind himself that being a murder detective didn't have to be a twenty-four hour a day job, even if it did feel like it at times.

The waiter arrived with their drinks: a gin and tonic for Sarah and a large glass of cabernet sauvignon for him. As the drinks were being placed on the table, he spotted Morrow and his wife getting out of a taxi. A few moments later, they joined them at the table.

Introductions were made. He guessed Morrow's wife, Emma, was around the same age as her husband – mid-forties – but she could easily have been ten years younger. She was dressed in a chic trouser suit and a pale silk blouse, her blonde haircut stylishly short. Morrow was dressed similarly to Denning: a smart blazer-style jacket over a white and blue patterned shirt, and a pair of cream chinos.

Morrow ordered a Glenfiddich with ice; Emma opted for a vodka and lemonade, with no ice.

'I was just saying to Matt that this is a lovely restaurant,' Sarah said. 'I think I came here a few years ago, shortly after it opened. I'd always intended to return one day.'

'It's one of our favourite haunts,' Emma Morrow replied, smiling at her husband. 'The head chef's from Bali, so the dishes are a fusion of Thai and Balinese. Not that I could ever hope to tell the difference. It's handy for Justin too, with City Hall just down the road. We really should make a better effort to try other places but finding the time is always a problem these days, especially now Justin's political career's taking off.'

Denning wasn't sure what she meant by 'taking off', unless she saw his membership of the Police and Crime Committee as some kind of move into the big league.

'We're the same,' Sarah said. 'Matt's job can be relentless sometimes. And I've recently been asked to head up an off-shore investment portfolio. Some evenings we're so shattered when we come in, we just want to flop in front of the telly.'

'That's like me,' Emma said. 'When I get in from work most evenings I just want to enjoy a nice glass of wine and a good book.' She looked at her husband. 'Justin's the total opposite: he's blessed with boundless energy. He's like a puppy. I struggle to keep up with him sometimes.'

'How's life at Bishop & Willett?' Morrow asked Sarah.

'Still the same. Long hours and rubbish money, but the bonus makes it all worthwhile. What about you? You've set up on your own, someone told me.'

Morrow smiled at his audience. 'There's nothing more rewarding than working for yourself. Luckily, I've got a good team to handle the day-to-day running of the company, which frees up time for me to devote myself to politics.'

A different waiter arrived to take their order.

'What about family?' Morrow asked once the waiter had left. 'You've got a son, haven't you?'

Denning was slightly taken aback to discover Morrow knew he had a son. Maybe Sarah had mentioned it in passing. 'He lives with his mother,' Denning replied. 'I usually spend every other weekend with him. However, domesticity's not always easy when you're in the middle of a murder investigation.'

'I suppose you're both in the same line of business.' Morrow's eyes darted between Denning and Emma.

'Sorry?' Denning raised his eyebrows.

Emma smiled. 'I'm a barrister. Though it's mostly corporate stuff. Dull as ditchwater, but it helps pay the mortgage.'

'Sometimes I feel like giving up work and becoming a kept man,' Morrow said, smiling at Denning. His comment was greeted by three hollow laughs.

After a further ten minutes of polite small talk, the waiter returned with their food. Denning had opted for the Thai fish curry, which appeared to come with a separate plate of rice and green beans. Sarah was having lemon chicken with a green papaya salad. He couldn't remember what the Morrows had ordered, but it looked appetising.

'What persuaded you to go into politics?' Sarah asked Morrow.

'It's something I've always been interested in,' he replied. 'But it was Emma who persuaded me to run for the GLA.'

'I was fed up with him shouting at the telly every time a useless politician appeared, so I said, why didn't he do something about it.'

'I really feel I'm making a difference,' Morrow said. 'It's well worth the personal sacrifice.'

'And the Police and Crime Committee?' Denning asked.

'They were looking for members to fill committee places, and with Emma's background I'd met a lot of solicitors and barristers over the years. Getting their take on law and order has always been fascinating, but it's useful to see things from the other side of the tracks too.' He smiled at Denning. 'I think the police do an excellent job, for which you guys never seem to get the thanks you deserve. It's important you've got the right support, and to know that politicians are behind you. Hopefully that gives you the confidence to do your job better.'

Denning wanted to ask him why, if that was how he felt, he had backed Harrison for the DCS's job, when there were other, better candidates. But he knew Sarah would throw him one of her 'warning' looks that told him he was stepping out of line. Instead, he said: 'Thank you. It's always good to know someone's watching out for us.'

'I did briefly consider a law career myself,' Sarah said. 'The money's good, but the work is so unpredictable. I like to know what's around the corner when I turn up at the office every day.'

Emma laughed. 'I mostly did it to keep my father happy,' she replied. 'He was a judge before he retired. My brother had no interest in going into law, much to our father's disappointment, and I was always a bit of a daddy's girl. And the advantage of corporate law is the hours are much more stable. The cases tend to last longer, so it's easier to build up a routine. Though, I have to admit, there are times I wouldn't mind the cut and thrust of a nice murder case.' She turned and smiled at Denning. 'Justin tells me you're working on a big murder case at the moment.'

'I'm sure Matt doesn't want to talk shop,' Morrow said. He was replying to his wife, but looking at Denning when he spoke.

'It's not a problem.' Denning was slightly flattered that Emma was taking an interest. 'Justin's already aware of the details: a retired DCI was murdered. It's a tricky case.'

'Then there was that journalist,' Morrow added. 'It was on the news earlier. Is she one of yours as well?'

'We're looking into that too. Though obviously I can't say much about either case.'

'Naturally,' Morrow said. 'Though I have asked DCS Harrison to keep me up to speed with everything. If we can be of any help, please let me know. Obviously a case like this is going to attract a lot of media attention.'

Denning was curious. Why would Morrow request Harrison to keep him up to speed with operational matters? There was no reason for him to know the progress of an ongoing murder investigation. 'Have you known DCS Harrison long?' Denning asked.

Morrow shook his head. 'I don't really know him at all, to be honest. At least not in a personal capacity. He came and spoke to the Police and Crime Committee shortly after I was appointed to it, and we seemed to hit it off. He's got some good ideas and he's a pragmatist. I wanted to learn all about the Met: how it works, how things could be improved. Ian was very helpful in educating me.' He looked round the table as though addressing a hustings. 'I don't want to be the kind of Assembly member that sits in an ivory tower making decisions that affect people's lives without having some idea of what I'm talking about. The Met's been through some difficult times – I'd like us all to move forward and build a decent future for Londoners and their police force.'

Denning wasn't sure whether he was expected to applaud, or just nod politely. It was an impressive speech. Only it wasn't clear who Morrow was trying to impress.

Emma Morrow signalled for the waiter to come over. She asked everyone if they wanted more drinks. Sarah asked for another gin and tonic, and Emma requested another vodka and lemonade. Morrow ordered another whisky and ice. Denning suddenly realised he'd finished his wine, so asked for the same again.

As Emma and Sarah chatted about the pressures of work and how best to smash the glass ceiling in their respective workplaces, Morrow turned to Denning. 'I've heard good things about you, Matt. You work well, you get the job done with minimum of fuss and you're professional. Plus, you're a graduate. That's the way ahead in the Met these days. Frankly, if you haven't got a degree, you might as well forget about any kind of promotion.'

Denning wasn't sure how to take his words. Compliments always made him uncomfortable. He wanted to point out Harrison had felt differently during their run-in the other day, but this wasn't the right place to bring that up. He also thought this was a slightly unfair assessment: there were plenty of people in the Met, even in his own team, who had worked their way up.

By the time they left the restaurant, it was gone ten.

Denning wasn't sure if it was down to the booze or the food, but he felt quite mellow. Despite his initial misgivings, he'd now revised his opinion of Justin Morrow; the man wasn't quite the arrogant twat that first impressions had suggested. Despite himself, he'd enjoyed their company. What's more, he could see the advantage of having someone like Morrow on his side if it came to a fight between him and Harrison. Hopefully that wouldn't be necessary, but it was useful to have something in his armoury that he could rely on if he had to.

In his mind he was already planning their next get-together.

Chapter Thirty-Five

If Jon was surprised to see Molly standing in the kitchen later that morning, then he didn't let it show. She'd taken the bus to Finsbury Park after she'd left Denning and had a wander round, breathing in fresh air and clearing her head.

She still couldn't believe Mags was dead. She'd never liked the woman, and had made no secret of it, but she couldn't get over the fact that she'd been murdered. Even a hard-faced bitch like Mags didn't deserve to end her life in some car park, alone and scared.

'Home early? Don't tell me they've sacked you?'

'Mags is dead.'

He sat down at the kitchen table, suddenly turning white. 'Jesus! I saw on the local news that a woman had been found murdered, but I had no idea it was Mags. What happened?'

She told him what little she knew about the murder. 'I've been suspended for the duration.'

'Can they do that?'

'I was the last person to see her alive. Taken in combination with our history, I'm probably their main suspect.'

'You are joking, aren't you?'

She looked at him. 'Of course I'm joking. Well, sort of joking. I don't think they believe I had anything to do with her murder, but they know I spoke to her last night.'

She was suddenly aware of Jon looking at her. 'She was alive when I left her.'

'It's not that. It's just… Well, I can see why they might think you're too closely involved. You knew her, you were working with her on this Colin Meek story. I did try and tell you to tread carefully.'

'Thanks, Jon, that's very helpful.'

'I don't mean that. All I'm saying is, you have to remember you're a detective and not a journalist. You're answerable to people. What about Denning? What does he have to say?'

'He was there, holding Betty Taggart's coat tails for her.'

Jon put his arm round her. 'I'm sorry.'

'About me? Or Mags?'

He removed his arm. 'That's not fair, Molly.'

She buried her head in his chest. 'I'm sorry. I didn't mean that. This is just all so awful. It's like being in the middle of some kind of nightmare.'

He hugged her again as she began to cry.

–

Molly slept badly that night; twisting and turning and chewing recent events over in her head. When she awoke next morning, her head was pounding from lack of sleep.

Jon was already pottering in his man shed by the time she wandered downstairs. She rummaged in the kitchen cupboards looking for cereal, and contemplated what she was going to do with all the free time that was about to come her way, when her mobile pinged with a text message.

It was from Denning.

He wanted to meet her.

Chapter Thirty-Six

The coffee shop was quiet, despite it being a weekend. Baboushka's was a former greasy spoon that had been transformed into a trendy eatery on Crouch Hill. Molly liked to go there with Jon sometimes. On a quiet Sunday morning, when she wasn't working, and he wasn't sleeping late, they would sit at a window table reading the papers and watching the world passing by. There was a selection of quirky artwork on the walls, with hefty price tags attached. Most of the pictures looked like they'd been done by local schoolchildren, and perhaps they had; Molly had never bothered to ask.

They were sitting at a table near the back today, Molly sipping a caramel latte and Jon a cappuccino. Denning sat there staring at an Americano. She couldn't be sure, but she suspected he was suffering from a hangover.

'Firstly, I want you to realise that McKenna had no option but to suspend you,' Denning said. 'This is in no way a comment on how you do your job.'

Molly looked at Jon as she sipped her latte.

'Her hands are tied over this. It's nothing personal.'

Her first thought, when he'd texted her earlier that morning to suggest they meet, was to tell him where to go. Politely, so as to ensure she still had a job to return to when all this was over, but firmly enough for him to get the point. Betty Taggart had pissed all over her, and he'd stood there in her office letting her do it.

But Jon had said Molly should at least hear what he had to say, so she'd relented. However, she'd insisted that Denning came to her, and had suggested the coffee shop they were currently sitting in.

'So you don't think I killed Mags then?'

He looked up from his coffee. She noticed one of his eyes was slightly bloodshot. 'It's not about that. We can't be seen to be compromising an investigation by having someone on the team who was a friend of the victim.' He blinked and shook his head. 'Someone who knew the victim…'

Jon had stayed silent up until now. He'd insisted on coming along; partly out of curiosity to meet this Denning she was always going on about – something she denied – and partly because he wanted to hear what he had to say. He promised he wouldn't go weighing in unprompted, and would allow Denning to argue his case before making any contribution to the conversation. She knew he'd never be able to keep that promise.

'So why are you here?' Jon asked. 'I don't think Betty Taggart needs someone to fight her corner for her. From what I've heard, she's pretty adept at fighting her own battles.'

Denning looked at Jon, then returned to his Americano. 'McKenna doesn't know I'm here. In fact, it's very likely she would disapprove if she knew what I was doing. But I think there's a possibility these murders could have something to do with the abuse allegations Colin Meek made thirty years ago.' He paused while a staff member tidied the table next to them. He waited until they'd disappeared behind the counter before continuing. 'This has nothing to do with your suspension. Except that it puts you in an advantageous position.'

She glanced over at Jon, who raised his eyebrows. 'How, exactly?' she asked.

There was a little amaretto biscuit on the saucer, next to the oversized coffee cup. Denning broke the biscuit in two and dipped one half in his cup. 'It's about Magda Kilbride and the story she was working on.' He popped the soggy biscuit into his mouth. 'It *could* be significant, especially in light of how she was killed.'

'Go on.'

'We've found a link between Buckfield and Colin Meek.' He told her what Trudi had discovered, and how it tied in with Buckfield. 'It looks as though Buckfield, as SIO at the time, was responsible for having the investigation dropped. However, I suspect Buckfield was leaned on. I'm guessing whoever did that was fairly high up in the Met.'

'Colin said that he thought one of the men involved could have been a senior police officer,' Molly said.

'That's the other thing.' Denning sipped his coffee. 'We need to speak to Colin Meek.'

'Why?'

'He's the obvious link between the two.'

Molly shook her head. 'No way. I admit, he's had his problems and he's no stranger to a prison cell, but he's not a killer. I honestly don't believe he's got it in him.'

'He's been in and out of jail most of his life for one thing or another. That changes people.'

Jon banged his cup on the saucer. 'Even if you buy that shit, it might give him a motive for killing Buckfield, but not Mags. She was trying to help the geezer, for fuck's sake.'

'Not if he thought she was using him,' Denning argued. 'If he thought he'd been betrayed by her and by the detective who should have believed him, but ended up being responsible for having him publicly branded a liar. If he felt Magda Kilbride had let him down too.' He looked at Jon and Molly. 'It's likely she knew her killer. I suspect there are very few people she would have traipsed across London to meet in the middle of nowhere at night, and you said yourself she wanted to speak to Colin. What if he got in touch and asked her to meet him? Was she the kind of person who would have agreed to do something like that?'

Molly wasn't convinced. 'I don't know. Maybe. She looked over at Jon, trying to second-guess what he was thinking.'

'Mags was certainly the kind of person who wasn't averse to taking risks,' he said. 'But still...'

'I can't see Colin killing Mags,' Molly said. 'Let alone Buckfield.' But she couldn't be sure. At least not a hundred percent.

'You think Buckfield could have approached Mags with the story?' Jon asked.

'Maybe his conscience got the better of him later in life and he felt guilty for the way the case was handled?' Denning shrugged. 'We'll probably never know. All we do know is that we have two people connected with this story who are now dead.'

'Then you need to reopen the case,' Jon said.

'We need to get permission first. And I can't see McKenna or anyone else agreeing to that unless we can prove the original investigation was deliberately sabot-aged, and that's not going to be easy.'

'What do you suggest?' Molly asked.

He lowered his voice. 'We need to keep this from McKenna, but I want you to continue looking into these allegations. Follow up what Magda Kilbride started. Try and find out if there's any truth in what Colin Meek claimed and who was involved in both the abuse and the cover-up.'

'How?'

Denning looked at Jon. 'You're a journalist. You must know where to look for things that people have tried to bury. Magda Kilbride thought she was onto something. We need to know what it was she'd discovered.'

Jon sighed. 'It's a big ask. This could ultimately lead to a dead end.' He threw a glance in Molly's direction. 'We don't know if Colin Meek was telling the truth. Even if we accept that Buckfield was pressured into dropping the investigation, that doesn't mean there's evidence of a cover-up. It could have been dropped due to half a dozen reasons: police budgets being one of them.'

'OK. Then if that turns out to be the case, we drop this angle and don't take things any further. But if there is any truth there, we need evidence to make it official. And the two of you are well placed to find that evidence.' He finished his Americano. 'It's not like you haven't followed your own instincts in the past. Last year, for instance: the murder of those women. Your investigation found the link to the Bermondsey Ripper, and that led us to find the killer.'

Molly thought about this. She knew Denning was taking a risk. If McKenna or Harrison found out he'd asked them to do this, both their jobs would be on the line – Denning's and hers, and she was already on suspension. But there was something about Colin's story that needed looking into.

'We'll do it.' Molly nodded at Jon. 'I'll speak to Colin again. Persuade him to talk to you. We'll try and uncover whatever Mags had found out so far and get to the truth of this.' She was aware of Jon shaking his head; a slight furrowing on his brow. 'We have to do this. If there has been a cover-up, then we can't just sit back and do nothing.'

Denning smiled. 'That would be a great help, Molly. Probably best if you contact me directly and don't discuss this with anyone else in the team. Even Trudi.'

'OK,' she said, still looking at Jon.

They finished their drinks. Denning paid at the counter. He checked his watch and told them there was somewhere he had to be.

As soon as he'd left the coffee shop, Jon turned to Molly. 'Are you mad? Do you know what you've just agreed to?'

Molly signalled to the young woman behind the counter that they'd like the same again. The woman nodded back at her.

'You heard Denning. If we're not careful, Colin could end up getting accused of this. He's the kind of person who would probably confess to killing them just because he thinks it's an easy way out.'

'That's assuming he didn't kill them.' Jon was shaking his head again. 'Molly, you're not thinking this through. Denning has as good as handed you a poisoned chalice here. If this all goes tits up, it'll be *your* tits on the chopping block. I think Denning's using you here. He knows you're concerned about Colin. He's not prepared to stick his neck out to protect him, but he's happy for you to do it.'

'Oh, for Christ's sake, Jon. He's not asking us to do anything illegal. He's only asking us to check out a few facts. Like what you used to do every day when you were at the *Echo*. And can you stop going on about my tits?' She pulled her jacket over her chest. 'Look, I'm going to do this anyway, with or without your help. It would be easier with.'

'Because you want to impress Denning? I dunno why – he didn't seem too bothered about doing you any favours when Betty Taggart frogmarched you out the building yesterday.'

'Don't be so childish. He explained that. And he's asked for my help. Firstly, that can't have been easy for him, and secondly, it says a lot that he trusts me enough to ask.'

Jon tutted and turned his head to look out the window. The young woman arrived with the coffees, placing them on the table and taking away their empty cups.

Eventually Jon turned back to face Molly. 'OK. You win. We'll look into this. We probably owe it to Mags if nothing else. And I think I know someone who might be able to help.'

Chapter Thirty-Seven

Lambourne House had been built in the middle of the eighteenth century for the third Earl of Lambourne. It was a few miles south of Theydon Bois, and surrounded by several acres of verdant parkland. Beyond the parkland was a golf course that shared its name.

The third Earl of Lambourne had been a notorious rogue, by all accounts, and had only inherited the title after the death of his elder brother in a hunting accident in 1742. It therefore seemed fitting that Alfie Kane had chosen the venue to officially launch his new homeless charity.

Denning had read the profligate earl's biography on a brochure that was available free of charge in the impressive entrance foyer. The house was now owned by a charity and open to the public during the summer months. It was also available for private hire.

After leaving Molly and her brutish-looking boyfriend, he'd driven out to Essex, relying on his Sat-Nav to find the house.

He'd parked his car in the gravelled car park at the front of the impressive mansion. An efficient-looking woman in a smart suit had greeted him at the top of the steps leading to the entrance, checked his name on a list and given him directions to the garden at the rear of the property. She had also pointed to a pile of brochures stacked on a table beside a marble fireplace that would tell him all about Lambourne House and its characterful history.

He walked through an ornate drawing room and out of a set of French doors to the garden. The section closest to the house was dominated by a large marquee. Smartly uniformed waiters carried glasses of champagne on silver salvers, while security personnel hovered discreetly, trying their best to blend into the background.

There were six-foot vertical banners dotted around the place proclaiming the name of Kane's charity, Safe Haven.

He spotted McKenna standing by the entrance to the marquee, sipping a glass of champagne and talking to an attractive woman in her late thirties. There was no sign of Kane.

'You're here at last,' she said when he approached. The woman she'd been speaking to smiled at Denning and told McKenna she'd catch her later, before disappearing into the marquee. He declined the offer of champagne from a passing waiter. 'Not drinking? It's good stuff, this. Bollinger.' She raised the glass in his direction and he suspected it wasn't her first glass of the day. 'No shop's own brand for Mr Kane.'

Denning felt his stomach grumble.

'This is all a bit OTT,' he said, gazing over the elegantly manicured lawns. The whole place looked like a classier version of Kane's Essex mansion. Which was probably why he'd chosen the venue for the launch.

McKenna snorted. 'You were the one who wanted to blag an invitation. I had to ask DCS Harrison on bended knee if I could bring you along as my plus-one.' She took another lengthy sip of champagne. 'You're not his most favourite person in the world at the moment, by the way. If you do bump into him today, try and be nice to him.'

'So he is here then?'

'Oh yes, by special request of Alfie Kane himself.'

Denning raised his eyebrows.

'Well, more Mrs Kane than Mr. Seems he knows Kane's wife, Marianne. She runs her own PR company. That was who I was chatting to when you pitched up. Actually a very nice woman. She organised this whole event.'

'And she has an eye for a rogue...'

McKenna waved a finger at him. 'Now, now, that's not very kind. We *are* here as his guests, after all.' She finished the champagne and looked around for a waiter. 'Which reminds me: why were *you* so keen to come along? I thought Kane was the devil incarnate as far as you're concerned.'

'I'm curious. What's he really up to? This whole charity launch – the reinvention from gangster to philanthropic businessman. Sorry – I just don't buy it.' He still wasn't entirely sure why he was there. Yes, he was curious about Kane: how he came to be where he was, and why he had been allowed to get away with breaking the rules time and time again. The man had created his own legend, but how much of that was myth and how much based on reality, however distorted? Was his success a result of an armed robbery from over twenty years ago? If so, then there would have been plenty of loose ends to tidy up, Buckfield possibly being one of them. His instinct told him there was something rotten about Alfred George Kane and he wanted to find out what it was.

'People change, Matt,' McKenna said. 'If they didn't then we might as well abandon the whole concept of reformative punishment.'

She helped herself to a passing glass of champagne.

'I thought you believed in locking 'em up and throwing away the key?' Denning said dryly.

She took a sip from her glass. 'Perhaps you don't know me as well as you think. Anyway, I thought you were the one with the clever degree in philosophy and criminology. Didn't they teach you about rehabilitation at university?'

'Maybe I was off that day. And it was psychology I studied, rather than philosophy.'

'Well, pardon me.' She reached over and touched his elbow. 'Look, take my advice – keep a low profile. Have a wander round the gardens and appreciate the serenity of this place.' She nodded at the brochure in his hand. 'I see you're interested in the history of the house and grounds. Well, why not make the most of it? They're open to the public during the summer. You could come here with Sarah and that kid of yours. Make it a family day out.'

'Jake.'

'Sorry?'

'The kid's name is Jake.'

McKenna just shrugged and drank some more champagne.

'Come to think of it,' Denning said, voicing something he'd been wondering about since he'd got there. 'Why are you here?'

For a brief moment, she seemed uncharacteristically embarrassed, but then she just gave another shrug. 'Harrison asked me to come along as his guest. A kind of clumsy apology for being an arsehole the other day.' She noticed the look on his face. 'Yes, I know, but hey – it's free booze.' She doffed her half-full glass at him.

'So you're his plus-one, and I'm yours. That's not awkward at all.'

She laughed. 'You're not exactly my "plus-one". You asked me if you could come along, and I swung it with Marianne.'

'And I'm very grateful.' He did wonder why Harrison would ask McKenna along to what was supposed to be a social event? And what exactly was Harrison's relationship with Kane's wife? 'Where's Harrison now?' he asked.

She pointed inside the marquee, where he spotted Harrison chatting to a group of people, clearly enjoying himself on the free booze almost as much as McKenna. Kane was standing immediately behind him, next to Marianne Kane. They were talking to what looked like journalists. Under the circumstances, it was probably wise if he were to avoid any contact with Harrison. Having been warned to stay away from Kane, it wouldn't look good if he was seen here today.

'Seriously, you don't buy this reformed character crap, do you?' Denning asked. 'OK, I accept that people change, but someone like Kane, crime's in his blood. He couldn't change if he wanted to. And I'd still put money on him being responsible for the attack on Gordon Lomax.'

'Not this old chestnut again. You've been told to drop it. Lomax isn't our problem. We've got two murder inquiries on the go. And Cairns, or Lomax, or whatever his name is, has asked you not to press charges.'

'We still don't know what happened to David Cairns.'

'Whatever happened, Matt, it's not our problem.'

They were interrupted by Marianne Kane approaching. Her husband was a few feet behind her, chatting to a guest.

'Hi Liz, sorry I was called away before. I had to speak to some people from one of the papers.' Marianne Kane extended a hand in Denning's direction, and McKenna introduced them. 'Nice to meet you,' she said. She spoke with an educated accent, polished and professional. Unlike Kane, it sounded authentic rather than the result of elocution lessons. She was smartly dressed in a tailored grey pinstriped suit with a white shirt underneath. She reminded Denning of Emma Morrow.

A moment later, Alfie Kane joined them, shaking McKenna by the hand as his wife introduced them, and then turning to Denning. 'Matt, isn't it? Good to meet you again. Sorry we couldn't chat much the other day. Hope I was able to help.' He had a beaming smile on his face. 'If you'll excuse me, I can see someone is trying to attract my attention, so I'll catch you all later.' He headed back into the marquee and towards a group of men standing next to a small stage.

'It's good of you both to come along today,' Marianne said. 'I've been talking to Ian. We'd very much like to get the police on board with this charity. So many young homeless people find themselves on the wrong side of the law, simply because they're desperate or ill. It would be so helpful to change that mindset amongst the police, and treat homeless youngsters with compassion and not assume they're criminals.' She smiled warmly at them. 'I'm sorry, I tend to get carried away sometimes. I'm not suggesting you're personally responsible for how our homeless people are treated by the law. But there's so much that could change just by adopting a different approach.' She glanced towards her husband, who was talking to the men by the stage. 'This means so much to Alfie. I know it's something close to his heart. We just want the charity to be a success.'

Kane called his wife over. She smiled at Denning and McKenna, and said she'd see them inside the marquee in a few minutes.

McKenna turned to Denning. 'Like I said: charming.'

'I'm still not sure what she's doing with someone like Kane.' Even with the edges smoothed, he was still a rough diamond. 'And what happened to the first Mrs Kane?'

'You can get that thought out of your head right now. They divorced some time ago. She's living happily in Majorca with her second husband, apparently.'

There was a sudden announcement asking everyone to enter the marquee. Denning and McKenna headed in. Kane was standing on the small stage at the front of the marquee, a microphone in his hand, Marianne standing on his right. There were more vertical banners on the stage advertising Kane's new charity.

Kane addressed the crowd. 'I know what it's like to worry about not having a roof over your head. When I was a child, my mother brought us up single-handed, dependent on the state to keep us safe. We lived in continual fear of the bailiffs coming round, taking away what little we had. I know the importance of having security and safety. That's why we've set ourselves a target of ten million pounds by this time next year. This will enable us to build a state of the art hostel for homeless men and women in East London. Whilst this won't eradicate homelessness, it will significantly reduce it in the capital.'

Denning had stopped listening. He was thinking of the hypocrisy of the situation: Kane with his mansion talking about the pitfalls of being homeless. But he had to hand it to the man: he had clearly learned some of his wife's PR skills.

He looked at Kane on stage addressing his audience: confident and assured. Kane, who had been all smiles when they'd briefly spoken earlier, but who had been quick enough to report him to Harrison the other day.

Kane's wealth was built on the back of a successful haulage firm, but what if they were to go over the company with a keen eye? Would they discover the business was being used for something illegal? And even if it was legit, there were still questions to answer. For instance, what was the story with Kane's former boss, Bernie Michaelson, and had Kane had a hand in his demise? Or what about Kane's relationship with Buckfield? Or Lomax?

Denning could see Harrison standing near the front, smiling his admiration. Did Kane still have friends in the Met? Did Harrison know the truth about Kane? Did Denning, for that matter? Local villain makes good. Denning refused to buy it. But was McKenna right? Was this down to some kind of irrational prejudice on his part?

Denning had seen and heard enough. He told McKenna he was leaving. She waved a hand at him. She either hadn't heard him, or didn't care.

He exited back through the house. The woman in the foyer who'd greeted him when he arrived asked if he'd enjoyed himself.

'Very interesting, but I've seen enough,' he told her. He could see from the bemused look on her face she didn't know if he was referring to the house or the charity launch.

Chapter Thirty-Eight

Barry Tasker was sitting in his favourite armchair beside an ancient gas fire that seemed to chuck out more fumes than it did heat. He was drinking from a tumbler that looked like it contained Lucozade, but it could have been a whisky and something; Molly couldn't tell. The house was in Greenwich, not far from the Royal Observatory. It smelt musty, as though it needed a good airing.

'It's been too long. And you've put on weight.' Barry's face had broken into a wide smile the second Jon had walked through the door. But his face was lined and yellow, his skin papery thin. There was a metal walking frame beside his chair.

Prior to his retirement, Barry Tasker had been the editor of the *London Echo*. He was Jon's former boss. But their relationship was closer than that: for almost fourteen years, Barry had been Jon's father-in-law. Despite the marriage having long-since ended, the two had remained good friends.

Jon smiled at Barry and placed a hand affectionately on his shoulder. He introduced Molly, who shook his hand. Despite his frail appearance, his handshake felt like a steel grip. 'Good to meet you, Molly. Jon has mentioned you on occasions, but I know so very little about you. Please, both of you, sit down, and let me get you something to drink.' He made an effort to get up.

Jon waved him back into his chair and said he'd do it, then headed into the kitchen. Molly looked round the living room. 'Cluttered' would have been the best word to describe it. Photographs and objets d'art littered the room. Every tabletop seemed to be covered with either framed photographs or clunky ornaments. According to Jon, Barry's wife had died ten years ago. Nowadays, he was dependent on a daily carer to ensure he ate and washed.

She spotted a wedding photograph of Jon and Jenna, Barry's daughter. They both looked young. Young and hopeful.

'It's lovely to meet you, Molly. I'm so glad Jon has at last found someone who can make him happy. How has he been recently?'

'Yes, he's been alright,' Molly said. 'He has his bad days and his not-so-bad days.' She was never sure when Jon was having a bad day, if she was honest. He worked hard at keeping things to himself, bottling them up. Usually the words 'I'm just tired' were code for another bout of depression, and then the black clouds would descend.

'He always suffered from dark thoughts. Jenna used to find it difficult. I think, in the end, it got too much for her. She started blaming herself for Jon's dark moods. The more she blamed herself, the more distant he became.' He sniffed, and there was a look of sadness in his eyes. 'I was always very fond of Jon. It broke my heart when he and Jenna split up.' He shrugged. 'It was nobody's fault, of course, just one of those things, but I was sad, for both of them.' There was a faraway smile on his face. 'Jon needs a woman in his life. He needs someone to look after him. Left on his own he thinks too much…'

Molly wondered what Jenna was like. She knew Jon's marriage to her had been the longest and least unsuccessful of his four marriages. And the only one that had produced a child: a daughter called Rowan, that he rarely mentioned.

'And then losing his job at that bloody newspaper,' the old man continued. 'He was a damned good journalist. We all gave so much to that paper, and look how they repaid us.'

As if on cue, Jon returned carrying a tray of tea and coffee. He placed the tray on the coffee table and passed round the mugs. Molly spotted a couple of dead moths floating on the surface of her coffee, and wondered when the mugs had last been used.

'The Meat Rack,' Barry said suddenly. 'That's what you're asking about. Boys – mostly boys – were procured, for use of a better word, from various locations in and around the West End. A particularly popular location was the West End Arcade in Soho. Boys, and we are talking boys – most would have been aged eighteen and under – were offered money, expensive gifts and whatever else in exchange for "entertaining" older men. I mean, it wasn't always sexual. Some of these men just enjoyed the company of teenage boys, some used to just photograph them in various states of undress. There was a particular group of men who were after something else. They were unofficially known as the "Dashwoods", after Francis Dashwood, the founder of the notorious Hellfire Club in the eighteenth century. They even used to have handkerchiefs with the letter D elaborately embroidered on them as a means of identifying themselves to one another.' He looked at Molly, sadness in his eyes. 'You've spoken to Colin Meek, so you know what went on. I don't need to go into further detail. We were all aware of the stories. These were powerful men – establishment figures who thought they were untouchable.' He paused, stared at his coffee for a moment. 'They *were* untouchable. That was the thing. They were and they knew it.'

'But who were they?' Molly asked.

'We never knew names, not for certain.' Barry drank his tea, seemingly oblivious to the moth corpses floating on the surface. 'We were tipped off about Colin Meek. I had a couple of reporters follow it up. They spoke to Meek, but he made for a poor witness. His account was unreliable and inconsistent. The police just issued a stream of "no comments". But despite that, we decided there was enough of a story. It would have been safe enough to run with, as long as we didn't name any names, which wasn't difficult as we never had any; apart from Robin Sims, and he was old news by then anyway. There had been rumours about this for years. Everybody had heard them, but no one was brave enough to go public with the story. It wasn't just Colin. There were others believed to be involved, though no one else could be persuaded to come forward. Apart from that one lad that later admitted he'd lied. Which was all very strange in itself.'

'Did you run the story?' Molly asked.

He shook his head. 'I had a visit from two of your representatives one evening.' He smiled at Molly. 'They said it would be "in our interests" to make sure the story didn't go ahead.'

'Seriously? What did you do?'

'Well, I was never one to give in to threats or bullying, so I told them where to go. We still have a free press in this country, just about. I told them we would go ahead with the story and if they didn't like it then too bad. OK, I may have used slightly fruitier language than that.'

'What happened in the end?'

'Orders from on high. Lord Fraser, who owned the *Echo* in those days, ordered me to spike the story.'

'Did he give a reason?'

'He said it was potentially libellous and wasn't of any public interest. That was rubbish, of course. We hadn't included anything in that story that was libellous. We'd checked it all over with the paper's lawyers beforehand. Naturally, I disagreed with him, but that was that. I was overruled.'

'You think someone got to him?' Jon asked.

The old man shrugged. 'Possibly. Perhaps he was nervous about running the story, or maybe he was worried about advertisers pulling out. I don't know. It was shortly after that he sold the paper to Moreton Media, and the focus shifted from serious news to celebrity gossip. Then the bottom fell out of the newspaper industry. Levison...' He looked over to Jon. 'Inevitable redundancies. I mean, the paper's still going, but it's little more than a comic now.'

Molly thought about this. It still didn't prove anything. The paper could have dropped the story simply because it wasn't strong enough. On the other hand, if Barry had been ordered to drop the story, then there was the definite possibility that order was made to cover something up.

'There was a rumour that one of the boys was killed. Do you think there could have been any truth in that?' Molly asked.

'These were powerful men,' Barry said. 'With good connections, if the rumours were to be believed. These boys, on the other hand, had nothing. Most didn't even have families who wanted them. If these men had wanted someone to disappear, it wouldn't have been difficult to arrange.'

She watched as his frail hand shook as he sipped his tea.

'But I don't know about a murder. If it happened, then it would be almost impossible to prove.'

'I don't suppose you can remember the names of the officers who visited you?' Molly asked.

He shook his head. 'It was thirty years ago. Sorry.'

'What about the men in question? Any names?'

'It would be mostly guesswork on my part. Meek said he didn't recognise any of the men, apart from Sims, and he'd probably seen him on the telly a few times. There was always the possibility the story would have flushed them out, but equally, the rumour of it might have been enough to drive them underground.' He leaned in closer. 'I have to warn you both – if you are going to go after this story, you need to be very careful. Whoever these men were, they clearly weren't without influence. They evidently had the police on side; they were possibly able to exert influence on a newspaper proprietor, and they managed to silence the only other witness to come forward. Colin Meek was destroyed after this. I'm only sorry I wasn't able to play my part more, but it was taken out of my hands.'

'What happened to this other witness?' Molly asked. 'Jason Wainwright?'

Barry shook his head slowly. 'I don't know. Like I said, it was all very strange. He came out of nowhere with his claims that he'd been one of the boys who'd been abused, then he just vanished again, claiming he'd lied. There were rumours he was on the make, but I often suspected there was more to it than that.'

Molly was now determined to find this mysterious Jason Wainwright and find out what he had to say.

'It's too late for me to do anything now,' Barry continued. He looked at them, sadness in his eyes. 'The diagnosis isn't good. Six months to a year, the specialist said.'

Jon reached over and touched the old man on the arm. 'I'm so sorry. If there's anything we can do.' He looked over to Molly. 'Get in touch with us.'

Barry shook his head again. 'I've come to terms with it now. And I've had a good life. I just want to keep going long enough to walk Rowan down the aisle in July.'

Jon's face flushed suddenly and his hand trembled against the mug. It was clearly news to him that his daughter was getting married.

'I'm so sorry,' Barry said. 'Didn't you know? I thought Jenna would have told you. I asked her to tell you. About Rowan, I mean. Not about me. I was always going to tell you that myself. But I kept putting it off.'

Molly could see Jon looking at the old man. The double whammy of discovering his former father-in-law was dying along with the news his only daughter was getting married and his invitation to the wedding had got lost in the ether, would hit him hard. Hard enough to knock him into another depression?

'You know what Jenna's like,' Barry said. 'She has a terrible memory. I'll bet she *thinks* she's told you. Or she thinks I have.' He smiled awkwardly at the pair of them. 'Well, there now, I have.'

'I should get in touch with Rowan,' Jon said. 'Otherwise she'll think I don't give a toss.'

Barry shook his head again. 'She would never think that. She knows you love her.'

Molly could read Jon's face: the look on it said otherwise.

'I'll tell you what I'll do,' Barry said, 'I'll look over my old files – they're all archived in boxes in the cellar – and

I'll see what I can dig out. There will be a lot of guess-work. But I can let you know when I find something interesting. I feel it's the very least I should be doing, especially after letting that boy down all those years ago.'

'You'll be raking up a lot of skeletons people will be expecting to keep buried,' Molly said, remembering what he'd said about his visit from the two detectives.

He smiled at her. 'They can threaten me all they like now, Molly. What have I got left to lose?'

Jon was staring at the pattern on the fussy carpet. It was likely he was still thinking about his estranged daughter's wedding rather than anything else. He would need hand-ling with care for a while.

'Thank you, Barry. That would be very helpful.' She looked at Jon, who raised his head and managed a smile.

Molly shook Barry's thin hand while Jon gave his ex-father-in-law a hug. She then offered to take the moth-encrusted mugs back to the kitchen and wash them, but Barry insisted they let him clear up.

As they were leaving, he said to them: 'Be very careful... Some of these men may well be dead now, but their families aren't, and they won't be happy that you're looking into this again. I'm an old man who hasn't got long to go. But you've got your career ahead of you, Molly. Make sure you know what you're doing.'

As they headed back to the car, Molly had a horrible feeling they had bitten off more than they could chew.

Chapter Thirty-Nine

Molly emailed Denning as soon as they got home. She gave him an abbreviated version of what Barry had told them. She noticed an email from the NCA telling her that there were no unsolved Missing Persons cases on file that matched Tommy's description. If Tommy had ever existed, no one had bothered to report him missing. Another dead end, but she had to admit it had always been something of a long shot.

She headed into the kitchen where Jon was sitting at the table staring into space.

'Everything OK?' she asked.

He looked up and smiled. 'Everything's fine. What did Denning say?'

'Nothing much. He didn't answer, so I left a message.' She sat down next to him, placing a hand on his arm. 'So what's next?'

'I dunno. Wait for Barry to get back to us with whatever he can dig up from his files.' He stretched his arms. 'Would be helpful if we could get some names.'

'I'm going to track down this Jason Wainwright. Find out why he changed his story.'

'If you can get hold of him.' Jon was staring into space again, seemingly lost in whatever thoughts were going on inside his head.

'Are you thinking about Barry? Or Rowan?' Molly got up and headed to the sink, pouring herself a glass of water. 'I'm sure Rowan will be in touch with you before the wedding. It's not until July, that's months away. Plenty of time for her to contact you.' Molly did wonder if she should go behind his back and contact his daughter on his behalf. She could explain the situation, and how Jon would love nothing more than to walk her down the aisle on her big day. Then again, did she really want to interfere? If it all went wrong, Jon would blame her. And perhaps Rowan didn't want her father to give her away, especially if they'd had no contact for a while. She'd asked her grandad and maybe that was what she wanted.

Molly thought about her own dad; the very last person she'd want to give her away on her wedding day. Not that she wanted a traditional wedding. In fact, she didn't want any sort of wedding at the moment, not that there was much chance of Jon going down on one knee now or in the foreseeable.

'Actually,' Jon said after a minute, 'I was thinking about Mags.'

'Mags?'

'She had a pretty shitty life when you think about it. Most of the men in her life treated her like crap, then she goes and gets herself murdered. I'd say that was pretty shitty.'

Molly sighed, unsure what to say. She couldn't help thinking that Mags was probably responsible for a lot of the shit that had happened in her life, and there was little point being hypocritical now she was dead. 'Mags liked taking risks. Maybe she just took one risk too many and her luck finally ran out.' Molly realised she sounded hard, so tried for a more sympathetic approach. 'I'm not saying she deserved what happened to her. And hopefully we'll catch whoever did it.' She looked at Jon, sure he was thinking about his daughter as much as he was thinking about Mags. But it was probably easier for him to focus on something he couldn't change rather than on something he could.

Molly was standing by the sink. 'Do you know if she had any family?'

'There was her mother. I don't know if she's still alive. By all accounts, they didn't get on. Apparently she threw Mags out when she was sixteen and pregnant.'

'Mags has a child?'

He shook his head. 'She lost it.' He sighed. 'She went off the rails for a bit: drugs, drinking too much. Sleeping around. But she got herself sorted out. Got her head together, got into uni, got herself a good degree and then ended up at the *Echo*. It helped her to turn her life around. For the most part.'

Some of this Molly already knew, but some of it came as a surprise. To her, Mags was just somebody that came into their lives, caused trouble and then disappeared again. She never thought of her as having had a past. 'I'm sorry.' Though even as she said the words, she knew they sounded hollow. She wanted to feel guilty for how she'd treated Mags, but she couldn't. She kept thinking back to that last night at the Jericho Bar: Mags trying to rile her by mentioning Bex. Bex, whom she thought about every day; the friend killed by a monster because Molly let her walk home alone after a night out.

Mags knew what buttons to press to get a reaction, and Molly had hated her for that.

But that wasn't what Jon wanted to hear. She needed to try and assuage his guilt for both their sakes.

'At least she had friends,' Molly said.

'I don't know that she did. Apart from me, and I'm not sure I count as a friend.' Jon sighed. 'In the grand scheme of things, I didn't exactly treat her well myself.'

'Jon, we've been over this. You can't change the past.' She tried to offer him a smile, but her lips remained stubbornly downcast. She knew about his brief involvement with Mags, from many years before. Raking it all up again now wasn't going to help anyone. It certainly wasn't going to help their relationship.

'I suppose the police will have contacted her mother as next of kin?' Jon asked. 'That's the usual procedure, isn't it?'

'If Mags's mother is her next of kin,' Molly said, 'then she'll have been officially informed about her death. As soon as her body's released she can make arrangements for her funeral.'

'That's if anyone knows how to get hold of her mum.' He looked at Molly. 'I don't think even Mags knew where she was.'

'I know it's not always easy, but the team will be doing their best to find her.' She touched Jon's arm again. 'However, I don't want to sound insensitive, but there will have to be a post-mortem, and it may be that the body isn't released until after the investigation is finished. Possibly not until after it's gone to court.' She looked at Jon. 'It's not uncommon for a defence brief to ask for a second, independent, post-mortem.'

'I'd like to go to her funeral,' Jon said. 'I think we should.'

Molly wasn't convinced. This was guilt talking: not so much guilt about Mags and how he'd treated her during their brief dalliance, but guilt that he had lost contact with his daughter; a daughter who was now getting married and didn't want her father to be a part of that.

'We need to stay focussed, Jon. In light of what Barry's just told us, we need to speak to Colin again.'

'We have to accept the fact that it's possible Colin could have killed Mags,' Jon said. 'Your mate Denning certainly seems to think it's a possibility.'

'Denning's just keeping his options open,' Molly said. 'The truth is, he doesn't have a clue who killed Mags at this stage. It might not even be linked to the story she was working on. We could all be barking up the wrong tree here entirely.'

'Or, on the other hand, we could be about to go looking for a killer. With you officially off the case, it's not like you could call on back-up to save our arses if it all goes pear-shaped. We could potentially find ourselves sitting ducks if Colin Meek is a killer and he decides to come after us next.'

Molly wanted to say something in response, but she knew Jon had a point. She would just rather not admit it.

Chapter Forty

Denning was sitting at his desk checking emails. Even though it was Saturday, the case was still active. There was a message on his voicemail from Frances Hynd, asking him to phone her back. She explained that she'd been on holiday, and had asked whether he had found David after all these years? He wasn't sure what he was going to tell her. It wasn't like he could offer her good news.

The team had been poring over hours of CCTV; reading and re-reading witness statements; trying to track down missing mobile phones, and constantly digging until they found that one clue that would lead them to a break-through. This was the reality of police work: dull, monotonous and repetitive. They now had access to Magda Kilbride's laptop. There were entire documents devoted to her investigation into the high-profile paedophile gang, complete with a list of possible suspects. Unfortunately she had used initials rather than names, so they had little to work with.

There were still waiting for Magda Kilbride's post-mortem report. Denning would chase that up first thing on Monday morning, though it was unlikely to contain any surprises. They were almost certain she had been killed by the same person who killed Buckfield.

Denning had gone straight to the office from Kane's charity launch. He had expected McKenna to get in touch asking where he'd disappeared to, but the only message on his phone had been from Justin Morrow, hoping he and Sarah had enjoyed dinner, and asking if Denning wanted to join him for a game of squash sometime.

Denning had replied, saying he'd be happy to arrange a game, and suggesting another meal. Sarah had clearly been taken with Emma, and was keen to invite them round to the flat for dinner sometime.

He rubbed a hand over his eyes. His head still throbbed, yet he was sure he'd only had a couple of glasses of wine with dinner last night. He had a vague recollection of Morrow ordering brandies at one point, and it was possible he may have had a couple. Maybe more. He wished he could remember…

He looked over the contents of his inbox, hoping it would focus his mind. There was a message from Molly outlining what she and Jon had uncovered. They were fast workers.

They'd spoken to someone who had tried to cover the original story in the press. It was clear from what they'd been told that the story had been deliberately spiked in the papers, as well as being formally dropped by the Met.

This in itself was clearly suspicious.

But how did it tie in with Buckfield? Had Magda Kilbride spoken to him? Had he approached her? Perhaps suffering from guilt for having stopped the investigation into an organised child abuse ring? But according to Dr Baker, his brain was too addled by booze to be capable of that sort of rational thinking.

None of it made sense.

Denning's thoughts returned to Kane. The success he enjoyed and the ease with which he'd evaded justice suggested he'd been more than lucky. And that hadn't been down to chance.

Kane and Buckfield.

Kane and Harrison.

Even the usually shrewd McKenna appeared to have been taken in by the superficial charm and the 'reformed baddie' persona.

Then he remembered something Molly had mentioned in her email.

Bringing it up on the screen, he quickly reread it.

> The boys were known as "The Meat Rack",
> and would be picked up from an amusements
> arcade in Soho called West End Arcade.

He searched through his notes on Kane. In the early 1980s, Kane had bought a lot of Bernie Michaelson's old property empire, shortly after Michaelson was killed. A lot of that property had been based in Michaelson's old stomping ground of Soho. Denning dug through the bit of paper that had been neatly stacked on one corner of his desk. He'd skimmed over it when he'd first received it – it had made for some interesting background reading on Kane – then put it aside to be filed at a convenient moment.

Scanning over the list of properties Kane had owned in the eighties and early nineties: a couple of bars, a nightclub, a casino, then he saw what had jumped out at him: an amusement arcade called West End Arcade.

What would Kane have wanted with an amusement arcade?

He'd initially thought it would have been a means of laundering illegal money, but surely the other venues would have been more suitable for that.

Suddenly everything seemed to tie together. Kane was providing underage boys to older men. Perhaps this had been something started by Michaelson, and seen as a lucrative earner by Kane, so worth continuing. Or had Kane also been an active member of the circle? A paedophile himself?

He reached for his mobile and phoned McKenna. 'Are you still at Kane's?'

'I'm in a taxi heading somewhere for lunch. What the fuck happened to you? One minute you were standing beside me, next minute there was just a Denning-shaped space? Get a better offer, did you?'

Her speech was slightly slurred, and he suspected the free champagne had been appreciated. At least she wasn't driving. 'I'm at the office,' he said. 'I've found something out about Kane.'

There was a heavy silence from the other end of the line and he wondered if she'd hung up.

Then he heard her voice, loud and clear, as though she were in the room with him. 'This is turning into some kind of obsession, Matt. You have to give it up.'

'We know that the Security Direct robbery links Kane and Buckfield,' he argued. 'And Kane is potentially linked to a whole lot more, including a rumoured paedophile ring dating back to the eighties. We need to bring him in for questioning.'

Another silence. 'We don't know for certain that there's anything to link Kane and Buckfield with Security Direct. The allegations were never proved.'

'It can't be a coincidence that Buckfield resigned from the force shortly after the allegations were made?'

'There could have been any number of reasons why Buckfield left the job. It's not uncommon for DCIs to leave early, trust me. And good luck trying to prove Alfie Kane was mixed up in some kind of dodgy kiddy-fiddling gang.'

'OK. Even if we give Buckfield the benefit of the doubt over Security Direct, Kane's name keeps cropping up in connection to both the attack on Gordon Lomax and the allegations Colin Meek made thirty years ago. Buckfield's name is linked to that too.'

'We don't touch Kane until we've spoken to Harrison,' she said, almost shouting down the phone.

'It's got nothing to do with Harrison. He shouldn't even be involved in this investigation.'

'It's more complicated than that.'

Denning found himself cursing under his breath. 'Harrison is too close to Kane. I'm not suggesting there's anything improper. He just can't see what the man's really like. He's blinkered.'

There was another pause. It sounded like the taxi had stopped and she was getting out; he could hear her arguing with the driver about something. After a second he heard a door slam and McKenna's voice came back on the phone. 'You're the one who's blinkered, Matt. Forget Kane.'

He told her what Molly had said in her email, being discreet about how he had come by the information. 'It proves Kane's part of this.'

There was an audible sigh from the other end of the phone. She was standing on a busy street somewhere, probably trying to finish the call before heading into wherever she was having lunch. 'We'll need more than this if we're going to go after Kane. What you've got is little more than circumstantial. You get proof that Kane was part of this gang, or was directly connected with it, and then we can think about bringing him in. This needs to be rock solid with no wriggle room. Even then I'd still have my doubts.'

She ended the call.

He stared at his phone for a while; thinking she might call back. But then realising she wasn't going to.

Finding proof wasn't going to be easy. Kane was clever. If Denning wanted to find proof, he was going to have to look very carefully.

But he had a pretty good idea where he might find it.

Chapter Forty-One

Colin was waiting for them in the same South London park where Molly had met him last time. He was sitting on a bench not far from the entrance, luckily some distance from the children's playpark. Molly tried hard to dismiss the sinister thoughts going round her head: the abused becoming the abuser. Colin liked parks. After spending so long inside various prison cells, he probably appreciated the green, open space. The proximity of a children's play area was nothing more than coincidence.

'I've brought a friend,' she said, introducing Jon. 'He can help us.'

Colin looked at him, slightly wary of a stranger entering his personal space, but he shook the proffered hand just the same.

The park was busier this time. There were a few joggers weaving their way round the paths, as well as families enjoying the early spring sunshine. She could hear a football match taking place somewhere nearby.

She'd brought something to eat. The last time she'd been in the park, she'd spotted a picnic area not far from the lake. She suggested they headed there to talk, hoping this would put Colin at his ease, and make him more likely to open up.

It had taken some soft-soaping to persuade Colin to meet her again. He'd heard about Mags's death. Although she hadn't been named yet, it wouldn't have taken much for him to put two and two together and know she was the journalist who had been murdered.

Colin had initially been unwilling to meet, insisting he had nothing more to say to her. Without actually spelling out that it was only a matter of time before he received an official visit from the police, she let him know it was in his best interests to talk to her again. If the police were to formally question him about Mags's murder – which was a definite possibility – it would look so much better if she were able to put a good word in for him.

Reluctantly, he'd agreed to meet her.

'Do they think I did it?' he asked, once they were sitting down at a picnic table. She'd brought sandwiches and crisps. Jon had a can of Stella, while she and Colin had a Coke and a Fanta.

'I'm not part of that investigation,' she said truthfully, 'but I know the officers who are working the case, and they won't come after you if you promise to be honest with me.'

Colin opened his can of Coke and nervously drank it. He kept flicking glances in Jon's direction, unsure why she'd brought along a shaven-headed gorilla for company. Perhaps he thought Jon was another detective, and maybe it was better if he believed this chat was somehow official.

'I told you everything last time. I thought you believed me.' He looked from one to the other, opening the packet of sandwiches and staring at them, as though unsure what they were. She'd bought him cheese and tomato: it seemed a safe bet.

'We not only believe you, Colin, we think we might be able to prove what happened to you. But we will need your help to do that.'

'What about Tommy? Can you find out what happened to him?'

She looked at Jon. There was still nothing that suggested Tommy had even existed, let alone that he'd been killed. 'It would help if you could tell us more about him, Colin. His surname, or where he came from? A description. Anything.'

He shook his head. 'He was just Tommy. That's all anyone ever called him.'

'We want to get justice for him, Colin,' Molly said. 'But until we have more details, the chances of identifying his killer are slim.' She looked at him, hoping he might be able to provide some more information. Something. But Colin just looked blank. She wasn't going to get anywhere pressing him for details he either couldn't remember, or had simply never known in the first place.

She offered him a smile, but he didn't react. He ate the sandwiches without comment, and she didn't know what else she could say.

'What about Mags?' Jon asked. 'Did she ever say who first put her on to this story ?'

He shook his head again and ate the sandwich. Jon opened his mouth to ask something else, but Molly put her hand on his arm. Sometimes his old journalistic instinct took over and his line of questioning could become aggressive. That would just scare Colin off, and they needed him onside if they were to get anywhere.

'Did Mags say anything to you about whether she'd managed to locate any of these men? Could she have spoken to one of them?'

He looked up from his sandwich and spoke with his mouth full. 'Do you think whoever killed her will come after me?' His eyes darted between Molly and Jon, then looked behind them to see if there was anyone else in the picnic area. There was a family at another table, chatting and laughing between themselves, and not paying them any attention.

'We don't know for sure if Mags was killed because of the story she was working on,' Molly said, 'but it's possible. In which case, anything you can tell us will help catch whoever did it.'

'You do think it was me, don't you?' He stared at Molly, ignoring Jon completely. 'You think I killed her.'

Molly could sense Jon wanting to speak. She knew he wanted to broach that possibility, see how Colin reacted. Her hand was still resting on his arm, but she could only keep him quiet for so long.

'Did you kill her?' he asked. He was looking directly at Colin, trying to make eye contact, which with Colin was always like trying to hit a moving target.

A squirrel jumped onto the picnic table, eyes focussed on the food, but alert to any sudden movement. Molly tore off a section of crust and threw it on the ground. The squirrel quickly jumped off the table, grabbed the crust and disappeared into the surrounding shrubbery.

Colin had stopped eating. He let his sandwich drop onto the picnic table. The squirrel reappeared – or maybe it was a different one, Molly couldn't tell – its eyes fixed on the sandwich. Jon swished it away with a swipe of his hand. Colin stared at the departing squirrel, then looked at Jon. 'I didn't kill her.' He turned to Molly. 'Honest, I didn't kill her.'

He stared at the remains of the sandwich; flecks of cheese had spilt out onto the table. 'Not her.'

Jon and Molly looked at each other. 'What do you mean "not her"?'

256

He lifted his head. 'I think I might have killed someone else.' His gaze flickered between Molly, Jon and the sandwich.

It was Jon who spoke first. 'Who did you kill, Colin?'

They had to wait until he answered. 'There was this man. He used to work in the arcade. I never knew his name. I think he might have owned the arcade. I don't know. I never really spoke to him, not properly.'

'What happened?' Molly asked. She had a bad feeling about where this was heading.

'I saw him. In the street. A few days ago. I recognised him – he hadn't changed very much – except he was older. I followed him, found out where he lived.'

Colin stopped speaking, as though that was all he had to say on the matter.

'Go on,' Molly prompted. 'If you don't tell us what happened, we can't help you.'

He finally met Molly's eyes. 'I went back the next day and waited for him. When I saw him coming towards me, I attacked him. I couldn't stop. He was lying on the ground, and I don't think he was breathing. I just… I panicked and ran away. I don't remember what happened after that. I just remember waking up at home and being sick.'

Despite being a middle-aged man, he looked for all the world like a helpless child. 'But I didn't kill Mags. I know I didn't.'

'The man's name is Gordon Lomax.' Molly spoke calmly, trying to keep the situation as normal as possible. Colin had just confessed to a serious assault, and she should notify Denning, assuming the case hadn't now been passed on.

'He's OK,' she said. 'You didn't kill him, but he was badly injured. The police will need to speak to you about this, but if you're right and this man was even partly involved in the abuse, then you could say there were mitigating circumstances.' She wasn't sure the courts would buy that, but a good defence brief could make a strong argument for it. But with Colin's record, taken along with the seriousness of the assault, it was likely he'd be looking at a custodial sentence.

'I'm going back to prison,' he said, as though reading her mind. 'Last time I got out, everybody said I'd be back and they were right.' He looked at Molly, pretending Jon wasn't there. 'I'm going back inside.'

Molly wanted to reassure him further, tell him he wasn't and that everything would be all right. Be she couldn't lie to him. After all the shit life had thrown at him, the last thing the poor sod needed was to be lied to by another police officer.

'I'll do my best to protect you, Colin. But I can't promise you anything more than that.'

Taking her mobile from her pocket, she phoned Denning.

Chapter Forty-Two

Denning rang the doorbell and waited.

Lomax had discharged himself from the hospital – that much he'd found out from a phone call – against his doctor's advice. But he was an adult, and had signed the requisite forms absolving the hospital of any responsibility should anything happen to him, so there was nothing they could do to stop him.

As he had nowhere else to go, his house in Highbury was the obvious place to look for him.

Only it wasn't his house. It belonged to David Cairns: legally and morally.

It was a few minutes before the front door opened and Lomax stood there, looking Denning up and down. Even though he'd felt well enough to discharge himself, he still hadn't fully recovered from his injuries. There was a pained look about him, though that could have been because Denning was standing on his doorstep.

'What now?' he asked.

His left eye was still bloodshot, but the bandage had gone from his face to reveal a nasty cut; there was a possibility it might leave some permanent scarring. His arm was still in plaster and the bruising on his cheek looked like a ripened plum.

'Can I come in?'

'No. Next question?'

'OK, let's stand on the doorstep and have our conversation right here. The neighbours already think you're a source of local intrigue, so let's really give them something to gossip about.'

Lomax poked his head out the door and glanced up and down the street. It was the weekend, so people were around: cars were being washed and gardens being tidied. An eager beaver two doors down was giving their front lawn the first cut of the year.

'Right. You've got five minutes. Not a second longer.'

The house was like a time warp. The wallpaper in the living room looked like it had been put up in the 1970s, while three of the four walls were lined with bookcases. It was David Cairns's home rather than Gordon Lomax's. Lomax had failed to stamp his personality on the place, despite having lived there – like a cuckoo in the nest – for over twenty years.

Denning sat in a dusty armchair opposite an old-fashioned television. Lomax stood by the fireplace, one arm in a sling, the other resting on the mantelpiece.

'You're feeling better then?' Denning asked. 'Or at least well enough to leave your hospital bed?'

'What's this about, Denning? I've told you I don't want to press charges, and I've explained about Cairns, so I don't know what the fuck you're doing here.'

'Firstly, I no longer buy your story about Cairns committing suicide. I've been speaking to Frances Hynd, David's sister. She lives in Wester Ross in the north of Scotland now. She's in her nineties, but still sharp as a tack.'

'Very interesting,' Lomax said witheringly. 'I told you, David hated her. Called her an interfering old cow and wanted nothing to do with her.'

'That's not quite how she sees it,' Denning said. 'She admits they had a falling-out some time ago, but they were still in contact with one another, more or less, right up until he disappeared.' He paused, waiting to gauge Lomax's reaction. Lomax just looked at him, not giving anything away. 'What's more interesting is that she insists her brother would never have killed himself. According to her, he was a practising Catholic, and it seems they take the whole death by suicide thing quite seriously. So that does – once again – raise the whole awkward question of what really happened to David Cairns.'

Lomax stood by the fireplace saying nothing. Irrespective of whatever Frances Hynd had said, they still had no proof that David Cairns had come to harm, other than by his own hand. And Lomax knew that. It was time to fire his next salvo. 'But that's not my main reason for calling round to see you. It's about the assault on you the other day.' He smiled at Lomax, and glanced at the antique clock on the mantelpiece: his five minutes would soon be up, so he'd better be quick. 'You'll be pleased to know that someone has confessed to assaulting you. It would appear he recognised you.' He was getting a reaction now. A hand went up to the bruise on his face. He subconsciously stroked it, before flinching.

'I've already made it clear that I—'

'Yes, I heard you. But you may no longer have any say in the matter. Your attacker recognised you from over thirty years ago, when you ran an amusement arcade in Soho on behalf of Alfie Kane. The West End Arcade. Does that ring a bell?'

Lomax stared at Denning. Beneath the purple bruising, his face was turning red. 'Your time's up now, Denning. I want you to leave. You have no authority to be here.

Unless you want to arrest me for fraud, or impersonating a dead academic, I suggest you get the fuck out of this house.'

'I can certainly do that, if that's the route you want to go down. Although I'm guessing you would prefer it if we didn't look too closely at Dr Cairns's disappearance, as you never know what we might uncover. However, I'd rather talk to you about the West End Arcade in Soho. Just in case the assault has damaged your memory, let me remind you – this was where teenage boys were picked up and offered to predatory older men, who then physically and sexually abused them. Technically, that doesn't make you a paedophile. An enabler, perhaps, But I doubt whoever you end up sharing a prison cell with will worry too much about the distinction.'

'You're talking crap,' Lomax said.

'We both know I'm not. I have it on very good authority. The man who attacked you is willing to testify. This will go to court and everything will come out.'

Molly had called shortly before he'd left the office, confirming what Denning had already suspected. Her phone call had been very detailed. Colin Meek was willing to cooperate, though Molly couldn't guarantee how well he'd hold up in court. But it didn't matter. Lomax would be willing to talk. Denning suspected he was the sort who would say anything if it meant keeping his own backside out of the fire.

'Let's cut to the chase here, Lomax, because clearly neither of us is in the mood to waste each other's time. I'm not interested in you. I want Kane. He owned the arcade, and I'm willing to bet he knew what was going on. Am I right?'

Lomax sat down on one of the other dusty armchairs. He rubbed a hand over his face, seemingly impervious to any physical pain this time. He let out a deep sigh. 'Of course Kane knew. There was nothing much he didn't know. I had no idea what was going on: I swear to you. It was only afterwards I found out what the score was. By then it was too late.' He was still pawing his bruised face, then gave a slight shake of the head. 'Kane sold the place in the early nineties, after the police began sniffing round.'

'But Kane knew what was going on? He knew what the place was really being used for?'

Lomax nodded. 'He owned a couple of knocking shops in and around Soho. He saw the arcade as an extension of that. He knew about it. I'm not saying he was a party to it, but he knew it went on. But I promise you, I had nothing to do with it. If I'd known what was happening to those lads, I would never have agreed to run the place for him.'

Denning knew he was lying. Colin Meek had clearly stated Lomax was well aware of what had gone on, but if that was how he wanted to play it, then Denning was happy to humour him in return for being told what he needed to know. He wanted Kane, and if that meant having to put up with Lomax's bullshit, then Denning was happy to play the long game.

'Why was Kane able to get away with it for so long? The local police must have been known the score?'

'Why do you think?'

'Kane had police protection?'

'He called it his tame pig. We never had a name. But Kane had someone on the inside who would tip him off if any flack was about to fly his way. It started off with the local plod just turning a convenient blind eye to whatever was going on in and around Soho. Then it seemed to escalate. As Alfie got more ambitious, he asked for more and more favours.'

But just how far had Kane pushed it? 'Did one of those favours include keeping his name out of Security Direct?'

'I suppose so. I was never around for that. I stopped working for him as soon as I knew what was going down at the arcade. Kane said nobody left his employ without his say-so. I was scared. Then David topped himself and I saw an obvious way out. I knew as long as I kept my head down, I'd get away with it. And I did, until that bloke attacked me the other day.'

'Could that officer have been Buckfield?'

Lomax shrugged. 'I honestly don't know. We never got a name.'

Denning was thinking on his feet. If the police insider had been Buckfield, and Buckfield's conscience had got the better of him, urging him to share what he knew with a journalist, things would have looked bad for Kane at the worst possible time. Just as he was about to launch himself as a generous philanthropist, Magda Kilbride's story would have exploded and destroyed his credibility faster than he could blink. That would be reason enough to want both Buckfield and Magda dead. But he still needed hard proof.

'I need you to make a formal statement. You knew Kane back in the day, before he decided to reinvent himself as Lord Bountiful, saviour of the dispossessed. You can confirm he knew what the arcade was being used for, and that he had links to a serving police officer. It'll be enough to bring him down.'

But Lomax didn't look convinced. 'Are you mad? I'd be lucky to last a week. Kane knows people. Don't be fooled by the respectable businessman image – Kane is still the ruthless operator he always was.'

Denning had never doubted that for a second, but it was reassuring to have it confirmed by someone else. 'We can arrange witness protection for you. A new identity – that shouldn't be too much of a stretch for you. You've already been living a lie for the past two decades.' He sat forward on the chair, placing his hands in his lap. 'This is your best bet at getting out of the mess you've got yourself in. When this goes to court, it's all going to come out – David Cairns, the West End Arcade, the lot. Your life won't be worth living. How long do you think you can go on squatting here for?' He waved a hand around the musty living room. 'David Cairns has family – they'll challenge whatever rights you think you have to stay in this house. Kane will more than likely come after you now he knows you're still alive. You're fraudulently claiming Cairns's pension, and probably more besides.' He paused, to let it sink in. 'I could go on.' But he didn't need to. He could tell from the look on Lomax's face that the message was hitting home. 'You haven't really got a choice in this, have you, Gordon? Nothing would change for you. You'd just go on living someone else's life somewhere else, but with the security of knowing no one can come after you.' He sat back on the chair. 'Or you can stay here, living a lie and looking over your shoulder every day, knowing it's only going to be a matter of time before there's a knock on the door and you find someone standing there you really don't want to see.'

Lomax was staring at the carpet, holding his head in his hands. Eventually he looked up at Denning. 'OK. What do you need me to do?'

Chapter Forty-Three

It wasn't quite a typical 'roses-round-the-door' country cottage, but it was pretty, in a quaint, rural village kind of a way. Built of mellow brick, it sat back from the main street, surrounded by a colourful garden. At some point in its history, the original windows had been replaced with aluminium double glazing, which slightly spoiled its charm.

Robin Sims had long since retired from politics and now lived in a village in rural Sussex, not far from Robertsbridge. He was on the electoral register, so his address hadn't been difficult to find.

Sims wasn't particularly pleased to see Molly and Jon when they knocked on his front door that Sunday afternoon. Jon had phoned ahead saying he wanted to interview Sims in order to get his side of the story from thirty years ago – insisting he felt Sims hadn't received a fair hearing at the time. He mentioned *The London Echo*, though had been deliberately vague about whether he still worked for it. Sims had reluctantly agreed to be interviewed, but the look on his face suggested he might now be having second thoughts.

'Like I told you when you phoned, I'm not keen to talk to the press. You stitched me up once before and I don't doubt you'd do the same again if I gave you the opportunity.'

'Mr Sims, this is not a stitch-up,' Jon said. 'I'd just like to get your take on the events of thirty years ago, and give you an opportunity to give your side of what happened.'

'I suppose you'd better come in, seeing as you've travelled all the way from London.'

He led them through the tiny cottage and into a pretty garden at the rear of the house. There was an expansive view of the Sussex countryside beyond the hedge which surrounded the property. An elderly-looking Jack Russell hobbled over to greet them.

Sims gestured towards a wrought-iron table and chairs that sat on a small patio. 'Take a seat. Would you like tea or coffee?'

They sat at the table, both declining the offer of a hot beverage. Sims joined them at the table.

Sims looked well preserved for seventy-nine; slim, with a glistening dome of a forehead, and sharp eyes that danced between Molly and Jon. He had a slightly croaky voice, that made Molly think of an old oak door swaying on rusty hinges.

The decrepit dog hopped up onto the patio, and wandered towards Jon, who reached down to rub its head.

'Don't mind Cerberus,' Sims said. 'He'll fall asleep again in a minute. He's half-blind, and partially deaf, but he's got a healthy curiosity about him.' Sims blinked at his two visitors. 'Which paper did you say you were with again?' He addressed the question at Jon, but was looking at Molly when he asked it. Jon had introduced her by name when Sims had answered the door, but had deliberately not said what she did for a living. It might be easier if Sims assumed she was a fellow journalist, at least for the time being. She was happy to let Jon lead on this; keeping quiet until she felt it was appropriate to speak.

'I used to work for *The London Echo*, but I'm freelance now.'

'Yes,' Sims said, still looking at Molly. 'I phoned them yesterday after you got in touch, and they told me that you no longer worked for them. But the paper gave me a reasonably fair hearing thirty years ago, and Barry Tasker was always an honest and decent editor, so I'm willing to give you the benefit of the doubt until you give me reason to think otherwise.'

'The accusations against you, Mr Sims,' Jon began. 'Was there any truth in them?'

Sims stopped looking at Molly and turned his attention back to Jon. 'Why do you ask that?'

'You never sued for libel. That would have been my first reaction. You wouldn't have been the first politician to take a paper to court and win.'

'And not the first one to lose either,' Sims said. 'Besides, it would have meant having my personal life dragged before a judge and jury. I'm a very private man, Mr Kavanagh. I would have found that extremely painful. And in return for what? A few thousand pounds from a newspaper? The damage would have been done.'

'But there's always the worry that people would believe you were guilty of what the papers accused you of. The stain on your character – the whispering. You would have had the opportunity to stand up in a court of law and challenge all that.'

Sims traced the ornate pattern on top of the table with his finger. The dog was lying underneath, snoring loudly and oblivious to what was going on. 'At the end of the day, what was so awful about the accusation? I know, a different era; less tolerant than today's more permissive attitude towards sexual indiscretions, but even so...' He let the rest of the sentence trail off.

'Are you saying there was some truth in the story?' Jon asked.

'I'm saying that with the passage of time, I've had the opportunity to think about my life.' There was a very slight tremor in his voice when he spoke. 'The newspaper article focussed on the more prurient aspects of my private life, and... my personal proclivities. They made me out to be some sort of pervert. Yes, I'm fully aware that the age of consent between men was twenty-one, and the man I was involved with was below that age. Technically, that makes me a pervert in the eyes of many, and perhaps I was. But if I'd been having a relationship with a young woman of the same age, in the eyes of the law at least, I wouldn't have been doing anything wrong.'

'I'm not here to stand in moral judgement on you,' Jon said. 'The lad's age was largely immaterial. You belonged to a government that had preached about personal morality. Many people saw that as hypocrisy.'

'Perhaps,' he said. 'But I ended up paying a high price for that hypocrisy. That newspaper story cost me my political career. Not to mention the damage to my name and reputation.'

It was difficult not to feel sorry for him. Molly couldn't help thinking about all the politicians who got away with far worse than an indiscreet liaison with an underage rent boy. But Sims had known what he was doing. It was no use him playing the victim all these years later. From underneath the metal table, the dog made a noise halfway between a bark and a whimper. When she glanced down, it looked like it had made the noise in its sleep.

'Did you know a boy called Colin Meek?' Molly asked. She was aware of Jon shooting her daggers, but she'd kept quiet for long enough. She had no interest in raking up an ancient newspaper story that Sims had as good as admitted was mostly based on truth. They needed information. 'This would have been around the same time.'

Sims looked at Molly and shook his head. She sensed that he resented her presence there. Sims was of a generation where women took their cue from men, and in his eyes, she was there as the support act to Jon's leading role. 'I'm sorry, I don't recognise the name.'

She suspected he was lying. 'He was one of a number of teenage boys who were regularly abused by a group of older men.' She paused, feeling slightly guilty at her directness, but knowing they didn't have time to waste on empty pleasantries. 'He claims you were one of them.'

She was still aware of Jon looking at her. There would be harsh words and icy silences on the car journey back to London, but this was part of a criminal investigation, and he was along for the ride in his capacity as a civilian. She *could* make it official if she had to.

Sims was looking at Jon now, either hoping for a more sympathetic approach, or wondering why some woman had suddenly taken the line of questioning in a totally different direction. 'There were a lot of false allegations made about me in the aftermath of that story. A lot of people making money by running to the newspapers claiming they'd had sexual encounters with me. Some of the less prurient stories even managed to make it into print.'

'That doesn't answer my question, Mr Sims.'

He slowly turned from Jon and looked over at Molly. 'I'm sorry, I forgot to ask which newspaper you're with. Or are you another freelancer?'

'I'm with the Metropolitan Police,' she said, feeling honesty was the best way forward. 'We're investigating a historic case of child abuse that may be connected to an ongoing murder investigation.'

If he was shocked, he didn't let it show. 'Oh. I see.' He shook his head, and looked down at the dog, who had suddenly scrambled onto its legs and was looking up at him, trying its best to wag its tail. 'I was never involved with that. I knew about it. And by that, I mean I'd heard rumours. But that sort of thing never appealed to me. It's all just a bit…' He searched for the word. 'Wrong.'

Molly wasn't sure if she believed him. Colin had insisted Sims had been present on at least a few occasions. But it was possible Colin had misremembered; maybe he'd seen Sims in the papers or on the telly and put two and two together to reach five.

Then again, it was just as possible Sims was lying.

'But you knew about the abuse?' Molly asked. 'And you knew who was involved?'

Sims was making a fuss of the dog, scratching it behind the ears. The dog made a whimpering noise, but it seemed to be borne of pleasure rather than discomfort.

'This is what you really want to know about, isn't it? You're not interested in what happened to me. You want to dig all this up again. I'm afraid you're wasting your time. I know nothing about those rumours, and I don't know who was involved. Just like I told the other journalist.'

'Other journalist?' Jon leant his elbows on the metal table. 'What other journalist?'

'Some woman. Magda something or other. I approached her to ask if she could help me write my memoirs. She said on her website that she helped to write and research biographies. She seemed very enthusiastic at first, but then she started going on about what she called "a high-profile paedophile gang" that my name had been linked to. I told her it was all nonsense, but she kept going on and on about it. Claiming she'd uncovered evidence I'd been part of it at the time this newspaper story broke. The more I denied it, the more she went on about it. It quickly became obvious she wanted to stitch me up, so I paid her for the work she'd already done and asked her not to come back. She kept contacting me for a while, asking me questions. It was only when I said I'd contact my solicitor that she finally left me alone. I didn't hear from her after that.'

'When was this?' Jon asked.

'About six months ago. Maybe a little longer.'

So, he was the one who had approached Mags, setting up the whole chain of events that had resulted in two deaths, including very likely Mags's own death. Molly had to appreciate the cruel irony of it. Sims probably thought he could control Mags; make sure she kept to his side of the story. He'd clearly picked the wrong person if that had been his plan.

'You were writing your memoirs?' Molly asked.

'I wanted the truth to come out, before I was too old to tell it.'

'And what exactly is the truth?' Molly asked. 'There was a young lad, we think his name might have been Tommy. Something happened to him. It's possible he was murdered.'

He looked at them; his face fell. 'I know nothing about that. I admit, I was aware of what was going on. A fellow politician – he's dead now, so I'm not going to say who he was – he used to attend these parties. He asked me to go along once. He promised me it was all very discreet. They were protected by some very powerful men. He didn't name them, but he said they would ensure nothing ever came out.'

'So even though you were a politician – a man in a position of power and able to help people – you decided to keep quiet about serial child abuse?' Molly was trying not to raise her voice. Sims was old and this had happened years ago. But that didn't excuse any of it. 'You could have stopped it.'

The dog was looking up at her, its watery eyes blinking in confusion at the sound of a raised voice. Sims sat there in silence, knowing there was nothing he could say. It was Jon who spoke. 'Mr Sims, you have to tell us what you know. It isn't too late to do the right thing.' He leant his elbows on the table again, looking directly at Sims. 'You said you wanted the truth to come out. Well, this is your chance.'

The dog was doing its bark/whimper thing again. Sims shooed it away with his hand. 'What could I do? I was one man. And a junior minister. I didn't have any political clout. If I'd made this public, I'd have been destroyed. These kinds of things went on all the time back then. As I said to you – it was a different era.'

But Molly still wasn't buying it. He had covered up a crime, which was a crime itself. If Jon hadn't been there, she might have arrested Sims. She still might, as she was sure he was holding back the truth from them.

'But you do know the names of some of the men involved in the gang?' Molly asked, refusing to let him off the hook entirely. 'There was a judge. The boys called him "Judge Dredd", like the comic book character.'

'Most of the men involved will be dead now. Or very old. Too old to face justice for what they did.'

'Mr Sims, Magda Kilbride is dead – she's been murdered. It's possible that whoever did it could be targeting anyone involved in the original cover-up.' She looked at him. 'For your own safety, I'd advise you to tell us what you know. You could still help to get justice for these boys. Boys who are damaged men now.'

'I only met him once. The judge. He was introduced to me by a mutual acquaintance.'

'What was his name?' Molly demanded.

The dog had returned and somehow managed to clamber onto Sims's lap, where Sims patted it affection- ately. 'I don't want it to get out that it was me that told you. The man in question is still alive. There may be repercussions from his family.'

'Mr Sims, if we believe you have information about a crime and refuse to assist us with our questions, I can have you arrested and formally questioned in a police station. In which case, I couldn't guarantee the press not finding out and the whole sorry tale becoming public knowledge. If you think things were bad for you thirty years ago, they will be a lot worse this time. Are you really willing to go down that route?'

Sims played with the dog for a while, stroking its neck and rubbing its muzzle while the dog made happy sighing noises. Sims was clearly chewing things over in his head, weighing up his options before realising he probably didn't have any.

'Boswell,' he said eventually. 'The judge's name was Grayson Boswell.'

Finally Molly felt they were getting somewhere.

Chapter Forty-Four

The atmosphere in the room was electric, like a thunderstorm was about to burst from the sky. Kane sat opposite Denning and McKenna, his solicitor on his left. McKenna clearly wasn't happy. And neither was Kane, though he was doing a first-rate job of pretending otherwise. The only person who didn't seem bothered by it all was Kane's solicitor.

'These are very tenuous reasons for asking my client to come down here today,' she said, eyes darting between Denning and McKenna. 'Luckily for you, he is more than happy to help the police in any way he can.' She paused and looked directly at Denning. 'However, your grounds for bringing him in are highly questionable, and we will be raising the matter with your superiors.'

The last comment was directed at both of them, though the solicitor had now turned her gaze towards McKenna. McKenna was twiddling a pen between her fingers and saying very little. This was never a good sign.

'Mr Kane doesn't deny having once owned the West End Arcade,' the solicitor continued, 'nor having employed Gordon Lomax to run it. But he insists he had no knowledge of what went on there, and you have no evidence to prove he did. Additionally, he denies ever knowing former DCI Frank Buckfield, and certainly played no part in his murder, nor that of Magda Kilbride, whom he had also never met.'

'We have evidence that links you to Buckfield,' Denning insisted. He pointed to a photocopy of Gordon Lomax's statement.

'A pack of lies written by Gordon Lomax, who – as I have already made clear to you – my client had cause to dismiss from his employ for theft. I would suggest that Mr Lomax has some kind of axe to grind and has been presented with an opportunity to do precisely that.' The solicitor sat with her arms on the table. Kane looked cool under pressure; too cool. There was something about his demeanour that told Denning he knew he was going to get away with this, and Denning began to feel that maybe he had a point.

Denning could sense McKenna wanting to bring the interview to a close. There was an iciness emanating from her that lowered the temperature in the room. She wouldn't give him eye contact.

They had the written statement by Lomax, which Denning had initially thought was dynamite, but McKenna had wanted Lomax to be formally interviewed before they hauled Kane in to confront him with Lomax's accusations. 'He'll be well prepared,' she'd argued. 'We need to make damn sure we are too.'

He'd thought they had been. He was certain they had enough to nail Kane, and at least make him sweat. Now, however, he'd allowed doubts to creep in and rock that certainty.

'We know you had dealings with DCI Buckfield,' Denning said. 'We have good reason to believe that you were bribing him to provide you with information about any police operations that may impact on your business interests. We also believe former DCI Buckfield was about to reveal all this – and more besides – placing you in a very difficult position. This gives you a strong motive for his murder.'

Denning had wanted more. CCTV from outside Buckfield's flat had so far failed to show anything, and the post-mortem report on Magda Kilbride had failed to show up anything significant, either: no DNA had been found on the masking tape, and the only wound was the one to her throat. Her phone still hadn't been found.

Kane had willingly surrendered his phone, saying he was happy for them to check his calls and texts, but Denning didn't honestly believe they'd find anything incriminating on it.

'And you don't deny owning the arcade where Gordon Lomax procured teenage boys,' Denning continued. 'That links you to the story Magda Kilbride was working on.'

Kane smiled. He slipped a sly wink in the direction of his solicitor. It was brief enough to be almost imperceptible, but Denning had noticed it out of the corner of his eye. 'I certainly owned the arcade,' Kane said, fixing Denning with his smile. 'Gordon ran it for me, and for the most part did a good job – until I found him with his hand in the till. However, I was totally in the dark as to what went on there. Gordon was paid to run the place. I acquired the property as part of a portfolio of properties from a former employer who needed to raise capital quickly. It was in a good location and a profitable business, but my ambitions took me in a different direction. If I'd known it was used for something like that…' He screwed his face up in an exaggerated display of disgust. 'Well, I would have had it closed down immediately.' Kane sat back on his chair. He was dressed in a dark brown leather jacket, with a Kenzo black woollen pullover underneath. The scent of his designer aftershave lingered in the airless room. 'I really would like to help you all I can, but I'm afraid there's nothing more I can tell you.'

He was good. Denning couldn't deny Kane knew how to handle himself under pressure. But he'd had practice. It was becoming obvious they weren't going to make progress and Denning was aware of the clock ticking and McKenna's patience wearing thin. They could only hold Kane for twenty-four hours. His lawyer was smart; she'd know how to play the system. And then there was McKenna. Somewhere in the back of his mind was a gnawing doubt that he'd called this one wrong. The evidence against Kane was circumstantial at best, and entirely dependent on Lomax's written statement. He'd left a message for Lomax to get in touch, but there had been no reply. They were clutching at straws, and both Kane and his smart solicitor knew it.

Denning could feel a crick developing in his neck. He was about to request a break, to give him a chance to stretch his limbs and let him and McKenna plan a last-ditch plan of attack, when there was a knock at the door. McKenna paused the tape as a member of the MIT support staff stuck their head round the door and handed McKenna a sheet of paper with something written on it. She quickly scanned the paper, then flicked a withering look at Denning. He'd tried to read what was on the paper, but she'd been too quick for him.

'OK, Mr Kane, you can go.' McKenna's voice was unsmiling.

The solicitor offered a curt nod of thanks in her direction.

'Thank you,' Kane said, smiling at McKenna. 'If you think I can be of any further help, please don't hesitate to contact my solicitor.'

As they stood up, his solicitor said, 'I'm afraid we will be lodging an official complaint with DCS Harrison, as well as the deputy commissioner.' With that, she led her client out of the interview room and into the corridor.

McKenna turned to face Denning as soon as they'd left the room. 'Well, I'd call that a monumental fuck-up. What would you call it?'

'Why did you terminate the interview?'

She handed Denning the piece of paper. He read it, then scrunched it up into a tight ball.

Lomax had withdrawn his statement. What little they had on Kane had just melted away to nothing, like snow on a red-hot griddle.

'He's guilty,' Denning said. 'Of something.'

'Oh I don't doubt he's probably parked his Mercedes on a double yellow on the street outside, or nicked a bag of Jelly Babies from Woolies when he was kid, but I think we can safely assume that what he didn't do was murder Frank Buckfield and Magda Kilbride.'

Denning wanted to argue; fight his corner and defend his decision to bring Kane in, which he still believed he'd been justified in doing, but there was no point. McKenna had clearly made her mind up. His first thought was to go straight round to see Gordon Lomax and throw the book him, but what would that achieve?

As they left the interview room, McKenna said: 'I have a feeling in the pit of my spleen, that we haven't heard the last of this.'

Predictably, she wasn't wrong. Within an hour of returning to the MIT office, there was a phone call from Harrison to join him in his office immediately.

'I've just had Kane's solicitor on the phone.' He was standing by the window. There was no suggestion of anyone sitting down. 'What the hell's going on? You were told not to go after Kane, and yet you did.' He was looking at McKenna when he spoke, refusing to look at Denning. 'Do you realise how this makes us look?'

'We had evidence that suggested Kane may have been involved in the murders of Frank Buckfield and Magda Kilbride,' McKenna said. 'We had to act on that.'

'Yet your "evidence" turned out to be nothing more substantial than a half-baked confession from a known criminal? That's not how this works, Liz, and you know that. How long have you been a senior officer?'

Although Harrison's ire was being directed at her, McKenna remained calm. Despite her faults, she would cover Denning's back for as long as he let her. But he wasn't afraid to fight his own battles. This was his fuck-up, and he was fully prepared to own it. 'It was my decision, sir. I persuaded DCI McKenna to back me. I take full responsibility.'

Out of the corner of his eye, he could see McKenna shaking her head, but he ignored her. He told Harrison about his suspicions concerning Kane, especially in light of what Lomax had told him. 'I feel we were justified in bringing Kane in for questioning.'

'Up until your star witness got cold feet. Even if Lomax hadn't withdrawn his statement, you can't go after someone like Alfie Kane without strong grounds.' He nodded at McKenna. 'I'll leave you to sort this mess out, Liz. I've made my feelings clear.'

The meeting was over.

As soon as they left his office, Denning turned to McKenna. 'I appreciate I've put you in a difficult position.'

'That has to be the understatement of the decade, Matt. You've really fucked this up.'

He wanted to fight back, but he didn't have the strength to argue. This was an exercise in damage limitation, and he was the damage that had to be limited.

'If that's how you feel, then I think you're making a mistake.'

'Do you? Well, thanks for sharing that with me.' They'd reached the lifts at the end of the corridor. McKenna jabbed the button with her thumb. 'You were told to leave Lomax alone, but you chose to ignore that order. You now appear to be pursuing what looks like a personal vendetta against Alfie Kane, for reasons known to only yourself.' She paused, sighed and shook her head. 'Look, I'm very sorry, Matt, but I'm going to appoint Neeraj as SIO on the Buckfield and Kilbride investigations.'

She looked at him just as the lift doors opened. 'You should be grateful we're already an officer down, otherwise I would be suspending you.'

Chapter Forty-Five

Denning finished work early. There had been no point hanging around the office and making his humiliation complete. His team would have received the news by now and would be raking over its significance, trying to unpick the finer details. McKenna would have given them the bare bones, leaving their imaginations and idle gossip to flesh out the rest. He'd been with that particular MIT for less than a year and it had taken him that long to be accepted as part of the team, let alone to earn their respect as its leader; and now all that work was potentially compromised. First Molly is suspended, then he's demoted. The team would certainly have enough to talk about.

Neeraj would have taken over as SIO by now. In all fairness, he deserved a break. He had been chasing promotion for some time, and had recently been turned down for a couple of inspector jobs, lack of experience being cited as the reason. Neeraj was a good detective, despite sometimes forgetting the subtleties that went with the job. But if Denning was being honest, he resented the fact Neeraj was getting his break at his expense.

He was in a quiet pub on the South Bank, not far from the former industrial monolith that was the Tate Modern, drinking a bottle of Italian lager and glancing at his watch every few seconds. He felt like he was on a date, nervous about being stood up. But he needn't have been: he looked up to see Morrow striding towards him, carrying a glass and a bottle of mineral water. Morrow sat down at Denning's table. 'Matt, how's things? Thought any more about joining me on the squash court sometime?'

Denning struggled to find a smile. 'Yeah. I'd be up for that. It's been a while since I've played, though.' Rugby had been his game, though he hadn't played it since school, when he'd been in the First XV.

Morrow opened the bottle of sparkling mineral water, and poured it into the glass.

The pub's clientele mostly consisted of professionals from nearby offices making the most of a leisurely lunch break. There was a menu on the table, but Denning's appetite had deserted him.

'Emma tells me Sarah's suggested we do dinner again.' Morrow sat back in his chair and sipped his drink. 'We've got quite a bit on at the moment, but next month sometime would be good.'

Denning nodded. He hadn't asked Morrow to meet him because he wanted to spend the afternoon making small talk. But equally he couldn't exactly just come out with it. He wanted to ask a favour, and that would take careful handling.

'Thanks for agreeing to meet me. Sorry to drag you away from whatever it was you were in the middle of.'

Morrow smiled and shrugged. 'Nothing that can't wait. You said you wanted to chat.'

'I'd appreciate it if we could keep things off the record.'

Morrow nodded. 'Of course.'

'Well, it's a bit awkward. I don't like going behind people's backs, but I have to talk to someone, and you seemed the obvious choice.'

'Shoot.'

'I have concerns about DCS Harrison.'

Morrow took another sip of his drink then cocked his head to one side. 'In what way?'

'I suspect he has links to Alfie Kane. Kane's a former criminal who may have been involved in an armed robbery. I'm not suggesting Kane is in any way abusing this relationship, but I think this is something he should have disclosed before being appointed to the post of DCS. And I don't trust him.'

There was a pause while Morrow digested this. 'And none of this has anything to do with your recent run-in with him, Matt?' He offered Denning another smile, although this one failed to reach his eyes. 'I've just had a lengthy phone call with Ian and he mentioned the situation. This wasn't in connection with you, incidentally, and he didn't go into any details. I don't know the ins and outs of it, and I don't want to. It's none of my business. But I'm sorry to hear you've got a problem with Ian. I can only once again reassure you that he's a good officer. I know he's got lots of ideas, and that can be unsettling for any organisation that's, well, set in its ways I suppose.' He placed his glass on the table and looked at Denning. 'From what I hear he's doing a good job.'

'I'm not denying that.' Denning was trying not to sound defensive. 'I just have concerns about him. How much do you know about his background?'

'I didn't appoint Ian. I admit I recommended him, and I have always enjoyed a good working relationship with him. I can't speak for this Alfie Kane character, but

I can tell you Ian is very sociable. He likes to get to know people. Perhaps you're reading too much into his relationship with this Kane.'

'Perhaps.' Denning wasn't sure where the conversation was heading. 'But there's something about him I just don't trust.'

'I'm not sure how I can help.'

'To be honest, Justin, I'm not sure myself. I think I wanted to sound you out. It's no secret DCS Harrison and I haven't hit it off. I'm sorry if that places you in an awkward position.'

Morrow seemed to chew over this for a moment. 'No awkwardness on my part, Matt. I respect you as a police officer and as a friend. I also respect your opinion. However, you have to know I can't be seen to be taking sides here.'

'I'm not expecting you to take sides.' He rubbed a hand over his head.

'Maybe I could have a word with Ian, though, as I say, I wouldn't want to be seen to be interfering in a murder inquiry. To be honest with you, Matt, I'd like to help, but I'd really rather not get involved.'

Denning knew he was fighting a losing battle. He was placing Morrow in a difficult situation, and placing a strain on their burgeoning friendship. 'Look, forget I said anything. I've just had a bad day.' He took another sip of lager. 'That game of squash – let's find a time when we're both free and make a date.'

—

Molly was sitting in the living room, enjoying a glass of Pinot Grigio. Jon was in his shed, either writing or pottering. She didn't really care; she was appreciating some time to herself.

They were still digesting what Sims had told them.

According to what they'd discovered from an internet search, Grayson Boswell had retired from the judiciary ten years ago. He'd had a fairly unremarkable career, mostly focussing on family law and child welfare cases, though he had covered his share of criminal cases over the years. However, his entire career had been without controversy, and he was well respected by his colleagues. He was widowed, and had two children, though there was little information about either of them. No address was given, and he didn't appear to be listed on any electoral register anywhere. Probably sensible for a former judge.

There was nothing to suggest he'd ever been involved in any kind of organised child abuse. But then, it was hardly something he was going to advertise.

Jon had left a message with Barry to see if he could come up with anything on Boswell, while Molly had remotely logged onto the PNC and searched his name, but nothing had come up. Not even a parking fine.

There was always a chance Sims had been lying; trying to save his own neck by throwing them a random name that would take the heat off him. Neither she nor Jon had fully bought his assertion that he had never been involved with the group itself, though even if he had, it was unlikely he had ever been a key player. But she could tell he'd been holding stuff back from them. Perhaps Mags had managed to get the truth out of him, and that was why he was now so guarded?

The thought of Mags made her think about Jon.

She knew he'd tried to contact Rowan, which had meant speaking to his ex-wife. She had given him short shrift, making it clear he wasn't welcome and asking him to stay away from the wedding for Rowan's sake. It was likely that whatever else he was doing in the shed right now, part of it involved licking his wounds.

Ever since their meeting with Barry, Jon had been more subdued than usual, bottling things up and telling her he was fine, when he clearly wasn't.

She always felt like she was treading on eggshells when it came to Jon's former wives and their families. She'd always known that becoming involved with a man twelve years her senior meant there would be the inevitable baggage, but there were times it felt like Jon had more than most. Mostly it wasn't a problem, except when it was – like now.

If anything, Colin's story had served as a welcome distraction: something for Jon to throw himself into. A reminder of his life as a journalist. On the drive back from Sims's house, he'd been fired up with enthusiasm to see this story through to its conclusion.

But what was that conclusion? Even if they could track down Grayson Boswell, he would be a very old man now. And their chances of locating any of the other men involved were slim. If Sims was unwilling to give up any names, then there was little chance of Boswell doing so. Jon was still convinced Barry would unearth something from the *Echo*'s archive, or from his few surviving contacts from the good old days, but Molly couldn't bring herself to share his optimism. It was thirty years ago, and there had been little more than rumours to work with even then.

She was startled by a muffled trilling sound, and realised her phone had slipped under a cushion on the sofa. She just managed to dig it out and answer it before it stopped ringing. The number on the screen wasn't one she recognised.

'Hello, Molly Fisher?'

The voice on the other end sounded slightly agitated but with a professional calm, as though it belonged to someone used to dealing with crises. 'This is St Thomas' Hospital here.'

Molly could feel her heartbeat quicken.

'We've got a man here who's in a bad way. We found your name when we looked on his phone. We weren't sure who else to call.' There was a pause from the other end, but Molly was already guessing where the phone call was heading. 'We believe his name's Colin.' There was another pause. 'He's tried to kill himself.'

Chapter Forty-Six

Denning returned home in a heavy mood. He couldn't face telling Sarah about the situation at work. He was still struggling to get his head round it himself. Besides, it wasn't fair to burden her with his problems.

He was watching TV in the living room when she came home.

'You're back early,' she said, dropping her keys into the ceramic bowl on the table by the front door. 'Run out of murders to solve?'

He offered a feeble laugh. He couldn't believe he'd wasted so much of the afternoon. At least he'd made something for dinner, even if it was only a pasta dish.

Sarah perched on the arm of the sofa, and muted the TV with the remote. 'Is everything OK? You seem a bit subdued.'

'I'm fine.' He smiled for her. 'Busy day, that's all.'

She got up from the sofa, then disappeared into the kitchen area and started fiddling with the coffee machine. 'I had another phone call from Emma today,' she shouted through.

He wasn't in the mood to talk about the Morrows. He was already regretting his hasty promise to join Justin on the squash court.

'What did she want?'

The coffee machine started grinding itself into life.

'She's asked me to join her women's networking group. I said I'd think about it and let her know. It might be useful – she knows a lot of people.'

'Why not. I'm sure I'd join a men's networking group if such a thing existed.'

'It does. It's called patriarchy. And it's been serving you well for centuries.'

There was no counter to that.

Sarah reappeared a few minutes later carrying two cups of coffee. She handed one to Denning, then sat on the sofa opposite and drank hers. 'I like Emma,' Sarah said. 'In a way, I kind of envy her.'

'Envy her? How?'

'Well, maybe not envy exactly. She just comes across as so confident and together. The sort of person who never gets fazed by anything. Then there's her and Justin. And she and Justin are quite the power couple. Talk about life in the fast lane. You really feels he's going places.' Sarah sipped her coffee. 'And yet they're such down-to-earth people. Very likeable, don't you think?'

Denning shrugged, Justin's words from earlier were still buzzing round his brain – *I'd like to help, but I'd really rather not get involved.* He didn't blame Morrow. Denning had placed him in a difficult situation, testing their embryonic friendship with an impossible request. But still, he could have at least pretended to be more sympathetic. And then there was his relationship with Harrison. What was the deal there?

Denning and Morrow. Morrow and Harrison. Harrison and Kane… Everyone seemed to be connected somehow, like that absurd six-degrees of Kevin Bacon nonsense. Did Morrow know Alfie Kane? He hadn't recognised the name when Denning had mentioned it earlier. But that didn't mean anything.

'Emma and Justin?' he said. 'They seem alright. I can see why he went for someone like Emma: she's got drive, ambition. They're a good match.'

'Did you get the impression the other night that she's the driving force in their relationship? I suspect she's the one who persuaded him to go into politics in the first place.'

Denning sipped his coffee. Sarah made it stronger than he liked. He'd always meant to politely point it out one day, but the opportunity had never arisen and it was easier just to accept it. Perhaps that was his problem: he was always too willing just to accept things rather than challenge them head-on.

'I'm not so sure,' he said. 'Justin seems quite driven himself. But I don't suppose it will hurt his career having a dynamic wife beside him.'

'It hasn't done your career any harm.'

He offered another weak laugh. The coffee was so strong he could feel his head begin to throb. Or maybe he was tired. If he was, the coffee would see to that.

'I had such a lovely time the other night,' Sarah said. 'It's good to socialise. We never seem to do it these days, unless it's work-related. I told Emma we should all go out somewhere again. On us next time.'

'What did she say?'

'She's going to get back to me. Apparently she's got a lot on her plate at the moment. She's going to be starting on a new case soon, and then there's all that stuff with her brother.'

Denning drained his coffee cup. There was a black oily trickle at the bottom, which made him wince. 'Her brother?'

'Weren't you listening the other night? She was telling us that her brother died a few months ago. He had a heart attack – apparently it was very sudden. She's having to sort out his estate. It's taking up a lot of her time. It would appear that her brother was a bit of a hoarder. She's spending every other weekend clearing his house of decades of accumulated junk. Then there's her dad – he's got dementia. It must be tough for her, especially as she was always so close to him. But to look at her, you'd never guess anything was wrong. She just takes it all in her stride.'

'Maybe not such an enviable life after all,' Denning suggested.

She playfully screwed her face up and shook her head at him. 'On the subject of families, have you phoned Claire to find out what the arrangements are for Jake?'

He was trying not to think about it. Claire was still talking about her and Jake moving to Devon to be closer to her mother, who was recovering from a stroke. There were times he felt like his life was spinning out of control, like a meteorite hurtling towards the Earth at a million miles a second.

'I'll call her later. It'll be dinner time soon. Jake doesn't like having his routine upset.' The truth was, he didn't want to phone Claire. He couldn't face another fight, not so soon after his run-in with Harrison.

Sarah sighed. She was still sipping her coffee, though it must have been getting cold by now. 'Jake moving to Devon might be for the best.'

'How did you reach that conclusion?'

'He'll have a better quality of life, for a start. And you'll still get to see him. Probably just as much as you do now.' She drained the rest of the coffee and placed the mug on the table between the sofas. 'He can stay here whenever he likes. Once we move and get a bigger place, he can have his own bedroom. It could work out well all round.'

Sarah took the mugs back to the kitchen. He heard her putting them into the dishwasher, before heading upstairs to get changed out of her work suit.

Denning wasn't sure he shared Sarah's naive belief that everything would work out all right. If Claire moved away and took his son with her, with the hours he worked, he would never see Jake. He didn't want Jake to grow up without a father. He didn't want the same distant, awkward relationship with Jake that Buckfield had had with his son.

Buckfield's son.

There was something he'd remembered. Something he'd meant to chase up at the time but had forgotten about.

Denning searched for his phone, finding it in his jacket pocket. Swiping it to bring it to life, he quickly flicked through his contacts list, hoping he'd saved the number.

Chapter Forty-Seven

It had turned unseasonably chilly the following day. Winter was clinging on for one last gasp before finally giving way to spring. Gavin Buckfield was dressed in a heavy woollen overcoat and grey striped scarf. Denning wore a padded Barbour jacket. The wind was blowing in from the east, and was dragging the temperatures down accordingly.

They were walking by the Regent's Canal, immediately to the north of King's Cross station. Gavin Buckfield worked nearby. The once rundown area had been transformed into an eclectic mix of shops and offices. There was still building work going on around them, reminding Denning that London was a city in a constant state of flux.

'It's easier to talk away from Mum,' Gavin Buckfield said. 'I don't like discussing Dad when she's around. She still likes to pretend he was some great heroic cop, even if the truth was nothing like that. It pains her to face up to the reality of what life was really like married to him, and I don't see the point in making her life now any more uncomfortable than it needs to be.' He stopped by a bridge over the canal. 'I'm not under any such illusions, however. I saw my father for what he was, warts and all. I suppose I loved him, despite everything, even if he was never an easy man to love.'

Denning was grateful Gavin Buckfield had agreed to meet him. He'd sensed when they'd first met in his mother's living room that Gavin had wanted to tell him more. He'd meant to follow it up, though part of him had preferred to wait for Gavin to get in touch. When he hadn't, Denning decided to follow up on his hunch.

'I appreciate the job takes its toll on people, Mr Denning,' Gavin continued, 'and I accept that my father was a flawed human being, but none of that excuses his behaviour.'

They were standing on the bridge looking into the cool dark water below. Denning still wanted to know exactly what Buckfield's behaviour had been. He was convinced that that was the missing piece in this puzzle.

'We've been over your father's old cases with a fine-toothed comb,' he said. 'We were initially convinced that the reason for his murder lay with a former investigation he'd worked on. But we haven't found anything to suggest he was killed by someone he'd helped put away.' He paused. 'My gut feeling is that this has nothing to do with revenge and the answer lies somewhere in your father's personal life. And I think you might have some idea where we should be looking to find it.'

They were on the move again; the Siberian wind was too cold for standing around. Gavin was walking towards an open space with a row of old railway arches at one end and a Victorian warehouse at the other, which had been converted into a bar and restaurant. Despite the chilly weather, there were people out and about, either sitting on benches, or dining alfresco at the various outdoor eateries that were dotted around the place.

'There was a whole other side to my father's life,' Gavin said. 'One he worked hard to keep hidden from his colleagues and his family.'

'This isn't about prying for the sake of it,' Denning said. 'And I know it's uncomfortable to talk about. But there's a real danger the investigation will stall if we don't get a breakthrough soon. And now we have another murder that may be linked to your father's, we're under pressure to make an arrest.'

'My father had been having an affair,' Gavin said. 'In fact, he'd had several, or at least I suspect he had.' They'd stopped again. Gavin Buckfield was staring at some scaffolding that was being dismantled from around a smart new office development. 'That was the real reason my parents split up: my mother discovered he was seeing someone.' Gavin paused, looking Denning in the eye. 'A young man. A teenager. My father was in his late forties at this point, so you can imagine our shock, especially for my mother.'

'He admitted this?'

'My mother had found evidence. I don't want to go into details, but she confronted him. He denied it at first, but then admitted the truth. However, I think that was just the tip of a nasty iceberg. I've often suspected he also used rent boys for a while. He would have known how to get hold of them easily enough. He had spent time with the vice squad and was based in Soho in the early eighties.'

'Do you have proof he used rent boys?'

'No.' He sighed. 'Naturally it wasn't something we spoke about. My mother didn't want to know either. They were already sleeping in separate beds by this time, and virtually living separate lives. Eventually, they agreed an amicable divorce. I mean, I suppose he did love my mother and obviously they had two children, but when your proclivities lie elsewhere, it's hard to maintain the façade.' He looked at Denning. 'I didn't hate him. Not if I'm honest. I felt sorry for him, and in many ways wished I'd made more of an effort to keep in touch with him latterly, especially when it became clear his life had fallen apart. But whatever there had been in our family, it was long gone by the time he died.'

Denning was thinking this through. It raised a number of interesting questions. He was certain the Soho connection was relevant. A direct link to Kane? Perhaps something else?

'This affair your father had. How long did it last?'

He shrugged. 'Years, as far as I know. I even knew the guy. I mean not well, but he went to the same school as me. Jason Wainwright. My dad introduced me to him once as the "son of a friend". He told me he was teaching him self-defence. It wasn't even a convincing lie. I didn't believe him at the time, but I had no reason to think it was anything improper. I didn't know the truth then, and to be honest with you, Mr Denning, I don't think I want to know now.'

Denning thanked him. He promised he'd keep Gavin posted with any progress, and tried to reassure him that they weren't far off making an arrest, even if he didn't actually believe the last point himself.

Chapter Forty-Eight

Colin was conscious now. Molly and Jon had rushed round to St Thomas's the previous day only to be told he was still unconscious, but should make a full recovery. 'An overdose,' the nurse had said. 'Paracetamol. More than likely a cry for help.' She'd informed them that if someone was serious about ending it all, they threw themselves under a train, or jumped off Beachy Head. An overdose usually meant they wanted to be found in time. But she wished they wouldn't use paracetamol: 'it did such terrible damage to the liver.'

Molly had phoned ahead this time to make sure it was OK to visit. She would come by herself; Jon had enough to occupy his thoughts at the moment, and this called for a sympathetic approach, which was never one of his strengths.

Colin was lying in bed, still half-asleep, but alive and, as they'd got to him in time, hopefully with little lasting damage.

He opened his eyes when Molly sat on the chair beside his bed. A nurse had pulled the curtain round the bed to give them some privacy.

'Molly?' He blinked a few times, then tried to sit up. She arranged his pillow and helped him get comfortable.

'What happened Colin? Why did you do it?'

He blinked at her again. Whatever words were trying to form themselves in his head were clearly destined to remain there. He just looked at her, unable to speak.

'It doesn't matter,' she said. 'It's more important that you're OK. But you gave us a scare, Colin. You've got to promise me you'll never try something like this again. You might not be so lucky next time.'

But the last thing Colin needed right now was a lecture. She smiled at him instead. 'We're making progress. We've got a name now. And soon we'll get others. What's more important is that we've got proof this gang existed. We can prove that you were telling the truth.'

He smiled back at her. But she could see there was an emptiness there, as though he didn't really care anymore. She wanted to tell him to trust her, but she felt like she'd already let him down.

He closed his eyes again, clearly still tired and groggy from having had his stomach pumped the previous day.

'I'm sorry,' he said. 'I'm sorry for everything.'

'You've got nothing to be sorry for.'

But it wasn't that straightforward. There was still the matter of the attack on Gordon Lomax. They could plead mitigating circumstances, but with his record and the viciousness of the assault, she wasn't optimistic about his chances. The suicide attempt would mitigate in his favour – they would argue it showed remorse – but it would still be a tough sell.

Molly promised Colin she'd come back and see him. For now, all that mattered was him getting better.

She left the hospital and turned her phone off silent. There were two messages: one from Denning, with some interesting information about Jason Wainwright, and another from Jon to say that Barry had been in touch.

He'd found the names of the police officers who had tried to persuade him to drop the story. Jon had checked the names out. It seemed the DS had retired some years back, but the junior officer was still working for the Met. And was now in a very senior position.

Chapter Forty-Nine

The house looked deserted, but Denning knew there was someone at home.

He walked up the path and knocked on the door. A few seconds later, Lomax opened it and glowered at Denning. 'What is it now? This is turning into harassment.'

Denning had wanted to make this official: have Lomax dragged to a police station and formally questioned. He wanted him charged with fraud, deception, lying to the police, and if there were any way of proving it, the murder of David Cairns. Instead, he would settle for answers, at least for now.

'I want to ask why you withdrew your statement,' Denning said. 'You owe me that at least.'

Lomax sighed. He looked like he was going to tell Denning to piss off, and slam the door in his face. Then he relented. He opened the door and let Denning in, leading him through to the same fusty sitting room as before. It was so hard to avoid David Cairns's presence in the house. He seemed to ooze out of every corner, as though his ghost haunted the place.

'I didn't have a choice,' Lomax said. 'You have to understand that. Once Kane knew I was the one who dropped him in it, I would have been a dead man walking. You can talk all you like about giving me police protection, but nowhere would have been safe from Kane. It was only ever going to be a matter of time until he tracked me down.'

'What's to stop me telling Alfie Kane you've changed your mind again, and have submitted a written statement outlining everything you know about his dodgy business dealings? How would you rate your chances of survival then?'

'We both know you wouldn't do that. Even if you did, he'd never believe it, not now.' Denning could feel his patience wearing thin. 'I want the truth, Lomax. We've spent too long twatting around each other. Either you tell me what really went on in the West End Arcade, or I'm dragging your backside down to the nearest police station and acquainting DS Anna Klein with all the lies you've been telling ever since you walked into this house. Including the mystery of David Cairns's disappearance.'

'You're bluffing, Denning. If you were going to arrest me, you'd have done it before now.'

'Well, maybe I was giving you the benefit of the doubt before. My patience is running a bit thinner now.'

He could tell Lomax knew he wasn't bluffing. Lomax looked like someone who knew he'd run out of good moves. He was caught between the pincer movements of the police and Kane, and neither of them was going to blink first.

'I told you everything last time you were here. What more do you want?'

'The truth. And I'm going to stay right here until I get it.'

Lomax sighed, realising he was beaten. 'I ran the arcade for Alfie, plus a bar he owned nearby in Wardour Street. But he was never a part of it, and nor was I – I swear I wasn't!' He rubbed a hand over his face. The bruising was beginning to die down now, but the nasty red gash on his cheek still looked raw and painful. At least, Denning hoped it was painful.

'I'd select the boys,' Lomax continued. 'Always willing ones, no one was ever forced into doing something they didn't want to do. Anyone who says otherwise is lying. These boys were nothing. They were either runaways, or they'd been in and out of trouble all their lives. Most of them came from shit homes. A lot of them were sleeping rough. That's why they came to the arcade: to get picked up. They were well looked after. You have to believe that. Those lads were up for earning a bit of cash. And some of them did very well out of it. I know at least a couple of them were set up in their own flats, rent paid and everything.'

'In return for what?' Denning asked. 'Being treated like meat for rich older men who knew what they were doing was wrong?' Denning kept any hint of emotion from his voice. He wanted to shout and scream and throw Lomax against the wall, but that wouldn't achieve anything. He needed to get answers, and Lomax was the only one in a position to give them. 'I doubt these men were doing it out of some misplaced altruism. They were abusing those boys. And they were just boys.'

'I was never involved with anything that went on,' Lomax argued. 'I dealt with an intermediary who knew the men involved. I never met any of the men. They didn't come to the arcade. I would simply pass their details on to this intermediary, then arrange when the boys would get picked up. I made sure those lads were well paid.'

'When will you get it into your head, this isn't about the money, Lomax? This is about abuse, exploitation and a massive cover-up. Those boys' lives were destroyed, and you played a part in that.'

Lomax looked uncomfortable. The lie he'd been telling himself for the past thirty years was being challenged, and he was being confronted with the uncomfortable truth of what had really gone on.

'You can't pin all this on me. I only played a small role in this. But you won't go after the bigger boys, will you, because it's easier to pick on people like me.'

'Who was this "intermediary", Lomax? Was it Kane?'

'Of course not.'

'Then who was it?'

He shook his head. 'You don't need to know. He's dead now anyway, so there's no point in me giving you his name.'

And then the penny dropped. 'It was Cairns, wasn't it? That's how you really knew him. All that crap about you helping him with research for a book. What happened? You found yourself down on your luck, so you black-mailed him? Insisted he gave you a roof over your head in return for you keeping quiet about him procuring teenage boys for fellow paedophiles? Am I close to the truth?'

'If you've worked it out, why are you still here?'

'Look, I'm not interested in Cairns. I want to know about Alfie Kane. What was his involvement in all this?'

Lomax sat on one of the old armchairs, his head in his hands. 'He was never part of it. Truth be told, it disgusted him. But he knew some of the men involved. Don't ask me how he knew them, but that's why he allowed the arcade to be used. It was beneficial for him to have this knowledge, and the power it gave him. These were men with considerable influence. One of them was a senior police officer. That's why the police never got involved in what went on at the arcade.'

'The senior police officer: it was Buckfield, wasn't it?' Denning could feel all the pieces beginning to slot into place. 'Buckfield never received backhanders from Kane: just his silence.'

Lomax didn't reply. He didn't need to; Denning was able to work it all out for himself. It explained how Kane had avoided jail; how his part in the Security Direct job was never fully investigated, and how his dodgy business practices had been overlooked. Blind eyes were conveniently turned whenever he needed a bit of discretion.

'I don't know.' Lomax shook his head. 'All I do know is that Buckfield used to drink in one of the bars Alfie owned in Wardour Street. We knew he was vice squad for a time. Sometimes he'd be there with a young lad. Sometimes they'd be joined by other older guys too. It was pretty obvious what the score was. Alfie had just purchased the arcade from Bernie's widow. I don't know whose idea it was: Kane's or Buckfield's, but shortly after that Kane installed me as manager of the arcade and asked me to keep an eye out for any young lads that might be on the lookout for earning a bit of easy cash. David acted as the intermediary. He was polite and quiet, so the boys trusted him.'

'Why was Buckfield killed? Was he threatening to reveal all about Kane? The man was ill. Dying. Maybe he felt he had nothing to lose?'

Lomax shrugged. 'You'll have to go figure that one out for yourself, Denning. I know for a fact Kane didn't do it. He didn't need to. Buckfield was scared of him, scared of what he could say. Even if none of it could be proved, it would have destroyed Buckfield's reputation.'

'And as long as you were off the scene, Kane felt relatively safe. But then Colin Meek chanced along. The man who attacked you, you recognised him, didn't you? That's why you were so keen not to press charges. You knew it would all come out.'

He sighed again. 'I'd bumped into him the day before. I didn't recognise him at first, but when he spoke to me I realised who he was. Meek was a troublesome little shit. He was always causing problems. He stole from some of the men. Tried blackmailing a couple of them. In the end he had to be threatened into behaving. Someone told him one of the boys had been killed and he would be next if he stepped out of line again. It did the trick. He left the scene shortly afterwards, and no one saw him again. There was a rumour he was inside for something. I hadn't given him a moment's thought in thirty years until I saw him that day.' He shook his head again. 'Now you know everything.'

Denning knew it alright. The whole sorry, sordid story had been laid out before him. The only thing it didn't do was point him in the direction of the killer of Buckfield and Magda Kilbride.

Chapter Fifty

'You should have run this by Acting DI Neeraj. He's running this investigation now.'

McKenna was behind her desk. The look on her face told Denning all he needed to know about the mood she was in.

'Molly Fisher has confirmed it. Two police officers tried to put the frighteners on a journalist. One of them was DCS Harrison. He worked for Buckfield. Back in the late eighties, when Buckfield was a DI, Harrison was a detective constable. They worked together in the same nick. I've checked.'

They were in her office. He'd filled her in on what Molly had found out so far. To say she wasn't happy that Denning had gone behind her back and asked Fisher to "go rogue", as she'd put it, was something of an understatement.

'You're sure it's the same man? It's a fairly common name.'

'There was only one Ian Harrison in the Met. The name fits, the age fits, and the general description fits. I've spoken to someone who used to work with him years ago.' He looked at McKenna. 'It's definitely him.'

She thought about this, drumming her fingers on the desk and pursing her lips. 'And this has nothing to do with the fact you don't like the bloke?'

'Personalities have got nothing to do with this. I think Harrison has questions to answer. Firstly, why he kept quiet about his connection with Buckfield, and secondly, about why he's so pally with Kane.'

'He isn't,' she insisted. 'Friends with Kane, I mean. He knows Marianne from before she married Kane. And you're not suggesting there's anything going on there.'

'But he's friendly with Kane now. We saw that this weekend when he was hanging round with Kane at the charity launch.' He leaned in towards her, placing his hands on her desk. 'Doesn't it worry you? Alfie Kane is a former criminal who seems to have an unhealthy relationship with the police? First Buckfield and now Harrison. And those are just the ones we know about.'

She rubbed a hand through her hair. 'What do we know for certain? DCS Harrison once worked under Buckfield? So what? He wasn't working under him when he was killed. And whatever else, he is our boss. He could have the pair of us out of here on our jacksies if the mood took him. And you're already skating on very thin ice, Matt. Buckfield was being blackmailed by Kane? We've only got the word of Gordon Lomax that that's the case. You can see how piss-poor this all sounds.'

'We're missing the point here, Liz. Harrison was around at the time Kane was blackmailing Buckfield. I'm damn sure he knew what was going on at that arcade. OK, maybe he didn't know just how involved Buckfield was, but he must have asked himself why Buckfield wanted the Colin Meek investigation knocked on the head, and any journalists thrown off the scent. And he must have wondered about Buckfield's relationship with Kane. He was a detective. He must have known which questions needed asking. And now he's cosying up to Kane at garden parties. He's playing us for fools.'

'Watch it, Matt. If you step out of line again, you're going to get yourself suspended. The fact you've asked Molly Fisher to look into these claims by this Colin Meek bloke while she's suspended is serious enough. But to start throwing around wild accusations about a detective chief superintendent is a sure-fire way of kissing goodbye to your career.'

'We need to speak to Harrison. We need to ask him about his connection with Buckfield, and how much he knew about why the Colin Meek case was dropped. If he doesn't play ball, then we go over his head and speak to the commissioner's office.'

'Cool your jets here. What we need to do is to tread carefully before we all end up out of a job. Harrison is a senior officer. We can't go behind his back with nothing more than unsubstantiated gossip. We need hard facts.'

'Let's speak to him, then. Hear what he has to say and take it from there. At least give him a chance to explain himself.'

She stared into space for a moment. 'I'm not happy about this. Pissing off a DCS. When I first started out, that was a disciplinary offence. You'd be out on your arse for doing that.'

'But what about our role as detectives? The need to serve justice? Isn't that why we joined the police in the first place? The old days of closing ranks and automatically deferring to top brass are gone. Now we need to be accountable and above board. How can we look ourselves in the eye knowing we've failed to hold one of our own to account, if it does turn out to be the case?'

'OK. We speak to him. We get his side of the story, and ask him to explain himself.'

'And if he can't give us a satisfactory explanation?'

There was a brief pause before she answered.

'Then we kick his arse.'

—

Harrison was in no mood for small talk when they knocked on his office door later that day.

'This is inexcusable,' he barked at McKenna. 'The two of you need to be out there finding the killer of Frank Buckfield and Magda Kilbride, not running to me with tales.'

Credit to McKenna; she stood her ground. 'The fact is, sir, we've come into possession of evidence that suggests you were more involved with Buckfield than you led us to believe.' McKenna and Denning were both standing, there having been no offer of a seat made to either of them.

'What *evidence*?' He spat the word out as though it were a bitter pill.

'You were one of two officers who visited Barry Tasker and warned him to drop the story into Colin Meek's claims,' Denning said. 'We suspect DCI Buckfield ordered you to do it, but it still amounts to conspiracy. Barry Tasker will be happy to identify you as one of the officers involved.'

'Who the bloody hell is Barry Tasker? I've never bloody heard of him.'

'He was the editor of *The London Echo*,' McKenna said calmly. 'He's retired now, but he remembers the incident well.'

Harrison's face turned white. 'I still don't know what the hell you're talking about,' he said, but Denning detected a sudden change in his tone, suggesting he knew very well what they were talking about.

'The story was subsequently dropped, or "spiked" as they apparently call it in the trade,' McKenna continued. 'At the request of DCI Buckfield. We have strong reason to believe that this was because he was one of the perpetrators.' She hadn't bothered to add a 'sir' at the end of the sentence this time.

Harrison eyed them both for a minute, keeping his focus mostly fixed on McKenna, but Betty Taggart was the mistress of the gimlet stare; it would take more than an intimidating look from Harrison to make her blink.

'DCI Buckfield was a good man,' he said weakly. 'He was a solid detective and a generous boss. He recognised talent and he made sure you got rewarded for that talent. That was back in the days where the only way you got promoted beyond desk sergeant was by being bloody good at your job. It was down to merit, and not by having a fancy degree or a pair of tits.' His face had turned from white to red now. 'Frank Buckfield was dedicated to the job. He gave everything he had to it. He never deserved to have his name and his reputation blackened by those bullshit corruption allegations. The two of you should be looking for his killer. Why the hell aren't you?'

Once the rant was over and he'd stopped shouting, McKenna said quietly: 'Nevertheless, we do have evidence that links DCI Buckfield with a paedophile gang. And we have evidence that suggests you were complicit in the cover-up that saw the investigation into Colin Meek's claims being dropped. If we take this higher, it would more than likely be a disciplinary matter at the very least. In fact, you'd be lucky to come out of this with your job and pension intact.'

Harrison sighed heavily, and shook his head. 'OK, so I knew there were rumours about Buckfield and his perverted friends, but that was none of my business. I took him at face value. I owed him. When I joined this job, I was looked down on by everyone above me. I'd been chucked out of the army when I was nineteen. I only got into the Met by the skin of my teeth. It was Frank who took me under his wing and gave me the opportunity to make something of my life. He recommended me for promotion. I'm only sitting here now because of him.' He looked from Denning to McKenna. 'Frank Buckfield was a bloody good detective.' Harrison rubbed his hands over his face. 'Kane didn't remember me. We'd only ever met on a few occasions, mostly when Frank was around. Kane barely noticed me, but I clocked him. A wide boy on the make. And I watched him lie and con his way to the top. Everybody suspected he was responsible for putting that bullet in Bernie Michaelson's brain, just as everyone suspected he was behind the Security Direct robbery. But we also all knew he was untouchable. It wasn't just Frank he had in his pocket, there were others too. I thought if I could get close enough to Kane, gain his trust, I could find some way to bring him down. For what he did to Frank, if nothing else. Kane destroyed his career. He turned a good detective who was respected by his colleagues, into that pathetic, wretched drunk, whose body you found rotting in that shitty flat. He deserved better than that.' Another shake of the head. 'I couldn't believe my luck when Kane started sniffing round Marianne. She used to work with my ex, so I saw a way in through her. I was sure that, given time, I could find proof Kane had been behind the Security Direct job. Maybe more. I just needed time.' He looked at them both pleadingly. 'What do you suggest I do?'

'Tell the truth.' Denning said.

'How the hell can I let any of this become public knowledge? I'd be destroyed. My career ruined. This is all I've got.'

'I'm sorry,' McKenna said coldly, 'but that really isn't our problem.'

Chapter Fifty-One

It was a working lunch. At least that was how they described it so it didn't look like they were taking time off during a busy murder investigation.

Molly was sitting with Denning, McKenna and Neeraj. The restaurant was McKenna's choice; an Italian place she liked to frequent in Wanstead, where the waiters were attentive and easy on the eye. It was fairly busy, but she'd asked for a table at the back, where it was quieter and there was less chance of them being overheard.

Neeraj was still adjusting to his new role as Acting SIO, and kept nodding towards Denning and McKenna for approval.

Molly felt awkward. She was officially still on suspension, so couldn't come to the MIT office, but it was clear to everyone she remained a part of the investigation. The lunch meeting had been a suitable compromise suggested by Denning. A chance to catch up and share theories, without having to make things official.

'Harrison has referred himself to the DPS,' McKenna said. 'We'll be given a temporary DCS until the commissioner can appoint a permanent replacement. I can't see Harrison surviving this. Shame, I think he was just coming into his own.'

Molly wasn't sure if she was joking, but smiled anyway.

A waiter appeared and took their order. No one seemed to be particularly hungry, apart from McKenna, who ordered lasagne. The others were happy with sandwiches and paninis.

'How's Colin?' Denning asked.

Molly thought Denning was looking tired. Trudi had told her about his demotion from SIO. It would have been gruelling for someone like Denning. Apart from the loss of face, there was the potential damage to his career in the long term. But with Harrison out of the way, there was always the chance he could claw back some of the lost respect.

She filled them in on his progress. 'He'll be OK. Hopefully no lasting damage. At least, not physically. The hospital has referred him to their mental health support team, and are recommending he gets counselling. In some ways this could be the best thing to happen to him.' She poured a glass of water from a carafe. 'What about Lomax? Is he still determined not to press charges for the assault?'

'It'll be a tough call for Lomax,' McKenna said. 'If it goes to court, everything will come out. He'll end up going down for his role in the paedophile ring. Not to mention the whole sorry saga with David Cairns, which is going to raise a whole load of difficult questions for him.'

'What is the real story there?' Molly asked. 'Do we buy this suicide claim?'

It was Denning who answered. 'No. I'm almost certain Lomax is lying about that, just as he's lying about his limited role in the paedophile ring. Proving anything will be difficult though, without a body.'

'We've checked, I presume,' McKenna said. 'Any suicides from around the time Cairns went missing.'

'There's nothing on file that fits Cairns's description,' Denning said. 'But we'll keep looking, maybe widen the area. He could have travelled to another part of the country to kill himself.'

'Or if he drowned, then we might never find his body,' McKenna offered.

Denning nodded. 'It's going to take time to search thoroughly. But we need to be confident we can conclusively rule out suicide before we start talking anything else.'

'What about Tommy?' Molly asked. 'I know it's tenuous, but if there's any truth in that claim, we need to investigate it.'

Molly noticed Denning look at McKenna before he answered. 'I don't think this Tommy was killed. It looks like one of the men made the story up to frighten Colin. Possibly some of the other boys too. It would have been a good way of keeping them in line. They were already frightened, vulnerable boys. They knew they were dealing with rich, powerful men. It wouldn't be difficult to convince them that one step out of line and they could easily disappear. How many of them would have been missed?'

'But these boys must have had families,' Neeraj said. 'Somebody would have missed them.'

'I'd like to think that was the case, Deep,' Molly said. 'But sometimes people just fall through the net. Most of these boys had either been abandoned by their families or never had any in the first place.'

The waiter returned with their food. For a few minutes they all ate in silence.

'I think Jason Wainwright is worth speaking to,' Denning said eventually. 'He and Buckfield were lovers back in the day. He might be able to throw some light on this.'

'I'm already on to it,' Molly said. 'I've got an address for him.' She looked at McKenna. 'I'm just not sure if I'm allowed to speak to him. At least officially.'

'Speak to him, Molly,' McKenna said. 'You can tell him it's off the record, if it makes him more comfortable. At this stage, all we need is confirmation that Buckfield deliberately killed the investigation. If we need to bring Wainwright in at a later date, then we can cross that bridge when we come to it.' McKenna looked around the table. 'The paedophile ring,' she said. 'How many names have we got so far?'

Denning was chewing a beef and mozzarella panini. 'Apart from Buckfield, we know that David Cairns was part of it. Possibly Lomax too, though his denial was pretty resolute.'

'Robin Sims is another possibility,' Molly said. 'But, like Gordon Lomax, he's strenuously denying any involvement. He did give us the name Grayson Boswell, though.' She looked around the table. 'He's a retired judge.'

'Well, at least two of those men are now dead,' McKenna said, shoving forkfuls of lasagne into her mouth as she spoke. 'Do we know anything about this Judge Boswell?'

Molly filled them in on what she and Jon had found out about Grayson Boswell so far. 'It seems he was diagnosed with dementia a few years ago, shortly after he left the bench. No idea of his current whereabouts, except that it's very likely he's in a nursing home somewhere.'

'Then we can probably rule him out,' McKenna said, pausing mid-forkful. 'Assuming the dementia's genuine, and not some clever ruse.'

'Are we any closer to finding out why Buckfield was killed?' Neeraj asked, ignoring McKenna's dry humour. 'The journalist woman too? I assume we now accept that they were killed by the same person?'

'I think they were killed to keep them from talking,' Denning said. 'The stuff with the masking tape was just to try and throw us off the scent, and make us think we were looking for a random serial killer. The post-mortem report on Magda Kilbride confirms that it's definitely the same killer, but there was no obvious connection between the two victims. Our killer assumed we wouldn't link them. But someone wanted them silenced. As soon as Magda Kilbride's story was published, it would destroy the reputations of a lot of once-important people. I believe she was way ahead of us. I suspect she wasn't far off identifying some of the big names involved in the paedophile gang. We'll never know exactly how much Buckfield told her, but I reckon it was enough to send her looking under all the right stones.'

'Do you really think she was close to making some sort of breakthrough?' Molly asked. In a way she hoped that was true. It would have been some kind of vindication for Mags. It was possible her story could still be told, especially if Jon was willing to finish what she'd started.

'She'd struck lucky finding Buckfield,' Denning said. 'I think Buckfield had decided he'd lived with the guilt of what he'd done for long enough. He wanted to salve his conscience before he died.'

'But I still don't get it,' Neeraj said. 'Why should any of these old blokes care enough about this shit getting out to want to murder two people? There's not much chance of any of them going down for these crimes now, even if we could persuade the CPS to bring the case to court.'

'It's not just the men themselves though,' Denning said. 'Some of them had families. Those families may have wanted this kept under wraps. Particularly if they had a lot to lose.'

He suddenly put his half-eaten panini down and looked at Molly. 'How did you know Boswell had dementia?'

Jon had done the digging there. She tried to remember how he'd found out about it. 'His daughter gave an interview for a magazine about a year ago: the difficulties of living with dementia, that sort of thing.'

'Did this article mention anything about his daughter?'

Molly screwed her face up, trying hard to remember. 'She's a barrister, I think. She mentioned something about following in her father's footsteps.'

Denning was still looking at Molly. 'Can you remember her name?'

She thought back to the article in question. Jon had found it online and shown it to her. 'Emma something.'

All four had stopped eating now. McKenna was staring at Denning, waiting for him to speak.

'Emma Morrow's father was a judge.' He was rubbing a hand over his tired-looking eyes.

'So?' McKenna held a forkful of lasagne mid-air.

'Her father's got dementia.'

Chapter Fifty-Two

Morrow was working from home that afternoon, catching up on paperwork, apparently. Denning had phoned and asked if they could meet. He had been deliberately vague about the reason. Morrow had suggested he called round to the house, and they could chat there.

The Morrows lived in a tall Georgian townhouse in Highgate, with an impressive view over London from the upstairs windows. There was a blue plaque on one of the neighbouring properties, stating that someone famous had once resided there. The Morrows' house may not have been quite so distinguished, but it was clearly worth a lot of money. Denning suspected it was the kind of place Sarah would have liked, even though it was so far out of their price range that they were more likely to live on Mars than live in a house like that.

'Can I get you a drink?' Morrow asked.

Denning didn't want this to feel too much like a social visit. 'I'm OK, thanks.'

They were in Morrow's office, at the back of the house, converted from a spare bedroom. There was a large antique mahogany desk at one end by the window. Denning sat on a comfy leather armchair next to the desk. Morrow turned away from his computer and faced him. Denning saw that the computer screen seemed to consist of excel spreadsheets with streams of figures.

Classical music blared out of a hidden stereo system: Wagner's *Ride of the Valkyries*.

'Emma still at work?' Denning asked.

'She should be back soon,' Morrow informed him. 'We're going out for dinner again this evening. To be honest with you, Matt, a quiet night in would be a blessing sometimes.'

Denning nodded his agreement. 'That's one of the prices you have to pay if you want to be a serious political player.'

A quick search on the internet had confirmed that Emma's maiden name was Boswell, and that her father had been a respected judge. If what they now knew about Grayson Boswell was true, then that respect was about to disappear.

But there was nothing to suggest that she had ever known about what her father had got up to in his spare time, just as Buckfield's son had clearly had his suspicions about his father, but had certainly never guessed the extent of what he had got up to. These men would have worked hard to keep their secrets buried as much from their family as from the outside world.

'How's Emma's dad?' he asked.

If the question caught Morrow off guard, he didn't let it show. 'He's OK. Well, he's as OK as you'd expect under the circumstances.' He kept on typing.

'He's in a nursing home, isn't he? That can't have been an easy decision for Emma.'

Morrow turned back to his computer screen. He started to tap at the keyboard, though there was a brief second when he seemed to pause mid-tap and his finger gave a slight twitch.

'Not easy,' he said. 'Not an easy decision at all.' He was staring at the screen, seemingly lost in his figures. 'But you do what you can for your parents, don't you, Matt?'

'Yes, I suppose we'd do anything to protect someone we loved.' If Morrow wondered how Denning knew about his father-in-law, he never asked.

It seemed obvious once they'd established the motive for Buckfield's murder wasn't revenge, and had connected it with Magda Kilbride's murder. Someone wanted them silenced, and who had the most to lose from the story getting out?

Kane would certainly have wanted his connection to Buckfield and his knowledge of the paedophile ring kept quiet. But he would have more than likely tried to buy them off. Or set his solicitor on them. He wouldn't risk getting blood on his hands these days: not now he was playing at being the respectable businessman.

No. The real threat would have been to someone young and ambitious. Someone whose carefully laid out plans would be knocked for six by the revelation that his much-respected father-in-law was actually a degenerate paedophile.

And Justin Morrow had planned it all. Pushed on by his ambitious wife, he couldn't risk letting the truth come out. He had too much to lose.

Morrow stopped typing. He tilted his head at Denning. 'What's all this about, Matt? You said you wanted to talk. I presume you didn't want to engage in small talk about my father-in-law's health.'

'No. Well, in part, perhaps. But I mostly wanted to talk to you about Frank Buckfield. And Magda Kilbride. We now know who killed them. And why.'

'You're not suggesting Grayson did it.' A hollow laugh. 'But then, I'm guessing you're not suggesting that, are you?'

Denning was trying to remain calm. Morrow was taking this in his stride, which meant either he was one cool customer, or Denning had called this wrong. But he knew he wasn't wrong.

Morrow just stared at Denning. There was no flicker of emotion, just the piercing gaze of his pale blue eyes. 'That's insane. I didn't kill anyone. I'm also a friend of the police.' He smiled again. 'I'd like to think I'm a friend of yours, Matt. And I look after my friends. Just ask Ian Harrison.'

'Except Harrison is no friend of yours. It was convenient for you to have someone who was able to keep you up to speed about what was going on in the Met, especially during a murder investigation. You knew all about Grayson and his predilections, just as you knew Buckfield was likely to spill the beans as soon as Magda Kilbride started sniffing around that story. I suspect Harrison knew the truth about Grayson. Either Buckfield told him, or he worked it out for himself, and persuaded you to back him for the DCS's post, even though he was clearly out of his depth in that job. You're not without influence, you and Emma. You said you're a friend of the police, well that's true. Does your friendship base also include someone at New Scotland Yard who may have some influence when it comes to internal promotions – Assistant Commissioner? Deputy Commissioner? Am I warm?'

'That's crap, Matt. As I've already told you, Harrison got the job because he was the best candidate. I'm sorry you and he clearly don't get on, but that's more down to you than him.'

'Maybe. But that's not the point. The point is, he had something on you. And that's the secret that so many people have worked so hard to cover up.'

'My father-in-law is an old man. A sick man. He doesn't deserve to be on the receiving end of these lies. And that's what they were – lies. Some journalist making up stories to make a name for herself, and bribing Buckfield with booze to get him to say whatever she wanted. How is someone in Grayson's condition expected to defend himself from that?' He looked at Denning. 'She contacted Emma; this Magda whatever her name was. She said she had proof about Grayson, Buckfield and Christ knows what else. She wanted to talk. We threatened her with legal action, but that didn't stop her. Even with Buckfield out of the picture, she came back, insisting she was going to run the story. Emma persuaded her to meet that night. We were going to offer her money. A lot of money. And for a second, it looked like she was going to take it. But what do you know: we'd found the only bloody journalist in London who had integrity.'

Denning almost felt sorry for him. Almost… 'You know I have to arrest you, Justin. There's no way of keeping this low profile, unfortunately.'

'I'm sorry, Matt. I really am.'

But Denning had had enough. 'Justin Morrow, I'm arresting you for—' Then there was a crash and everything went black.

Chapter Fifty-Three

When he came round, the room was empty. Music was still playing on the stereo. *Ride of the Valkyries* had given way to another piece of music, something loud and classical that Denning didn't recognise.

He found a remote on Morrow's desk and turned off the stereo. Then he grabbed his mobile and phoned Neeraj. They needed to find the Morrows, and quickly. He explained what had happened, and Neeraj confirmed he was on his way.

There was a heavy glass ornament on the floor, slightly smeared with blood. He guessed it had been Emma Morrow who'd whacked him, the sound of her arrival being drowned out by Wagner.

Denning felt a lump on the back of his skull, which was damp and sticky to touch. He looked at the blood on his fingers and tried not to think about how much worse it could have been.

Had they known he was on to them? If so, how? Had he inadvertently tipped them off during dinner? He remembered Justin asking him about the investigation – he'd even mentioned Magda Kilbride's murder, which Denning had thought strange at the time. Was this Morrow's way of looking for a lead? Had the whole dinner suggestion been nothing more than a ruse to see if the police were on to them?

There was a sick feeling in his stomach. He should never have gone there without back-up. He had been banking on having a civilised chat with Morrow. His intention had been to try and convince him to come down to the station and make a statement quietly and without any fuss. He'd learned his lesson with Kane. Discretion was preferable to going in all guns blazing. He hadn't banked on Emma Morrow having other ideas.

He searched the office to see if he could find some clue as to where the Morrows might have gone.

Their passports were in a drawer in the desk. At least that meant their options were reduced. It would be difficult for them to leave the country without passports. But they had money, so they weren't entirely without options. He checked over the rest of the house, hoping he might find something. But there was nothing obvious.

Twenty minutes later, Neeraj was knocking on the front door. Denning also spotted McKenna getting out of her car, and a squad car pulling up behind her.

'Where are they?' Neeraj asked, not bothering with pleasantries.

'I don't know, Deep. Someone – probably Emma Morrow – smacked me on the back of the head, then they both legged it.'

Neeraj had already run into the kitchen, then poked his head into the two elegant downstairs reception rooms in case the Morrows were sitting watching telly and Denning hadn't bothered to check.

He returned to the hallway and noticed the blood on the back of Denning's head. 'You alright, boss?'

Before he had a chance to answer, McKenna burst through the front door. 'We've notified ports and airports, as well as Eurostar. They won't get out of the country.'

'They've left their passports behind, so if they *are* plan-ning on leaving the country they're going to need a contingency.'

'Or a helicopter,' Neeraj added.

'There's nothing to say they don't have access to both,' McKenna countered.

'Do we think they planned this? Did they know we were on to them?' Neeraj asked.

'Emma Morrow left work earlier. No one can get hold of her.' McKenna looked at Denning. 'We reckon someone tipped her off.'

'Justin Morrow could have phoned her to tell her I was on my way. That might have rung an alarm bell with her. I imagine she put two and two together, and realised their luck was about to run out.'

McKenna was shaking her head. 'My money's on Harrison. He's still hanging around like an old man's scrotum. He probably feels he's got nothing to lose now.'

'I don't think they'll try to leave the country,' Denning said. 'Not without their passports – at least not immedi-ately. It's too risky. I reckon they'll lie low for a while and plan their next move. We've obviously caught them by surprise, and they strike me as the kind of people who like to plan their moves.'

McKenna was staring at the back of Denning's head. 'Do you need to go to hospital?'

He could still feel the lump on his skull. Emma Morrow had given him quite a whack. 'No,' he said. 'I'll be fine.'

–

Back at the office, the team was going over all the options. There was a picture of Justin and Emma Morrow on

328

the whiteboard; their names written underneath in red marker pen.

'Justin and Emma Morrow,' Neeraj said, addressing the room, but flicking awkward glances in Denning's direction. 'We think one or both of them is responsible for the murders of Frank Buckfield and Magda Kilbride. Also an assault on DI Denning earlier today. Their present whereabouts are unknown.'

Denning lightly fingered the lump on his skull. At least the bleeding had stopped.

'We need to find them,' Neeraj continued. 'We have to explore the possibility they may be being shielded by someone. If so, we need to find that someone.'

Denning's first thought was Harrison. But he was currently attending a disciplinary meeting over at New Scotland Yard. He would be eager to distance himself from Justin Morrow now that yet another of his so-called friendships had turned out to be toxic. Harrison would be desperate to try and save whatever was left of his career, though the best he could realistically hope for would be a hefty demotion.

'Who do we think did it?' Kinsella asked. 'Him or her?'

Neeraj shrugged. 'My money's on him. He was trying to save his career. But she's certainly guilty of covering it up.' He nodded at Denning. 'We reckon she's the one who slugged Matt, so she's not walking away from this scot free.'

'I suspect she's the driving force behind him,' Denning suggested. 'That's not to say though that he isn't capable of acting off his own bat.'

'What about friends?' Trudi asked. 'If no one knows we're looking for them, then maybe they're staying with someone who's completely unaware they're shielding two suspects in a murder investigation.'

'We don't know who their friends are,' Neeraj replied. He threw another glance in Denning's direction.

Denning was sure there were some people sitting in the room who probably thought he and Sarah counted as friends of the Morrows. The lump on his skull would have told them otherwise.

'We need to speak to Emma Morrow's work colleagues as well as Justin Morrow's fellow Assembly members,' Neeraj continued. 'We're not going public with this yet, as we don't want to panic either the Morrows or whoever might be assisting them.'

'An appeal might help,' Kinsella suggested. 'Get something out there – social media at the very least.'

'It hasn't been ruled out, Dave,' Neeraj replied. 'If there are no sightings or clues to their whereabouts in the next twenty-four hours, DCI McKenna has suggested we go public. But until then, we keep this low key. They're out there somewhere. We need to keep focussed and keep looking.'

Denning was impressed by how well Neeraj was running the briefing. Yes, he could be an arse at times, but the old saying about someone rising to the challenge seemed to apply. He was proving he had what it took to make a good Senior Investigating Officer. Denning hoped he wouldn't fuck things up between now and his next interview with the promotion board.

'What about family?' Cormack asked. 'Has anyone spoken to them?'

'Justin Morrow's parents live in France,' Neeraj said. 'We think they may try and head out there when the heat's off. We don't know much about Emma Morrow's parents.'

'As far as I know, there's only her father,' Denning said. 'And I don't think he's in a position to help them out.' He explained to the team about the dementia, and her father being in a home.

But if Denning thought about it, then would Emma Morrow really be prepared to leave her father behind? If one of the reasons behind all this had been to protect his name, then surely she wouldn't want to abandon him at this stage?

'Actually, maybe we want to try and find Grayson Boswell. He's the key to this. I think we should at least speak to him.'

'You said he's gone gaga,' Kinsella argued, 'so what would be the point? He's not going to be able to tell us anything useful.'

'It's worth a try, Dave. And right now we need to explore every possibility. Trudi, can you get in touch with Molly and find out which nursing home Grayson Boswell is in.' Denning suddenly realised he was barking orders at the team as though he was still in charge. He looked over at Neeraj, who just nodded his approval.

Kinsella was right: according to the information Molly had given them, plus what Sarah had told him, Boswell's dementia was pretty advanced. It felt like a long shot, but right now that was all they had.

Chapter Fifty-Four

The nursing home was a converted Victorian villa in St Albans. A modern extension had been grafted on to one side of the main building, and no attempt had been made to blend the two together. The home overlooked a garden to the front and – inappropriately, Denning thought – a cemetery at the back.

He and Neeraj showed their IDs to the receptionist and were asked to wait in a seating area for the manager. They were greeted a few minutes later by a dark-haired man in his fifties who introduced himself as Kevin Pettiford, the home's manager. Denning had phoned through the previous day, explaining that they wanted to speak to Boswell and it was urgent. Despite some initial protests, the home had agreed.

'Mr Boswell hasn't received any visitors for a few days now. The last time his daughter came to see him was almost a week ago,' Pettiford explained. 'You are aware that Mr Boswell is very ill. As I told one of your colleagues on the phone yesterday, he has dementia and—'

'We know,' Neeraj interrupted. 'We only want to ask him some questions. We need to find his daughter and son-in-law urgently, and it's possible he might be able to help.'

Pettiford looked at them both as though he was about to change his mind about letting them speak to Boswell.

'We realise he's unlikely to know much,' Denning said. 'But if we could just have a quick word?'

'OK,' Pettiford said. 'But if he gets distressed or confused, you have to stop the questioning. Understood?'

Denning agreed they would. Pettiford led them through to a large, open-plan lounge, with a wide bay window at one end, and an archway leading to a smaller lounge at the back. The room mostly consisted of high-backed chairs and a television that played silently against a wall in the corner. The view was over the garden at the front rather than the cemetery at the rear.

Half a dozen or so residents were sitting in the lounge. Some of them still seemed to have an alertness about them, and looked up as Denning and Neeraj entered. One or two smiled, perhaps thinking they were getting visitors.

Others sat staring into nothingness; their brains now somewhere that nobody could hope to reach. Grayson Boswell was one of them.

Boswell sat in a chair beside the window. He was gazing at the dancing pictures on the silent television but didn't seem to be taking any of it in. Pettiford lightly tapped Boswell on the shoulder, smiled at him and introduced the two men. 'These gentlemen would like to talk to you about your daughter,' he said.

Boswell looked at Denning and turned his head to focus on Neeraj. He squinted his eyes very slightly, then turned back to stare at the television.

Pettiford left them to it, but reminded them again not to upset the old man. Just before he left the lounge, he spoke quietly in the ear of a care worker who was sitting by the door. They both looked over at Boswell, making it clear that police or not, he expected his words to be heeded.

Boswell was a wrinkled, shrivelled creature of a man, dressed in an old woollen cardigan and a pair of flannels. His bald head was peppered with red marks and purple splodges. He looked a bit like a tortoise and barely resembled the man whose photograph Denning had been staring at less than half an hour ago. Pale, glassy eyes gazed up at them without acknowledging they were there.

Denning was unsure what to think. They were there to ask about Emma Morrow, but there was something else too. Denning was curious to see the man who had damaged so many lives. In his mind, Boswell had become a monster. He thought if he could see him in the flesh, he could confront him with what he'd done, and somehow make him face up to the misery he'd caused. But looking at the withered old man sitting before him, he just felt pity. And disgust.

'Mr Boswell,' Denning began gently, 'We want to talk to you about Emma.'

A brief flicker of something seemed to stir behind his eyes at the mention of his daughter's name. 'Emma...?' a weak, reedy voice came out from somewhere near his shrunken chest.

Denning had read up on Boswell. Like Buckfield, he'd been well-respected in his profession. He had possessed a razor-sharp intellect, and was renowned for his compassion and fairness. But, like Buckfield, there had been another side to him that he'd worked hard to keep hidden.

He found it hard to reconcile the once-powerful, intelligent man with the pitiful shrunken figure sitting in the armchair.

'Your daughter, Emma,' Neeraj prompted. 'Do you know where we can find her?'

The old man continued to stare at Denning. 'Do I know you?' The dull eyes twinkled and something, somewhere in what was left of his brain clicked, but failed to make a connection. To his knowledge, they'd never met. Denning had never appeared before Boswell in court, and he was sure their paths had never crossed socially. Maybe he reminded Boswell of someone he once knew.

'Your daughter,' he said. 'We need to find her. Can you help us?'

'Edward,' he said, still looking at Denning. 'It's Edward, isn't it?'

Denning shook his head. 'I'm a police officer, Mr Boswell. My name's Detective Inspector Denning.'

'It's pointless, boss,' Neeraj offered. 'We're wasting our time. The old man doesn't know shit from piss.'

Denning was aware of the carer by the door looking over at them, a wary look on her face.

Boswell was still staring at Denning. 'Edward,' he said again. He was saying the name with some conviction, as though he was certain Denning was who he thought he was.

'Let's go,' Neeraj said, the impatience clear in his voice. 'It's obvious he doesn't know where they are.'

Denning agreed. He looked into Grayson Boswell's eyes, but there was just an emptiness staring back at him. Neeraj was right: Boswell was unable to help.

Chapter Fifty-Five

Back in the MIT office, he told McKenna they were trying to find Emma and Justin Morrow as a matter of urgency.

'So, the old man couldn't help you?'

'Not in any obvious way,' Denning replied.

'Meaning?'

He thought for a moment before replying. 'Something he did say. Could be nothing…'

'OK. Any little nugget of info would be useful right now.'

'I'll need to make a couple of phone calls.' Denning was thinking aloud.

'Right, well you do that. Meanwhile, I've got a meeting with the bigwigs over at New Scotland Yard to discuss what has now been officially labelled "The Harrison Situation", and I'm already running late.'

He suppressed a smile. 'Don't forget to tell them it was nothing personal.'

McKenna told him to keep her informed of any progress, and to make sure he ran everything by Neeraj first. 'At least let the poor fucker think he's still in charge,' were her parting words as she headed towards the lift, glancing at her watch and cursing.

Denning returned to his desk. He phoned Sarah. She was at work, and slightly surprised to receive his call.

He remembered something she'd mentioned about Emma Morrow's brother.

'Anything wrong?'

'Sorry to bother you at work, Sarah. Emma Morrow's brother, do you know his name?' He was acting on a hunch that had, at first, felt like clutching at straws.

There was a pause from the other end of the line. 'I'm not sure.' Another pause. 'Eddie, or Teddy, or something. Why?'

Edward Boswell was Grayson Boswell's son. *Was that what the old man was trying to tell them?* Maybe even subconsciously part of his brain still functioned. Or maybe he genuinely thought Denning was his dead son.

'You mentioned she was sorting through his estate. Did he leave her any property in his will?'

'He had a house somewhere. Emma was trying to sell it. What's this about, Matt? Has something happened?'

'Did she say where this house is?'

There was another pause. 'No. I could phone her and ask. I mean, if you were thinking we could buy it, I'm sure she'd offer us a good price.'

'Don't bother, it's nothing important.' He thanked Sarah and ended the call. She would be wondering what that was about. Word still hadn't got out that the Morrows were wanted in connection with two murders, but it would be common enough knowledge soon: either they'd be arrested and it would make the news, or McKenna would insist on putting out a public appeal. The only problem with the latter option was that it could potentially make them really go to ground, or try to find some way to leave the country.

He googled the name Edward Boswell, finding a recent obituary for Edward Maynard Boswell. He'd been headmaster at a private school near Oxford, and had died six months ago from a sudden heart attack.

There was a reference to Emma, and to the fact that Edward's father had been a high court judge. There was no mention of any other family.

Denning noted the name of the school, searched for their phone number online and called them. The phone was answered by a secretary. He explained who he was and that he needed an address for Edward Boswell. After the secretary informed him Mr Boswell was deceased, he patiently explained he needed to find the last known address for Mr Boswell and it was urgent. It took him the best part of five minutes and a lot of persuasion to convince the secretary to part with the information.

Edward Boswell had lived in a village just outside Didcot called West Moreton. He noted down the address she gave him, thanked her for her help, and brought up Google Maps on his computer screen. West Moreton was a tiny village, consisting of what looked like two main streets and a pub.

He picked up the phone and dialled the number for Thames Valley CID.

Chapter Fifty-Six

The gym lay off the Mile End Road, situated in the arch of a railway viaduct. Every so often a train rumbled overhead.

Jason Wainwright ran a youth boxing club on a Tuesday lunchtime.

He was in good shape: muscly, but toned rather than bulk. His head was shaved, and there was a colourful tattoo of a dragon on his left shoulder. The boys in the group were bursting with hormones and adrenalin. They were mostly in their late teens or early twenties, and either training or watching from the sidelines as other boys trained. The vast room stank of teenage sweat.

Jason smiled when he spoke, but Molly could see there was sadness in his eyes. 'I knew Frank,' he said to her. 'He was good to me. But it was all a long time ago.'

'I'm not here to judge, Mr Wainwright, I just need to know the background to the case. You had a relationship with Frank Buckfield and now he's been found murdered. We're looking into his background, and your relationship may be relevant.'

He frowned and glanced around him before nodding towards a door in the corner, 'Look, can we talk somewhere else?'

Molly looked around her. A dozen pairs of ears were trying to tune in to their conversation. He led her towards a small room just off the main area of the gym, stopping en route to buy a can of Fanta from a drinks machine by the door. Once they were in the small office he opened the can and took a long drink, then belched. He wiped sweat from his forehead with the back of his hand.

'When I was young I was in a bad way,' he said, launching into his life story as though it explained his behaviour. 'My parents chucked me out the house as soon as I turned sixteen. I'd been in trouble with the police before my fifteenth birthday. I already knew Frank. I'd been at school with his son. Frank helped me out the first time I was arrested – offering me advice and warning me to get my act together. Then I bumped into him when I was hanging round Soho scamming punters for a bit of ready cash. I knew what he wanted. He never hid what he wanted me for and I never made any bones out of the fact I was in it for the money. I wasn't gay. It was nothing like that.' Another bead of sweat had formed on his forehead but he ignored it this time and let it trickle down his face. 'Frank understood that. He was never going to leave his wife, and that suited me.' He looked at Molly. 'I was in it for the money,' he repeated.

'I'm not really interested in that, Mr Wainwright,' Molly said. 'I want to know why you lied to the police about Colin Meek? You told them you knew about the abuse he and other boys experienced back in the 1980s, then you changed your story. Why?'

He sat on a chair. 'I'm not proud of what I did back then. Jesus, I'm not even proud of what I *was* back then – just a fucked-up kid who did what other people wanted in return for a few quid. Frank knew this. There were times he looked like he wanted things to get more serious, but we always knew what it was.'

'So why lie?'

He sighed. 'We'd finished with each other by this time. But he knew I still needed money. He came round to the bar I was working in, and said he needed a favour. He wanted me to make a formal statement saying I'd been one of the boys who had been abused. Then I was to make another statement saying that I'd lied. He promised me there would be no repercussions for me, and it would seriously undermine the case against this other lad. It was Frank's idea.'

'And he paid you?'

He stared hard at the floor. 'I needed the cash.'

Molly had heard of this sort of thing before: discredit one of the witnesses and a case was immediately weakened. If one witness admitted to lying, then there was a strong chance other witnesses were lying too. It was devious but it worked. But it should never have been allowed to happen. Colin's testimony should have been strong enough to have been believed on its own, but it was always going to ultimately boil down to his word against that of some very powerful men. Once he was discredited, there would be little or no chance of the case ever getting as far as a court. 'You were happy to go along with this?' she asked, a slight edge to her voice. 'You were prepared to help destroy the life of a young lad who was telling the truth?'

'Look, it was years ago. I was a fucked-up kid myself. I knew what went on. I also knew you'd have to be pretty fucking stupid to tangle with blokes like that.'

'Or just very brave, Mr Wainwright.'

He looked at her. His face fell. 'OK. I know I shouldn't have done it. I know it was wrong. If I could take it back I would, but I can't. And what would be the point anyway? The damage is done now.'

'Not necessarily.' She smiled at him. 'Frank Buckfield is dead now, but that doesn't mean you can't come forward and tell the truth.'

'What would that achieve?'

'It would prove that Colin Meek wasn't lying all those years ago. It would mean that people might finally believe him.'

He shook his head. 'I don't know. I don't know that I want all that raked up again. I've got a nice life now. I'm married with a couple of kids. My wife knows nothing about my earlier life, and I'd prefer to keep it that way.'

'It's your call, Mr Wainwright. And it's your conscience. Obviously I could charge you with lying to the police and deliberately obstructing a serious criminal investigation, but, like you say, it was thirty years ago and what would be the point?' She looked at him. 'This has to be your call.'

She left the gym. She wanted to phone Denning to tell him that they now had confirmation that the original investigation had been deliberately scuppered. But there was someone else she needed to tell first.

She took out her phone and called Colin.

Chapter Fifty-Seven

It took them just over an hour to drive to Oxfordshire. Numerous traffic jams and road works had initially slowed their journey, but once they were out of London, the traffic had thinned out, allowing them to make up for lost time. Neeraj asked him questions en route, some of which he could answer, but some of which were dependent on guesswork.

Denning had spoken to someone from Thames Valley CID who had agreed to meet them at the local station. Denning had stressed that no one was to approach the house until he got there. They had insisted on more details, concerning whether the Morrows were dangerous. He had only contacted them out of courtesy. South Oxfordshire was outside the Met's territory; if they required back-up, it would be Thames Valley who would be expected to provide it.

'We don't know for sure anyone's going to be there, boss,' Neeraj argued. 'And it's a long way to go on the off-chance.'

Denning agreed, but this was all they had right now. Justin and Emma had to be somewhere. Her brother's house was empty and, according to Google Maps, reasonably isolated. It would have been the perfect place to lie low until they'd decided on their next move. But Neeraj might be right: this could turn out to be a complete waste of time.

'Don't you think we should get back-up?' he asked. 'I mean proper back-up, like armed response.'

'They're not armed, as far as we know. Anyway, we need to confirm they're actually there before we do anything.'

They were met at Didcot Police Station by a DI Phillip Eaves. Eaves was in his late forties, with slightly receding hair and a podgy, freckled face. He'd travelled down from Thames Valley's operational HQ in Kidlington to meet them. 'DI Denning,' he said, shaking Denning's hand. Denning introduced him to Neeraj, who returned his handshake. They were chatting in the car park at the rear of the station.

'I've spoken to my boss. The house is an old farm cottage on the outskirts of the village. It's about three miles from here.' He nodded at Denning's Focus. 'Shouldn't take you long to get there. We've kept away from the house as you requested,' Eaves said. 'But we did swing by the estate agent and borrowed a set of keys, just in case there's nobody there and you want to have a look around. They weren't happy about it. They insisted we had to sign for the bloody things.'

'Don't they know this is a murder inquiry?' Neeraj insisted.

Eaves laughed at this. 'They have their rules, same as the rest of us.'

He made to hand the keys to Denning, but Neeraj grabbed them, asserting his authority on the situation.

'Thank you,' he said. 'We'll make sure you get them back.'

'Should be easy enough to find,' Eaves said. 'Head north through the village. The cottages are on the right just as you leave the village.'

'Cheers,' Denning said. He was keen to get on his way.

'You've got my number,' Eaves said. 'Give me a call if you require any back-up. We can have a team there in minutes.'

Denning looked at Neeraj. 'I'm hoping that won't be necessary, but thanks for the reassurance.'

'Technically, someone from Thames Valley should be accompanying you. If anything goes wrong, it'll be our knackers on the block.' Eaves was sweating slightly, and looked worried.

'We just want to interview them,' Denning said. 'We're not expecting there to be any trouble.'

'You mentioned a murder investigation,' Eaves said. 'A pair of suspects on our patch – we really should be handling this.'

Denning tried to reassure Eaves that this was nothing more complex than a routine inquiry. He was beginning to regret notifying Thames Valley in the first place.

They thanked Eaves, promising to get in touch if there was a problem, then headed off in the direction of West Moreton, Denning having already programmed the location into his sat nav.

It didn't take long to get there. The roads around the area were bordered by trees and tall hedgerows, but there was little traffic.

A few minutes later and they were driving through West Moreton. It looked exactly as Google Maps had shown, complete with village pub.

They continued south towards the outskirts of the village. They passed an old barn and then there were just fields on one side of the road, and a small wood on the other side. Denning thought they'd gone too far, despite the sat nav saying otherwise. Then a second later they turned a sharp bend and spotted a couple of redbrick cottages set back from the road, separated by a small strip of grass and an overgrown garden.

'I deffo think we should call for back-up,' Neeraj repeated. 'We don't know they're not armed.'

'We don't know they're even in there,' Denning countered. 'You said yourself this could turn out to be nothing.'

Denning drove past the building and parked the car beside the entrance to a field about ten yards away. They got out of the car and headed back to the house. In his head, Denning had planned how events would pan out. They would knock on the door, either Justin or Emma would answer, and he would ask them to come back to London with him. There were two officers and more could come quickly if requested. But Neeraj's concerns about them possibly being armed rattled round his brain, repeating itself on a loop.

He knocked on the door, trying to make sure his hand wasn't shaking.

There was no answer.

He knocked again, but still no answer. They were out and this looked like another wasted journey.

Neeraj held the keys up. 'We might as well have a look around whilst we're here.'

They unlocked the front door and went in. They entered a long, narrow hallway with a set of stairs leading up to the first floor. The house smelt musty as though no one had been there for a while, but it was clean and warmer than Denning would have expected. 'The agent said they hadn't done a viewing here for a few days, so no one's been here for a while.'

The kitchen was at the back of the house. There was a fresh pint of milk and some food in the fridge, and bread in a bread bin on a worktop. 'I reckon they've been here and have since legged it,' Neeraj said.

'Let's look round the rest of the house,' Denning said.

The small living room at the front contained a sofa and a couple of easy chairs. There was no telly. Everything felt very bare. Either Edward Boswell had lived frugally, or Emma had cleared the house of most of its valuables.

Upstairs were two bedrooms and a bathroom. All the rooms were clean but almost empty; just some pieces of furniture that had yet to be removed. The bedclothes in one of the rooms were slightly rumpled as though someone had recently been sleeping in the bed. There were some toiletries in the bathroom. They'd obviously hurriedly packed before they'd left the house.

'They're not here,' Neeraj said.

'No,' Denning replied. 'But they were, and I have a feeling they'll be coming back.'

He looked round the house. 'Unless they know we're onto them.'

'But why would they?' Neeraj said 'No one would have tipped them off we were coming.'

'Unless the estate agent said something.' But Denning thought this was unlikely.

They were just about to leave and give this up as a lost cause when Denning heard a car approach. He glanced out of the front bedroom window and saw a red BMW coming down the road from the opposite direction to the way they'd come. The car stopped outside the house. They stepped back from the window so they could observe without being seen.

Justin and Emma got out of the car. They obviously hadn't seen Denning's car, parked a few yards away. They headed straight into the house. Neeraj looked at Denning. They should call for back-up, but if they alerted the Morrows to their presence then they'd risk losing them again. He was trying to dismiss Neeraj's suggestion that they might be armed. They were a middle-class, professional couple caught up in something way over their heads: they weren't the sort to carry a gun. But then, one of them had slit the throats of two people in cold blood. They were clearly prepared to use violence if and when they felt it was necessary.

They heard the key turning in the lock, then the front door slowly opening. Denning peered through the bannisters and saw that they were carrying bags of food. They both looked tired and slightly dishevelled.

He waited until they were in the kitchen and signalled to Neeraj to be as quiet as possible and follow him downstairs. From the narrow hallway he could hear the two of them talking in the kitchen. Emma was saying something about getting fake passports, but Justin was suggesting they stayed where they were, keeping their heads down until the dust settled; insisting they were safe for the time being.

Both looked startled when they saw Denning and Neeraj standing in the doorway to the kitchen.

It was Justin who reacted first. Grabbing a bag of shopping from the table, he picked it up and swung it at Denning. Denning stepped back as the shopping smashed into the doorway, scattering tins and cartons everywhere. The momentary distraction gave Morrow the opportunity to open the back door and leg it into the garden.

Emma Morrow stood where she was, still slightly shell-shocked. She opened her mouth to speak, but Neeraj was already reading her her rights.

Chapter Fifty-Eight

Denning followed Justin Morrow out the back door. He was running along a stone path towards the front of the house, presumably heading for the car, but then realised he must have left the keys in the house.

He turned his head and threw a glance in Denning's direction, then ran across the road towards the wood opposite the house. Denning shouted after him to stop. He didn't know why Morrow was running and where he expected to go.

Denning chased after Morrow, trying to work out what was going on in his head. Did Morrow have a plan? Or would he just run and run until he ran out of steam? Denning was fit, but so was Morrow: all those sessions on the squash court would have built up his stamina.

The wood wasn't particularly dense, but there was no obvious path through it. They were running past shrubs and rhododendron bushes and dodging the odd protruding tree stump. Denning felt his face being slapped by low branches and something scraped against his ankle, tearing at the flesh. He ignored the sharp pain and carried on after Morrow.

Denning was gaining on him, but Morrow was fast.

Morrow glanced behind him. The distraction caused him to trip over a tree root. He crashed to the ground and cursed. Denning was on top of him a moment later, pulling him up by the shoulders, telling him to stop being an idiot and give himself up. Morrow was struggling with him, trying to break free of his grip. Then he stopped.

For a second it looked like he was going to be sensible and accept his luck had run out. He looked at Denning, smiled, then punched him in the stomach. Denning doubled up and let go of him. He managed to grab hold of Justin's jacket, tearing it at the shoulder, but Morrow wrenched free of his grip. He ran off, fighting his way through the shrubbery until Denning could no longer see him.

Denning got his breath back then gave chase. After a few seconds, he spotted Morrow in the distance. He'd stopped at a fence. He looked round at Denning again, then started climbing over the fence, cutting himself on some barbed wire.

Denning was almost upon him when he disappeared over the fence and vanished from sight. It was only as Denning approached the fence that he saw the ground beyond it suddenly dropped away. Several feet below there was a railway line.

A dead end.

Denning had reached the fence now. He was standing at the top of the cutting looking down onto the track. The cutting was about fifteen feet deep. There was a metal bridge at one end while the track curved out of sight at the other.

'Justin,' he shouted. 'It's over. There's nowhere left to run.' But Morrow was already clambering down the embankment, ignoring Denning. Denning knew he had to call for back-up. The idea of chasing Morrow onto a busy railway line was foolhardy. Morrow was almost at the bottom of the embankment now. He briefly glanced up, then turned his head to look at the railway line, clearly trying to gauge the level of risk. Four lines of railway track lay between him and the far side.

Then he dropped down beside the track, skidding slightly on the stony ballast that spilt out from between the concrete sleepers.

Denning didn't know how frequently trains ran along the line, but he assumed they were fairly regular.

Morrow was on the track now, looking in both directions, still trying to gauge his chances. The bank on the other side of the track was just as steep, though slightly more overgrown: bramble bushes and dense undergrowth blocked his path to the top of the far embankment. But the insanity of running along a main railway line was obviously not an option.

Reluctantly, Denning decided to follow him. If Morrow did manage to clamber up the other embankment, he'd never catch him. It was a risk.

He'd just climbed over the fence when he heard it.

Blasting out like a clarion.

A second later, he saw it rounding the bend to his left, speeding towards London; moving fast.

Morrow saw it at the same time.

He was almost across the tracks to the bank on the other side when the oncoming train rounded the curve, heading straight along the cutting.

Another claxon cry of the horn blasted out, followed by the sound of brakes being applied in earnest.

A harrowing screech like a million nails on a blackboard.

It would have taken less than a second to jump out of the way. He could have made it. Just.

Instead, Morrow turned and looked up at Denning. Denning was sure he saw him smile, just for a moment, before the train smashed into him at around a hundred miles an hour.

Chapter Fifty-Nine

Emma Morrow was sitting in a cell, her knees pressed against her chin, staring into space. The usually confident barrister seemed subdued, as though the stuffing had been knocked out of her.

She'd been officially informed about her husband's death. Mercifully, she wouldn't be expected to formally identify whatever was left of his body. She was shaking, but there were no tears.

A doctor had examined her and said she was in shock, but was otherwise fit enough to be questioned.

Denning, McKenna and Neeraj were in McKenna's office now, going over what had happened, and where they went from here.

According to Neeraj, when he'd arrested her, she had exercised her right to silence. Even when Eaves had arrived with back-up from Thames Valley CID, she'd had nothing to say.

She'd blamed everything on Justin. He'd committed the murders single-handedly, and without her knowledge. The first she'd heard of it was when he confessed to her over the phone, shortly before Denning had turned up to arrest him. She'd come straight home from chambers to confront Justin, had seen Denning, panicked and hit him over the head with the first thing that came to hand. She was very sorry for that. It had been nothing personal and she hoped Denning hadn't been badly hurt. Everything since then had been Justin's idea and she'd gone along with it because she couldn't think of a way out of the mess he'd created. She had fully planned to convince him they should hand themselves in once he realised how hopeless their situation was. Her solicitor had backed up her version of events, and she had signed a statement to this effect. Then she'd been officially informed of her husband's death, and hadn't spoken since.

'Do we accept what she said?' McKenna asked.

Neeraj shook his head. 'She knew the score. I reckon they were in this together from the start.'

'Could she have killed them herself?' McKenna asked. 'It would have been easy enough to overpower an inebriated Buckfield, and Magda Kilbride didn't have much muscle on her.'

Denning had given this some serious thought on the drive back from Oxfordshire. It would have taken a lot to persuade Magda to meet someone in the middle of nowhere in the dead of night. She would have been more likely to have trusted another woman. Even then she would have been wary. But that didn't mean the Morrows weren't in it together. Emma could have persuaded Magda to meet them, and then Justin had done the actual killing. It was a theory.

'I don't think we'll ever know the true story,' Denning said. 'Even if she was the one who killed them, we're going to have a hard job proving it. But she has the strongest motive. I get the impression Boswell was one of the main players in the paedophile ring, and he's probably one of the few men who are still alive. If the truth came out, it would have destroyed Emma as much as it would have her father. Perhaps more so.' Denning could still feel the lump on the back of his head. 'I honestly think that's the reason they did it. I mean, yes, there's the damage to them and their careers, but I really believe – deep down – she wanted to protect her father's reputation. The thought of people talking about him, calling him a pervert; his final days being made hell by reporters trying to get a picture of him, or worse, trying to speak to him. The double humiliation of the truth coming out alongside people seeing him with dementia.' He sighed. 'If you loved someone that much, you'd go to any lengths to protect them.'

McKenna nodded. 'Do you think she'd always known about her father?'

It was a good question. Gavin Buckfield had always had his suspicions about his father, but hadn't wanted to know the truth. Emma Morrow was a barrister, someone used to reading people and getting the truth out of them. It was likely she'd known all the time, even if she'd chosen not to believe it.

'Why kill Buckfield and Magda Kilbride?' Neeraj asked. 'Why not kill Sims?'

'Sims could be relied upon to be discreet,' Denning said. 'Or at least have his silence bought. He only named Boswell after Molly and her partner forced his hand. Buckfield was always the weakest link: a retired copper with a drink problem and a conscience, and Magda Kilbride wasn't going to let the matter drop, even after they tried to bribe her.'

'CCTV has shown the Morrows' car en route to the sports centre on the night in question,' Neeraj said. 'No indication of who was driving. Once the images have been cleaned up we'll have a better indication of whether it was him or her.'

'It doesn't matter,' McKenna said. 'She's going down. Maybe not for murder, but certainly as an accessory. And the truth will inevitably now come out about her father, so it's all been for nothing.'

'I think she planned for Justin to go all the way,' Denning said. 'Parliament, government perhaps. They truly saw themselves as some kind of power couple.'

He could still see Morrow's face. The look that said *I know it's over.*

It would haunt his dreams for a while, but in time the memory would fade.

He was about to head back to the main office when McKenna stopped him in his tracks. 'Matt, there will have to be an inquiry, I'm afraid. It'll be a formal investigation, but there won't be any finger-pointing.' She threw him a smile, albeit it a brief one. 'Everybody knows there's nothing you could have done to save Morrow.'

He saw Morrow's face again, but blinked the image away. The more often he replayed that final scene, the less potent it would be. He smiled back at McKenna, touched by her kindness.

'But it shouldn't interfere with your reinstatement as SIO,' she added. 'I'll have to run things by Harrison's replacement, though I can't see that being a problem.'

He thanked her and returned to his desk. Trudi was chatting to Neeraj.

'Coming to the pub?' she asked Denning.

'Just got to finish some bits and pieces off first,' he said.

'Molly's joining us,' Trudi added, by way of an incentive.

'I'll see you in there.'

He logged on to his computer and checked his emails. There was one from Anna Klein. He quickly read over it and typed a reply. This was good news. But it could wait. The pub couldn't.

He quickly checked the BBC News website.

There was something about Alfie Kane. He'd been in the local news today: smiling for the camera and boasting about the charity launch the previous weekend.

Kane was a clever bastard, Denning had to give him that. But he'd slip up one day. And Denning would be there, waiting to bring him down.

There was also a brief piece about Morrow's death. He wasn't mentioned by name, but there was already a lot of speculation about what had happened, and rumours circulating on social media as to why.

An inquiry into Morrow's death was the last thing he needed. He would rather forget what had happened and move on. But they would need to establish whether it was suicide or accidental death.

He didn't know the answer to that one himself, not for sure.

Had Morrow meant to kill himself?

He could have jumped out of the way in time, his survival instincts kicking in at the last moment. Or had he been confused? Using that last fraction of a second to think through his options, had fear and panic frozen him to the spot? Could Denning have done anything? Stopped him? Been quicker?

Justin Morrow's face popped into his head again. He remembered their planned squash match, which he would now have to delete from his diary. Or maybe he'd keep it there as a reminder of the fragility of human life and how he shouldn't ever take that life for granted.

Chapter Sixty

Molly was sitting in the pub nursing a pint of Kronenbourg. This wasn't their usual pub, which was closed for a refit, having just been bought by one of the big pub chains, but a quieter one a few streets away.

Betty Taggart had put fifty quid behind the bar, insisting the first couple of rounds were on her. She apologised that she couldn't join them, but she had another meeting with the Deputy Commissioner's office.

The atmosphere was lively enough.

Neeraj was laughing at one of his own jokes, or at an anecdote he'd just told – she couldn't be sure as she was only half listening. Dave Kinsella was talking to Ryan and Trudi, neither of whom looked impressed by his banter.

Denning hadn't put in an appearance yet, but that was nothing new: he usually turned up late to these gigs and then left early, spending the duration looking like he wished he was somewhere else.

Truth be told, she'd rather not be there herself. Colin was being discharged from the hospital that day, and she wanted to be there for him. She'd even suggested to Jon that Colin could move into one of their spare rooms. His response had been firm enough to persuade her otherwise. But the thought of Colin returning to a lonely bedsit made her heart sink.

Trudi sat down next to her. 'You look like you're miles away, mate.' She clinked her pint glass against Molly's. 'Anyway, cheers. You're officially back on the team.'

'Yes.' Molly smiled and drank some more Kronenbourg.

'What did Betty Taggart say to you?'

'Nothing much. Just said she never thought I'd killed Mags and welcome back to the team. I'll be at my desk first thing tomorrow morning. Just like nothing ever happened.'

'Well, to be fair, she couldn't have said much else, could she?' Trudi gave her a cheeky grin. 'And none of us believed for a minute that you offed Magda what's-her-name. Well, maybe Dave had his suspicions, but he's an arsehole at the best of times.'

Molly laughed. 'I don't know, Trudi. Why do I still get the feeling I'm here on sufferance?'

Trudi rubbed her arm affectionately. 'Look, old Betty Bollocks-face had no choice but to suspend you. But you've got to forget about it. You're part of the team, and that's what matters. Everything else is just shit.'

'I'm not talking about the suspension. Well, OK, maybe that's part of it. But it's more than that. Sometimes I feel like I'm not really cut out for MIT. It's such a tight team, I'm not always convinced that I fit in.'

'You're being paranoid. We all feel like that at first. Apart from Betty Taggart, I was the only woman in the team when I joined. That took some getting used to.' She jerked her head at the group spread round the table laughing raucously at someone's joke. 'Can you imagine what it was like working with a load of alpha males? There were days when it felt like I was going to drown in a sea of testosterone and sweaty armpits. I mean, if you think

360

Dave's got some questionable hygiene issues, you should have smelled some of the blokes I had to work with. But they're like all teams: once you've proved you can do the job, they accept you whatever you are. And you *have* proved you can do the job. Several times over.' She smiled at Molly. 'Now, drink your pint and stop behaving like a twat. Next round's on you.'

Molly thanked her and gave her a playful peck on the cheek. 'Which reminds me: how are you and Charys? Is divorce still on the cards?'

Trudi laughed. 'I forgot to say: I'd read that whole situation wrong. She wasn't seeing someone else. She was planning a surprise fortieth for me.'

'How did you find out?'

'My mum rang me and mentioned it. She'd forgotten it was supposed to be a secret.'

'And you didn't suspect anything?'

'No. But that might be because I won't be forty for another year. Charys got the date wrong.'

They both laughed, only for Dave Kinsella to ask what the joke was.

By the time Denning appeared, Molly was on the point of leaving. He thanked her again for all the work she and Jon had done chasing up Colin Meek's claims, and offered to buy her a drink. She politely declined, saying there was somewhere she had to be.

–

She arrived at St Thomas' to discover Colin had been discharged half an hour ago. She thought about calling round at the bedsit, but that would have felt a bit like stalking. He had her number: he could get in touch anytime he needed someone to talk to.

She still wasn't sure what she was going to tell him about Boswell. She'd promised Colin justice, but all they had to offer was an old man with dementia who probably couldn't remember anything about the events of over thirty years ago and so would very likely never be put before a jury in his state, assuming he lived long enough for the case to go to trial.

They could go after Robin Sims: if it went to court, there was a chance Sims might be found guilty, despite his insistence that he had nothing to do with the paedophile ring. But was it really worth it? Sims had, at best, been a minor player. Boswell was another possibility, but he was too ill to stand trial.

As for the other men involved, even if they could get names, the chances were that most of them would be dead now, or in a similar state as Boswell.

Perhaps justice would come from elsewhere. The press, rather than the police. Jon was determined to finish what Mags had started. They had enough evidence for Jon to run the story. Maybe it would be enough for Colin to see his name vindicated?

Chapter Sixty-One

Sarah was drinking a glass of wine when Denning arrived home that evening. She was already two thirds of the way through a bottle of Chablis.

He hadn't even taken his jacket off yet. 'What happened? It was all over the news. Something about Emma being arrested and Justin's dead.'

He hung his jacket on the coat rack. 'You know I can't discuss that, Sarah.'

'I don't want to know the ins and outs – I just want to know what happened. It said on the news that she'd been arrested and that Justin had been killed.'

He sat down on the sofa next to her and put a hand on her arm. 'Emma's been arrested on suspicion of murder. She and Justin were believed to have been involved together. The details are still sketchy at the moment, but it looks like we'll be charging her with either murder or with being an accomplice.'

'What about Justin?'

'It looks like they were working together, though we'll never prove which one actually did it.'

'No. I mean, what happened to him?'

Denning headed into the kitchen and reappeared with a wine glass. He emptied what was left from the bottle into the glass. 'I don't really want to talk about it. Let's just say he's dead and leave it there.'

Denning knocked back the wine. He was tempted to go back to the kitchen and open another bottle, but getting pissed wasn't going to make matters any easier. He understood what Sarah was feeling. Her burgeoning friendship with Emma had been brought to an abrupt end before it had even had a chance to develop.

'What's going on, Matt? I've tried ringing Emma, but it goes straight to voicemail. I can't believe she's involved in a murder.'

'We don't know all the facts yet, but she's certainly involved in either covering it up or assisting an offender.'

Sarah drained her wine glass. 'What'll happen to her?'

'I don't know. It's unlikely she'll be bailed.' He looked at her. 'Whatever your feelings for Emma, don't forget two people have been murdered. Any sympathy would be better directed at them than at Emma Morrow.' And then there was the fact she'd whacked him on the back of the skull with an ornament.

But he immediately realised he was being unfair. None of this was Sarah's fault. He reached out and hugged her. 'I'm sorry. I know that sounds brutal. I know you and she were friends. But neither of us can avoid the reality of the situation. Emma Morrow is very likely going to prison for a very long time.'

Chapter Sixty-Two

Next morning, Denning was back on Arundel Road, standing on the pavement outside number twenty-four. The area immediately in front of the house had been taped off, while a specialist team worked in the back garden, using ground-penetrating radar to scan the area. They'd had to wait for a dry spell, as damp soil could give an inaccurate reading. Denning had neither the scientific expertise nor the inclination to disagree with them, so had left them to get on with it. He asked them to let him know the moment they found anything.

Joyce Lindsey had already popped across to say hello, and ask how he was. In reality, she'd wanted to know what was going on, but was trying her best to be subtle about it. Denning had fobbed her off by saying they weren't sure what they were looking for, but they'd know when they found it. It was close enough to the truth. Joyce had wandered back indoors, but had made the offer of a coffee, if Denning wanted to come over.

'Save you standing round in the cold,' she'd said. He'd thanked her, and had been momentarily tempted to take her up on her offer, but he wanted to be on hand if the search team found anything. He watched her wander across the street towards her house, throwing occasional glances over her shoulder; worried she might miss something.

He looked round to see DS Klein approaching. She was wearing a fashionable-looking raincoat and a pair of knee-high boots. She twisted her head towards Joyce, who was walking up the steps to her front door.

'What did she want?'

'Just a concerned neighbour,' Denning said. 'I suspect this is the most excitement they've had round here for years.'

Klein laughed. 'Lomax is down at the station being interviewed right now. He's sticking to his original story, I'm afraid, and I don't think he's going to deviate from it. He's had twenty years to perfect this story. He knows it off by heart now.'

She glanced in the direction of the house. The gate at the side that led to the back garden was open, and it was possible to catch a glimpse of white-suited SOCOs moving around.

'These boys don't come cheap,' Klein said. 'I'm just glad it's coming out of your budget and not ours.'

Denning smiled at this. He'd been working on a hunch, little more, but something that kept niggling at him.

David Cairns.

Frances Hynd's insistence that her brother would never take his own life. A former colleague of Cairns's at Queen Mary's had confirmed this. She'd often talked to Cairns about his depression, and he'd assured her it was something he'd learned to live with. His faith gave him the strength to get through the dark times. She'd agreed with Frances Hynd's assertion that Cairns was unlikely to have killed himself.

But it had been more than that. A feeling when Denning had been inside the house. He could almost *sense* David Cairns's presence. He'd joked to himself about Cairns's ghost haunting the place, and even though Denning didn't believe in an afterlife, that's exactly what it had felt like. Cairns had never left that house, at least not the grounds. Denning was sure of it.

But the team had been there for the best part of an hour and the garden wasn't that big. It was possible Lomax had been telling the truth, and Denning had called it wrong.

Even if he had, it was the least of his worries at the moment.

It had been a week since Morrow's death, and the official inquiry would be starting soon. Despite McKenna's assurance that he had nothing to worry about, he couldn't escape a slight feeling of dread. He was going to have to relive the details. Not that he hadn't been doing that every night since it happened. Sarah had been trying her best to be sympathetic, but even she'd bombarded him with a thousand questions, mostly variations on why Justin had done it and what would it mean for Denning's career. She'd also asked about Emma, and what was going to happen to her. He either couldn't or wouldn't answer these questions, and made it clear he didn't want to talk about it. Eventually Sarah had taken the hint and let the subject drop.

'This could still turn out to be something and nothing,' Denning said. 'But at the very least, you've got enough to charge Lomax with fraud and failing to report a death.'

As things stood, Lomax was currently CID's problem. If the ground search threw up anything of note, then they would be looking at a murder inquiry, and MIT would take over. Not that his team would welcome a cold case like this. He could already hear Dave Kinsella muttering about time-wasting and squandering resources. But they couldn't ignore a murder, even if it was decades old and the victim had very likely been a paedophile.

'We'll have a lot of fun with Lomax,' Klein said. 'I'd say he's looking at a prison sentence no matter what happens.'

'Well that's probably just as well.' Denning nodded at the smart but slightly dilapidated property in front of them. 'David Cairns's nephew has been in touch. Turns out he's a solicitor specialising in property law. He's already served Lomax with an eviction order. He claims the house legally belongs to his mother, Frances Hynd, as Cairns's next of kin. Looks like Lomax is going to be needing somewhere else to stay.'

Klein gave him a wry grin. 'Life does have a habit of catching up with you, doesn't it? Lomax probably thought he'd get away with this for the rest of his life. It's only by chance he was found out.'

'Nobody's luck lasts forever,' Denning reflected grimly. Not even Alfie Kane's, he thought. Despite Harrison's statement, they still didn't have enough to go after Kane. Not yet. But Denning knew that if he was patient enough, Kane would trip himself up sooner or later.

'I was wondering,' Klein said, throwing him another wry grin. 'Assuming you're not too busy, would you like to go out for a drink sometime? No strings… just two detectives swapping work stories.'

He tried not to appear too taken aback. He unconsciously rubbed his thumb over his wedding ring. She must have spotted it: she was a detective, after all. 'Yes,' he heard himself saying. 'That would be nice. You've got my number.'

Before the conversation could be allowed to develop, one of the SOCOs appeared down the side path. As they drew closer and removed their mask, Denning saw that it was Sheila Gorton. She approached Denning and Klein, greeting them both, then turned to Denning. 'Well, you're either going to be very popular or very unpopular with your colleagues, DI Denning.' She looked over at the house. 'They've found something. We'll need to do further tests, to make sure it isn't someone's dog, but they're reasonably confident it's human. I would suggest the body's been burned and the remains buried quite deep under a gravelled area at the rear of the garden.' She unhooked her mask from her ears. 'It looks like we've finally found Dr David Cairns.'

Chapter Sixty-Three

It was a damp day in April. There were only a handful of mourners gathered in the crematorium, while the celebrant read out a hastily written eulogy. Mags hadn't been religious and wouldn't have wanted anything that stank of hypocrisy.

Molly looked around her to see if there were any familiar faces, but she didn't recognise anyone. She didn't really expect to. Jon had said there were one or two people there he knew from his days on the *Echo*, but others were either drinking buddies, or professional funeral crashers. Or had possibly turned up early for the next funeral and couldn't be bothered hanging around the cold and draughty waiting area by the main doors.

Jon sat looking ahead. It wasn't long until Rowan's wedding and most of his attention was focussed on that.

Rowan had been on an extended holiday in New Zealand, staying with friends and working as a barista. Upon her return to the UK three weeks ago the first thing she'd done was to phone her dad and ask him to her wedding.

It seemed she hadn't said anything to her mother about not inviting Jon, and Jenna had had no right to suggest otherwise. Jon hadn't wanted to cause a fight between mother and daughter and told Rowan he had more than likely got the wrong end of the stick. Molly wasn't sure

Jenna had deserved such diplomacy, but it was easier for her to keep out of it.

The wedding was only a few months away. Naturally, Molly had been invited, despite telling Jon she had nothing to wear. It was only a little lie. In truth, she wasn't sure she wanted to go. She belonged in a different compartment of Jon's life, and she didn't think she was quite ready to meet his other family just yet.

Mags's mother was sitting in the front row, sobbing into a paper hanky and being comforted by a man she didn't seem to know.

The coroner had agreed to release Mags's body, as Emma Morrow's defence team weren't contesting the specifics of her death, and the lack of DNA meant there was nothing for them to challenge.

They'd struggled to trace her mother, though an illicit check of the PNC had helped point them in the right general area. Mags's mother had a number of convictions ranging from shoplifting to assault; the last one being three years ago. She was no longer living at her last known address, but a former neighbour had a phone number for her, and someone had finally managed to track her down.

Whatever history had passed between mother and daughter had clearly been forgotten as she'd wailed like a banshee at the news of her only daughter's death.

Jon and Molly had agreed to write the eulogy. Barry had helped, as they realised the three of them were probably the only people who ever really knew Mags. Barry had known her longer than anyone, and was able to offer up some useful notes about her early years as a journalist. Barry was too ill to attend the funeral. He was still hoping to make Rowan's wedding, even if it meant turning up in a wheelchair. His health had taken a sudden turn for the worse in the past few weeks, but he told them he was never short of optimism.

They'd phoned Colin to tell him about the funeral, and ask if he wanted to come along, but there had been no answer and he hadn't replied to their messages.

Molly wasn't sure if Colin was still at the bedsit in Herne Hill, or if he was even still in London. She suspected he just wanted a bit of time alone. Jon's article would be coming out later in the year, once Emma Morrow's trial was out of the way. Colin would have his moment of glory then. He would likely have to stand trial for the attack on Gordon Lomax, but the extenuating circumstances surrounding the case, along with his attempted suicide, would work in his favour. Colin had already spent several years in prison because of Lomax, any sympathetic judge would certainly take that into account.

The celebrant ended the short service with a few words about Mags's life and her career. A photo of Mags half-smiling for the camera sat on the coffin. It was the same one downloaded from her website that had so recently adorned the whiteboard back at the office. She looked quite attractive in the picture, which Molly suspected was down to the skills of the professional photographer that had taken it.

As soon as the celebrant finished speaking, the curtains parted and the coffin made its slow journey towards the furnace.

Molly could never pretend she'd liked Mags, but she felt something close to sadness when the coffin finally disappeared. She'd never liked endings. The best part of a journey was the start, not the final destination.

When the service was over, they headed out into the drizzle. Molly wanted a cigarette more than ever, but fought back the urge. She linked arms with Jon and suggested they headed to the pub with the other mourners to remember Mags's life, but Jon wasn't in the mood. Perhaps he was feeling guilty, or was grieving for the woman he once knew. She couldn't tell and she didn't want to push it.

They were about to head back to the car, when Molly spotted a figure skulking by a tree, dressed in a black hoodie and staring over at them. It took a second or two before she recognised Colin. She headed over to speak to him, Jon following in her wake.

'I didn't want to come inside,' he said. 'It's not like I really knew her. But I felt I should at least say goodbye.'

'It's OK,' Molly said. 'You didn't have to come if you didn't want to.' She reached out and touched his arm. 'How are you?'

His mouth twitched into a smile. 'I'm going to be all right. I've spoken to someone from Victim Support, like you said. She told me there's a chance they could reopen my case.' He seemed very matter-of-fact about it, as though discussing compensation over a car accident. But then, he'd had years to live with this, and to try and come to terms with something most people would struggle to even understand.

'That's good.' Molly looked at Jon, who nodded. 'We'll do everything we can to help. And you know we're here if you need us.'

Colin smiled. 'You're very kind.' He jerked his head towards the chapel. 'It was down to her. In the end, I should be thankful for her help.'

Molly looked over towards the low concrete building that backed on to the chapel. There was a tall chimney sticking out the rear of the building with smoke coming out of it.

'Yes,' Molly said. 'We should all be grateful to her.' She looked at Colin, trying hard not to feel sorry for him; hoping this was the opportunity he needed to finally get his life sorted out. Somehow, however, she doubted it. In reality, the chances of his case being reopened were slim. Though if Mags's story were ever to see the light of day, the ensuing publicity might persuade CAIT to at least look into it.

'Can we give you a lift anywhere?' she asked.

Colin shook his head. 'I'd rather walk back, thanks. I enjoy the fresh air.'

The rain was lighter now, but it was still dull and overcast.

Molly wished him well and asked him to keep in touch. He promised he would.

As they headed back to the car she glanced behind her. He was still standing against the tree, seemingly lost in thought.

'What are the chances of bringing anyone to justice?' Jon asked. 'Honestly?'

She let out a long sigh. 'Who knows? I mean how much, if any of this, can be proved after all this time? Once Emma Morrow's case goes to court, there's a chance the truth might come out. And if a courageous journalist were to run the story...' She smiled Jon. 'But at the end of the day, it will always be Colin's word against that of some very powerful men. Powerful men and their powerful families. And in these kinds of situations, the powerful invariably tend to win.'

They'd reached the car now. Jon dug in his pocket for the key.

'Colin will have the chance to speak up in court,' Molly said. 'People will hear about what happened to him and the others and they'll be listened to.'

But Jon didn't look convinced. The cynical journalist, she thought. But did that make her the cynical cop? She preferred not to think about it.

He unlocked the car and she climbed in. Jon started the engine and pulled away.

As they were heading out of the small car park beside the concrete chapel, she glanced over to where Colin had been standing, but there was no sign of him.

A letter from Graeme

Many thanks for reading *The Darkness Within*. I hope you enjoyed the latest outing for detectives Denning and Fisher.

Even before I'd fully developed the story, I knew I wanted to bring Mags back from *Know No Evil*. There was something about the character that intrigued me. It was a difficult decision to kill her off, and not one I took lightly, but I feel it was the right decision for the story.

Another character who appeared in the first book – albeit fleetingly – was villain-turned-businessman Alfie Kane. Every good detective needs a nemesis: Holmes had Moriarty, and now Denning has Kane. We haven't heard the last of him.

However, *The Darkness Within* was always going to be Colin's story. I wanted to explore what happens to someone when they've been denied justice and then have to live with the consequences. I also wanted to write about a character who was damaged and – on the surface at least – not entirely likable. By the end of the book, there's hope for Colin, so perhaps all is not lost for him.

I'm already planning the fourth book in the series, where someone from McKenna's past comes back into her life, someone she thought was dead...

If you enjoyed *The Darkness Within*, please leave a review on Amazon, Kobo or Goodreads, and please recommend the book to your friends and family as nothing helps to promote a book like a word-of-mouth recommendation. I love hearing from readers, so please get in touch via my website: www.graemehampton.com, or follow me on Twitter at @GHam001, or on Instagram @graeme_hampton.

Thank you,
Graeme

Acknowledgments

As always, there are so many people I'd like to thank for helping me bring this book into the world.

Firstly, thanks as always to Keshini Naidoo, Lindsey Mooney at Hera Books for their tireless contribution to *The Darkness Within*. Your support and enthusiasm for my books means everything. Thanks also to everyone else who worked on the book, from editing to jacket design – your contributions help to make this a better book.

Thank you to Laurence Daren King and everyone at Jericho Writers: your advice, suggestions and guidance are very much appreciated.

I would also like to thank Graham Bartlett for answering my questions about police procedure and the complex organisational workings of the Met. Graham's website: www.policeadvisor.co.uk is an excellent resource for any crime writer, and is highly recommended. Any factual inaccuracies are mine alone.

A massive thank you to Christine Warrington for reading over the manuscript prior to publication and spotting any errors, and to Gary Metalle, Jessica Dyson, Tracey Caswell and my fellow Hera scribes for their kind words and encouragement while I was writing *The Darkness Within* during what has been a very challenging year.

Finally, I'm eternally grateful to all the book bloggers and readers who were good enough to review my first two books. Your reviews help get the books noticed and this in turn helps to build my readership.